D1569550

Other Books by Mary Austin

THE LAND OF LITTLE RAIN

ISIDRO

THE BASKET WOMAN

THE FLOCK

LOST BORDERS

THE ARROW MAKER

CHRIST IN ITALY

THE GREEN BOUGH

LOVE AND THE SOUL-MAKER

A WOMAN OF GENIUS

THE LOVELY LADY

THE LAND OF THE SUN

THE MAN JESUS

THE TRAIL BOOK

NO. 26 JAYNE STREET

THE AMERICAN RHYTHM

THE LAND OF JOURNEYS' ENDING

EVERYMAN'S GENIUS

THE CHILDREN SING IN THE FAR WEST

TAOS PUEBLO

STARRY ADVENTURE

EARTH HORIZON: AN AUTOBIOGRAPHY

ONE SMOKE STORIES

THE FORD

THE FORD

MARY AUSTIN

Foreword by John Walton

UNIVERSITY OF CALIFORNIA PRESS
Berkeley · Los Angeles · London

University of California Press
Berkeley and Los Angeles

University of California Press, Ltd.
London, England

Copyright, 1917, by Mary Austin
Foreword copyright © John Walton 1996

First California Paperback Printing 1997

Library of Congress Cataloging-in-Publication Data
Austin, Mary Hunter, 1868–1934.
    The ford / by Mary Austin.
       p.   cm. — (California fiction)
    Originally published: Boston : Houghton Mifflin Co. ; New York :
Riverside Press Cambridge, 1917.
    ISBN 0-520-20757-2 (alk. paper)
    1. Labor movement—California—Owens River Valley—Fiction.
2. Land use—California—Owens River Valley—Fiction. 3. Feminism—
California—Owens River Valley—Fiction. 4. Owens River Valley
(Calif.)—Fiction. I. Title. II. Series.
PS3501.U8F67   1997
813'.52—dc20
                                     96-14396
                                          CIP

Printed in the United States of America
1 2 3 4 5 6 7 8 9

The paper used in this publication meets the minimum requirements of
American National Standard for Information Sciences—Permanence
of Paper for Printed Library Materials, ANSI Z39.48-1984. ⊚

And he rose up that night, and took his two wives, and his two womenservants, and his eleven sons, and passed over the ford Jabbok. And he took them, and sent them over the brook, and sent over that he had. And Jacob was left alone; and there wrestled a man with him until the breaking of the day. And when he saw that he prevailed not against him, he touched the hollow of his thigh; and the hollow of Jacob's thigh was out of joint, as he wrestled with him. And he said, Let me go, for the day breaketh. And he said, I will not let thee go, except thou bless me. And he said unto him, What is thy name? And he said, Jacob. And he said, Thy name shall be called no more Jacob, but Israel: for as a prince hast thou power with God and with men, and hast prevailed. . . . And Jacob called the name of the place Peniel: for I have seen God face to face, and my life is preserved. And as he passed over Penuel the sun rose upon him, and he halted upon his thigh.

THE BOOK OF GENESIS

FOREWORD

John Walton

Mary Hunter Austin (1868–1934) was a woman of her times whose work is especially relevant for our own. Her life and art were rooted in turn-of-the-century events — the capitalist transformation of the western frontier, the marginalization of Native Americans, the struggle for women's rights. At the height of her career in the 1920s she traveled in the society of Herbert Hoover, Margaret Sanger, H. G. Wells, Lincoln Steffens, Martha Graham, and Ansel Adams. Her work was praised by Joseph Conrad, William Butler Yeats, and George Bernard Shaw. Yet this daughter of a Civil War veteran pioneered the modern roles of feminist, environmentalist, advocate for Indian and Hispanic minorities, historical preservationist, bilingual teacher, and organizer of the arts communities in Carmel and Santa Fe. She wrote about these issues with a sharp moral vision that continues to invigorate readers a century later.

Mary Hunter was raised in Carlinville, Illinois, by an austere Methodist mother, Susanna Graham, and Captain George Hunter, a local attorney. Her father's health had been ruined by military service, and he was often confined to his study. Mary was devoted to her father; her committment to a literary career was formed during the days when they read aloud from classics in his well-appointed study. But tragedy entered her life at age ten, with the death of her father and younger sister within months of each other — events that nurtured Mary's life-long spirituality. Susanna carried on with the captain's Civil War pension and a nursing job of her own that put Mary and her older brother Jim through Carlinville's two-year Blackburn College. In 1887 Jim went west, and Susanna decided to follow, moving the family to the out-skirts of Bakersfield, California, where they took up homesteads.

Here on the dirt farms of Kern County, with the Tehachapi Mountains rising dramatically from the south-ern end of the San Joaquin Valley, Mary's writing first flourished. Although she taught school for a time, her preoccupation was riding the countryside, observing the physical environment, and coming to know the sundry Indian, Basque, Chinese, and Mexican peoples of the land. At twenty-four she published her first short stories about these modest folk in the San Francisco-based *Overland Monthly*.

It was in Kern County, too, in 1891 that she married Stafford Wallace Austin. A refined young man who had graduated from the University of California, an uncom-mon achievement at the time, her husband was never-theless a dreamer and dilettante. And Mary, even in her early twenties, was rebellious, and driven — in the par-lance of the time, a "woman with views." Their odd mar-riage might be explained by Mary's desire to escape Jim and Susanna's condescension at home and by the nov-elty of Wallace's attentions, which must have been flatter-ing to a plain, overserious young woman. In the follow-ing year the couple moved to the Owens Valley on the eastern slope of California's Sierra, where Wallace took up a series of jobs, notably as Register of the U.S. Land Office, while Mary wrote, taught at the Inyo Academy, struggled with the ill-conceived marriage, and began to raise a daughter, whom they soon realized was retarded.

Mary's Inyo County years mark her formation and emergence as a writer of national prominence. From 1892 to 1906 the Owens Valley was still a frontier community. With characteristic intensity, Mary threw herself into the fine features of this desolate land — the miners' doleful stories, strange itinerant shepherds, the desert landscape and wildlife, a Mexican American village, and the language and life of Indian *rancherias* where respectable white women did not go. Highly readable nearly a century later, her stories were collected in *Land of Little Rain* (published in 1903 and still in print), *The Basket Woman* (1904), and *The Flock* (1906). Although written in New York during a later phase of her life, *The Ford* (1917) was fundamentally a reflection on her experience of frontier development in Kern and Inyo — of the social forces at work, the winners and losers, and their character.

Kern County was the locus of ill-gotten land holdings such as the vast Miller-Lux properties, of pitched conflict between leaseholders and the Southern Pacific Railroad that led to the Mussel Slough massacre chronicled by Frank Norris in *The Octopus* (1901), and of a subsequent oil discovery that converted the agrarian community into a rough-hewn boomtown. Just one hundred miles northeast, but over the trackless Sierra and reached circuitously via Carson City or Mojave, Inyo County's Owens Valley would soon play a key role in Southern California development. For it was the stream-laced Eastern Sierra slope and the Owens River that attracted the water seekers. Initially U.S. Reclamation Service planners located a site for an irrigation and power project; agents of metropolitan expansion from Los Angeles followed on their heels. The Owens Valley–Los Angeles controversy, a rural-urban struggle of epic dimensions that began at this time, has persevered throughout the century, resulting in a monumental aqueduct supplying 80 percent of Los Angeles water, legendary grassroots rebellion, precedent-making environmental action, and Southern California urban sprawl as we now know it. In the years leading up to publication of *The Ford*, Owens Valley citizens protested Teddy Roosevelt's decision to cede the Reclamation Service project to Los Angeles' designs for urban development some 240 miles to the south. Mary Austin lent her talent to the resistance movement, with trenchant critiques in the *San Francisco Chronicle*, and Wallace joined other public officials in letters and petitions to Washington. Although the local struggle in 1905 failed, it began a tradition of debate and action that would be elaborated in the 1920s and 1970s, until the valley finally obtained a measure of justice.

The Ford is set in fictional Tierra Longa Valley, a composite of Kern and Inyo Counties circa 1905. Oil discovery leads to a stampede of ruthless speculators. Agents from San Francisco (rather than Los Angeles) maneuver behind the scenes to grab land and water rights. The valley's great land baron conspires with "government men" and urban predators in an aqueduct scheme to export the ranchers' water supply. Citizens form a committee to block the powerful urban-landlord alliance but fail to see and act on their common economic interests. The specter of power confuses the provincials, and the desultory locals are saved only when the city turns elsewhere for its water. Although the story ends with an uncharacteristic resolution of conflicting interests, the plot boldly draws the frontier dilemma.

The Ford is most animated when it turns to an explanation for this pattern of acquisitive power and yeoman deference. Local farmers and townspeople are weighed down by "their invincible rurality . . . how by as much as they had given themselves to the soil, they were made defenseless in this attack upon it." Captives of the land, they lack a vision for themselves and an alternative to the land baron's master plan. "It isn't the Old Man's capital that the people of the valley are up against, so much as the *idea* of it, and their idea of the situation, or their lack of ideas. . . . The greatest common factor of the Tierra Longans was their general inability to rise to the Old Man's stature; they were inferior stuff of the same pattern." They are simultaneously ingenuous and vaguely ambitious. Like Wallace in Mary's own life and the Brent family in *The Ford*, they hope "to get into something" but have no idea what that something might be. In a lyrical passage she observes, "Capital went about seeking whom it might devour, yet such was their strange illusion about it that they believed that if once they could lay hands on it, Capital could be made to run in their harness, breed in their pastures. To those who owned Capital, and set their brand upon it, it ate out of the hand, but its proper nutriment was the content of poor men's pockets. They railed upon it as wolves that defile the corners of the woodman's hut, and it was the sum of

all their desire." The words convey to us what Ambrose
Bierce called "an unexpected interest [in her] tang of
archaism" and a clear moral injunction. Capital is avari-
cious, and the grave error of common folk is to expect
anything but exploitation at the hands of power. Bold action requires ideas, and frontier society generated no
compelling alternatives to individualism and commer-
cialism.

Although this evaluation may underestimate grassroots initiative and exculpate urban colonialism, it re-
veals a fundamental truth neglected in romanticized accounts of the American West but confirmed by historical
research. Our pioneer settlers were never oppressed
peasants defending communal bonds. Rather, they were
precarious entrepreneurs anxious for commercial development. The men, at least, were Progressives in the
spirit of Roosevelt's expansive regime. They welcomed
federal intervention that promised regional development
and later quarreled with Los Angeles mainly over their
right to share in the fruits of growth. Women more often
understood the self-exploitation underpinning pioneer
society. As Mary Austin observed in her autobiography
Earth Horizon (1932), "There was a spell of the land
over all the men. Men talking together would inevitably
express the deeply felt conviction, 'Well, this country is
bound to go ahead sometime; just look at it.' Women
hearing it would look at one another with sharp — or
weary — implications of exasperated resignation." If, by
today's standards, she neglected government involve-
ment in frontier society, if urbanization and the state
were outside the range of her analytic concerns, she anticipated by many decades our own understanding of

frontier development and the social class and gender divisions it fostered.

In 1906, when Los Angeles won its first engagement in the Owens Valley water war with the right to build an aqueduct, Mary Austin left her husband and Inyo County for good, committed her daughter to an institution, and began a new life in Carmel's emerging artist community. At thirty-eight she was a recognized, self-supporting writer with broad interests in religion, Native American lore, history, and stage direction at Carmel's Forest Theater. As a professional writer, she soon found it necessary to take up residence in New York, where publishing deals could be more conveniently arranged to provide a regular income. Eventually she settled in Santa Fe, where for the balance of her life she wrote continuously and devoted her time (and her estate) to the local arts community, historical preservation, and the Hispanic–Native American population.

The Ford stands out among her thirty volumes of short stories, novels, and biography as perhaps her best characterization of American society and a reflection of the formative influences on her writing. It shows her strength, her compassion as far as it went, her impatience, and her determination to get on with the work at hand. And that work helped build a cultural foundation for successful environmental movements of recent years in Inyo and Mono Counties just as it continues to inform feminism, ecology, and Native American studies. Her legacy is a new understanding of the American West and the diverse participants in its creation.

Suggested Reading

Austin, Mary. 1903. *Land of Little Rain.* Boston: Houghton Mifflin. Reprint, Albuquerque: University of New Mexico Press, 1974.

———. 1932. *Earth Horizon.* Boston: Houghton Mifflin.

———. 1987. *Western Trails: A Collection of Short Stories by Mary Austin.* Selected and Edited by Melody Graulich. Reno: University of Nevada Press.

Fink, Augusta. 1983. *I-Mary: A Biography of Mary Austin.* Tucson: University of Arizona Press.

Kahrl, William L. 1982. *Water and Power: The Conflict over Los Angeles' Water Supply in the Owens Valley.* Berkeley: University of California Press.

Stineman, Esther Lanigan. 1989. *Mary Austin: Song of a Maverick.* New Haven: Yale University Press.

Walton, John. 1992. *Western Times and Water Wars: State, Culture, and Rebellion in California.* Berkeley: University of California Press.

THE FORD

BOOK FIRST

THE FORD

FROM the first Virginia had insisted on playing the Angel. She stood straight, with her feet wide apart and her hands on Kenneth's shoulders; her hair blew backward in the wind out of the Draw, and her eyes were shining. Kenneth had his arms about her waist and tugged and strained. The part of Jacob had been conceded to him in his right as shepherd of the lamb-band, browsing in the deep meadow of Mariposa beside the creek which did duty as the brook Jabbok.

A somewhat older, rather overgrown and gangling boy lounged on the sandbank and umpired the play in a way that the Brent children sometimes found annoying. Ever since Frank had come back from San Francisco the last time, he had shown as much superiority toward the democratic play of Las Palomitas as he dared without being left out of it altogether. He suffered the necessity of all despots of keeping himself provided with an occasion for exercising his dominant humor.

"Go on," commanded Virginia to her adversary, "say it."

Kenneth butted his forehead into her breast bone and gripped with his arms.

"Tell me," he panted, "thy name."

"There!" cried the exasperated Virginia. "You've got the words all wrong again!" She relaxed her pose and turned in swift appeal to the umpire, as she was not above doing when it suited her. "It's 'Tell me, I *pray*, thy name.'" Virginia had made the play out of a book called "Bible Stories for the Young," and quoted freely from her own composition. She twisted about to assure herself of Frank's recommendation. Kenneth slipped his arms down to her hips; suddenly the Angel lay sprawling on the pebbly border of the Ford. She gave one astonished squeal as she went down. The little Romeros, who were not supposed to associate with the white children of Las Palomitas except on sufferance, from their gallery on the crumbly bank of the Wash gave a shrill little whoop of delight. They had not understood very well what the play was about, and when they saw Kenneth looking scared and Anne running to gather Virginia in her arms, they changed to a note of soft commiseration.

Virginia was dazed and shaken by the fall, but her eyes were blazing.

"It's no fair," she cried; "you have to play it the way it *is*. . . . Look there what you've done," she triumphed.

She had abraded her elbow on the pebbles and it was beginning to bleed a little. The four Romeros came down from the bank; nobody could have had the heart to deny them a closer view of so interesting an occasion. Virginia, at any rate, had n't; she turned up her sleeve to show the extent of her damage; the eyes of Ignacio Stanislauo expressed the compassion of a Raphael cherub for an early Christian martyr.

"Me — I feex him!" he cried. He dashed off up the creek toward the wet meadow where the Mariposa came out of the Draw. The four other Romeros were divided between loyalty to the chief of their clan and hopeful curiosity over the outcome of imminent war among the Gringos.

"It says, 'Tell me, I pray, thy name'!" Virginia was implacable. "I was trying to get you to say it right and you took advantage of me."

Kenneth, between the flush of victory and embarrassment at having hurt a girl, found it impossible to explain that the connotation of "I pray" in his mind made it a word admissible only at the bedside and on Sundays.

"Ought n't he to say it right?" Virginia appealed to the company. "It's in the Bible," she brought out irrefutably.

"Aw —" Kenneth was taken suddenly with a sense of world-old feminine evasion. "It's in the Bible that the Angel could n't be throwed. That's the way with girls, they want to *play* they are angels, but the boys have to do all the pretending."

A diversion was created at this juncture by the return of Ignacio Stanislauo with a handful of the pink-veined leaves of *yerba mansa*. He poked them at Virginia persuasively.

"You put this on your arm, he won't hurt you no more . . . *siempre, siempre* . . . my mother tole me."

Ignacio's mother being an Indian it was indubitable that she should know the virtues of all herbs. It was true he had seen her use the *yerba mansa* only for burns, but it was all one to Ignacio Stanislauo if he could serve the Gringos. Even Frank came back into the community of interest to watch the shaping of the poultice, for which Anne demanded his handkerchief.

"It's silk —" he began to protest.

Anne looked at him; there was not the slightest trace of persuasion or compulsion in her tone.

"It's bigger than mine," she said, "and Ken has n't got any."

Virginia being comfortably swathed in it, was restored to her normal consciousness of ascendancy.

"You could n't do it again," she notified Kenneth; "not if I was looking out for you."

"Aw, go on," Frank scorned; "do you want a fellow to throw you twice?"

Anne was swift in placation.

"We could play Moses and the Hebrew children," she suggested. "The Romeros could be Pharaoh's army." That had been one of their successes of the summer before, even though the little Romeros had been obliged to lie down in the sun-warmed, sandy shallows for the Red Sea of Mariposa Creek to roll over them, for nobody minded if Ignacio and Francisco and Pedro Demetrio and Carmelita and Manuela came home with their clothes soaked and sun-dried. Now at the end of February the oldest of the tribe tested the water with his bare toe and opined that it was too cold.

"The very idea!" Virginia found it unspeakable that the Romeros should develop an independent point of view; what was to become of half their entertainment? "You can just splash about," she conceded.

But nobody made a move to begin. The truth was that the children were outgrowing the age of make-believe, though none of them knew it. The littler Romeros lined up, looking at her apologetically, like so many dark, bright-eyed little birds on a bough. In the silence they heard the click of horses' feet coming down the Draw.

The meadow of Mariposa Creek lay close up under the Torr'. It was more than a mile from the ranch house and was kept clear for the lambing ewes on account of the lush grass and the strip of windy dunes that fenced it from the valley. At the upper end of the meadow, where the creek came out in soddy runnels under the fern, the Torr' began. It rose from the mesa that closed the southern end of Tierra Longa, with the smooth, lovely swell of a woman's breast. Where it abutted on the flanking range, the Draw opened narrowly and winding. It led by intricate, roundabout ways to the mysterious region of cities and men, brooded over by a perpetual haze of heat, known in Tierra Longa as "over beyond." The little-used wagon road trailed like a dropped thread across the Mariposa and down to Arroyo Verde, islanded by its green fields in the opal-tinted valley. At this season nothing came into Tierra Longa by way of the Draw except an occasional prospector on his way to the Coast Ranges, or a wool-buyer from Summerfield. The clink of shod hoofs, then, on the stones of the Draw, and the half-glimpsed figures behind the thick ranks of the chaparral beginning to be fretted by young leafage, had the exciting charm of the unusual, the mysterious. Unconsciously the children drew all together at the edge of the shallows. The dogs that from the bank had been interested, one might almost say intelligent, spectators of the play, got up now uneasily and walked their accustomed round of the flock that frisked and fed in the meadow.

The riders came out of the Draw, bending to avoid the buckthorn branches. They forsook the beaten track and skirted the spongy meadow where the creek issued from the hill. A third horse with the pack fell to cropping the wet grass where he found it; he was practiced in that business and did not waste himself on detours of investigation. The two men dismounted and began to poke oddly about in the black, pasty loam under the fern.

As the taller of them turned below the willow hummock, the children saw him lift a handful of the oozy earth almost to his face as though to taste or smell it. Halfway in the act he had his first sight of them, their frank, staring curiosity. He made no startled movement, but slowly he let the hand drop and the wet slime trickle from his fingers, toward which he did not so much as glance aside, though they saw him wipe them stealthily upon the tall fern. Without turning or taking his eyes off the children he spoke to his companion, and in a moment the two of them came riding directly to the Ford.

This companion, who rode foremost, was so much a part of what they were accustomed to see moving about the great spaces of Tierra Longa, sandy-colored and trail-weathered, in garments of no noticeable cut or color, that they took scarcely any notice of him; it was on the tall man that all their attention hung.

He was both thin and tall, the thinness accentuated by the drooping black mustache, which reached, swallow-pointed, below his chin and followed the lines of his huge *tapaderas*. One of his eyes, of an extraordinary opaque blackness, had a slight cast which seemed to render it capable of going on with a separate intelligence of its own, ruminating when the other was observant, quick when it was still. His clothes also were black; soft hat and curly *chaps*, as black as the blackest wether of the flock, quite enough to have established his singularity in a country where even the human inhabitants took on the tawny colors of the soil. Out of the depths of his coat the polished ebony handle of a revolver protruded.

As the pair let down the bridles of their horses at the Ford, they swept the whole of Tierra Longa before their eyes came to rest on the children huddled like antelope under the shallow bank, with a fixed, bright curiosity.

The sandy man picked out Kenneth at a glance.

"This the way to Brent's ranch?"

"Over the hill there." All the children turned to show him, with their concentrated gaze, the white walls of the ranch house behind the blue haze of the figs and the pink of the orchard.

"Boss at home?" It came as one word really like his former question, but at Palomitas they heard little else than the clipped speech of the ranges.

"They're cleaning out the ditch." Kenneth strove to be accurate; he had no notion as yet of an incentive to be anything else. "They'll be done by this time." The chorus turned as one to point the westering sun behind the Coast Range.

"Ask him how far it is to Agua Caliente," the dark man suggested as though he found himself unpossessed of the communicating medium.

"Two miles by the lower field, three by the ranch house," Anne interpolated freely; she resented the indirect speech as including them all somehow in the tribe of the Romeros.

"Ask them if old man Rickart is at home." The dark man insisted on an unusualness of address that began to make itself felt even with the children, not bred to any kind of fear or favor. They waited this time for the question to reach them by way of the sandy man, and then for Frank to whom it pertained to answer it.

"My father is in San Francisco," he condescended at last, not without an appreciation of the possible effect it would have on his interlocutors. That it had its effect was evident from the quick centering of their attention on him. The pair looked him over with a kind of stealthiness which extended even to the wordless communication which passed between them.

"When's he calculatin' to get back?" the sandy man wished to know, this time without any audible prompting.

"He's going round by Summerfield first." Frank allowed himself the air of being deep in his father's affairs.

"Oh!"

"Huh!"

These two remarks appeared to be struck out of his listeners as the note of their respective metals. "Huh," said the dark man with an intensifying of the husky whispering which affected all his speech. All the little Romeros shivered to hear it. The strangers reined their horses; they rode up out of the Ford and gained the Ridge which lay between the meadow and the house; they had their heads together as they disappeared over it. Ignacio Stanislauo crept up to Virginia with whom he acknowledged a community of dramatic interest.

"That black man — he ees *un diablo*." He made the Roman sign, mixed with a native Indian gesture of repulsion.

Virginia clutched at the suggestion in an ecstasy of shudders.

"Get out!" Frank cut her short. "They're prospectors. That's why they were so anxious to know if my father was at home. I'll tell Dinnant. He'll soon let them know that we don't allow anything of that sort at Agua Caliente." Tom Dinnant was the warden of the Rickart principality which ran all along the wooded Coast Ranges almost to the Bay. It was the boast of the elder Rickart that he could drive his beeves to market on his own ground; but he maintained it strictly his own, he permitted no trespassing.

Frank turned and began to walk back toward the lower field where he had left his horse tied. The little Romeros, seeing there was no more entertainment to be got out of the Gringos for that day, scattered down the creek to look for *taboose*. Anne and Virginia had their arms about each other.

They had come up out of the Wash to the grassy flat where the ewes were, and it was feeding-time. Scores of white lambkins tugged at the maternal fountain. Here and there some reluctant mother had been reconciled to a changeling by the skin of her own dead lamb sewed over its body, the little dried legs dangling pitifully. All across the meadow they heard the blether of distracted ewes inquiring for the lambs that, answering each to its familiar *baa*, trotted unsatisfied at its mother's heels until by some accident she turned and muzzled it. Finally the field was all atwinkle with white wagging tails that went slower and slower until they ceased from repletion. It was a sight none of the children could resist, though they might see it every day from the middle of February on until weaning-time. They waited now until the dogs, seeing the lambs begin to frisk about again, had set the flock in motion.

There was nothing that made it particularly a hardship for Kenneth to herd the lamb-band in the naturally fenced meadow of Mariposa. Once or twice over the trail, the sheep traveled it with eagerness in the morning and with the docility of habit at night. On this afternoon the other children had come out to keep him company.

Now, as they turned in all together behind the bleating ewes, some instinct, working in them as subconsciously as the spring, set the girls off toward the upper trail which Kenneth was forbidden to take with the sheep; it led to the entangling gullies of the Torr' where the ewes lost their lambs or tired them with much running. Kenneth regarded this defection with dismay; faint lines of cleavage threatened their democracy of play.

He executed a sudden change of front in the face of Frank's detected maneuver to join them. "Aw! — Come on . . . don't be tagging the girls all the time."

Anne repaid him over her shoulder.

"The sun's over Baldy," she reminded. "You know what you'll catch if you are as late as you were last evening."

Kenneth knew perfectly, but he thought it unsisterly of Anne to refer to it. Besides, he could have got the ewes in early as easy as not the night before; he had merely wanted to find out if that roadrunner really had a nest in the camisal. Virginia followed up the advantage. She called to the twins, whom nobody ever thought of addressing as though they had more than a single identity.

"You know what you *won't* get, if you're late to supper."

They knew, of course. They would be turned over to

the charity of Sing Lou, and whatever Virginia might have left of the dessert. Against that alarming contingency the lamb-band had a diminishing interest. They felt it necessary, however, to lag behind it for another quarter of an hour, just to prove to Virginia their scorn of feminine adjuration, shying stones at the bob owls that with the twilight began to come out *whoo-hooing* at their burrows. Kenneth was pleased to have Frank to himself on any terms, pleased enough to go lightly along with running jumps from hillock to hillock, saying nothing. Now and then one or the other of them whistled to the dogs or answered the owls at their mating. As they came up over the Ridge, a long, mole-like rise of the land running from the foot of the Torr' far out into the valley, they made out the figures of two riders and a led horse, moving up the river road toward Palomitas.

"It's those two prospectors." Frank was certain. "They must have turned across the flat as soon as they were out of sight of us."

"What for!" Kenneth wondered.

"They meant to cross the river farther down, so Dinnant should n't see them. Now they find they've got to come back to the bridge." It seemed a reasonable explanation. "They will probably camp in the willows and cross after dark." Frank gave a snort of contempt. "A lot of good that'll do them!"

Kenneth admired Frank's perspicacity immensely.

"What'll Dinnant do to them?" He hoped it might run to shooting or something equally exciting.

But Frank preferred to wag his head portentously, saying nothing.

The flock turned of its own accord into the beaten

track that led past the lower fields to the lane between the orchards. The sun behind the Coast Range had turned it airily blue and filled the valley with a diffused, mellow light.

The mesa here was dotted with oaks, all in tender leaf, and about its dimpled hollows ran drifts and drifts of white forget-me-nots. Over the flats there was the delicate flutter of cyclamen; they swarmed and hovered above the damp places. As the flock shouldered along the fenced field, it checked and crowded on the edge of the old wash of Vine Creek. Kenneth quickened the docile ewes with his voice, he whistled up the dogs; for answer the flock rolled back along the fence, blatting confusedly. Above the blether the boys caught the rush of descending waters. They knew in an instant what had happened. The men had been busy cleaning the ditch and had turned the water back in its ancient channel. Nobody had remembered about the lamb-band.

"You'll never get them across." Frank was familiar with the ways of sheep.

"I got to." There were never any two ways to Kenneth. He had been told to bring the sheep home below the house. The waters of Vine Creek tore along, dark with the dust and rubbish of the abandoned years, with the noise and motion of a great cat worrying a bone. With all its volume and swiftness the creek was not so deep in places that the sheep could not have crossed in safety if they could have been persuaded to cross at all. But before the boys had discovered the difficulty, the leaders had turned back along the bank, and the check had served to dissipate the shallow impulse of their daily habit. They had forgotten that they had set out to go to the corral. Somehow a gently sloping declivity always incited the lambs to play; they ran now in all directions leaping and bunting. The boys and dogs together dashed out and around them. Three times they headed the flock toward the shallows, and each time their silly fears halted the leaders on the edge of the rushing water and communicated to those pressing from behind.

"If we could get old Ringstreak over," panted Kenneth.

Ringstreak was the bellwether, a scraggly, captious ancient of the flock. Suddenly Frank dashed into the bunch after her; he seized the wether by the rump, crowding and jamming her through the huddle and into the stream. As he scrambled up on the farther bank with the astonished wether, he heard Kenneth's cry behind him above the blatting of the flock. By his precipitance one of the lambs had been crowded off the bank into the deep water.

It went over and over — one brief little choking *baa*, and then the steady gurgle of the water. The flock broke from the bank again, every ewe calling distractedly to her own lamb. All at once the orphaned mother concluded that her own must be in the place where she had last fed it, and tore back toward the meadow with the whole excited train at her heels.

The boys looked at each other across the brown ripple; far below them they could still see a white object bobbing and turning.

"Ah, won't you catch it, though . . . won't you just catch it!"

The tone in which Frank measured the completeness of the disaster dangled him just out of reach of it. Suddenly his horse whinnied from the fence where he had tied it earlier in the afternoon. "I got to go home," he announced.

A sense of insupportable forsakenness kept Kenneth speechless. He was used to Frank's method of taking himself out of trouble; what staggered him was the want of any sense of obligation to the senseless flock. He turned and began to run blindly back after the sheep. When he stumbled, the pressure on his chest broke into dry, gasping sobs. He was aware as he ran of the penetrating, musky scent of the little white gilia that opens after the sun goes down; he could see the flutter of petals between his hot eyelids and the earth. The dogs had halted the ewes before he came up with them, and by degrees he was able to turn them, blatting a continuous, mild protest, along their earlier track.

Kenneth's legs twinkled back and forth to keep them in the way, but at ten and a half there is a limit to what legs can do. He was quite spent when they came again to the bank of the Wash. Suddenly lights broke out in the corral at the top of the lane; they heard the tinkle of the bellwether on the upper bank. The sheep had forgotten their fears and remembered that they were going home; one after another of them took the crossing, the lambs scrambling after. Once in the orchard lane they would not turn again, or if they did the dogs could hold them.

The lost lamb harried Kenneth's sense of responsibility. His father, he knew, expected him to bring *all* the flock in. He took the time, then, to run along the bank, peering and calling. He could not imagine that the lamb would be dead so soon.

He saw it at last, washed on a bar on either side of

which the creek slid smoothly over hollows, old trout pools before the waters were put to work in the ditches. He felt the pull of the stream as it closed over his ankles. He was not afraid, — all the children at Palomitas could swim, — but he had been running with his eyes close to the ground; he had not noted the withdrawing of light from the sky. Now, as he looked up with the drowned lamb in his arms, he saw it dark; pale darkness like obsidian above, and thick blackness around the foot of the Torr'. Dark seemed to flash on him and blind him. He slipped, perhaps; he felt the hurrying snake of Vine Creek wrap about his knees. For an instant the waters went over him . . . and then the roaring of it in his ears was silenced by a shout from the bank above. John Grant, the head shepherd, was calling to him from the bottom of the orchard and his lantern made sudden day again.

Kenneth scrambled up somehow and trotted dripping along the trail with the lamb still in his arms. The blether of the ewes sounded faintly from the corral. His day's work was over; he had a faint feeling about his middle which made him think of his supper. John Grant swung the lantern over him as he came into the lane.

"Well, of all the —" he began; he left off, "flabbergasted," as he said afterward at the bunk house.

"I had to get this one," Kenneth explained carefully, "down by the old swimming-hole. . . . Do you suppose my father will whip me?" he asked after an interval in which John Grant appeared to have trouble with his throat.

"Whup ye? . . . Whup ye? . . . ye little . . ."

But they had come plump into Mr. Brent running

down the lane. He had left the ditch earlier than the
men, and he had just learned that the water had not been
turned back. He snatched Kenneth to him, lamb and
all. The boy gave a shout.

"It beats . . . it beats!" he cried; "I can feel it." The
heart under his hand had given a feeble thump.

"They're all in, sor," Grant was saying, "'t is not two
men could have done it." Kenneth began to cry. He
thought it was because he could not feel the lamb's heart
again. "He wants to know will ye whup him, sor?"

Mr. Brent made a strange noise in his throat. He took
the limp body from the boy's hand and turned it over
to the head shepherd: "We'll save this one, too," he
promised.

There was nothing more said as they walked back
through the orchard-scented dusk. Kenneth held fast to
his father's hand, and by what came to him from that
warm pressure he knew that somehow the question of
whipping had been quashed. At the door his mother
came through the square of light to meet them; he had
forgotten about his mother. She could never forgive any
sort of blundering. He wanted to tell her at once that
John Grant would be able to save the lamb, but he could
not frame a beginning. His father put up a hand quickly.

"He's dripping wet," he warned her.

She sheered off, drawing back her dress.

"What in the world —" The light streamed from the
door full onto him. "Why, the boy's drowned!" She
had one of those terrible flashes of insight which all they
at Palomitas dreaded. "You turned the water — you
put the child to a man's work and then you can't even
remember . . . " She snatched at her son's free hand.

Kenneth stood between them, as he knew himself too often, miserably, the source of mutual accusation. He did not know at first what checked the flow of recrimination, but as he crossed the threshold he saw that it was the presence of the tall black man whom he had last seen riding in the valley. He looked even taller without his *chaps;* his hat was off, and around the dead blackness of his hair ran a shining crease where the heavy sombrero had rested. As they looked at each other, Kenneth was aware of the cast eye taking him in on its own account with a complete and sinister intelligence.

II

WHETHER it was due to company, — in the person of the dark man, — or the mere effect of putting his father in the wrong, a form maternal solicitude often took with her, Kenneth was disposed to make the most of his mother's commiserating frame, of the nearness of her lovely arms as she helped him to dress, the softness of her bosom and the faint scent of her hand under his chin as she brushed his hair. It was a moment of dear and satisfying intimacy, the more so as he felt it somehow commensurate with the evening's adventure, — of which the rescue of the drowned lamb had been the least considerable item,— and he prolonged it even to the risk of the impatient "There, there!" with which she too often met his flooding sense of her wonderfulness.

He was swimming in that sense when they came, with her arm about his shoulders, some minutes later into the dining-room, caught up to appreciations of her charm which gave him for once the sharp, dividing test of manners in his father's rising to draw her chair for her, and the dark man's lumbering up after his host and dropping down again without having discovered what it was about. Between the Brents and their guest widened, in the act, the rift of social distinction.

Under the arm of Ah Sen, the Chinese boy who was helping his plate, Kenneth looked across to Anne. There passed between them the swift, excluding communication of childhood which swept their visitor aside and apart into the limbo of their mother's "that sort of people." It was gone in a flash as it had come; the overlying consideration was to make Ah Sen understand that invariably and on all occasions one wanted a great deal of gravy. When he had leisure to attend to it, Kenneth was aware that the conversation going on about the board afforded his mother new and subtle opportunities for presenting his father in the light of being very much to blame for things as they were. She was leaning forward a little to bring her interest to bear on their guest, and Mr. Jevens, who was blowing his coffee with both elbows on the table, gave her the whole of his good eye which burned like a black, phosphorescent hole in his sallow countenance.

"Literally made in a day, ma'am, fortunes made in a day," he assured her. He waved his cup as though it were some sort of fairy wand by which such riches came into being.

"But where so many are made," — Mr. Brent attempted to stem the flood of fortunate instances, — "there must be many lost also."

Mr. Jevens waved his prestidigitating cup over the objection.

"Doubters, doubters," he protested; "them that don't know their opportunity when they see it. There are people," — Mr. Jevens's manner admitted that, though it was nearly impossible of belief, it was so, — "people who need a lot of convincing to allow themselves to become rich — there was Delancy, he did n't take any stock in it anyway you could fix it, turned down offers and offers. Hogs and alfalfa was good enough for him any day. Finally comes a man from Santa Anna. He'd been through the oil boom down there and knew what was what.

'Never mind,' says he; 'you keep the land and give me
sixty per cent of what I can get out of it.' Mrs. Delancy
she was after him. 'What harm will a few holes do your
old land anyway?' says she. 'I guess your alfalfa don't
reach down to where the oil is.' So Delancy gave in. He
made them bore in the old horse corral so's it should n't
stop the seeding any — and now," — Mr. Jevens flicked
it off the ends of his long fingers which, like his person,
were tipped in black, — "now Mrs. Delancy and the
girls are in Paris."

Having drawn off nearly the whole of his coffee at a
gulp, Mr. Jevens put down the cup and looked about for a
new point to hang his relation upon. Mrs. Brent held it
out for him, with a sharp little needle-like dart in it, such
as her husband too often winced under. It appeared even
now to have passed over Jevens to whom it was addressed
and struck at its accustomed mark.

"And yourself, Mr. Jevens, — you've not let all these
opportunities by you!"

"Me, ma'am!" Jevens coughed modestly behind his
hand. "Not having either land or capital, not to say
what you'd call capital," — he had the air of taking off
his hat to it, — "I did n't expect to come in for the big
prizes, but still — but still —" He modestly permitted
his manner of not being altogether displeased with himself to say what it would to them.

"But how can you — without land or capital — much
capital?" Mrs. Brent played with her salad and an appearance of making conversation for politeness.

Ah Sen was taking away the plates for the dessert,
which maneuver appeared to give Mr. Jevens some concern as to whether or not he should hold on to his knife

and fork. He changed his mind at the last moment and rose in his own estimation by discovering that he had done the correct thing in letting them go. It lifted him for the moment to a plane where he could expand graciously to his hostess.

"Stocks, ma'am, stocks. You get in on the ground floor when the company is formed, and you sell on the rise . . ." He finished the remark directly to his host. Mrs. Brent relinquished the subject as beyond her. "Twenty thousand . . . a cool twenty thousand . . . and in four months." Mr. Jevens fairly spread it on the table for them. "It's a matter of knowing your opportunity when it comes to you!" He leaned back in his seat and resisted visibly the impulse to tuck his napkin into the front of his shirt.

Mrs. Brent looked across at her husband. "You see!" she seemed to have said.

There being no more pudding to be got out of Ah Sen on any persuasion, Kenneth's interest wandered from the conversation about the room in search of entertainment. It was a low L-shaped room, made by tearing out one of the thick adobe walls in the old Spanish hacienda, with great smoky fireplaces and narrow slits of windows. The walls had been tinted over many times and the peeling of the various coats made strange, shadowy shapes of beasts and birds. Secretly Kenneth's fingers had often helped out the suggestion of his quick fancy. Now as he looked at his latest effort, under the flicker of the lamp, he was reminded of the drowned lamb bobbing in the rush of Vine Creek, neck and heels together.

He wondered if John Grant had been able to save it, and decided that he would go at once and see. He caught

Anne's eye with the thought and the two of them wriggled simultaneously. He felt for her foot under the table which came promptly to meet his and shoved vigorously. Anne's chair creaked a little and she giggled.

"If you can't be still, children," their father commanded, "leave the table."

They got up, gravely folding their napkins.

"It will be in the bunk house," Anne whispered at the door; nothing else had passed between them and no more was needed.

There was a fire in the bunk house stove, for though it was the end of February, the ewes had not all lambed yet and it was necessary for the head shepherd to be up with them at all hours. Nights on the Torr' were chilly often, on into April. They found the drowned lamb wrapped in a rag of old blanket under the stove; it blatted freely and moved its head.

Anne hunted about until she found the nursing-bottle which was kept for orphans, or for unhappy firstlings whose mothers refused to suckle them. When they had warmed some milk, John Grant put a dash of brandy in it. The men were still sitting about the dismantled supper-table — obviously under the spell of the sandy man who had come down the Draw with Mr. Jevens. Finding him there the children understood that the two strangers stood, or wished to be thought to stand, in the relation of employer and employed. Hank Sturgis, the teamster, sat opposite the sandy man and played the part of chorus to what the others lapped up with avidity.

"How did they first come to know it was there?" Hank prompted as a means of keeping the stream flowing.

"First off it was a couple of fellows had been around

Santa Anna, when the boom was on there; they was fishing up Cedar Crick, an' they see what was considered signs. So they had an expert up, sayin' nothin' to nobody."

"Of course!" interpolated the chorus to a circle of appreciative nods —

"And the upshot of it is they got six wells down, runnin' a thousand barrels a day."

"Them owning the land, I take it?" Peters, the ploughman, contributed.

"Ownin' nothin'. They bought it offen the fellow what did — sayin' nothin' to nobody —"

"Well, I reckon not," agreed the chorus with a grin.

"There ain't no law compellin' a man to shoot off his mouth about what he expects to make out of what he's buyin' —"

"If they was, where'd business come in, that's what I'd like to know!" Peters demanded of the company in general. Nobody seemed to know where it would, indeed.

"The original owners held it for sheep pasture, and they was tickled to death to get twenty-five an acre for it — and now she's runnin' a thousand barrels a day." The sandy man, who answered to the name of Collins, was as pleased as though he had done it himself.

"What they talking about?" Kenneth demanded of Anne over the lamb which had managed a resuscitating wag of its tail.

"Coal oil, silly. It comes out of the ground."

"Truly-truly!" There were times when Anne's information was more interesting than reliable.

"Ask father! It's like an artesian well."

Kenneth revised a sketch impression of barrels running

at large across the sheep pasture, by what he recalled of the smooth, pellucid flow of the Agua Caliente well.

"What I want to know," demanded Peters, "is where ye'll be when Standard Oil catches you?"

"We ain't a-worryin' about that until it does."

"And then 't won't do ye no good. I seen old John D. onct, and if you think he ain't got his little eye on ye —"

The lamb had finished the bottle and the children, being forbidden to linger in the bunk house, wandered out into the soft dusk. They sat down on the edge of the *patio* under the Banksia rose starred over with hard, tiny buds. Now and then a gust of air wandering down from the Torr' brought them the strong smell of the sheep and the rustle of young leaves in the chaparral. Dan, the house dog, got up from his bed and came and lay down beside them. The square light of the open door spread out sharply on either side and was lost in the pomegranate bushes.

"I say, Ken," — Anne looked at him with a mixture of interest and a determination not to be imposed upon, — "were you nearly drowned?"

Kenneth wriggled with embarrassment, working a toe into the hollow of the other foot.

"I guess so," he confessed.

They were silent for an interval in which it appeared they had somehow slid along the stoop toward one another.

"Ken . . . " very softly.

"Well, what!"

"I would n't have liked it if you had been drowned."

"Oh, shucks," said Kenneth; "I would n't 've liked it, neither."

They did not know how it happened, but they were so close together that it seemed quite natural for them to be holding hands under the fold of Anne's apron, and something in the warm clinging of Anne's fingers made him think of his mother.

They sat so, quietly, until their father came out and sent them off to bed. He was looking very tired after his day in the open, as he often did, hiding his desire for sleep from their mother's deep irritation with it. As they kissed her now for good-night, she was in the brightest of her evening moods, trying as she did on so many occasions to give to the habitual gathering a status which it had n't intrinsically for any of her family, and succeeding now in it only by the help of Mr. Jevens.

The light had been moved from the dining-table to the piano, and by some subtle arrangement the whole room had taken on for the moment the air of being not, as it actually was for the rest of them, a casual and transient retreat, but the center of a settled existence. To whatever suggestion of this sort it had for him, Jevens had responded handsomely. He sat far back in his chair, fingering his swallow-tailed mustache.

"A man'd ought to know when to quit," he offered oracularly. "I've had my slice of luck, and now I'm looking for a tidy ranch."

"Oh — a ranch!" There was an upward note in their mother's voice; it was as if she saw, across the heads of the children whom she kissed without remarking what she had so often protested Las Palomitas did n't offer her in any case, a Way Out. They were so accustomed to her talking of Palomitas as if they were all aching to get rid of it, that it waked in them not even a habitual resentment.

The room in which Kenneth slept was in the older adobe part of the ranch house; it had been, when Las Palomitas itself had been a Spanish hacienda, a chapel; his dresser was backed into the space where the altar had stood between the little niches in the walls for saints. In those days there had been a border painted on the walls in primitive reds and blues, and an attempt made, in successive whitewashings, to preserve it as a finish to the room — but more and more the whiting had carelessly encroached until now the scrolls and saw teeth showed faintly here and there like the traces of the gay Spanish life that had gone on once about El Torre Blanco. Often just as the boy would be dropping asleep, it came out for him quite plainly. He made it out now, lying staring awake with the excitement of his adventure with the sheep, the struggle in the water, and the arrival of the strangers.

At the foot of his bed there was a little window a foot or two square, which had never had a glass, but was protected by a pent which opened up and down like a box lid, to keep out the rain. It was open now upon the flank of the Torr' where the wind moved on the leaves of the chaparral as upon waves, and the rounded backs of the live-oaks bulked like strange, huge creatures come up out of the sea to graze. In the mingled light of the stars and a paling moon, the shadows of the pepper trees moved on the faintly illumined wall, and the face of the dark man, with the extra intelligence shining in his misdirected eye, shaped out of them. Kenneth recalled Ignacio's characterization of him as *un diablo;* it seemed not unlikely. By association he recalled along with it something which had not been in his mind for several days.

On the east side of the house where the ground was too broken for cultivation, the camisal came down to the garden fence. There was a little gate there by which one went along past the cultivator sheds and the horse stalls to the corrals, without the trouble of opening and shutting heavy gates. The space cleared for this convenience became a sort of limbo where rubbish was dumped and small farm creatures, that died of themselves, were buried. Whatever was given, the camise and the wild cucumber took and converted into green leaf. In two seasons it had grown quite over the place where they had buried Shep, the herd dog. Shep was the father of all the herd dogs on the place, a very patriarch of dogs; he had known everything that it was necessary for a sheep dog to know, but he could not know outside his kind. On such a night as this he had slipped the collar which he regarded as an indignity, and eaten of the poisoned meat put out for the wild cats and cougars that troubled the Palomitas flocks; and though he had come whining up to the house for help in the early light, there was nothing that could be done about it. The blatting of the flock going out to the morning pastures had drawn his last bark out of him, and he had become, in a very little while, the source of a singular and secret experience. About the time Kenneth was able to pass, without a choking rush of tears, the spot where Shep had been buried, there began to steal over him the suggestion of Shep's being still alive there, of revisiting, as dead men were said to do, the scene of his extremity.

On the morning that the old dog had come groveling with pain to the *patio*, Kenneth had prayed very earnestly that he might not die, and now by a queer reversion of the faith that had suffered such a shock, he became convinced that the dog's life was really going on there in the cleared space back of the garden and the corral. It was only a few days after this recrudescence of belief that he had been strolling along the trail there, when the thought came to him, "What if he should be chasing me now?" And in an instant he found himself running toward the gate in a panic of fear. He knew in his secret soul that nothing could be more unlikely, but he could not pass that way again without thinking about it, and anticipating the start and the delicious thrill of causeless terror. It grew very shortly into a game with strict observances. When he came by the sheep corrals as far as the buckthorn bush, he was safe; from that on to the garden gate there was no knowing what might catch him; but the moment the gate clicked to behind him and the bean rows began, there was an end to his panic. Of real fear he knew nothing whatever, of night or darkness, nor even of the bears and cougars which still by night visited the sheepfolds of the Torr', but he would not for worlds have confessed, even to Anne, the appetite he had for the sharp clutch of his breath and the race with the nameless dread and the relief of safety.

Now, as he saw the tops of the camisal all lifting and fingering with the wind, the sense of his incompleted evening's adventure came back to him with the recollection that it had been days since he had had an opportunity for the game he played with fear. Suddenly at the thought, he slipped out of bed and into the moccasins upon which he had compromised between his own passionate wish to go barefoot and his mother's insistence on shoes. He let himself noiselessly out of the little window.

The light had gone out in the living-room at last, and there was nothing astir in the garden but the bean leaves flacking against their poles. Just outside the gate the Fear waited for him. It gathered immensity with the night. The thumping of his heart startled him with the illusion of padding feet. By the time he came to the end of the horse corral the game had broken bounds; it had all the night and the windy space for its own; it would not, he was dreadfully aware, leave him at its accustomed corner. He plunged on, tripped and fell. It was upon him now, the Thing that had almost snatched him hours before in the rush of the waters. The panels of the horse corral were wide apart. Lying there in the discarded litter where he had fallen, Kenneth's courage took flight; with a little clucking noise in his throat he rolled under the panels and lay panting while the Fear went by.

Heaps of fresh fodder lay about; he could hear from their stalls the steady munching of the horses . . . and then voices. Mixed with the darkness and his state, they took on terrifying strangeness. It was not till he heard the stirring of the hay on the other side of the heap that he identified them as the voices of Jevens and his companion. They had come out to their camp bed which they had thrown, no doubt at their host's suggestion, on the hay. Nobody in those days thought of offering beds to their chance visitors any more than of refusing them a meal. Kenneth heard their preparations for the night, and then the voice of the sandy man, pitched low for caution.

"How'd ye make out!"

"They'll bite. The madam's hooked already. He ain't so easy."

"He'll loosen up. I got it out of the men that the place is mortgaged for all it'll stand. And ranchin' don't agree with her."

"It would suit my plans better," Jevens calculated, "if it was n't mortgaged so much. What's the good of them sellin' if they come out with nothin' in the end of it?"

The sandy man made a rusty, chuckling sound. Kenneth could hear how he laughed by the rustle of the hay.

"It'll be a reason for their sellin' to *us*, that we can afford to give 'em something. But it's got to be *pronto, pronto*. The Old Man himself will be gettin' on to it."

"Not him. He's had every foot of the range experted, and this side of the valley don't interest him none. What'd you do with them samples?"

"In the cayac." The sandy man stretched himself audibly. There was silence for a time and then a remark broken by a long, yawning sigh. "If we don't get no more rain than we've been gettin', he'll be eatin' out of our hand before October."

A low, steady sound answered him; the dry stems of the alfalfa creaked under the sandy man and presently Jevens took up the sound on his own account, improving upon it in variety and volume.

The talk had hardly interested Kenneth, but the cessation of it did. He must get back to bed, and he knew he would never have courage to attempt the camisal path again that night. He meant to creep on to the sheep corral and down by the wagon sheds to the house on the other side. The dogs would know him.

He rolled under the panel noiselessly, but as soon as he was on his feet again, the Fear was up and after him. It brought him into the sheep corral in a short, dry agony of sobbing. It leaped upon him. It took voice at last and barked. It licked his face . . .

When his breath came back again, there were his father and John Grant with the lantern bending over him.

"Boy, boy . . . " Kenneth felt arms around him and yielded himself to simple crying.

"He's been walking in his sleep, sor." Grant swung the lantern across his face. Flora the dog fawned on him. Kenneth understood that his father and Grant had come down for a last look at the ewes, more than twoscore of which had not yet cast their lambs. But he did not try to have them understand how he came to be there.

"Poor little man, no wonder, after such a day." Mr. Brent took off his coat and wrapped it about the boy's pajamas. He lifted his son in his arms, and Kenneth's hand went about his shoulders.

He turned up his face as the men moved on their round and saw the pale remnant of the moon like a broken boat, and the great constellations which his father had pointed out to him, wheeling to their stations. The night wind blew down from the Torr' in a steady current. It was all a solemn stillness except for the mutter of the mothering ewes and the click of a wooden bolt sliding into place . . . but by the time his father laid him in his own bed, he was past knowing anything about it.

III

On clear days the outlook from Palomitas took in the
flat glimmer of the marshes in which the river lost itself
at the far end of Tierra Longa. Always one had the
town in view and the green-lined squares of the quarter-
sections which fringed the creeks between the Agua
Caliente fence and the green, meandering smudge the
river made on its way down from the west flank of the
Torr'. It was a little river, but swift and full, beginning
with the best intentions of turning mills or whirring dyna-
mos, with the happiest possibilities of watering fields and
nursing orchards, but, discouraged at last by the long
neglect of man, becoming like all wasted things, a mere
pest of mud and malaria. Not but that it did its best
with such opportunities as were offered it. The Caliente
Ditch, taken out above the branding-pens, watered a
great green oasis of alfalfa, and the "Town Ditch"
turned the original purlieus of a Spanish roadhouse into
a green, murmurous hive out of which scarcely any betraying roof lifted in that clear air. Far below all these
its surplus waters made a glittering hieroglyphic between
the poisonous greens of the tulares. In wet years it went
on beyond these and reached the sea.

It was one of the certainties to which Kenneth seemed
to have been born, that the figure of the watery waste
spelled much to his father, that, in moments when they
faced it together, as they did, following the lamb-band
past the Wash of Vine Creek next morning, seemed wondrously shared between them. He could not, of course,

understand that his father was looking at that almost untouched valley as a man might at his young wife, seeing her in his mind's eye in full matronly perfection with all her children about her; but the warmth of that vision communicated itself to the hand that his father held and expressed itself in sundry little hops and skips of satisfaction.

It was at breakfast that Mr. Brent had announced his intention of walking with Kenneth and the lamb-band as far as the Wash. By adding that as soon as school began he would put one of the Aguilar boys to the herding, he had precipitated one of those displays of Mrs. Brent's hostility to Las Palomitas which the children were beginning to feel as a hidden thorn on which the family life might be impaled at any moment.

"I don't know," she coldly charged, "why, if the boy is to be brought up as a sheep herder, you bother with school at all."

"There ain't going to be no school," Kenneth had announced inelegantly, pleased with being able to deliver a piece of news and at the same time somehow range himself on the side of his father. "The Scudders have sold out. Frank told me."

The item had been overlaid in his mind by the adventure of the day before; however, if he had saved it with the notion of bringing it out with the greatest possible effect, he could n't better have chosen the time. His mother laid down her knife and fork, let them fall even with a little clatter on her plate.

"Steven! Steven!" she called across to her husband, almost indeed as if the significance of the incident had driven her to his side. There had been a five months' school insecurely maintained in the district by the residence in it of the required number of children of school age. The Scudders would withdraw six.

"Frank said his father offered them two hundred dollars," Kenneth eked out his effect, "and they swallered it whole."

"Swallowed, you silly!" Anne corrected, dribbling syrup on her cakes in a negligent ladylike manner.

"Well, I suppose if people insist on living in a place like this, that is what they must expect."

Kenneth was uncertain whether this remark of his mother's referred to the gustatorial feat of the Scudders or to the settled expectation, that sooner or later every homesteader would find himself elbowed out of it by a process which, however indirectly, could be traced finally to Frank's father.

Mr. Jevens chose to find in Kenneth's announcement an opportunity for sounding, as he had more or less obliquely all morning, the praises of a more favored region.

"That's one thing I will say for Summerfield" — it was only one of many which he had more fulsomely said — "that we have good schools there. Our schools are as well organized and equipped as any in the country." His tone had a slight sing-song which to one more sophisticated than Mrs. Brent might have betrayed the quotation from the honorific circulars by which the price of real estate was kept up in towns of California at that period. "Not," admitted Mr. Jevens, "that it matters much to me, but I can understand that to a man with a family — " He put his elbows on the table and blew on his coffee, and his unofficial eye appeared to express a degree of understanding which the other one by no means corroborated.

"I hear the Old Man ain't anyways friendly to home-steaders," he let out, unable to resist an occasion for getting, even in a small way, a knife into the character of the elder Rickart.

"Scudder took the chances a man must take on unirrigated land." Mr. Brent let the subject drop as he rose, excusing himself to his guest.

Twenty minutes later, as Kenneth stood with his father watching the lamb-band pour steadily down the track toward Mariposa, their eyes came to rest instinctively on the Scudder cabin, close up against the Rickart fence on the west side of the valley. Young trees about it spread a thin shade beyond which they could trace the pale green plantation of winter wheat, which already took on a prophetic tinge of yellow. It struck all at once, for the boy holding his father's hand, the note of the retarded season. Under the spring flush which had followed on two or three really satisfying rains, he perceived the bare bones of drought.

"Over west a ways," which was all their visitor had vouchsafed of the direction of his errand, he could see Jevens and his companion disappearing along the country road toward one of those coastward cañons within which it was sometimes possible to hear as in a shell the far-off roar of the sea. The trail of dust they made was over-matched a moment later by one that sped out from the lower Caliente gate and turned up toward the Torr', too much dust for a team to have stirred up at that time of the year. It puffed out from under the wheels and settled thickly in the lifeless air.

Kenneth tugged at his father's hand.

"Mr. Burke's coming."

Distracted from his study of the landscape by the name, Brent turned his attention toward the opposite slope where, spread out like a map, lay the headquarters of Agua Caliente, an inconsiderable oasis of house and garden in the midst of a great hoof-beaten space of branding-pens and breaking-corrals. Across it the buckboard, with its high shining top, turned into the Palomitas road.

Frank's father spent very little time at the ranch which was under the superintendence of a former fore-man, who was commonly believed to be maintained in the place because no better man would put up with all that Rickart expected of his subordinates. Whatever Cornelius Burke himself thought of his qualifications, he made no boast of them. The families at headquarters and Palomitas were on that footing which disclosed itself in Burke's inquiry, when he had at last come up with Brent and the boy, whether Virginia might n't come over to stay for a few days while her mother accompanied Burke to Summerfield. The boys would do well enough under Frank's tutor, but there was no woman about with whom a girl might be left, a girl, who, as her father admitted with a mixture of pride and excusing, might be up to almost anything in the interim.

"The Old Man sent for me," he offered in explanation. "It's about this oil business." He referred to his employer as the Old Man, just as he would have said the Duke, or His Excellency, supposing neither title to have been convenable; it was the only term allowed him in a democracy to express a state of affairs which the democratic theory explicitly disallowed.

"So," Mr. Brent pricked up a little, — "you think there is really something in all that?"

"Well, the Old Man's going in pretty strong."

"Oh, for *him* there's always something in it. I mean do you think they've struck a permanently producing field?" . . .

What followed was very much the sort of thing that had been said by Jevens. Burke, whose youth had been spent in the oil fields of Pennsylvania, added a personal touch. Kenneth looked the team over and adjusted a buckle tongue which he found hanging loose; the sheep herded by the dogs would be by this time safe in the meadow; besides, he wished to hear how soon they were to expect Virginia. His father came around at last to a subject of more immediate interest.

"Is it true that you've bought out Scudder?"

"The Old Man told me to close him out." Mr. Burke carefully tried the lash of his whip, looking down at it with concentrated attention. "There's no sense in him losing another season at it."

"He'd have proved up in two years if he'd got all the water that was coming to him. . . ." Mr. Brent broke off as not finding it worth while to discuss; everybody knew that before Scudder had filed on the land there had been water enough from Oak Creek to have maintained eighty or a hundred acres, and since that time it had been mostly turned off on the Agua Caliente pastures. He took up the phase of the matter in which Burke as a parent might be interested.

"It will break up the school."

"I'm not so sure; we got in on the census . . . Anyway, this young man that's teaching Frank, we can fix up

something with him, I reckon." Having put the matter in this hopeful light, the Superintendent of Agua
Caliente was disposed to include the unfortunate homesteaders in his genial optimism. "Scudder's lucky to get
what he did. It's going to be a dry year."

"Going to be? It is! Look at that!"

A flock of quail ran neck and neck across the orchard
lane with soft twitterings and cooings; a moment later
they were heard in the barley with their warning *Cuidado
. . . Cuidado!*

Brent shook his head over it. "They've not begun to
mate, and the grain is turning yellow."

"Well," — Burke was judicious, — "we've all of six
weeks yet. If it was to begin now and rain hard for two
or three weeks, it would save us."

"Yes, it would just save us."

Burke gathered up his reins and turned the wheels for
his neighbor to mount to him. "About those calves now
. . ." he was beginning.

Kenneth saw there would be no more for him in the
conversation. He set out for the meadow. John Grant
had given him a shepherd's crook that morning, fitted
down to a stock just the length for him; the curved iron
reached a foot or more higher than his head. The lower
end also was shod with iron, and he used it now as an
alpenstock, digging it into the soft earth and taking long,
skipping jumps with it. Suddenly ahead of him, under
the mirage-breeding mist, he saw close to the ground a
single brilliant flame, orange crimson; it moved a little
and flicked in the wind like a flame. The beauty of it
pricked him still for an instant, then he gave a shout.
In a moment he had snapped it short on its translucent

stem. It was the first of the golden poppies that spring
up so plentifully after rain; as he fastened it in his hat,
he was quite and completely happy.

Virginia came over that evening, with her things in a
suitcase, but it was not until the third day of her stay that
the children were together again. There had been a moment when Frank had swept them all into the common
tribal impulse with a proposal to ride over to the shearing-
sheds at Agua Caliente, an impulse which had been somehow mysteriously checked by a swift assumption of
superiority on the part of Anne, and a disposition of the
two girls to walk apart with their arms about each other
and their chins in the air. Frank thought Mrs. Brent
might be at the bottom of it; Kenneth set it down to
the general unaccountability of girls. But the last afternoon before Virginia's parents came back from Summerfield, John Grant came down to Mariposa to examine the
condition of the feed and set Kenneth free for the whole
of the afternoon. About four o'clock they found themselves, including the little Romeros, who must have had
the same sort of prescience for things going on at Palomitas as the buzzards floating in the thin blue above the
valley had for their particular prey, gathered at the
spring. Peters was cutting out the brush, which made
a cover for wild cats and an occasional lynx that preyed
upon the poultry yards.

The spring was a deep, cool fountain from which
water was piped for use in the house, and lay high
enough on the Torr' to show them the great green flank
of it, stirred by the wind, wavering like the fur on some
wild creature's coat.

The girls had arrived in time to stand out with Peters

for a buckthorn in which mourning doves had made their nest. It was all one to Peters if they could fix it with their Pa. Anne thought they could. The little Romeros quite approved of the exemption, since they meant to come back and rob the nest themselves the following day.

Anne, however, forestalled them. "If there's a single one of those eggs missing," she warned, "I shall know who did it."

Gringos undoubtedly carried things of this sort too far.

Frank and Kenneth found them all sitting on the stacked, springy brush; the air was full of the damp smell of the spring and the crushed fern. Now and then startled rabbits ran out of the brush under Peters's bill, and the little Romeros dashed wildly after. They fell all aheap in the middle of the clearing, to their amazement with the rabbit under them. Pedro held it out by the ears kicking and squealing. Anne cried out at them.

"Drop it!" Frank ordered.

Pedro took the rabbit under his coat, — what passed for a coat, — and made up his mind that if Frank tried any more of *that* on him, he would n't understand English.

"They'll only torment it when we are n't looking," Virginia protested. "Send them away."

"Be off!" Frank was magnificent. "We don't want any of you kids here anyway."

Ignacio Stanislauo took his cue. He waved his tribe away.

"Get out, you! *Vamose! Bastanta!*"

The younger Romeros burned in speechless indignation; it appeared that 'Nacio had turned traitor, but they were too used to obeying him. Besides, if anything more was said they might be deprived of the rabbit. They moved off by one of the threadlike trails disappearing in the camise, by which the woodland visitors came down to the spring to drink.

"Children are so cruel," Virginia offered superiorly to the company.

The Burke boys, who had come over to visit their sister, concealed their disgust. At any price it was worth being outside the jurisdiction of Virginia. They began to run in the clearing, jumping over one another very much as the rabbits leaped in the runways, but at every leap and tumble they came nearer to cover. Presently they disappeared in it, and a little later they were heard signaling the Romeros by low, cautious whistles in the chaparral. The line of cleavage had been effected at last. It was a natural limit of interest and outlook.

The oldest Romero made a brave effort to maintain himself in the new grouping. He came sidling toward the girls with something hollowed mysteriously in his palm.

"*Win-hah-topeék*," he announced, as though it had been a word of power. They looked with solemnity and saw lying there an inch or two of fleshy root and a small transparent-petaled flower. "My mother tole me — eet ees a sign," he nodded wisely.

"A sign of what, 'Nacio?" Virginia was always immensely taken with his retailed bits of Indian lore.

"*Un año malo!*" he wagged impressively.

"A bad year! But we know that already." The children felt slightly imposed upon. "Does n't your mother know something better than that?"

"Oh, but thees ees ver', *ver*' bad year; thees sign he

only come when my mother leetle . . . leetle . . . " He tried a sliding scale on his person as his sense of the remoteness of the period increased. "Then all the creeks go dry, all the deer she go — *pasear* — up the mountain, all the cattle die . . . See, eet ees begin." He tossed the fragment of *win-hah-topeék* dramatically toward the vault above the valley where the black specks of buzzards hovered over the moving flocks, sliding in and out of the distance on invisible wires.

Kenneth began to count.

"Four, five — seven."

"Over by the Gordo," Virginia pointed out.

"Seven on Mariposa Creek," Frank announced; "but that 's where John Grant lost a ewe yesterday." Nevertheless, he looked quite soberly with the others down the long groove between the hills, turning fawn and tawny where it should be green. From the edge of the chaparral they could hear the cry of the unmated quail.

"*Cuidado!* Have a care," translated Ignacio Stanislauo triumphantly. "He knows. *Cuidado!*" He returned the whistled warning.

Frank rolled over and lay staring up at the light withdrawing from the sky.

"Oh, well, what's the diff.? I'm going down to the coast in August, my father promised me. I shan't see any of it."

Anne looked down at him in measured indignation.

"If things were starving I'd care — whether I had to look or not. I can look with my mind just as well as I can with my eyes."

"Oh, of course —" Frank corkscrewed himself half into a sitting posture. "Of course I did n't mean —"

"And I *would* look," Anne finished with her chin cupped in her hands. "Even if I could n't help it, I'd look. I would n't pretend I did n't know what was going on."

Frank changed the subject to one which permitted the implication of reproach on his side.

"Why did n't you come to the sheds the other night?"

"Her mother would n't let her." Virginia was explicit. "She thinks we are too old to play with boys."

In the pause which ensued they accepted it after their several fashions; they would no doubt have found it out presently for themselves.

"I suppose we've just got to grow up," Virginia sighed; then her facile mind took flight. "What you going to be?" she demanded.

Kenneth had no doubt whatever. He should stay right on at Palomitas and have more sheep than anybody; but Virginia convicted him of a want of imagination.

"I shall go everywhere," she announced, "and I shall tell people what to do. I'm going to have them be kind to the poor and not let there be any little children crippled — or anything." Then, on reflection, as if she did n't see exactly where she came in herself, added, "perhaps I shall act in a theater and have them throw flowers at me."

The brilliance of this prospect took their breath away. It was not dimmed even by Frank's declaration that he meant to be rich.

"Are n't you rich now?" Anne was interested.

"Not like I'm going to be. I'm going to do like my father; I'm going to get after some of those fellows down there —" he waved his hand in the cloud-shadowed direction where the city lay, — "and I'm going to have them running."

Kenneth had a moment of wishing he had chosen this for himself; but Anne pricked the bright bubble in a way she had.

"They'd be running *away from you!*"

"Oh, I'll have them scared all right." Frank lay back on the brush and crossed his legs, with his hands in his pockets, as he had seen his father do.

"Well," said Anne, "I think it would be a lot more fun to have them running *with* you."

"Yes!" cried Virginia, "like a soldier, don't you know." The imaginations of all of them flamed up.

Kenneth looked at her admiringly. "I guess I'll be that kind," he chose again.

"Oh! and I'll inspire you — like . . . like . . ." Virginia cast about in her mind for an example; but Frank cut her short.

"It was Anne thought of it first," he insisted.

Nobody inquired about the future of Ignacio Stanislauo; perhaps he knew as well as they what was foredoomed in his blood.

Anne had to be persuaded a little. At last she confessed.

"I'd like to keep house and have children."

"Ho-ho!" Kenneth began to laugh; he had picked up somewhere, but he could n't say where, a faint savor of ribaldry as proper to such an admission.

Frank kicked out at him.

"Shut up," he said. "That's what women are for."

"Not all," Virginia held out. "I've seen in the papers, actresses are always Miss."

"Much you know about it!" But Frank would not explain himself further, chiefly because he could n't. He had, in his last stay in the city, clutched at the skirts of knowledge but not of understanding.

Kenneth had left off laughing to look at his sister in the light of Frank's acceptance of her destiny. So Anne was to be a woman. Somehow he had never thought of her as anything but Anne. He was struck now as he had never been before with the likeness to her mother in the curve of her cheek and the faint swell of her bosom under her gingham dress. She was not pretty as Virginia was, her eyes were too pale and the thick hair, drawn smoothly on either side her face, was ash-colored, but he saw how inevitable it was that she must turn out a woman.

They were all quiet as they trailed along after Peters to the edge of the camisal. At the upper gate of the *potrero* they heard the first gong for supper. Virginia measured the distance across it with her eyes.

"First one to the gate's the winner!" she cried.

Toe and toe she set off with Kenneth and Ignacio. When they brought up breathless, all in a heap against the bars, they turned to see Anne and Frank far behind them walking sedately.

"They never even started —" Kenneth began; but Virginia had n't noticed him. After one look back she began to walk off toward the house with her chin up as if nothing in the world was further from her thought than racing.

IV

Two singular and contradictory impressions mixed with
Kenneth's earlier years to make up for him the sum of
associative ideas called Home. One was the feeling he had
about the little room where he slept. It was as safe to him
as its hole to a fox. The deep adobe walls, the low roof,
the pepper tree scratching comfortably about its eaves,
more than all else the maternal flank of the Torr' glimpsed
from its little window as from a half-opened lid, had for
him the absolute quality of refuge. He came into peace
there, distilled delicately as from a vase that has once
held ambergris, and dropped as lightly into sleep as souls
into the faith that for so long had had its daily crisis between the niches in the wall.

The other reached him from without, through the thin
partition of the door that formerly had opened from it to
his parents' room. It was boarded across now, and with
a chintz curtain its deep recess served as a closet for his
clothes, but never for the purpose for which it was probably intended, to cut him off from their private dissatisfactions. It was close to the head of his bed, and often
at night, sometimes long into it, he could hear, like the
wearing of machinery left to run down unattended, the
guttering end of his mother's empty, unappreciative
days. It had become so early part of a great natural sequence that the free, rich life of Palomitas *was* empty for
his mother, that he had never attempted to account for
it. He supposed it must be so with ladies. He had
found himself even with a kind of tender commiseration

for her in a situation so little in accord with her disposition. It drove him from his father at times to perceive in him, as he was sure she did, the source of her discomfiture, and drove him back, with a sense of their mutual incrimination, in liking heartily what a lady so beautiful and charming as his mother so completely disliked.

For they were all of them, except Mrs. Brent, wholly and absorbingly interested in what went on at Palomitas. Life for them was lived out of doors; it was only lately that the children had begun to be embarrassed by her demand that it should be in a degree lived about the supper-table or under the lamp. Days for her were to be got through somehow; they were the excuse for, or the annoying interruption to, the real performance on which, for their mother, the curtain seemed never quite to go up. There was something expected of them which they were helpless to afford her, something vaguely indicated to them by the obligation of dressing for the evening meal, of playing the piano as she was teaching Anne rather futilely to do, and particularly of talking.

"She wants us," Anne had figured it out, "to be company."

There was very little of that at Palomitas to judge by, but certainly company, under the stimulus of their mother, always talked. In their small way the children had undertaken to rise to an expectation which their father's manner ever permitted them to think of as unwarranted, but the trouble was that they *had* talked. At the Ford, by the lambing-corral, they had met the day's occasion with its appropriate comment or debate. But where, indeed, — Anne put the matter succinctly for them both, — "when you are n't doing anything, is the talk to come *from?*"

Their mother, at any rate, found an unfailing stream of it which, after the house was shut and the children in bed, ran on in a kind of fretful gurgle behind the walled-up door of Kenneth's room. It seemed to have taken on a new and sharpening impetus after the return of the Burkes from Summerfield. They had come driving down the Draw after a week's absence with a distinct and distinctly maintained air of having been in the great world, to set up in this quiet cove of Tierra Longa an eddy of its tremendous stir. Things were doing out there, things which, even with his salaried position and perquisites, Mr. Burke thought it a pity a man should miss, things which he permitted them to guess rather than directly said, he had been sent for in order that he should n't miss. Treasures were being pumped up out of the earth, trips to Europe, houses in the city; better still, enlarged opportunities for involving yourself in the stir, for making, to a degree, a stir on your own account.

"Makes a man feel like he was *in* things," he confessed, "money passing like that; even if it does n't stick to you none, you feel it circulating." He seemed freshened and livened by the touch; he even handed it about for the moment to his hearers.

"You mean to tell us, then, that none of it *did* stick to you?" Mrs. Brent was watching him, Kenneth thought, almost as if she expected to detect it somewhere about his person.

Cornelius Burke was a tall, bony man with the blue, black-fringed Irish eyes which he had managed to pass on to Virginia without implicating her in the nose and chin between which a Fenian conspiracy was deferred by a bristling, square-cut, black mustache. His admiration for Mrs. Brent as a fine figure of a woman was just modified by resentment at her restless maternal anxiety. It was an implication of Brent's inability to bring his affairs to a successful issue, which as Brent's friend he was unwilling to admit. He dropped back, at her question, from neighborliness to his character of cautious agent.

"You have to be *in* the game for that . . . those yellow birds don't perch, I reckon, except where there's bird lime about. Not but what I'd be above taking a whirl if it came my way," he relaxed, remembering Virginia.

"You think, then, that it's a sound development, that it will hold out as it's begun?" Brent questioned. "These things have a way of slumping."

Burke grinned. "It won't slump yet a while, I can tell you. The Old Man's in deep. Deep."

Although they might have questioned its legitimacy, no one in his senses would have doubted the financial fatness of any venture so long as the Old Man remained in it. And the extent to which he was "in" was proclaimed very loudly within the week by the "Summerfield Clarion," and in Tierra Longa more personally by the fact that he had not discouraged, as his habit was, the favored ones in his employ from taking stock in the enterprises which circulated in his name, but even condescended so far as to indicate the companies in which he deemed it advisable stock should be taken. He had spread at last, as Tierra Longa had lingeringly hoped, as it believed he might so easily and humanly do, the mantle of his financial competency over their insufficiencies. It produced in certain of the community a kind of pocket loyalty, a dis-

position to find in the methods by which Agua Caliente
had been compacted, out of two or three loose-titled
Spanish grants, into one of the best cattle ranches in the
country, nothing more reprehensible than the acumen
upon which the success of their investments now hung.
Was n't the very relentlessness with which he had hemmed
in and starved, and at the psychological moment finally
bought out settlers in the adjacent grazing-lands, the best
of evidence that he would be able to maintain his interests
in the oil field? It was all a question of whether you were
against the Old Man in this game, or with him. If until
now you had found yourself in the first case, you could at
least measure by it what might be coming to you in the
second, if, as seemed wondrously the fact, he had decided
to let you "in" on his oil ventures. All down the valley
farms, and in the hill coves from which he had not yet
successfully dislodged the preëmptors, there ran the weld-
ing warmth which money makes, passing from hand to
hand. At Palomitas it was felt, however, that they were
unfairly and inexplicably out of it.

"We always *will* be, as long as you insist on living in a
place like this," Mrs. Brent would protest to her husband
in the biting hours when she worked off against him the
energies undischarged by tasks which she made it a
peculiar merit not to do. "Though I do live in the country, I don't have to *be* country," she had professed to Mrs.
Burke. "A woman has to keep up a standard; she has
only herself to thank if she lets herself down." And how
beautifully, by the aid of paper patterns and the mail-
order catalogues, she had kept up, she was as willing to
have known as to be commiserated on the extent to which
her family were n't able to keep up with her.

"I don't see," she would offer to her husband's heavy-eyed attention, "what we are living here *for*, if it is n't to find ourselves in a position to take advantage of such opportunities when they come along. And how *can* we when all we get by living here is just *living?*"

"It's all, my dear, we'd get by living anywhere, is n't it?" Brent had ventured.

"Oh! if you call this living! It's merely being alive. And the children; I'd like to know what *they* are to get out of it. You never seem to think of *them*. Not even a decent school."

She had him there, as Mr. Brent's silence seemed to imply. He wanted the best for his children.

"Even if you have n't any compunction about throwing *my* life away," she followed up, "you might think of Anne! I suppose I can't even take her to the coast this year."

"If you did," he reminded her, "she would n't in that case have got any schooling either."

"Oh, they'll get nothing whatever, either of them. I suppose I'll have to make up my mind to that!"

He had nothing, however, to offer her but the hope, dulled by much handling, of "getting things straightened out," of "seeing his way" to something which would be a little more commensurate with what she felt herself so richly entitled to. He was n't, if you came down to cases, he reminded her again, getting so much out of it himself. That touched upon the half-sensitized root of wifeliness.

"It's not " — she fell back upon the note of renunciation — "that I mind doing without things, if it only came to anything. I should n't mind not going anywhere, if I had the *price* of going to spend on something I liked

better. But I've *been* doing without . . . and now where
are we?" Her voice would break with it, the vexation,
the sincerity of her effort and the futility of it, to lay hold
on anything in her situation that approximated to what,
for her, were the values of life. "It is n't as if I did n't do
my part, Steven . . . the only part this kind of life gives
me a chance for. I've kept friendly with the Burkes —
a regular Biddy she'd be if it was n't for Cornelius — and
what I've done for Frank . . . His father would be sure
to put you on to something if only — Oh, it is too *stupid*
for anything . . . "

Sentences like these ran on and mingled in the boy's
mind with the tinkle of water dropping from the flume
and the riffle of the wind across the chaparral by which
the Torr' seemed to breathe. In that impressionable hour
between the day and dark, the two streams sunk and
watered the roots of being. Day by day, as the rains held
off and the year declared itself one of unrelievable drought,
a note of desperation crept into the question and recrimination that went on behind the walled-up door.

Early in April the curse of *el año malo* began to settle
down upon Tierra Longa, to be felt even by the children. Both at Agua Caliente and Palomitas they were
selling off as many wethers and yearlings as possible on
account of the scarcity of feed. For three days buyers
from San Francisco had been at the ranch across the river,
and now the drive was beginning; far down the road to
Arroyo Verde the children could count the columns of
dust where they went in bands of three hundred. In the
flat below, the shepherds were still busy parting out the
ewes; they spread, white from the recent shearing, scattering, like grains of corn in the popper, up the coast-

wise slope. The Palomitas's yearlings had been turned
out of the fenced pastures below the house, and far toward Saltillo the lamb-band fed under Juan Romero,
outside the fence.

All down the east side of the valley below the Brent
ranch, the range was government land, with here and there
a quarter-section bought by the owner of Agua Caliente
from the hardy homesteader who had wasted five years
upon it. Just which of the unfenced squares were owned
thus was a matter of conjecture, but enough of them to
keep out the wandering herders who passed in their
yearly round along the Saltillo hills. It was so easy for the
owner of land, that had been inadvertently grazed upon,
to institute a claim for damages that pared the profits of
a whole year's herding. On dry years the knee-high sage
and the curled dry "fillaree" between was not thought
worth the risk. That was why, when it had been determined to turn the Palomitas flocks on the unclaimed public pasture, they had been put in charge of Juan Romero,
who knew — not even the buzzards knew better — just
which of the invisibly divided squares had passed into
private ownership.

It was reported, indeed, that Romero, as the last of the
generation who had received the original grant of Agua
Caliente directly from the Spanish Crown, knew more of
its titles and boundaries than it would be convenient for
the Old Man to have made public. What he might or
might n't have got out of the Old Man on account of it
had been for long one of the settled speculations of
Arroyo Verde.

The drought crept on them slowly. The spring flood
came too early, with the rapidly melting snows, and

was gone too soon. The wild grass failed to seed: the buzzards thickened in the lit space between the ranges. The one good rain which was to have saved them dissolved in quick, impotent showers; by the end of June the streams were all shrunk well within their summer limits. Over all Tierra Longa a weight like a great hand was laid, moving up slowly toward the source of life and breath.

It turned out that, though there was no school at Palomitas, it made very little difference to Kenneth; he was to be kept at the herding. He remembered his father's curt "I can't spare him" as the point at which he began to react instinctively to the pressure from without, the impalpable threatening of the Powers. Whatever it was, he felt himself leagued with his father not to let it happen. Two of the men had been paid off early in the season; there were days when it did not seem possible one pair of legs could do all the running necessary to keep the hungry sheep at their short pastures. Evenings Kenneth would drop asleep with fatigue over his plate, starting awake with a feeling of his mother's immense and inexplicable graciousness in not taking it out of him for such lapses. Times he would be conscious of her hands about him as she laid him on his bed, and moved his lips gratefully against her sleeve, her bosom . . .

Anne, it had been decided, should ride over every day to have lessons with Virginia and Frank under the young tutor. Afternoons Frank would ride back with her to open the gates. The tutor modestly confided to Mrs. Brent that this was partly his own idea; he considered the society of girls excellent for Frank; it was softening. Much of his own softness, which was conspicuous, he owed to such influences. The tutor had not, however, seen his young charges racing up the lane with flying hair and lathered horses. Mrs. Brent had, and made it the basis of a struggle which went on the summer long between herself and Anne, in which Anne was continually losing ground. Not that Mrs. Brent debated or put commands on her. What she did was to put her into muslins and embroideries; she constrained her with nothing more palpable than paper patterns. Anne could reject the promptings of propriety with young scorn, but she was not proof against the feminine obligation of not "making wash." She was reduced by it before the end of the summer to a frame of behavior through which Kenneth could perceive the shaping outlines of a young lady. It was about this time that he noticed that his mother was not fretting about the trip to the coast with which she customarily broke the long summer at the ranch.

"I suppose I might manage it for you and Anne," his father had told her, "but I simply can't spare the boy."

"Oh," she resented, "I'm not *quite* unnatural! I don't want to spoil *all* my children's chances!"

Kenneth took it from this that Anne was getting on remarkably well in her studies with Frank. Whatever either of that gifted pair chose to dispense for his benefit, he received with unenvious admiration.

That year the buzzards drooped low and lower over Tierra Longa. Under the morning haze every hillock, every dying rump was black with them. The fences had been cut and all the cattle turned out to the bone-dry land. Mere crates of bones themselves, they tottered in the trails; they lay down at last with their heads pointed toward the course of the vanished streams, while the buzzards walked solemnly about and made occasional hoarse comments on the ripeness of their condition. The sheep fared better. They could be herded and restrained to their meager allowance of sapless, sun-dried grass. All up the camisal there were lacunæ, little natural clearings where only the deer had penetrated before, — *potreros* they were called, — which were opened up for the Palomitas flocks. Peters would cut lanes in the camise, and Kenneth would follow along the sharp stubble with the sheep. It was easier for him than for the men; he could creep in between the thick, interlacing stems and bring back the hunger-driven stragglers.

As they worked up the Torr' there was much of the high-growing chaparral of which the sheep could eat both leaves and bark, and tufts of bunch grass growing in the crevices of the rocks. It was hot, heart-breaking work. Days when they fed close to the Palomitas fence Kenneth would see the gaunt cattle watching them over the wires from their own gnawed pastures. There was something terrifying to the boy in the slender, pointed horns measuring his full length from tip to tip, and the famished eyes underneath. Although Peters reproved him for it, he could not forbear at times to push branches of the buckthorn under the fence. Nights after would often find him running down interminable close lanes of chaparral pursued by formless heads all slender horn and glazing, hungry eyes. Sometimes he would spy his mother at the end of the run and manage to cry out to her, then he would find her comforting him in his bed. Afterward he would hear voices, quarreling, it seemed, but he could never make out over what.

"You'll kill the boy, too, before you're done . . . What

is this place to you that you should sacrifice everything
to it? What is it to any of us? There is n't even a living!
Just a selfish craze you've got. I'll be glad if they do
foreclose. I'll be *glad!* Do you understand? It's taken
fifteen years of my life, but I'll not stay until it takes my
children!''

"It" was no doubt the terror which pursued him down
the blind lanes of sleep. Even his mother was afraid of it.

After Frank joined his father in San Francisco and
Mrs. Burke had taken Virginia and the twins away with
her to Santa Barbara, Anne used to come out to him in
the long afternoons as often as her mother would let her,
which was oftener than would have been permitted if she
had not — O clever Anne! — thought of bringing her
books along with the avowed intention of keeping Kenneth up with his studies. So they made sand maps for
geography and learned by heart the "Book of Golden
Deeds." The sun turned in his course and the days fell
cooler; people began to look prayerfully for the winter
rains.

In September they began cutting the post oaks to get
at the moss that clung like film to the lower branches.

Burke came over from Agua Caliente that day to offer
the consolation of company. Very little passed between
the two men beyond a prolonged handshake.

"I'm thinkin' the rain can't hold off much longer,"
Burke proposed as a likely topic.

Brent turned his hands outward with a gesture that
said that any time now would be too long for him. He
was a slighter man than his neighbor, but with a sort
of personal sureness before which Cornelius, with all
Brent's informality, felt often at a disadvantage.

"And yet," — Brent returned to a subject that was always in his mind, — "there's water . . . there's thousands of cubic inches of water . . . " His gaze wandering down the glittering hieroglyphic of the river completed the suggestion. "There's people, too, if they could only get together — why can't they get together?"

"And if they could, the whole bilin' of them would n't be the match of the Old Man."

"Ah, but why can't we get together *with* him, — why should n't all of our interests be identical? They *are* as a matter of fact; what I can't understand is why a man of Rickart's intelligence don't see it."

"Now, Brent, what for running mate would the lot of *them*" — Burke thrust out his hand toward the cluster of small ranches around Arroyo Verde — "be for the Old Man? There's that to think of."

"We're not so dull as that comes to." A glow began to come into Brent's pale face. "We have ideas, — I have ideas . . . There's no sense in our having times like this. There's water there . . . water goin' to waste . . . and stock dying for want of what the water would grow. Ah, look at it, Burke." Far down they could see the pale gleam of the mud flats in the tulares. "Thousands of cubic feet going to waste every year."

"Well, this is the way I look at it, Misther Brent; there's ideas goin' around loose, slathers of ideas, but the thing that counts is puttin' 'em through. I don't know what quality the Old Man's ideas are, but he gets 'em *through*."

"Oh — through — where? Ahead of the others, perhaps, but where? Your cattle are dying on your hands like flies, Burke. What can even Rickart do when the land turns against us? It takes all of us to fight that, but we are busy fighting one another. And the beasts die — starve — on our hands. We that took them out of their native state and taught them to depend on our care! Ours! You'll save — how many, Burke?"

"One in ten if we're lucky."

"And I — now . . ." He held up his four fingers; after some consideration he added the thumb to them. "I can hold out five weeks. If the rain does n't come by then, I shan't save any of them."

"The Old Man is sending me ten tons of alfalfa for the brood stock; I could spare you a couple if it's any help to you," Burke offered.

"Thank you kindly, Cornelius." Brent laughed again his short, light laugh, like a man quite at the bottom of things, secure only in the certainty that nothing worse could happen to him. "I think I ought to tell you that I could n't pay for it. I'm done, Burke. Morrow wants to foreclose."

"But, man, it's not half the value of the land!"

"That's why. Any other year but this I could raise the money anywhere." They looked quietly out at the shapely, sunny valley with the river winding down. "My wife's not been happy here either," Brent added as the last drop in the cup.

"'T is a hard country for women," Burke conceded. "Men love it, just, but women — they want different things. You've heard," he hinted, "that Rickart is sending me to Summerfield?" Brent nodded. "There's chances there, I'm told, for the pickin'. Maybe now —" Some deeper sympathy than words allowed prevented him from finishing.

Brent got up abruptly and walked to the edge of the veranda.

"That's it," he cried; "that's just it! Wherever the land flings us a handful of coin we run and scramble for it like beggars in the street. And she laughs — she laughs. I tell you, Burke, we've got to master her — we've got to compel her . . ."

Foreshadowed thus in the talk of their elders, the Brent children felt the approach of disaster. The Burkes added something to that the day they came over to say goodbye; for Cornelius was being transferred to Summerfield to have charge of Rickart's oil interests. Frank was leaving soon for the school for which his tutor had been fitting him. There was a sobering realization of change stilling the impulse of play, as they made for the last time the round of Palomitas. There were a good many pitiful little starved corpses in the camisal, and the air was black with buzzards.

At Mariposa the Ford was bone-white with drought.

"What fun we used to have here when we were little," Virginia sighed. It seemed to them that these things all happened a long time ago. "Oh, well, we'll soon all be together again. My father said so."

"What did he say?" demanded Anne with interest.

"He said if Jevens would give ten thousand more than the mortgage, your father would jump at it."

This was so far from being clear to Kenneth that he took the first opportunity to talk it over with Peters, who told him that it meant that Jevens was trying to buy Palomitas. Peters was a raw, red-looking man, with absurd yellowish hair sprouting about his crown and on his upper lip. He had the strength of a steer and not more than two or three motives, one of which, though he would have denied it, was a deep, sentimentalized attachment to his employer.

"But my father would n't let him have it — he would n't," Kenneth scoffed.

"Oh, well," — Peters was judicial, — "your paw's a smart man. A mighty smart man. I ain't much on this oil stock they talk about; got all the stock I kin tend to right here on Palomitas . . . kind o' stock 'at keeps itself above ground's all *I* kin tend to." It was Peters's one joke and he made the most of it.

"Hank Sturgis said the oil stock was going up; right up." Kenneth did not know what this meant exactly, though he heard it often enough; he was grateful to Peters for treating him to grown-up conversation.

"Oh, well, now," — Peters reached out with his billhook, — there were bright freckles as large as ten-cent pieces on his raw wrists, and tufts of reddish hair at the base of his fingers, — "it stands to reason that they don't know *how* it's going. But your Paw 's a master hand with stock, an' *if* he thinks it's better 'n any stock he's got right here on Palomitas, you ain't no call to worry none."

It was about this time that Jevens came back. Kenneth, bringing up the straggling lamb-band that they might have the first go at the long moss on the fallen oaks, saw him stalking Steven Brent across the fields, and a little shiver went over him as though Jevens might have been, what 'Nacio insisted on calling him, *El diablo negro.* But in the valley everybody was frankly glad to see Mr. Jevens.

To Arroyo Verde, where cattle men, with something in their eyes strangely like the look of the famished herds, sat about idly under the wide old sycamores and listened to the dropping of ripe fruit in the orchards round, Jevens was the incontestable evidence of places where, and occasions by which the normal procedure of life was still going on. "Over beyond," which was, in Tierra Longa, a generic name for the country beyond the Saltillo hills, there was still money clinking down the arteries of trade; it clinked revivifyingly for them in Mr. Jevens's pockets. Whatever happened to Tierra Longa there was still good money to be made in oil.

Those who had been so fortunate as to "get in with the Old Man" held on to all that the relation implied as the drowning to a rope. They took to hope as though it had been to hard drink. They tucked up their feet and let the drought go by them.

On the evening of his return Jevens supped at Palomitas, and addressed most of his conversation to Mrs. Brent, retailing incidents of his trip "over west a ways."

"But I did n't," he remarked, cooling his coffee in his saucer and supporting himself with his elbows on the table, "find just the property I was looking for. I don't know as I see anything which stuck in my eye like this little property right here." It must have been in the cast eye it stuck, for there was nothing that Kenneth could make out, in the one turned toward him, but a velvety, opaque blackness. "I don't know," he repeated, "as I ever see a property which stuck in my eye the way this does."

Kenneth heard his mother crying in the room that night. She cried with exasperation and hopeless hurt, and at times with a strange terror. It seemed a part of something that had been going on a long time, as if he might have heard it many nights before and only now taken note of it.

"But there ought to be *something* you could do. There is always *something*." Her voice rose out of sobbing. "After all we've wasted here . . . time and money . . . to have to be *turned* out. And it isn't as if you hadn't had an offer, as if you couldn't have gone on your own terms . . ."

"It wasn't really an offer," he could hear his father answer in a toneless patience; "we don't know that we'd have gotten out with anything in that case either. We could pull through if we had rain — just one good rain — God!" He broke off with the same note of bitter helplessness.

"It isn't *going* to rain . . . Why would Mr. Rickart send the Burkes away if he thought it would rain? If a man like that gives up, what's the sense of *your* holding on!"

"He isn't giving up. It's only that he's learned that he must have a bigger man, more scientific management. He's sending Burke to Summerfield to let him down easy."

"He'll make his fortune for him first, anyway . . ."

There was a silence in which Kenneth dropped almost into the pit of dreams. Suddenly the trouble broke out again with a torturing, impatient cry.

"Oh — you are going to *sleep!* You can sleep! And you don't know if the children and I are to have a roof over our heads! No wonder things go on the way they do when you don't have it on your mind any more than *that!*"

Kenneth sat up in bed struggling with his stupor; he was under the impression that this was addressed somehow to himself. Then he heard the trouble die away in dull sobbing and protesting, extenuating endearment. It mingled with the voices that pursued him down the labyrinths of drought and sleep . . .

V

It was n't in the least, as Anne had said, like an artesian well. It came up from the pumps in black, pasty gobs, and stank. That was Kenneth's first impression of the oil fields the November evening that Peters drove them down to Summerfield with their goods lumbering behind them in the wool wagon. They lay, the half-hundred wells, in the hollow of an old earthquake drop that took a curving line about the town and left it high on the up-tilted side. At the foot of the drop the waste of the river seeped away and the hollow climbed by degrees to the comb of the mesa, drawn all in fine puckers where the flocks had left it bare to the ruining rains. In the early dusk they made out the derricks each by his little, danger-red eye, like half-formed, prehistoric creatures feeling their way up from the depths to light, leaning all together with the slight undulations of the land, and seeming to communicate in low, guttering blubs and endless creak-ings, as though they plotted to tear loose at any moment and stamp out the little hordes of men who ran perpetu-ally about, or collected in knots among the sheds with their heads together.

There were crowds of men. The night the Brents had driven up, belated, to the hotel, they saw them standing weariedly about the bar like storks, puffy with want of sleep, and yet always with a tense, waiting air. Rows of men slumped in chairs in the dim-lit halls, trying to sleep, and outside in the street men walked up and down as though no such thing as sleep were thought of. Long after the Burkes had taken them in, for beds at the hotel were not to be had for any money, Kenneth could hear, louder than the wind on the Torr', the troubled murmur of the town.

It was not real trouble he made out in a day or two, but the milling of men about the oil interest like the mindless blether of the flock; it rose at times to the note of happy excitement. Men clustered like bees about the hive before the post-office and the bank; they collected in the streets and were cast back and forth between the trolley and the pavement by the passer-by, without any cessation of their absorbing talk.

To the Brent children, threading their way to school among them, there was, in spite of the widest individual differences, a curious likeness about all these gesticulating men; the likeness of all the hounds in the pack, of whatever breeds, at the parting of the quarry. Wherever there was news of a "strike," of a new company formed or an old one extended, they leaped and snatched at morsels of it, only to tear away excitedly at the least report of one in some other direction. They slavered with the desire of "stock," they gave tongue at the mere hint of dividends. And over all, through the streets, in the houses even, there was the penetrating, acrid flavor of oil. It came in at the church windows and gave to the Sunday quietness the effect of a lull in the market merely.

At Palomitas, the night after Mr. Jevens had bought the ranch, the rain began: a fine, long, growing rain. Clouds enfilading behind the Coast Ranges poured billowing down on Tierra Longa; they took the Saltillos. Hour by hour, as the wind bunted the flocked masses, the hilltops showed a spreading greenness; in the burnt camisal little green spears put forth from the immortal roots. The sheep, loosed to the wild pastures, ran frantically about; the grass, too short to nip, looked always longer in the far places. Kenneth ran with them, and begged, when he had time for it, to be left behind with his father until Christmas, but the advantage of the fall term at school had hurried his mother away with the two children. It was understood that Mr. Brent was to come on as soon as Jevens took possession, and "get into something."

If in the mean time Mrs. Brent had shrunk from the adventure of pulling up and transplanting her home, there was nothing in her manner which allowed her children to discover it. They saw her always leaning out from the little circle of their present circumstances, to drink the town; they copied as far as possible her eager attitude, though they did not know very well what it was about. Day by day as on their way to school they glimpsed the blue Torr' through gaps in the street above the undistinguished hills which divided it from Summerfield, they hastened to assuage their homesickness by ranging themselves on their mother's side.

"She belongs here, I guess," — Kenneth kicked at the late blooming succory which still came up through the sidewalks of by-streets in Summerfield. . . . "There's taboose along Mariposa Creek now, and cluster lilies coming up . . . she never even mentions it —"

"She wants us to like this better," — Anne gravely understood. "She's going to like it better herself whether it is or not."

"Is it better?" Kenneth wondered. Times when he looked up at the Torr' there was such a pull in his bosom that he felt he must set out for it that very hour.

Anne was disposed to make the best of things.

"There's school," she offered.

Yes, there was school; an absorbing, preponderating experience. With minds unwearied of print they had taken to it as ducklings to water.

"Anyway," — Kenneth returned to the point at which the conversation began, — "she belongs."

"Oh, she belongs, more than anybody." Anne was sure of her ground.

"More than Mrs. Burke!"

"I should say!"

"Mrs. Burke is a regular Biddy —" Kenneth did not know where this had come from; he knew it as one of those edged tools of grown-up judgment with which some unwritten law of childhood forbade them yet to play. Brother and sister gasped across it, scared and yet implicated in the mutual recognition. It was one of those moments by which the world outside them fell into order and perspective, but they neither of them knew what had set it in motion.

Anne, however, in spite of the pains that had been taken with her, was a little lady.

"She's Virginia's mother." She pulled them both back into the practical relation. What, indeed, would they have done, feeling their way about school society, without Virginia! Moments of confidence like this increased between them, for want of more objective interests.

That their situation was not, in a material way, anything like so good as at Palomitas the young Brents could n't help knowing.

The three little rooms into which they had to stuff their household goods, the scrappiness of all their ways of living, could n't have been borne except by the implication, in which all Summerfield was involved, of its being a concession to the process of growth. Everywhere one was met with the joyous extenuations of the "boom." You would n't have guessed either, from anything you heard in the town, that Summerfield had n't kept the oil fields up its sleeve awaiting the felicitous hour. This was an attitude that matched wonderfully with the high, eager mood of their mother's which the Brent children had recognized as the company sign. In the midst of it she had for them, quite unmistakably and in the superlative degree, the note of social fitness. She was tall, her thick hair had still a touch of brightness, and if it gave them sometimes a strange embarrassment to meet her as she appeared on the street, the waist a little too tight, the bust a trifle too full, a shade too much pearl powder under the veil, they did not fail to see in her what Cornelius Burke had defined for them as the fine figure of a woman. They believed quite heartily in the future which her manner created for them, and unassailably in their mother's being equal to any of the brilliant possibilities which were tossed up from time to time on the black, gurgling fountains under the derricks. At least Anne and Virginia believed and Kenneth accepted his faith at their hands.

And yet after he joined them at Christmas, their father did n't, unaccountably, "get into" anything. Things hovered, bright, irreducible promises that seemed about to fold their wings and rest upon the fortunes of the Brents, only to sail high over them at last and fix on the most unlikely quarters. By the end of the spring term he was still so far from being "in" that it began to seem, with so many good things flying over, failure must be owing to the quality of the intelligence with which Mr. Brent limed the twigs of his investments.

That somebody had said or suggested something of the kind began to be present to the children in unpremeditated attitudes of partisanship, in darts and flashes by which they felt themselves flung to one side or the other in the inexplicable urgency of affairs. A sense of that urgency rose about them in the crowded little room until it drove them quite literally against their father's breast and to his knee, only to be drawn back from that community of sympathy by the rising consciousness that it had been formed outside their mother's claim on them, and somehow incalculably against her interest. The trouble, whatever it was, seemed to be summed up for them in the current phrase that their father was n't "in" things, and that not to be in was somehow blamable.

"But I could, you know," he had more than once insisted. "Burke would give me charge of one of the groups of Company wells if I wanted it."

"You mean you'd be working for him?" Mrs. Brent had turned from shaking out the cloth to take in the full meaning of it.

"Well, in a manner — he has charge of all the Rickart Interests."

"Working for Cornelius — and I'd have to treat *her* as my employer's wife? I can't see what you're thinking of!"

"I'd be on the ground . . . Cornelius would give me tips . . ."

"And she would me . . . perhaps that's what you want. Perhaps you think I need to be told what to do for my family —" Exasperation mastered her. "After I've been willing to pull up everything and come here to make a new start, to have to come to this!"

"It's come to us," her husband reminded her. "If you don't like it, there's no need to think of it again."

They did think of it, however; it came up in talk over and over.

"I don't see why you should take *anything* from Cornelius," Mrs. Brent would expostulate. "Why don't you go to Rickart himself?"

"I did, my dear."

"You mean — oh, I'll not believe it. Steven, you've bungled matters somehow." She was sitting at the supper-table at which the absence of Ah Sen was conspicuous in the pushed-back plates and the spotted cloth which she tapped with a hand that the weeks of doing her own housework had not yet robbed of its rosy finish. The shaded glow of the lamp just touched her fine bosom and the beginning of the flush of exasperation along her cheek. "You mean he sent you to get a job from Cornelius?"

"My dear, you don't understand how men look at these things . . . better than I would jump at it. It's a chance to get in touch, to know what's doing. And the way we are situated —"

"Oh — what you can't see, what you *won't* see, Steven, is that it's the way we are situated that is the real trouble. After fifteen years . . . to have to edge in like that! It's only the proof of what I've always said, that with all I've done without, we haven't *got anywhere*. Fifteen years we've been at it, and here I am doing my own housework, and you taking anything Cornelius Burke gives us for charity!"

"Oh, my dear . . . charity! You do make us poor when you take it like that!"

"Oh, *take* it!" She pushed back her chair and stood up to her unaccustomed task. "Anybody can see how I take it . . . look at my hands . . . it's being in a position where we *have* to take it that I mind. I'll take it as well as the rest of you."

"Why, then, we'll take it as the best of jokes, — eh, kiddies!" He opened his arms to them, perhaps as a reminder to her that, at any rate, they were there and taking in everything in their several capacities. Perhaps also there was some deeper need of his for their sustaining arms, their young, loyal confidence. It was there that the situation stood when the spring term of school was finished and Kenneth went back to Tierra Longa for a visit with Frank.

He went up with Hank Sturgis in the supply wagon, along the road that wound and wound among the bare-topped hills, threaded all through their cañons with rivers of green. Kenneth had meant to lose no point of the way, especially after they struck into the southern spar of the Saltillos, but he went to sleep stretched along the feed bags soon after dark, and knew nothing of the Torr' until he saw its dark bulk above the *patio* of Agua Caliente, where Frank and the dogs leaped a welcome to him. Frank had come back from his own school two days before, taller and more citified as Kenneth saw him, a little subdued by the discovery there of several things that he had n't been able to do, and a little more insolent on account of the things he had discovered that his father's money could do. But to do him justice he was fond of Kenneth; the family at Palomitas had been the nearest thing to kin that he had known. He was as eager as his guest to review the familiar bosom of the Torr'.

Ken's pony had been kept at Agua Caliente in anticipation of this visit, and as they came clattering over the bridge into the Palomitas road next afternoon, it seemed incredible that they should n't find there all the familiar air and use of home. Over the scars of drought the year had woven a thin web of green, too thin for the wandering air above it to wake the stir and play of light by which the Torr' had seemed to breathe. Bare knuckles of rock stood out in the *potreros*.

At the orchard lane the boys struck upon the first slight traces of neglect; trees that had died out in the great drought of the year before had not been replaced; they rotted where they stood. Here and there panels dropped from the corrals, wagons and cultivators stood half out of the sheds. Whatever Jevens had meant to do with the place, he was no farmer. At the house there was no one about but Ah Sen, who cackled with delight. The pink tassel of his queue was replaced by a black string and his starched white jacket was neither starched nor white, but he would have hugged Kenneth if he had been allowed. He wished to know about everybody.

"You telle you motha, I likee more better cook for she. You telle black debble heap no savey." He included the disordered house in a wave of his lean, sallow hands.

It gave Kenneth a pang to see Jevens's cheap male belongings strewn about the familiar room, so identified with his mother's presence, as if she had suffered a personal violence. He turned for a glimpse of his own room and found it full of saddles and a litter of harness.

Ah Sen had baked a chocolate cake which he brought

out now with rusty creaking of affection. The boys accepted thick, soft slabs of it and went out sobered by the garden gate. With one consent they moved toward the spring. Here the chaparral had been spared by the drought; beside it lay the dried, stacked brush of the year before. They sat down on it looking out over Tierra Longa. All at once Kenneth's cake choked him. He felt inside him the tear of a creature too big for his breast. It terribly gripped and shook him.

"Oh, I say, Ken . . ." Frank was embarrassed. "Say . . . you don't want to take it like that. A fellow's got to get out and see things . . . he can't stick in a hole like this all his life."

"You shut up!" Kenneth blubbered; "that ain't what I'm crying for."

Frank dug his heel into the damp earth and took another tack.

"You're crying for your mother, that's what."

Kenneth did not know exactly what he was crying for, but it seemed likely.

"Well, you ain't got any to cry for," he retorted.

Frank was dazed.

"Mine died when I was born," he admitted rather soberly. "Say, Ken, . . . are they so great — mothers?"

"Uh-hu." Kenneth sat up swabbing his eyes with his cap. "I guess you'd cry if you had one," he justified himself.

Frank carefully fitted his heel into the hole he had dug for it.

"Say-y you know, Ken . . . your mother used to kiss me birthdays and Christmas, — *you* know. I kind o' liked it."

It was an admission that somehow extenuated Kenneth's tears. Insensibly they had got their arms around each other . . . but they started apart at the sound of voices coming down the Torr'. They came by one of the old paths that led up from the spring, and were followed by the sound of Jevens breaking through the tall chaparral, putting back its interlacing boughs to clear the way for a younger, slighter stranger.

"Hello-o!" he cried at sight of the boys; Jevens made a movement of withdrawing and thought better of it. "What you doing here?" He recognized Frank and paid him the deference due to his father's son, but he was plainly disconcerted. The young man who came out of the trail behind him was dressed for the part. Nothing could have been nattier than his corduroys, his puttees, and his soft flannel shirt. He chewed a twig of buckthorn and seemed mildly amused. The boys stood up and eyed him.

"Well, bub," he remarked to Kenneth, "you'll know me again, I reckon." He laughed quite cheerfully, but Jevens kept an anxious countenance. Two or three times they saw him hesitate as he went down the cut, looking back as if he had made up his mind to speak, and unmaking it.

"Well, I guess we will know him," Frank resented.

"I *did*," said Kenneth. "I saw him over to Summerfield!"

"What doing?"

"Expertin'." Kenneth had picked up the word without knowing very well what it stood for. "He came to see my father. His name is Hartley Daws."

That day at luncheon they mentioned it to Frank's

father. On the great lonely ranches a stranger was a grateful topic of conversation.

"He's an oil expert," Kenneth was proud to contribute.

Mr. Rickart pricked up at that. "So?" he said. Presently he laid down his fork and spoke to the Japanese boy who waited softly at the table.

"Send Tuyo to me," he ordered; and when a few minutes later the still, dark halfbreed fence rider drifted across the doorway he threw over his shoulder, as one throws scraps to a dog, commands in a Spanish Indian patois of which the boys understood only a word or two. They heard them again, master and man conferring in the soft, guttural speech late that evening in the *patio* between the two long wings of the Agua Caliente ranch house.

The next morning at breakfast all their plans for the day were changed in a twinkling, hearing Frank's father say to the fence rider that he was to go and tell the wife of Juan Romero that El Señor Viejo would ride over to eat *chile con carne* and *enchiladas* with her that noon.

Frank whooped with delight.

"Us, too, father, — us, too!" He dashed off at once to tell the stable man that they would n't want their ponies that morning. Señora Romero's *enchiladas* were worth much more than a morning's amusement.

They did not, however, find the ride, on which they set out about ten o'clock, entirely without entertainment. Mr. Rickart drove himself in the high-topped buckboard with the pedigreed bays. They struck into the Summerfield road below Palomitas and followed it for an hour. Here a faint, old wagon track swung out into the middle of the valley, visiting one and another of the quarter-sections which had been added to the Agua Caliente property by the half-starved homesteaders, lured there by the splendid possibilities of the land and driven from it by the inadequacy of human endeavor. It seemed this morning that the owner was bent on visiting each one of them.

Rickart was a tall man, made to look shorter by his exceeding stockiness of build. The squareness of his clean-shaven face was modified by the weight he had put on with years. The nose was beaked a little; the lips, if too full, were still finely cut; the puffiness under the eyes kept down with resoluteness. He looked meditative, uninterested, noted without seeming to see, and chewed perpetually on a seldom-lighted cigar. The angle of this cigar, as it went up and down with the working of his mind, made the perfect dial of his revolving thought. Now and then he halted the bays to adjust the fieldglass which he had brought, and though he yielded it easily to the boys when the impulse seized them to look, they did n't discover what, if anything, directed his searching glance. They fell to counting the whitening skulls left from the drought of the year before, and looked for buzzards sailing in the blue. They were down opposite the mole end of the Ridge, about a mile from it, when Mr. Rickart pointed out a badger to them. He was an ordinary brown badger, scurrying along nose to the ground on a fresh squirrel trail, and hovering over him were two crows and a hawk, meaning to be in at the kill.

"Beat him to it," Rickart suggested. The boys, tired with the inaction of the buckboard, piled out one over the other.

They saw the dust fly up where the badger had started

for the central hill, and the hawk circling low to catch any hopeful rodent which might escape by the side doors that came up at a distance from the citadel. The crows settled and stalked solemnly about; their concern was with the storehouse of grain that might be uncovered by the brown sapper. The boys were in time to snatch the badger back by the tail; there was no reason why they should have done this except that it was fun to see him snarl and snap, and it was as much as they were able to manage between them, so fast he dug, so quickly he snapped and swung. In the old days young gods might have done so to men for pure joy of their godhead. Kenneth had found a battered kerosene tin which he meant to fasten to the badger's tail, when Mr. Rickart called them. Frank as he ran administered a parting kick at the poor beast's head which left it staggering blindly.

"Ah . . . what you doin'!" So far their play had been pure sport; it was forbidden to kill badgers on any of the ranches on account of their service as squirrel exterminators, and Kenneth turned a little sick at the needless cruelty.

"What's the diff.? They ain't on our land," Frank retorted, as they ran.

They climbed into the open end of the buckboard and sat with their feet hanging out. Kenneth could see the badger still running blindly and stopping; he thought its eye might have been put out. That was how they missed noting that the objective of Mr. Rickart's drive was a man on horseback who could be plainly seen now rising from behind the Ridge.

They crossed his path in about twenty minutes, and were made aware of it by the slacking of the team. They turned to see Mr. Jevens's visitor exchanging greetings with Frank's father.

Mr. Rickart was looking regretfully at his unlighted cigar.

"You have n't got a light about you — oh, thanks." He held the match carefully to the brown roll. He dropped the match, however, to produce the twin of his cigar from his inner pocket, his special brand. "You're Hartley Daws, are n't you?" No young engineer could be such a fool as not to be flattered by the recognition. "I thought I had seen you at Summerfield. Blakely and Company tell me you did some good work for them. I'm Rickart, T. Rickart — That's my little property over there." He included the whole serried rank of the coast hills in his gaze. He had to have another match for his cigar, and set his watch by the stranger's.

"Well, it's about eating-time, I guess," he remarked; he gathered up the reins.

Mr. Daws's lunch was plainly tied behind his saddle in a brown paper that betrayed Ah Sen's hand.

Rickart must have had a kindly thought about it, for he checked his team to say, "I'm going over to the *ranchería* of one of my men for a Mexican dinner. If you're a stranger in these parts it might interest you, and there's always enough in the Señora Romero's pots for two. Her grandmother was cook at one of the Missions, and her *enchiladas* are the real thing."

The boys could hear him discoursing pleasantly to young Daws as he rode alongside, of the old Spanish régime in Tierra Longa.

They arrived at the Romeros' *ranchería*, which lay on the Saltillos side close up under the Torr,' about one, and

Ignacio Stanislauo was very glad to see them. He had a young coyote in a box which he was teaching to answer to the name of Tito.

The dinner was served in the *ramada*, the long, wattled hut under the wild grapevines. Chickens walked about in it quite unconcernedly and dogs and little Romeros lurked and dodged in deeper recesses of the vines amid which stood the original adobe hut. There was soup with forcemeat balls and *chile*, chicken with rice and *chile*, *frijoles* with *chile*, *enchiladas* reeking with *chile*, and little cakes fried in too much fat. For a relish there were *chiles tepines* in a dish. It was easy to see that Mr. Hartley Daws was not used to it, and that he was going to feel the effect of the amount of black coffee that he took to wash it all down. And all the time he was divided between what he thought of Mr. Rickart and what he was able to guess of what Mr. Rickart thought of him. Somehow the talk drifted around to Jevens.

"Made a tidy pile in the oil fields, I understand," Mr. Rickart was saying . . . "You would n't think a man would take to ranching at his age."

"Oh, a man like that gets notions," young Daws admitted. His manner went to say, "Would n't you like to know what notions?"

"It's a wonder he would n't get one that there's oil on this side too. It's much the same formation."

"There's nothing in that," the expert made haste to inform him; "oil's where you find it."

"Nothing in it whatever; I had the whole place experted years ago. Funny thing, though; only goes to show how you can fool the best of these experts, — no disrespect to you, Mr. Daws, — but I had a man down here from Gates and Woodward — you know Gates and Woodward, best men in the city. Well, there was a place on Palomitas, below Mariposa Creek where Brent had had a vat made — good stiff clay there — for sheep dip, and I'm blessed if this fellow did n't think he'd found oil signs. Petroleum in the dip, you know, — sent up no end of samples, — had me going, almost, until Brent heard of it and explained." If the stranger looked dashed at this, it was doubtless because of the discredit cast on his profession. "Nothing but sheep dip —" Rickart laughed reminiscently. "But, of course," he came back, "you fellows can afford to make a mistake once in a while, you 're so darned necessary to us. We have to have you, you know, and we have to take your word for it. Look at me now —" He launched into a long account of affairs at Summerfield which the expert drank up. Whether it was the confidential matter it had the appearance of being, it afforded Hartley Daws those occasions so dear to rising talent, occasions which you could already see shaping behind his flattered countenance, of saying, "As the Old Man remarked to me . . . "

"You might give me your card, you know," Rickart was saying at last as he laid down a bright new twenty-dollar piece on the Señora's worn board. "I expect to do a lot of development work in Summerfield this winter and I shall be needing —" He broke off, "It's my opinion that the field slews around to the southwest, — of course I'm only a layman, — but I'm pretty lucky in my guesses — pretty lucky —"

If young Hartley Daws did n't know that for making money the Old Man's guesses were better than most men's certain information, he did n't know much. He had pocketed the bit of pasteboard in exchange for his own, with the look of a man who fully appreciated that merely to have exchanged cards with T. Rickart was a better promise of professional advancement than anything Jevens would pay him for his day's work at Palomitas. Whatever else he had got by the interview, he took away with him a trick of the Old Man's by which, as he rode, his cigar went out as it traveled the whole round of his thought.

VI

THE visit to Agua Caliente returned Kenneth by the end of August to his family at the new town of Petrolia sprung up about the wells under the river bluff, there to find himself in the midst of old acquaintances. The Scudders were there, "squatted" on a strip of tillable land where the waste of the Summerfield Canal turned back into the waste of the river, with Addie, the eldest, looking as newly set in his mother's kitchen as the red geraniums which shored up the new-built bungalows in a predetermined prosperity. There, too, was Peters in his character of permanent employee of Mr. Brent's, taking on, as much of him as was visible between the black, oily stains, a deep purple tint of the perpetual embarrassment in which he found himself involved by the proximity of a "young gell," under which title he kept up through the children a kind of third-hand exchange of comment and compliment with Addie.

There, in the most geraniumed of the bungalows, was Cornelius Burke as Superintendent of Works, and there, if you choose to count him among acquaintances, was Hartley Daws. At least there he was announced to be in an eight-by-ten office adjacent to the old adobe roadhouse that had once been a resort of the Basque sheep herders on the circuit between Summerfield and Naciemiento. The office stood close up under the bluff where the road, winding down the crumbling face of it, forded the river waste between the willows, and the door, swinging open, never failed to draw the speculative eye to the

card rack opposite and the carefully conspicuous display
of the personal card of T. Rickart. For life proceeded
here, with whatever change of scene and decoration, as
at Palomitas, under the shadow of the Old Man. Success
was reckoned from him as distance from the Torr'. The
Old Man knew where money was as much as buzzards
know the place of carrion. If ever Hartley Daws ventured an opinion as to the underground direction of the
arteries from which the pumps drew up the black, stinking juices of an age decayed to lubricate the enterprise
of this, it was estimated, not by his standing as an expert,
but by the degree to which he might be supposed to be
"in with" the Rickart Interests. By the mere device of
carefully saying nothing when his patron's name was mentioned, Hartley Daws contrived to give the impression
that he was very deeply "in."

This was the question upon which all interest and
inquiry at Petrolia hung, a question endowed with the
capacity for involving Kenneth's family in a succession
of acute crises as rumor ran to and fro about wells which
failed and others that from narrow, iron throats belched
up great wasteful fountains — the question as to whether
this were not the time and occasion for Mr. Brent also
to get "in." Kenneth could see the whole tension of his
mother's life tightening over it as the skin tightened on
the knuckles clasping and unclasping under the evening
lamp in endless sessions of anxious talk. It was as if the
trouble which had been so long walled up behind the
boarded door at Palomitas had been let loose to circulate
in the house at Petrolia where the thin plank walls saved
the children nothing of its strained, discordant privacies.
Whatever went on in it could be heard from one end to

the other; at all hours the young Brents found themselves assailed by the fevers, drops, and perplexities of
the "boom." They fled from it unconsciously into that
absorbing world of school, where not always the most
careful parent can follow the young, racing minds; and
when all other refuge failed, to Addie. For Addie, though
she "talked oil," talked it with a high, unshaken confidence in the Powers, who, if they had neglected to do it
before, could be counted on now to turn the fruitful,
hidden stream squarely under Pop Scudder's twenty
acres of truck garden in the pit of the river waste, known
as "the Sink."

"'Cause why?" she would demand of the doubtful
Peters who found himself greatly put out at this juncture
on account of Mr. Brent's not having formed any opinion for him to hold. "'Cause my Pop's done used up all
his rights a-homesteadin' and a-timber claimin' and a-pre-
emptin'. He's served his time at them things and served
it honest, and I reckon they's a pay-day comin' round,
ain't they?" she would demand irresistibly. "'Cause it
don't take more 'n half an eye to see that my Pop ain't
no ways fitted for nothin' but them kind of things, and
I reckon Them That's Above," — this was as near as
Addie permitted herself the naming of any Powers, —
"They would n't let a body serve his time at what They'd
made him for, without They would tot it up for him one
of these days," she would conclude with a triumphant
logic that convinced Peters of having stood out against
the Heavenly Host. For it did not take even the half an
eye which Addie allowed to it, to see in Pop Scudder the
figure of the incurable, the temperamental pioneer; the
tall, stooping frame, sloped forward, not so much with

years as with following fast on Hope, the huge, toil-hardened hands curling in his lap like a child's as he sat listening with a child's bright fixity to Addie's leaping confidences, the pale, far-seeing eyes looking out from an expanse of whitened whisker as from the mist of his own dreams.

Addie had a way of heightening the prophetic effect of her utterances by always speaking of him in the third person even in his presence.

"He's been through such a lot, Pop has, it don't seem like it's worth anybody's time to go through so much without They're taking notice of it, and I do say, if They ain't, that this is the jumpin'-off place for my Pop. He 'll just go plunk!"

The tone with which she dropped her parent into the gulf, all her talk shot through with the knowledge of imminent, approachable Powers, seized upon the Brent children with dreadful, delicious shivers. It was alive with what, wholly unexpressed, had lurked for them in the deep lanes of the chaparral, around the sentient, breathing Torr'. Evenings they would escape from the endless gurgle of oil about the supper-table to snuggle on either side of her on the back stoop, with perhaps Peters as an appreciative but embarrassed third, to re-immerse themselves in the epic of Pop Scudder as in the essence of the Wild.

Kenneth admired Addie immensely. Her young body, slanted by years of homesteading, had the poise of a pine tree shaped by the wind; the flare of her bright-burned cheeks and sun-streaked hair reminded him of the gera-niums. He had vague notions of setting out with her some day in a white-topped settler's wagon on the track of ancient adventure, toward a claim which always turned out to be Palomitas. Times the dream would take and hold him all the night, and though he could not remember more than a fleeting fragment of it, he would wake with a warm tingling all through his body, which returned upon him at moments of the day when he would think of Addie. He thought of confiding this singular experience to Peters, with whom, in default of other companionship, he had grown exceedingly friendly.

"You're very fond of Addie, ain't you, Peters?" he chose for a beginning one clear Sunday morning when that born servitor was pretending, to save himself from boredom, that the stilled pumping engine really required his tinkering over it.

"Who? ME?" Geraniums were nothing to the color of Peter's indignation. "Now, looky here, young feller," — Peters had never called him that before, it was his utmost term of reprobation, — "who put that idee in your head?"

"Oh, nobody, — but you know you do stay a good while when father sends you up to the house for anything," Kenneth defended himself.

"'Cause why, young feller," — Peters's tone allowed its full measure to the blighting epithet, — "'Cause I got business there, that's why." He thumped so violently at the vitals of the suffering engine that Kenneth felt his friendly impulse at fault.

"Well, of course, Peters —"

That individual withdrew his still inflamed countenance from the belly of the engine to complete his justification.

"Of course, young feller, I got the highest respeck for

that young gell, — I don't know as there's any young gell I got a higher for, she's a young gell as any man might respeck, — but when it comes to bein' fond of her —" Peters hid the emotion which the suspicion occasioned him in the inwards of the engine.

"Well, of *course*, if you are n't, Peters," Kenneth excused, "you can't help it, can you? I just thought I'd ask." By some queer twist of the male consciousness beginning to wake in him, he discovered that if Peters was not fond of Addie he was not so very fond of her himself. He sat on a gunnysack wrapped about one of the lead pipes and kicked the sand until Peters came out of the engine again to say: —

"You might mention it to her, you know, — how much I respeck her, — if you was any way mentionin' me."

"But I don't think I will, Peters, because if I did she might ask me how I came to know, and then I might have to tell her. And a person don't like to be told that a person is n't fond of them if they are not fond of a person themselves." He considered that he had made himself perfectly clear and if Peters did n't understand him it would be due to his not having an affectionate nature. Kenneth felt that he had such a nature himself and that it had received a check.

By degrees that winter the situation at Petrolia cleared to Kenneth's opening mind. He discovered lines of direction in the human interest there, as well defined as the network of iron piping that ran from well to well and to the bat-ribbed, iron roofs of the reservoirs squatting in every coign of the hills sucking, sucking — He developed a kind of double consciousness toward it, of public, boyish interest in the activities of the oil fields, and a con-

tained, secret loathing. He knew to a certainty the output in barrels of every gusher, and attended with the
Burke boys the installation of every new engine and iron-
riveted tank; but there were days when he would dodge
away from the others after school to climb to the comb of
hills beyond the settlement, from which he could make
out the winter-capped tip of the Torr'. Here he would
walk for hours full of an absorbed, contemplative pleasure in which the piercing of the sod by the first faint
spears of the brodea marked an epoch, and the finding
of the first meadow-lark's nest a momentous discovery.
As he returned full of the importance of these things, the
talk of the supper-table fretted him with its inconse-
quences. He would slip away after it to the back porch
to exchange contraband items of news with Anne as to
the progress of wild bloom and the thin, ascending spires
of dust that marked where wandering flocks laid bare the
hills to the corroding weather. It was after such evenings
as this that he would dream of Addie and the white-
topped settler's wagon making way over those same hills
to the land of unproved delights.

Sometimes on Sundays his father would walk with him
in that direction, and by wordless consent they would
make for any point miles away where they saw the dust of
a flock rising, to refresh themselves with the familiar
knowledge of sheep, to exchange, with the nearly inarticulate French and Basque herders, news of the far
pastures, of lambing-time and the fluctuating prices of
wool. Sometimes they would sit for long, wordless sessions on a summer slope with their backs to Petrolia,
fronting the high, treeless barrows that lead the eye away
inland, handling the rich, crumbly loam of the hills as a

prospector fumbles pay-dirt between his palm and thumb, tasting its possibilities. On such occasions they renewed that common consciousness of the earth which had passed between them on the Torr' with the force of a revelation. Drought and disaster could pass away, and the rending, gutting hands of men, but the earth would not pass away nor the fullness thereof.

Life lets in light to men at least once, — to women many times, — but to men, always once; in the disturbance of equilibrium between youth and adulthood the gates are up and the floods come in.

If there had been anybody to read and help him shape his life to what that deep sense of the waiting earth and the will to abide by it, must mean, this would have been another story — but just because it is so common an occurrence for Life to speak to youth at this time and in this fashion — Oh, Youth, Youth! we say, and the word falls unheeded.

Sometimes at this period the feel of the purposeful earth would get through to him even at Petrolia, when the purple dusk crept up along the old river track and the wind would be crooning about the tall, iron trees — for does not iron come up out of the earth even as oak and pine? — and the little red spark, nesting in each, twinkled friendlily. Every half-hour the Summerfield trolley would peer from the top of the bluff with its one white eye, only to scutter away with a shrill, insect whine, and the derricks would talk together of the absurdities and limitations of men. But by day, and especially in the house, Kenneth found himself drawn into the coil of a practical perplexity over which Addie's confidence in the Powers floated as a bright, morning-fluttered flag.

"'Pears like you're kind of losin' your grip on Providence, Mis' Brent," she would say to that lady in the intimacies of the day's domesticity, in which no hints of her mistress ever taught her she was not a concerned and indispensable item. "An' you church brought up, too,'" she reproached.

"I've been waiting on Providence fifteen years," Mrs. Brent answered her, as every one finally did have to answer Addie, on her own ground.

"Hoo! What's fifteen years — when you think of my Pop?" Addie set her arms akimbo on her slim, slant body and prepared to expound the policy of the Powers. "Seems like They" — the impersonal plural referred to but one thing in Addie's vernacular — "They just let you go along a piece by yourself, kind of stumblin', an' sometimes it's a good long piece. But by and by, when you've come to the end of your string, They step in and save you. They just got to. An' that's right where Pop is now, Mis' Brent; he ain't good for nary 'nother move — 'n if you're looking fur one of the same to put with him, why, that's Mr. Brent."

"Oh!" — Mr. Brent's wife bit her lip over it; "so you think that Mr. Brent is at the end of his string, do you? Well, it's not your place to be running down your employer, and besides, Mr. Brent —"

"My land!" cried the unsnubbable Addie; "if you was doin' that well at Palomitas, why did you leave it?" Having reduced her mistress to silence and folded the tablecloth by catching the middle of the hem in her strong white teeth and bringing her arms together at the ends of it, she returned to her exposition. "If ever there was two men cut off'n the same piece of cloth — though maybe they was different ends of it — it's Mr. Brent and my Pop. Both of 'em just got to be monkeyin' with the dirt — and a-dreamin' and a-seein' the end of things and a-skippin' the middle. Only Pop, he could n't seem to get a-holt nowhar, and if Mr. Brent could n't make it with the holt he got — why, there ye are!'' There *they* are she meant, in a case so similar that perhaps Mrs. Brent was glad to sink the comparison in the saving consolation of Addie's confident ''An' of course they got to make it now; there's nothin' else for 'em.''

That Pop Scudder advanced in the public consideration, as the popular belief in the direction of the oil-bearing beds traveled toward his squatter's claim, was apparent even to the children, in the degrees by which he moved from the back porch, where he came to see Addie of evenings, to the front, where he was openly in consultation with Mr. Brent. There grew to be a little coterie of them meeting there by the end of the rains: men who lived forever at the fringes of affairs, snatching their living from unconsidered acres, that in their turn became considered and then not theirs — Jim Hand, who had fought so long for his surplus water right that he fought now even in his talk, his voice big and belligerent; Soldumbehere, who had seen the wild pastures close in homesteads and forest reserves until almost his only undisputed bit was the shearing-corral close up under the bluff below Scudder's truck garden; and other holders of contested rights, who came or ceased coming as their estimate of the chances of fortune in this combination varied. They talked much, and always of the same thing; were they, or were they not, in the oil district, and if they were, what should they do about it? They must have Capital;

and if they did, such was their deep conviction, Capital in the end would have them. Capital went about seeking whom it might devour, yet such was their strange illusion about it that they believed that if once they could lay hands on it, Capital could be made to run in their harness, breed in their pastures. To those who owned Capital, and set their brand upon it, it ate out of the hand, but its proper nutriment was the content of poor men's pockets. They railed upon it as wolves that defile the corners of the woodman's hut, and it was the sum of all their desire. All but Pop Scudder. Expecting nothing but to lose, he went through all the brave forms of resistance as a habit. He was no more embittered than a squirrel. He was constitutionally a homesteader.

The real question, of course, was whether there was oil under your land or was n't. If the fields extended toward the Sink, then the price of Palomitas, which still burned in Mr. Brent's pocket, would make an even balance to the titles of the land. It would become Capital; and the salt, barren acres an Investment. All this, more or less comprehended, played over the heads of the Brent children without superseding the immediate interest of Kenneth's being promoted in arithmetic and Teacher said he must have a new geog'aphy. It remained for the boy, however, to give the final fillip to the great indecision.

That winter the tule fogs came in to Petrolia. Not every year, but fitfully, season by season, thick, white, low-creeping fogs gathered above the flat tulares of the San Joaquin Valley, and beleaguered the bluffs of Summerfield. Rarely they rose to the level of the town, but this year they inundated Petrolia; men abroad in them

too much, hot with the fevers of the "boom" and chilled
from standing about on the damp ground, died of an in-
fection which seemed to travel on the thick medium of
the fog. The fear of it drove Mr. Brent's visitors into the
living-room, where, between her sense of their social un-
fitness and her anxiety to hear all that went on among
them, they were a source of many restless sallies on the
part of Mrs. Brent and a great annoyance to Kenneth,
who found he could n't do his examples with the talk
going on, and yet, in the presence of his father, dare n't
ask Anne to do them for him. He had tried that before
and knew what came of it. He sat idly and listened to
the high, quarreling voices of big Jim Hand, and idly
moved his pencil over the slate, moistening it from time
to time in his mouth, an old, half-forgotten, childish
trick. Something in the shape of the blot he was making
led him to complete the figure of a badger and so supplied the subconscious link of memory.

"If we could get a line on Rickart," big Jim was saying,
"that'd clinch it." There was that in his manner which
implied that such a line was to be got, but somebody was
neglectful. It was perfectly in the air that this somebody
was Kenneth's father. Brent, by reason of his employment, was supposed to be in a position to know Rickart's
plans, and not only had he failed to tap that source of
information, but a quixotic notion led him to shrug off all
discussion of it. He lifted his shoulders now in the habitual gesture, which dropped half-finished in a realization
of its futility before men at whose keyhole Rickart was
always figuratively listening and alert.

A sudden little impatient movement of his mother's
brought out in Kenneth's mind words that seemed to

pop up like automatons to the jerking of a string, words in his mother's voice, high and exasperated — "What's the use, Steven . . . what are we here *for* if it is n't to find out . . . to find a way *in* . . ." He saw her shut her lips over them now, but he knew they were quite audible words for him and Anne and their father; the recognition of them flashed electrically between those three.

"An' Burke won't give up nothin'," Hand quarreled on; "he must know what the Old Man thinks about it; though he's buyin' east *and* west, one of 'em is a blind."

The two ends of memory made connection for a moment in Kenneth's mind.

"Ho, *I* know!" the words slipped out almost under the compulsion of his knowing that he ought, perhaps, not to have uttered them. He felt himself suddenly embarrassed by the centering of attention on him and rushed on to brave it down. "Frank's father told Hartley Daws it swings south by west . . . I heard him. . . . Over at Romero's, having a Spanish dinner," he conceded to the eager question. "'Nacio's got a young coyote he's taming," he volunteered further, but found that the detail lacked interest.

"What were Hartley Daws and Mr. Rickart doing there?"

"Talking oil." He believed this to be quite the case, but Mr. Brent held him down with a question as firmly as with a hand.

"And you heard him say he thought the oil development would be south by west?"

Kenneth nodded. "Hartley Daws said so too," he added in confirmation, since his father seemed to require it; he had no idea that he had given them the impression

that Rickart and the oil expert had come together by
intention. Something had happened in the room that
seemed to make the occasion momentous. Kenneth felt
it swell in memory; "And Frank's father took some
papers out of his pocket and gave Hartley Daws one," —
he did not really know that this had been a business card,
— "and — and there was money on the table." If they
found the incident so significant as all that, of course it
must have had such a significance in the beginning. Kenneth leaned back in his chair and felt himself a valued
contributor to the evening's entertainment.

There was a silence through which Jim Hand's big
voice blustered like a bee through a summer afternoon.

"Well, in that case, Brent, I don't see what you are
waiting for."

"Well, gentlemen, I don't quite see myself."

They were waiting for something, though; they were
all tense with it. One of the men strange to Kenneth
seemed to have supplied it when he said, "What's the
matter with getting a move on us, then? Once you know
where the stuff is, you're losing money every day it's in
the ground."

"Daws will let us have the outfit as cheap as anybody."
Hand's voice was at strife even with his cheerful announcement. "I guess an expert that's good enough for
the Old Man's good enough for the Homestead Development Company."

Something seemed to be concluded as the men stood
up to go. Kenneth's mother stood up with them; she was
standing still behind his chair as Mr. Brent came back
from showing them to the door. Her hand went out to
his arm and rested there.

"Well, Molly —"

"Oh, Steven, — I suppose it is the thing to do —"

"Anyway, it's done — that is, it's begun."

"And Mr. Rickart knew all this time and would n't let you in, after all. It's too *mean*, I think, — the way Cornelius has acted — and the way I've put up with *her* —"

"But he might n't have known anything himself, Molly. I told you Rickart only put him here to let him down easy —"

"It's no excuse for his trying to put *you* down — though perhaps it is with that kind of a person."

This was n't the first Kenneth had heard of the changed relation that had come about between them and the Burkes; had n't the twins tried to put it over him more than once on the ground that his father was working for their father!

"But he has n't really —" Mr. Brent protested.

"Well, *she* has." Mrs. Brent laughed. "And she can't understand how I get on so well in society; the other day at Mrs. Steidley's reception she said —"

"Go to bed, son."

Kenneth found himself usually sent out of the room before interesting human bits of that nature. He calculated, as he kissed his parents good-night, that there would be time for Anne to work his examples for him going over to school next morning on the trolley.

Within a week it was known at Petrolia that landholders in what was known as "the Sink" had formed a Development Company with Mr. Brent coming in on a cash basis, and that operations would begin immediately.

The Brents were "in," oh, quite completely and over-

whelmingly "in." It leaked out in this connection that
the venture had been determined by a private tip from
the Old Man. For all you knew Brent was merely a
blind, and it was really Rickart's capital. Look at the
way their kids had been visiting back and forth — writing letters, too! Of course the Brents were "in" — on
the innermost inside.

With a movement like the rush of passengers to the
side of a listing ship, all the floating interest of Petrolia
rushed in the direction of the Sink.

VII

In the middle of the Easter holidays, one of those clear days when the sky went high and higher and great, rounded clouds nosed about the rim of the hills, Kenneth was making a kennel for his dog on the far side of the house when he heard the honk of a motor, from the hollow below the Rickart pumps. It was a sound that brought everybody to the windows, for in those days private motors were still a matter of rare curiosity, and this car in its glittering newness, as it skimmed and tilted over the undulating surfaces of Petrolia, was like some bright, insect-eyed creature of the day. Kenneth saw it wheel into position before the shed which answered for Burke's offices, and all the idlers running toward it as ants will run about some shining-backed beetle dropped in their midst.

He recognized Mr. Rickart getting heavily out of the car, but Frank must have dropped out on the other side, for it was not until Kenneth had covered half the distance from the house that he saw him. He gave a whoop and began to run; something happened to his heart that sent it flooding all through him, warm and watery. A rod or two from the motor it began to beat again, queerly in a hollow place far below him, for he saw that Frank had not moved toward him at all. It occurred to Kenneth that he would go quite around to the other side of the car as though a view of it had been his only objective, but he found himself pulled suddenly, irresistibly to Frank's side.

"Hello, Ken!"

"Hello yourself —!" He was conscious of Frank's quick paleness, and their hands were together, they scarcely knew how.

"Did n't you know it was me, kid?"

"I guess so —" Kenneth felt the need of a diversion. He laid his hand on the wheel guard to steady himself. "This yours?"

"Ain't she a beaut?" Frank began to explain the motor to him quite fully.

"Does your father let you run it?" To Kenneth this was the most enviable lot.

Frank looked about to see if the chauffeur were listening before he committed himself.

"I guess I *could* handle it —" he was beginning when Mr. Rickart came out of the office followed by Burke, and ordered the boys to pile in. Kenneth would n't for worlds have admitted that he was scared, as the car bumped away over the road reticulated with half-buried iron piping. They made the circle of Petrolia and swung away toward the Sink. Mr. Rickart's cigar stood at the corner of his mouth in an upward angle; he rolled it from time to time as he asked a question of his Superintendent. Kenneth could n't help hearing as they slowed down opposite the Homestead Development Company's borings. He tried to hear, in fact; for was not his own father in the same relation to the wells in the Sink as Mr. Rickart toward those in Petrolia. He would have liked to introduce them as he had seen his father do to strangers with a wave of the hand, but Burke had forestalled him.

The first boring had been made on Scudder's land; beyond the derrick where the men were still busy at it, they could see Jim Hand's scraper banking up a hollow for the oil which was expected daily to come bubbling out of the iron-throated well. They heard him quarreling with his team over the unfamiliar whir of the motor.

"What have they got?" Rickart demanded of the Superintendent; bulletins of the borings were as regular as from the bedside of royalty.

"Saturate sand; she's like to gush on 'em any day now."

"That all they got for taking care of it?" The Old Man waved his hand toward the shallow in the sand that Hand was scooping with his one plough team.

"They're not counting on having to store it —" Burke began.

"What are they counting on, then?"

"On the pipe line . . . Bailey says it'll be finished the end of this week; they'll have to sell quick, they need the money."

"And they're counting on the pipe line, eh?"

"Ain't we all?" Burke counter-questioned. "The tanks don't carry no more than thirty per cent of the output."

He referred to the line of tank cars that looped about Petrolia from the valley road, like some sort of Gargantuan-joint worm of the same prehistoric period that produced the derricks.

Mr. Rickart chewed his cigar.

"How deep's Brent in?" he wished to know, chopping the words short as if by that means he would have prevented them reaching the alert ears of Brent's boy.

"All in; the others had nothing but land."

"And they're counting on the pipe line." Something in the tone caused Burke to give a quick look at him and another at the boy.

Kenneth had an impulse to speak up smartly and say, what of it, since the pipe line was n't old Rickart's anyway; but dizzying loops which the car executed among the gopher hills absorbed him.

They swung back toward the bluff and stopped before Hartley Daws's office.

Burke climbed out here.

"I reckon this is as far as we go, Ken," he reminded the boy who was caught up in the rapture of flying.

"Me, too," Frank insisted; "I'll come home on the trolley."

Mr. Rickart nodded. "I guess you two got a lot of talk coming." He smiled on them not unkindly.

Instead of turning back, however, toward the Brents' house, Frank led the way across the low bridge and along the willow border. "A man 's got to have a chance to smoke sometime," — he flourished a cigarette case, — "have one, old sport." Oh, there was an air of cities about all he did; Kenneth found it irresistible.

"I have n't tried it yet —" he began, but he held out his hand.

"All the fellows in our school do. But you bet we keep it from Prexy, all right, all right. These cost me fifty the box, and maybe I don't have to do the Japanese juggle with my allowance to keep Dad from finding it out. Gee, but this is something like!" He leaned back against the foot of the bluff and blew rings. What he did n't know about himself was that, quite as much as the cigarette, he loved the flavor of secret indulgence. Smoking in public would cease to be a sporty thing to do and become merely a habit.

Kenneth whiffed at his cigarette gingerly and wished there were not such a sickish smell of the waste oil and the damp earth under the willows. The sun shone down on them warmly and the leaves kept up a soft, secret rustle.

The occasion seemed one for confidences and Frank rose to it.

"Well, old sport," he quizzed, "how's the girls?"

"The g — Oh, they're all right!" That was it, the tone had done it; they were not just Anne and Virginia; they were "the Girls." Any gentleman of thirteen will understand.

"'S Virginia as good a looker as she used to be?"

"Pretty fair." Kenneth had n't, to tell the truth, remarked his sister's friend lately; the phrase he copied from his father, and felt that he was getting on extremely well.

"Gee, but there's some swell skirts around Oakdale," Frank let him know.

All at once Kenneth realized that this was what he had been waiting for. Frank could understand him as no one else had done, not even Peters.

"Addie Scudder's working at our house — she's pretty — kind of . . ."

"Oh, you kid!" Frank tilted his hat against the sun and looked at his friend under the brim of it as a gentleman should.

Kenneth found himself richly embarrassed by the implication. He leaned his head against the bluff to correct a swimming tendency, and met it as gallantly as he was able. "I have the greatest respect for Addie," he announced gravely — "the greatest possible respect for her."

"Oh, of course —" Frank admitted the extenuating fact with a wave of the hand.

They looked at each other, a little at a loss how to go on with the conversation; they lay still and soaked in the warm light.

It came upon them there between a tremor and a sound — a dull rushing which grew into a steady roar as of wind or water or the bellowing of the plundered earth. They could n't make it out, — a sound so unrelated to the day, — but they heard shouting at the bridge, astounded, frightened. They understood that. They leaped out from the willows and across the bridge in time to see three or four idlers running out of the roadhouse, and Hartley Daws, hatless, starting from the door of his little office like a cuckoo from his clock.

All the lines of looking and running converged at the Sink, where now they saw arise the black vomit of the earth in a huge column that broke and rained backward on the green sod. They saw the waggling, broken arm of the derrick, whirled about like a twig in a freshet, and little drenched figures running aimlessly. The boys began to run, too; it seemed to Kenneth that he was running in a dream; his legs moved but he got no farther forward. Men came running up behind and passed them.

"Strike! Strike!" some one shouted.

"It's a gusher!" they heard Hartley Daws calling over his shoulder.

The grocery wagon went by at a gallop with Mr. Brent standing in it holding on to the back of the seat.

The boys clutched at the tailboard, felt it bumping cruelly at their chests and then ricocheted, with a final jerking halt, into the ring of astonished gazers about the precincts of the well. They stood off from the fine spray of the gusher, the fall of which veered a little and finally descended to the west into the hollow prepared for it. Jim Hand capered about, drunk with excitement. He was drenched with the sudden black rain and blood ran down his face from a cut in his forehead made by a falling bar of the derrick, though he seemed not to notice it; from time to time he would move to put his hand to his head as if in pain, but forgot the gesture in the repetition of an obsessing phrase.

"Thousan' bar'ls a day, thousan' bar'ls," — he clipped his words like a man far gone in drink. "Just look at her, look at her!" He caught sight of Brent and surged toward him. "What d' you think of that, Brent, what d' you think of it? Has the Homestead Company got oil or has n't it? Betcha there's a thousan' bar'ls." He waved his arms about as challenging all comers with the statement.

Brent caught him by the shoulders and forced his attention.

"A thousand barrels going to waste, then, you booby."

Hand threw him off with a foolish laugh.

"Tell you what, boys, there's no gusher like that in these oil fields. I tell *you!*"

"Take him away!" Brent ordered.

Two or three of the men led Hand toward his house; they saw him holding his head at last as if he had just discovered his hurt. Pop Scudder drifted over from the truck garden where he had been at the moment of the strike. He was looking startled and yet childishly pleased out of the ambush of his silver beard.

He chuckled a little indulgently at Brent as he surveyed the spouting rain. "What'll you bet she's eighty feet high?"

Brent could have struck him; instead he followed the old man's look across the space in which Mrs. Scudder moved toward them with the youngest Scudder still hanging at her skirts, one hand stayed to her flat breasts. She looked back at him, white, under all her weather exposure, with the facing of many fearful destinies.

"Well, mom, it's some blow-out, ain't it?"

"It sure air, Pop."

Something passed between them, with the homely words, of mutual consolation, the profound, extenuating look of the long-mated. They had n't really expected anything; they had known their luck would get the better of any fortunate circumstances at last; they had met too many times under its shadow not to make light of it. Steven Brent turned from them suddenly, sick with comprehension. He began to walk back toward Petrolia. Kenneth ran and slipped an unobtrusive hand into his father's; he understood nothing of what had happened except that his father was daunted by it. They could hear, as they went, Hartley Daws, to whom the boring outfit belonged, trying to save what he could of the derrick; the roar of the springing well cut off his orders grotesquely. It seemed a long walk back to the house, like a walk in a dream, with disaster clogged about their knees. As they mounted the hillock where their house stood, father and son could see crowds of people, notified by telephone, getting off the Summerfield trolley.

It was some time before the entertainment of the gusher as an event, and an event proudly and exclusively theirs, — for Addie was of their own household and they scorned the pretensions of the young tribe of Scudders, — was dissipated for the Brent children by the realization of it as a catastrophe. It gave them a strange sense of secret powers to see it swaying like a torch above the Sink, and a guilty sense of connivance when, at night, as the wind turned the fall in their direction, its steady, devouring roar made the thin walls of the bungalow to tremble.

The gusher decreased in height and volume during three days, and after that went on filling the shallow reservoir and keeping pace with the banks that Pop Scudder and Jim Hand piled against it. On Sunday the banks broke and the viscid flow began to eat up the tillable lands of the Homestead Development Company. That day the rainbow hope of the Homesteaders was broken and dissolved by an announcement in the local paper that the pipe line, which had been building to carry the surplus product of Petrolia to the Bay, would be in operation by the end of the week, and that the controlling interest had been leased by the company of which the Rickart group of wells was the representative.

In the "Clarion" the announcement was almost completely overlaid by extended reference to the Rickart Company's plans for subdividing and selling out in small parcels what was known as the Summerfield ranch property. This was a flat, unplanted acreage lying between the town and the foothills, which had been acquired by the Old Man after the way north had been closed to the cattle, and used as a halfway station between the range and market for the long-horned, milling herds. Since *el año malo*, however, the ranch had not been fully restocked, and with the improved irrigation, made possible by the recent release of capital in the district, the breaking-up of this tract into vineyards and orchards, marked, the "Clarion" assured its readers, the beginning of a new era.

Stirred as he was by every interest of the soil, the significance of the pipe line announcement might have passed over Steven Brent. But there was another and smaller sheet, which was, or affected to be, free from every form of pocket allegiance to the Rickart Interests, in which the original promise of the pipe line to be a common carrier, and the significance to the small oil producer of its preëmption by the Old Man was made as much of as possible, in view of the fact that nobody knew just how the thing had been managed. There was the usual suggestion of legislative connivance and private corruption, the usual veiled allusion to the local octopus, tempered by the realization that a free press, in order to remain free, must not render itself altogether obnoxious. Passed to Brent through the inflammable mind of Jim Hand, the item began to appear sufficiently alarming.

The announcement had appeared in the Saturday issue. Sunday morning there had been an informal meeting of the Homestead Development Company at the Brents' house, in which the querulous impatience of the stockholders at Brent's failure to get "next" to the Old Man's plans was kept in check only by the realization that Brent was still their one chance, through his connection with Rickart, of keeping "in" with the newer development. It led to Brent's walking over in the afternoon to discuss, so far as Cornelius would lend himself to discussion of his employer's affairs, the whole situation with the Superintendent.

"It seems to me, Cornelius," Mr. Brent allowed himself leave to say, "that you need n't have been so close with me. This hits our interests pretty severely."

"About the lease you mean? I did n't know myself — at least not in time to do you any good. And I did advise you —"

Brent moved impatiently.

"What's the use of that in the face of what we've got? You knew we were counting on the pipe line; Rickart knew it. It was in all the papers that it was to be a common carrier —" The men were standing in the Burkes' front yard, which, so far as the ordinary boundaries of a front yard were present to mark it off, might have included the whole of Petrolia. They could see from where they stood the Sunday crowd of sight-seers and the black geyser shaking above the Sink. Brent voiced his impatience with a touch of despair. "Eight hundred barrels running to waste! Good Lord, Cornelius, what are we to *do!*"

"You are kind of up against it," — Burke's sympathy was genuine. "You might get the Company to take over your product — but you know how the Old Man is. He does n't like his people to be mixed up with these outside interests. They're apt to be too much taken up with them. And then it looks like a tip, and that upsets the market. If you had saved your capital now, and put it in this Summerfield extension — that's a legitimate investment."

"Ah," said Brent, "if you had just given me the tip —

I suppose," — he turned the question hopefully, — "there would n't be anything doing now, in the way of a situation? I'm no good at this oil business, Cornelius, and that's a fact; I'm sick to get back to the land."

"Well, the Old Man *was* mentioning something about me having charge of the office," — Burke almost apologized; "but to tell you the truth, Steven, being tied up with this Hand outfit has n't helped you any with the Old Man . . . they're a bunch of pikers. . . ."

"So long as I am tied up with them," Brent took him up shortly, "I'll see the thing through with them."

Kenneth, who, with a disquieting sense of his father being at odds with circumstance, had been hanging loosely on his arm, felt the squaring of Brent's shoulders.

In spite of Brent's employment by the Rickart Company which had looked so hopeful a peg to hang fortune upon, the development of the next few days left the family more and more sickeningly aware how completely they had been deflected from the main line of prosperity. They were not "in" at all; they had never been "in."

It drove the children more and more to the open; in the little thin-walled house they were never free from the sense of their mother's impotent chaffing, and, whenever they saw the black torch of the gusher waving above the Sink as though it were shaken by the hand of disaster, from an uneasy consciousness of guilt. It was as though in their fumbling they had somehow turned the forbidden key, pressed upon the prohibited button. Always there was their mother's importunate —

"But is n't there anything you can *do*, Steven? I should think you could think of something to do!"

"There's only the pipe line . . . the courts would bear us out in its being a common carrier, I think, but *we* are n't in a position to carry it up to them."

"But how did Rickart get it? Get it away from him — Oh — if you would *do — anything!* Won't he buy the oil from you? It's perfectly *good* oil, is n't it? —"

Brent looked at her commiseratingly.

"What's the use of offering to sell a man what he knows you'll be glad to give him if he waits a bit." That arrested her.

"Give it to him!"

"When suits begin for damages — we're flooding the Wilts property — unless we can stop the flow." He threw out his hands with a hopeless gesture. "Do *you* think of anything to do, Molly?"

"If I did," she told him shortly, "I should do it myself. I should n't leave it to *you!*"

It did not, however, occur to Kenneth that she had found something, when he discovered her on Wednesday waiting for him at the close of school. She picked him up that way occasionally when it was a question of new suits or shoes, and as he was still at that age when new shoes would have been in order on almost any occasion, he supposed that might be what was in the wind. Especially as Anne was let go on directly home with Virginia. He was very pleased to go about with his mother on any account. There was no denying, as they went along the crowded street, the quality of her success. She had such an air of making her passage of the public thoroughfares a thing done for its own sake, and justified, that it brought out in Kenneth a manner before which even the Burke boys, who usually contrived completely to disown

any female of their families with whom they might be
caught walking, were abashed. He held his shoulders
straighter and preceded her at the crossings quite of his
own accord.

They did not, however, on this occasion turn in at the
shoe store, but kept on to the disused and partly recon-
structed dwelling which, until the two-story brick block,
to which the local paper had devoted a quarter of a
column, could be built, did duty as office for the Rickart
Interests.

It stood quite on the other side of the Main Street, a
little back from the sidewalk, in one of those grassless,
shrubby yards which characterized the pre-bungalow
period of Summerfield architecture. As they hesitated a
moment in the small square entrance, they had a general
impression of trousered legs moving to dispose themselves
more decorously on the advent of so fine a figure of a
woman. In the interval before any one came forward to
inquire her business, Mrs. Brent had time to get hold of
Kenneth's hand and to lose a little of that bright security
to which her shape, the hats she wore, and the admirable
line of her skirts lent such sanction. The strength with
which she clasped her son's small, perspiring hand suggested the sudden failure of her high determination, persisted in all the years at Palomitas, to treat the Old Man
as a neighbor, and a neighbor with no claim to any other
status. After all, who *were* the Rickarts? It was with a
drowning clutch on her old resolution that they were
ushered into his private office.

"Frank's somewhere about," Frank's father let fall to
Kenneth as soon as they had finished with the hand-
shaking; "he was here a minute ago." He was looking at

the boy as he spoke and Kenneth looked at him with that
half flutter of a smile between them by which these two,
when they met, recognized, without its occurring to
either of them to admit it, that they liked one another.
Kenneth supposed that the words were a permission to
take himself out of the way, but a look from his mother
detained him. The Old Man caught her halfway in it.

"And what can I do for you, Mrs. Brent?" was his
curt way of recognizing the suggestion of formality in her
visit.

"Ah, what can you? That's what I came about."

"In relation to — what?" The half gesture he made
to resume the dry smoke, left off in deference to the presence of a lady, seemed indefinably a movement to guard.

"The gusher, you know," — she was determined to be
bright with him, — "it's flooding us off the map, — unless you take a hand at it." The absence of emphasis
on the "you" had a world of feminine wile in it; it took
so many things for granted. Too many.

Rickart's response to it was distinctly colder.

"Young Daws seems to be doing all that can be done.
I sent him over four of my scrapers to-day."

"To cut off the flow altogether — but that cuts us off
just as completely."

Her voice made of the gusher a smaller matter than
Kenneth had ever imagined could be made of it, almost
an amusing matter. He was on the point of speaking up,
of protesting that it wasn't a matter you could just take
up between your thumb and finger, but the Old Man
spoke first.

"It's a risk we all run in a country where gushers are
frequent. One has to be prepared."

"We thought we were — the pipe line, you know."
She could n't quite keep it up; her voice trembled; the
smile with which she finished was a little awry. "We
could n't imagine you were going to swoop down on it
like that."

Rickart restored his unlighted cigar to the corner of his
mouth and revolved perplexedly. He leaned both his
hands on the rim of the desk before him and looked across
it at Kenneth. "Frank's somewheres around the back
yard," he explained; "you could look for him."

Mrs. Brent forestalled him again.

"We're going soon." One could see that she meant to
be brief and businesslike with him.

Rickart surrendered to the situation.

"Now, look here Mrs. Brent, I know what your husband thinks about that pipe line, and I want to tell you
that he's dead wrong."

"Then you will take over their product. . . ." She slid
the phrase off with a rising inflection.

Rickart paid the tribute of a flickering glance to the
cleverness with which she almost did the trick.

"The terms on which we've leased the line won't admit
of our carrying anything but our own output," he notified her. "I knew the small owners would kick — it
pinches them, and bad, too. But I want to say, Mrs.
Brent, what I have n't said to anybody here except Burke,
that it never was a question of the small owners and myself at all. It was a question between me and Standard
Oil. If I had n't got ahead of them, they'd have got ahead
of me, and then where would you be in any case?"

The troubled end of his cigar traveled its half-circuit
of perplexity in the corner of his mouth; he bore hard

with his spread fingers on the rim of the desk in his effort to make himself completely understood. "I'm sorry for your husband, Mrs. Brent. He's a man I have the greatest possible respect for. But this thing is a game. You've got to play it with the cards that are on the table. I did n't know to what extent Brent had mixed himself up with those pikers, but it could n't have made any difference if I had. I know a lot of yahoos like Jim Hand think us capitalists are just lying in wait for 'em at the crossroads to gobble 'em, but the fact is we're looking out to save our own skins the same as they are, only we look out *better*. It's not so easy as you think. I had to have outside money on this deal." He would not look at her as he destroyed her hopes, pressing them down one by one with a spatulate finger on the desk before him. "Brent ought n't to have gone in with that outfit," he concluded, "it's not his game."

"I don't know why you should think *that* of my husband." She was choking.

"Have n't I just said I've the greatest possible respect for him? . . . But he's a born rancher. It's a wonder what he accomplished there at Palomitas, beginning with nothing at all. Why did you let him quit?"

She blenched at that. "The place was mortgaged —"

"I know, I know —" He looked at her now and was relieved to see that she was n't going to cry. He could n't for the life of him understand why women did these things. "I was pretty hard hit myself, but if I'd known— Any sort of a ranching proposition now, I'd back Brent against any man. He had that ranch where it would have paid him big money in a few years. But he can't buck this game, Mrs. Brent. If you'd get him back to Palomitas —" He broke off as if remembering something. "I guess that's not possible — now." Any emphasis there might have been on the item of time missed her benumbed faculties.

"Then there's nothing —?" She rose.

He rose with her.

"Unless Daws gets her cut off — they could lay low a while. Now that you know there's oil there —"

She gave an unmirthful laugh.

"Oh, there's oil there, there's oil!" She got out somehow holding to Kenneth's hand. All the way home on the trolley she held it with convulsive clasps and shudders; something struggled up in her shaking the fine bosom, and was bitten back.

Kenneth felt for the note of sympathy.

"That old Rickart, I just hate him."

"Hush," she bade him; "somebody'll hear you."

They came down the bluff stumblingly; the thing that struggled in her had her by the throat. She turned aside at the bridge into the willows until they came to the place from which the boys had heard the first portentous roar of the gusher. For a moment Kenneth thought that she had it in for him somehow on account of the cigarettes; the half-burned stumps lay where they had dropped them; but he saw that she was crying; she leaned against the willow trunk and shook with sobbing.

Kenneth did not know what to do; his breast swelled against Frank's father; he thought that he would take it out of Frank one of these days. Suddenly he found that he was crying too. He slipped his hand under his mother's arm and leaned against her. She shook him off impatiently.

"What have you got to cry for?" But the affectionate gesture had touched the chord of self-commiseration; she struck the willow with her tender fist. "I can't bear it; I can't! To think that we've always got to be like this, always poor — and put upon. Never to have anything! Never to *be* anybody! It's *too* stupid!" The old intolerable cry broke from her. "I'll not bear it!" she reiterated; "nobody could be expected to bear it!"

By degrees her anguish worked away; she moved up and down muttering to herself. By and by she took a powder puff from her pocket and dusted her nose. She retied her veil. Kenneth understood that they were to set out for the house; he was terrified and ashamed as the young often are at any emotion in their elders. On the bridge his mother turned and looked at him for a moment. He knew as well as anything that she had it in mind to warn him not to mention the episode of the afternoon to his father, and though she did not finally, he also knew, better than anything, that she knew he would not. He knew it was unmentionable.

As they paused before the house for a moment their attention was arrested by the cessation of the rushing roar of the gusher, always faintly audible from the veranda as from the lip of a shell. Glancing away toward the Sink they could see the black column drop, bubble, and go out under the heap of sand which Hartley Daws's men had managed to draw about it and topple over the fountain's mouth. A moment it remained so, cut off as by the turning of a tap, for as long as they held a suspended breath to watch it. Then, with a swift, tearing sound, it tossed up gobbets of sand as a cork is tossed from champagne; the column shot up again and the figures of the men were veiled in the relentless, viscid rain. Years afterward it seemed to Kenneth in retrospect that the roar of the released gusher was but the signal to disaster which rushed in upon his youth from every side.

VIII

WITH the full disclosure of the Old Man's plans for parceling out the Summerfield ranch came other news and not less disconcerting. It was brought direct from Agua Caliente by the Ballards, Frank's sole kin on the mother's side.

Mrs. Ballard was a woman who had but one object in life, or at least but one which she allowed herself to speak of as an object, and that was to be a mother to poor dear Fanny's boy, who could n't bear her.

She was quite the mirror of fashion and the mould of that form which is accomplished in the middle forties by pushing all the superfluous flesh close up under the bust and keeping it there by means of a "straight front" and a heroic resolution.

About Ballard there was a paucity of ideas and a plentitude of coatskirt and whisker which seemed to bear her out in the way she continually lined him up and toned him down to his proper attitudes as husband to a woman whose sister had married T. Rickart. In seventeen years she had acquired a way of looking at him which said as plainly as possible that she would n't have thought of bestowing herself on him if she had had any idea that poor dear Fanny was going to make such a match of it. Occasionally, the Ballards had visited at Agua Caliente, where there had grown up an intimacy between Mrs. Brent and Frank's aunt, based on a common sense of their superiority to Mrs. Burke. Always it was at the back of Mrs. Ballard's mind that Burke's place should belong to her husband, not because of any fitness for it, but because of what she as a sensitive woman — so sensitive, my dear, it has positively been the ruin of me — could n't help feeling for her sister's son. Now that the turn of the wheel had brought them to Summerfield, still in a position of subordination to Burke, it gave a fillip to that intimacy to find the Brents in almost an identical case.

So it was to the Brents they came with the news, picked up at Agua Caliente, that Jevens had discovered oil at Palomitas. Over on Mariposa. Nobody knew whether or not it was a profitable flow, but it was oil. Men at Agua Caliente had seen it.

Something shriveled in Mrs. Brent as at a hot blast. She cried out against it.

"It's not true . . . I 'll not believe it!" In the midst of protest memory awoke; she was taken with one of those riving flashes of insight in which situations seemed under her hand to become hopeless by their clearness. "He knew it," she broke forth. "Rickart knew it all the time. He knew it while we were there. All the time we were struggling so . . . and with all I did for Frank. He knew there was oil and he never told us!"

"But you can't be sure," her husband warned her. "Why should he keep a thing like that from us?"

"Oh, don't ask me why. It was n't on his land. Don't talk about it."

The Brents had indeed stopped talking oil. They had had enough of it. Nevertheless, Mrs. Brent upbraided Addie as the nearest representative of the Powers that had played such a trick on them.

Addie flushed in their defense.

"Well, now, Miss' Brent, you can't expect They're going to be remembering always about human foolishness and taking account of it. They got to let men do some things for theirselves, ain't They? They done the best They could for Mr. Brent when They gave him the land and the liking for it; he had n't ought to have let go of it. They can't be lottin' all the time on human foolishness and meanness, like Ole Man Rickart's and my Pop's. They got other things to think about, ain't They?"

"Oh," Mrs. Brent flung back at her, "I suppose even God could n't help a fool."

Words like these flew wide over the children's heads and found their mark.

The story of Jevens and his Palomitas find grew, taking form and color from men's minds. It was said that Jevens had known all the time there was oil there; it fairly oozed out of the ground. Jevens had *not* known; Brent had thrown the place at him and he had taken it for charity. He had only a trace of oil and was trying to create a boom to sell his property. He had found abundance of oil and was trying to keep it quiet until he could make a deal with the railroad which had been surveyed through Tierra Longa these twenty years. Jevens had private advices that the railroad would go through at once if he could find oil. He had had the whole place prospected by Hartley Daws, who had reported that there was no oil. Then Jevens had heard of a meeting between Daws and the Old Man at Romero's. Naturally the Old Man did n't want oil discovered at Palomitas until he had ripped the guts out of Petrolia. He had made it worth while for Daws to report unfavorably; he was in deep in the pipe line; it was up to him to keep the price going. So opinion chopped back and forth like a wave in the wind.

Much of all this went over the children's heads. Trouble gathered about the Homesteader's Development Company, but was overshadowed in their minds by the immediate and pressing concern of Examinations. April lengthened into the rich warmth of May, and then there was Vacation; things transpiring in and about Summerfield made it eventful. The Rickart Land and Development Company began upon its brick block. It was understood that the Burkes were to move into town when it was completed, and Cornelius was to have charge of the office. The process of letting him down was being accomplished with due consideration. The Ballards moved to Summerfield. Ballard was to keep the books of the new concern with such disguises of his title and relation to the firm as was demanded by the interest which Mrs. Ballard kept alive in poor dear Fanny's offspring. First and last the Brents heard a great deal of the relationship, but it was plain that Ballard himself would have been much happier merely to have been an employee of Rickart's, peculating in stamps and stationery perquisites, servile to his face and cheaply disrespectful behind his back. Frank lived with his aunt that summer, in pursuance of his father's plan to keep him as much as possible out of the city. In July, Mrs. Ballard took them all, the two Brents and Virginia, over to Agua Caliente for an outing.

Almost the first of their rides was to see the oil well at Palomitas. It lay on the Ridge between the house and the Ford of Mariposa; a little trickle of the familiar black fluid oozed from it and wasted away into the creek. Near by, a second boring in which the drill had been broken and left, marked the limit of Jevens's hopes, or more probably of his capital. It had been decided that the railroad was not to come through Tierra Longa after all. In silence the children turned and rode on to the Ford. It looked smaller than they remembered it; the stones along its borders were blackened here and there with the sticky overflow of the well, thin rainbow films of oil floated on the surface of the water as it went hurrying by. Nevertheless, they dismounted and sat on the shelving bank with their horses picketed behind them.

"That nasty oil, it's over everything!" Anne broke out. "I wish we'd never heard of it!"

"It was just here we were, when we saw them coming out of the Draw that day." Virginia luxuriated in reminiscences. "'Nacio's *diablo negro!* That's what he was, prospecting for oil right on your own land."

They looked up toward the Draw with a touch of the old, half-fearful anticipation. Somewhere in its secret recesses the presence of death was announced by the wheeling of the buzzards low and steadily. The field nearest them was possessed by a ramping black stallion; half a dozen mares with their colts of that year ran in the *potrero*. There was nothing particularly amiss with the scene and yet over it and over all Tierra Longa was the indefinable impress of neglect. Prosperity had gone by them.

"— Just a black devil —" Virginia was dramatizing the idea when Frank interrupted her. He shied a stone into the dry gully leading down from the ranch house.

"Come out of that!" he demanded. They perceived a figure dodging there. "Oh-ee! 'Nacio!" they raised in concert.

Ignacio Stanislauo came out of the dry Wash and remained at his accustomed distance, at once both bold and shy. By almost the buzzard's instinctive sense he had seen them from the house and tracked them here. He had matured more than any of them in two years; he was slim and taller; he had the grace of the Spaniard, but you saw at once that his mother must have been an Indian. On the whole they were glad to see one another. 'Nacio was carrying a handful of mariposa lilies, such as grew airily at the tips of tall, wiry stems all over the mesa at this season. He slapped them gently against his leg as he answered them categorically on behalf of Manuela, Carmelita, Francisco, and Pedro Demetrio.

"You'll break them," Virginia protested; "give them to me if that's all you can do with them."

A certain reticence as of the Indian came over the boy; he sidled past her with a quick, unobtrusive movement and thrust the lilies into Anne's lap.

"They very pretty flor; maybe you like."

· Frank jeered a little. "Did you ever get left, Virginia!"

"Oh, well," Virginia flashed . . . "He knows what's good for him!"

This cryptic remark was rendered perfectly intelligible by the swift, wordless communication of youth. It meant that as Ignacio's father was working for Frank's father, it was inevitable that it would be to Ignacio's interest to please Frank, and that Frank would rather Anne had the flowers. This was perfectly plain to Kenneth, though he could not altogether account for it. Most boys gave things to Virginia; she was, for one thing, infinitely prettier. He was surprised to see that both Frank and his sister reddened; Ignacio Stanislauo carried it off better.

"I got to go back," he announced grandly. "I'm working for Jevens."

He was also more of a man than either of his former tormentors. He reached back in the pocket of the blue denims buckled about his slim waist, and drew out the makings of a cigarette. They watched him in fascinated silence as he caught the edge of his tobacco sack in his teeth and drew out the loop with a practiced finger. Kenneth was aching to have Frank restore the balance of accomplishment with a show of his silver case; when the snub came, however, it was even more effective than he had expected. Ignacio rolled his cigarette, standing with his feet apart in a manly attitude. They noticed that his legs were bowed already by the saddle.

"Smoke, Rickart?" His grown-up manner could not have been improved upon.

Frank was majestical. "I don't smoke in the presence of ladies."

A certain bridling on the part of the ladies present advised him that he had struck the right note. Kenneth felt that he would never have thought of anything so brilliant himself; such *nuances* were, however, lost on Ignacio Stanislauo.

"So long!" he saluted them; as he turned back up the gully, he paused just long enough deliberately to set a match to his cigarette.

"My goodness, Anne," Virginia giggled, "to think of 'Nacio being sweet on you."

"I don't think it's that," Anne protested; "it's just that this was my home . . . and the first time I've been back . . ." She had always stood up for the little Romeros more than any of them.

"Anyway, what if he was; you used to be sweet enough on old Ken." Frank was always swift to the rescue. "Remember how I caught you kissing him, last time we were here."

"He was telling me good-bye; we were nothing but children." Virginia felt herself injured.

"Bet you can't get him to do it again. Go on, Ken. Go to it," Frank scoffed. "What you afraid of?"

"I ain't afraid of anything," Kenneth averred hotly; "I just don't want to."

"Frank Rickart, you're the meanest . . ." Virginia executed one of those swift changes from indignation to cool philosophy under which Frank winced. "I guess you come by it honestly. When I think of the kind of thing your father does — that pipe line, and everything . . ." Virginia always cut right and left regardless of her own position.

"Well, I guess he did n't do anything to *your* father." Frank was driven to defend himself.

"Well, I guess it does n't matter *who* a person does a mean thing to. Persons ought to be fair just for fairness." Virginia's eyes were shining, the warm wind blew little tendrils of hair about her forehead.

"I guess my father can take care of himself," Kenneth advised her. Some floating straws of things heard at home in long, troubled sessions of the Homestead Development Company came uppermost in his mind and he seized upon them. "I guess Burt and Estes money is as good as anybody's. First thing the Rickart Company knows —"

"First thing you know we'll be late to lunch."

Anne's announcement brought them all to their feet.

As they set out by the upper road for Agua Caliente, she pulled out a moment and passed Kenneth on the off side. "You shut up!" she warned; "talking about things you don't know anything about."

As his sister rode on, Virginia fell in beside him. She lagged her horse until the other two were more than earshot ahead of her.

"What makes you such a stupid, Ken, letting Frank put a scare on you? What's kissing anyway?"

"I was n't scared."

"Well," — impatiently, — "that is n't the way to make folks think so, just *saying* you ain't."

"I did n't think you'd like it." Kenneth was conscious of having fallen into her bad graces . . . "I'll kiss you now, Virginia, if you want me to."

"Oh, my goodness, Kenneth Brent, did you think I'd *let* you!" She struck her horse viciously and gave him her flying dust.

In spite of such perplexing incidents they had a glorious week, and agreed solemnly, with young confidence in controlling destiny, that they would come there every summer for just such another so long as they lived. "No matter where we are or what we are doing, we'll just lay it down, half a world away," Virginia dramatized, "and come back to the dear old land." But if she had been able to foresee that never again would the four of them ride together at Agua Caliente, nor anywhere in quite the same relation again, she would have got just as much pleasure out of it.

The first thing the children noticed the morning that they came back to Petrolia, was a solemn, unfamiliar stillness as of a death in the family. It was the gusher that had died. Without warning it had fallen to half its height, bubbled there for a day and a half, dropped half again, shot up hissing far into the air with such force that the oil divided in a fine spray, stopped short, and with a final burst that tore the earth for yards about the throat of the well, it ceased to be. Nothing was left of it but the shimmering, stinking pool that spread far over the adjacent land and fouled the ancient bed of the river.

There was a sense of loss with it at first, and then relief. The relief was merely physical. The Wilts property-owners filed suit for damages; it was a just claim that the company would have been glad to compromise had there been money attainable. And there was no money. All that the rich promise of the future still brought to Petrolia was engaged in the building of tanks and reservoirs. When the Rickart Company had discharged its surplus, then the flow would begin again, to and from the markets of the world, oil going down in the great pipe line to the Bay and money coming in through its appointed conduits.

And in the mean time Wilts might get a judgment; or the oil spread all over the surface of the land might catch fire. While the gusher was going, it warned with its terrible menace the passers-by. Men carefully ground out their cigar butts in the dust of the road before they ventured within reach of its inflammable rain. But as it sunk into the earth and left the hillocks bare, they grew careless. A spark, the clash of an iron-shod heel on flint, might have set it off. Or it might have caught even from the incandescent wrath of Jim Hand. Day by day anger flared higher in him as he went about muttering, chewing the cud of his bitter resentment.

He was working by the day with his team on one of the great reservoirs in the hills; he, part possessor in one of the richest sections of Petrolia. Land — acres of land with oil under it! Oh, there was no doubt about the oil — and he was working for day's wages. It was plain that the Homestead Company would have to make terms with the devouring beast.

They must have Capital. There were two notable representatives of Capital in Petrolia. Rickart and the combination known as Burt and Estes, which had competed unsuccessfully with the Old Man for control of the pipe line. Both of them would presumably be interested in keeping other large interests out of the field; it was thought the ultimate argument with either would be the suggestion of an appeal to the other. The Homestead Development Company milled it over sitting around the Brents' dining-table, evening after evening. The talk of it mixed with all Kenneth's reading; it was sewn into all Anne's clothes. Their minds ran in a little track; they plotted and were wise over they knew not what.

The Brents must have known at last what they had let themselves in for; the deep distrusts, the limited imagination of Pop Scudder and Jim Hand. Brent stood out as much as he dared for an appeal to Rickart. He knew a little of the Old Man's weakness. If they put themselves unreservedly in his hands, they would be shorn, no doubt, but they would get something: the portion of faithful vassals. If they went to Burt and Estes, they would get the enmity of Rickart and what else besides? Who knew? Burt and Estes were reported to be but one of the chameleon forms of Standard Oil. With all Steven Brent could say, his wife reproached him for not

saying more. "Impossible," he told her; "Hand has already thrown it up to me that I'm working for the Old
Man. They'll think I'm making something for myself on
the side."

"The common thing!" She dismissed him. Of late she
had taken a new note toward her husband, almost of
apology, of reparation. It offered him no clue, however,
to her sudden anxiety to enroll their interests under
Rickart's banner. They settled at last the terms of a
mortgage which they might offer to Burt and Estes for
money enough to satisfy Wilts and to make new borings
on another part of the land, this time with adequate pro-
vision for the unexpected. It was all to be so secret; you
never knew what you might be up against if these things
got about. It cheered them greatly, the thought that
they might by this deal "put one over the Old Man."
The item of the pipe line still stuck in the craw of the
Homestead Development Company. They felt that they
were playing the game.

And then, before the arrangement could be completed,
it went like wild-fire over the Fields, that Rickart had
taken over the Wilts property, damage suit and all.
Somebody had leaked. Jim Hand came roaring up to
Cornelius Burke.

"You —— dirty, Irish spy, you!" There was the root
of an old racial hatred between these two. "You been
pussy-footin' around among your honest neighbors,
you —— —— ——."

"Go slow, go slow." Cornelius warned him.

"Slow as hell!" Hand retorted on him.

One great fist, red like a ham, shot out at the Superintendent. All the children saw it. They had come down to

inspect the installation of the new pumps at the Escondita group. They huddled together, fascinated to watch
the two great-bodied men turning and contorted in a
struggle from which issued a gasping stream of profanity. Cornelius fought cold and remembered his youth
in the boom days of Pennsylvania. Before the pump
hands pulled them apart, Hand was staggering sick and
dazed.

"Now, you rambunctious fool you, what's eating
you?" Cornelius demanded.

"Yah!" Hand snarled at him, spitting blood. "Pre-
tendin' you don't know. Ask *them*." He indicated
Burke's assistants with a wave of his hand on which the
bruised knuckles bled. "Ask anybody if it ain't well
known that you're nothing but a snooper and a spy for
that —— ——. You a well superintendent! You don't
know a well from a hole in the ground. You're just kep'
on to spy, you ——, I'll fix you for this." He took himself off muttering.

By noon it was known all over the Fields that Hand
had fought Burke for tipping off the Old Man to the
Burt and Estes deal.

Brent came over in the evening to exculpate the
Company.

"I'm mighty sorry, Cornelius; Hand's an unlicked
brute."

"I'm not holding it against you." Cornelius met him
cheerfully. "'T is a relief to a man's feelings to fight occasionally. Besides, if I'd known, I'd 'a' told, maybe.
'T would have been my duty." Burke had almost said
"juty"; his lip was cut, all the Irish stood out on him
like a hallmark.

"Perhaps. It's all a fight, I suppose. You have n't the least idea who did tell, have you?"

For a moment Burke seemed to consider; his unclosed eye traveled past Brent to Kenneth, who had come down with his father, and seemed to catch the boy's gaze for a moment of singular if fleeting intelligence. "No," he said; "no, Steven, I have n't. I had the wire straight from the San Francisco office to make the deal with Wilts and make it sudden. That's all I know."

"It's no use," Steven Brent told his wife that night. "We don't even know what's against us. We're on the wrong side of the carpet. All we see is ragged ends, and now and then a loose thread that seems as if it would start something. But we don't know what. It's a game, Business. And it is n't my game. I'm afraid ranching's all I'm good for, Molly."

"You were good at that," she told him.

It seemed a wonderful concession, for which he kissed her. He stood there for a moment with his arms around her; some of his care fell from him.

"We could have the ranch back on any terms almost," he ventured; "I reckon Jevens knows when he's got enough."

The children pricked and thrilled. Palomitas back! But it was too much even to dream.

"I don't know where you'd get the money for Palomitas, if you can't get it for the wells," she reminded him.

Brent turned away wearily.

"We'll get it," he assured her, "but we'll get it on their terms."

It was about this time that there began to be a great change in Kenneth. Anne noticed it first, and Addie.

"Calf love," Addie opined, "or growing pains; one or tother; makes 'em kind of mopy either way."

"Ken won't even look at a girl." Kenneth's sister was positive. "He does n't know what girls are *for !* "

Nevertheless, he moped; he fell silent in the house and took to spending long hours roaming the hills, where he would meet with the returning sheep herders, feeding their flocks down from the summer range in the high Sierras. He would tend a flock for such-a-one half a day while the herder dozed or went down to Summerfield for a jolly little claret drunk and a game of handball at Noriega's. He knew a few words of the lingo by which the French and Basque and Mexican herders communicate, and they trusted him instinctively. He was one to whom knowledge of sheep came as to musicians the handling of their instruments. Besides the secret relief to his mind, the work of herding saved him from a certain shame which he had begun to experience, as he grew taller and thinner, in the inadequacy of his lengthening limbs to anything that might reasonably be expected of them. Nothing suited so well with the languor of his rapid growth as walking at the head of a flock out of sight of the oppressive derricks, away from the loathed smell of petroleum, with his arms extended on the herder's crook which he laid across his shoulders, the dogs ambling friendlily at his knees.

He had room then to attend to the vague prickings of his instincts, sending up from below the plane of his consciousness, where they worked, vague, pleasing intimations, starts and warm floodings that mixed with the suggestion of presence that waits upon men in the vast open country. He did not know quite what it was that they shaped between them, the land and his instinct; at times if he would but turn his head he would see it there, and yet he did not turn. Glimmers of the dream he had, about setting out with Addie across the hills for the unnamed adventure, would wake in him, and set him to plaiting the tops of the sage together as he had seen the herders do in half-conscious stirrings of the house-building sense, widening his shelter for the invisible, unshaped companion. But when no flock afforded him the excuse of an occupation, he wore himself out, tramping as much as he thought his years demanded of him.

It was on one of these occasions that Anne, who was the only one of the household at Petrolia who knew much about them, climbed up to the lip of the Sink to meet his returning. This was Anne's birthday and a present had come by the afternoon mail. She showed it to him now as they sat there together looking out across the sunken oil fields to the bluff of Summerfield, wrapped in a cobalt haze, against the banked hills of fawn and purple. Anne's arm somehow seemed flat, not round like Virginia's, and the chased silver band struck Kenneth as an unsuitable ornament.

Anne was quite miffed at his want of appreciation. "Anyway I should like it," she affirmed, "because Frank sent it to me."

"Well, that's no reason for me to like it."

"Kenneth!" The tone had made her look up at him with a start of inquiry. "You and Frank have n't quarreled, have you?" They had neither of them seen young Rickart since he went away to school about the first of September. "He said you had n't answered his letter."

"Nor ain't a-going to . . . the snitch!"

"Ken! I don't believe it." The connotation of the word was only vaguely familiar to Anne; those two had never required many words, however.

"Nothing to me whether you believe it or not. You can send his rotten old present back to him for all *I* care." He swung himself out from the lip and began to clamber laboriously down between the brush and stones.

Anne called to him once; she ran fast on the trail to overtake him as it crossed his more difficult route. Then she saw that she had committed the unpardonable offense. The young have saved, out of their native savagery, wisdom enough not to look on one another's personal agonies. Kenneth's face streamed with tears, his breath came sobbing.

Anne darted past him quick as a rabbit.

"Beat you down!" she called back, running. But the moment the turn of the trail took her out of sight she began to go slowly. "I don't believe it," she insisted to herself. "Anyway, Ken ought to have kept his mouth shut." Presently she took the bracelet from her arm and put it in her pocket.

That night the waste from the Homestead gusher took fire. It was thought that Soldumbehere himself might have set it. He had come in that evening at sundown with the first of his flocks, and camped about six miles from his corrals. After supper he had left the sheep with the head shepherd and walked across to Jim Hand's. Soldumbehere knew almost nothing of the gusher; he had been gone since early in April, and though letters had been sent him, they were most of them following still on his trail through the Sierras. He walked across the dry, tindery grass lands and right through the drenched district, smoking and perhaps shaking out the sparks from his pipe. There was no moon; he guided himself by the derrick lights and the feel of the ground underfoot; Soldumbehere had made his wintering ground about the Sink for twenty years. He sat a long time at Hand's, three or four hours; there was much to be explained to him. Finally, when Jim let him out the door, they saw the fire running like serpents in the oil-drenched grass.

The Brent children knew nothing of it until morning; fortunately the fire set with the wind away from Petrolia; a thin line of it still burned toward the river bed, like a streak of light under a thick curtain of smoke, miles away. It burned out there by noon, but it had burned Jim Hand out of house and home. They had to run for it with the children and what they could snatch of the household goods. It burned Soldumbehere's corrals, and sheds and fences on the Wilts property. The Homestead Company was resigned. They had dreaded fire so long they were glad to have it over with. Rickart would demand damages again, but it was up to Burt and Estes.

Addie was almost cheerful over it; the more misfortunes the nearer they were to the turn. Even the Powers must finally exhaust their bag of tricks.

"Twice the fire, once the flood, and then the fortune," she quoted to Mrs. Brent, falling back on that wild lore which the earth-born cull from their wrestle with the untamed forces! It seemed to Kenneth, however, that his mother was not taking it so easily. It brought into her voice again that note of desperate rebellion which struck all through him with shivers of dreadfulness. He heard it sounding in the night through the thin-walled bungalow, the fretful sound of hopeless chiding. It went on for a week or more, issuing from his mother's room at night, the sharp, reiterated protest and the patient, low rejoinder.

"It's too much, Steven; it's too much. I can't go through with it. After all I've *been* through . . . the way we've been disappointed . . . and now *this* — when I thought I was done with it, after fourteen years. . . . Oh, it's too *stupid*. . . ." Then tears and the rising note again. "I won't go through with it. I tell you I won't, it's too much to ask of a woman. . . . Oh, what do you men *care!* I'm going to see Mrs. Ballard. She'll tell me something . . ."

"Marcia!" Mr. Brent must have been moved, indeed, when he called her that. "I'll not have that woman interfering."

"Well, I don't care! It's too much to ask of a woman . . ."

Kenneth would pull the bedclothes over his head to shut out the sound and lie rigid with misery. He thought that his mother's "too much" was all that had grown out of the trouble about the money and the way his father's plans were ground to powder between the Old Man and Burt and Estes.

IX

A WEEK or ten days before Cornelius Burke had removed his family from Petrolia, to be installed in the Summerfield office as a sort of a blind and buffer to the unfathomableness of the Old Man, there had been a conversation between him and Steven Brent, down by the pump house, which, as overheard by Kenneth, seemed to press more sorely still on his sense of injury.

It began with Cornelius announcing the expected arrival within twenty-four hours of the new Superintendent of Wells.

"What's he like?" Brent had wished to know.

"The recommendations he's got sewed onto him are something grand," Burke assured him, "but he's not one of us. You could hardly say that of any Easterner, Brent, that he'd be one of us." The repetition of the phrase and the slight blur that Cornelius's speech invariably took on with embarrassment caused Brent to look up a little keenly, but without saying anything.

"I'm thinking you won't get on with him, Steven, as you have with me." Cornelius took his pipe out of his mouth and worried it with a sliver from the rough planking of the pump house. "'T is not," he insisted, making as if the pipe had begun the argument and intended to hold out at it, "as if he would know what to do with you, being, as the saying is, neither the one thing nor good red herring; working for the Old Man as you are, and yet going cahoots with Burt and Estes. 'T is like he wouldn't know half the time whether you were their man or ours."

"I see," said Steven Brent. "The fact is, Cornelius, I've been my own man too long. I have n't got in the way of imagining such things."

"Exactly." The Superintendent had the air of rejoicing that they had at least that ground between them. "It was what I was saying to MacEvoy at the Mill when he was wanting some man who could be trusted to get out of the boys the work that you know in reason is in them. Mac knows so little about it that you would forget that you were working for him entirely. I think you'd like it, Steven."

"Meaning you think I'd better take it."

"I could get it for you as easy as talking."

"Thank you kindly, Cornelius; I guess I should n't have waited to be fired, in any case." There was no rancor in the look of deep understanding which passed between them. A saving commonness in Cornelius Burke made of defeat a not too unlikely adventure. "I guess I know when I've dished myself," Brent admitted.

"I'll speak to Mac this afternoon when I'm going in." Having got the better of his pipe, Cornelius forgave it and restored it to his mouth. "You're a man of talent, Steven, but you're wasted when you get board walk between you and the earth, and that's the truth."

When the Superintendent had taken himself off to the house, Kenneth remained shyly in his father's neighborhood hoping for some acknowledgment of the community of slight which the occasion seemed to create. For no good reason the Rickart Interest had turned its back on them. It was one of those moments in which the incident of sonship had been merged in their common maleness, the squaring of their shoulders against fate. Looking up to catch Kenneth's wistful attention fixed on him, Steven Brent put forth a hand to the support of the family bond.

"Well, old man —"

The boy flashed back at him a sudden bright comprehension.

"Mother'll like living in town a lot better."

The sureness with which he touched on the only point that really mattered, cast Brent back for the moment into the shadow of an anxiety by which he took Kenneth the more completely into his confidence.

"Ah, let's hope she will, son; let's hope she will."

Matters stood thus until about the beginning of the Rains, and in the mean time the children had their own problems.

"Frank's coming to his aunt's for Thanksgiving," Anne confided to Virginia, "and it's going to be perfectly horrid. Ken won't even talk about him."

Virginia was enchanted with the situation. "But of course, if he really did tell, I suppose we ought n't to have anything to do with him either." It never occurred to Virginia not to include herself in the tribal difficulty.

"I never did find out," Anne confessed; "I could n't somehow, in a letter. Anyway, I don't believe Frank meant to be mean; he might just have let it out the way Ken did."

Virginia sighed.

"If they could only stick each other with a sword the way men used to, and then forget about it! It's ever so much more sensible, *I* think, than spoiling everything with grudges."

They were sitting in her own room, and as she spoke, Virginia could n't resist a sidelong glance at herself in the mirror. She thought the way she was wearing her curls, tied high, gave a flowerlike droop to her head. Scraps of romantic reading floated through her mind, of lovely ladies leaning out of casement windows to watch the mortal struggles of knighthood in its prime. She thought of them as fighting for her favor, and then it occurred to her that it would be more interesting to think of Kenneth and Frank as her and Anne's lovers in some deadly feud; whichever of them lost her sweetheart would retire into a convent and devote her life to good deeds. . . . She knew better, however, than to speak of these things to Anne — Anne was so uppity when it came to talking of lovers.

Anne went and sat on the edge of Kenneth's bed that night after he had turned in, and had it out with him.

"I don't think it was any worse trick than you played on Dad," she insisted; "letting things out that way. Anyway, you've just got to do something; going on like this is as silly as Jim Hand. If you can't make friends with him you've got to lick him."

"Catch old Frank standing up to that," scoffed Kenneth. But he cleared the bedclothes away from his ear the better to listen to this seductive suggestion.

Frank gave her more trouble. "I did n't do anything except what is perfectly regular — in business," he protested. "I have to look out for my Old Man . . . everybody thinks because he is rich they can stick him for everything."

"Well he *is* rich . . . and my mother had always been kind to you. I should n't think you'd want her to be poor always . . ." Anne did n't spare him.

"But I never thought of that." Frank was appalled. "What do you want me to do, Anne?"

"Make friends with Ken . . . or else let him lick you. He's down by the old pump house this minute."

"Me! Fight old Ken — he's two years younger than I am."

"Oh," said Anne, "I don't believe that will make as much difference as you think it will."

But when the boys found each other, all Anne's cunning came to nothing before the swift, overwhelming fact of how glad they were to see one another.

Kenneth shuffled uneasily with his foot, but his eyes were shining . . . "Aw, go on," he said at last, "I don't want to fight you."

"I say, Ken . . . I never thought . . ."

"Neither did I . . ." Kenneth surveyed the tawny and black landscape. "Let's go somewheres," he offered.

"All right . . . Virginia's waiting up at the house to bind up my wounds."

At this characteristic touch a thin bubble of laughter broke between them.

"They're shooting a well over at the Escondita; we can just make it . . ."

So a peace was patched up which carried them over the week-end to Virginia's Sunday party which was to mark the farewell of the Burkes to Petrolia. Virginia's faculty for making an occasion of everything carried them to such a pitch of entertainment that it was not until Kenneth was well on his way home that he discovered that all the hollow had been retaken by one of the thick white fogs which at this season haunted the boundaries of ancient waters. Feeling his way home through the ghastly murk, Kenneth became aware, by striking his shins against it, that he had passed east of his proper

path and come up against one of the great pipes that led
to the reservoirs on the hill. He thought, however, that if
he felt along it he should presently come to a cross-line by
which he could trace his way back to the trail. He trotted
along, hoping for a clue, liking the quiet of the night
and the palpable smother of the fog which had swept
all the day's warmth into the hollow before it. Finally
the slope of the ground warned him that he must have
struck above rather than below the cross-line. He had
hardly appreciated this discovery until he came out quite
unexpectedly on the rise of the land above the wells, and
found himself clear of fog. It lay all below him, woolly
white under a watery moon, heaving a little and faintly
splashed here and there with derrick lights. All about the
rim the reservoirs clung like great ticks sucking the black
juices of the land, bloated with it to bursting. The pitch
of the corrugated roofs and the open vents gave them a
deliberative air, as though they calculated, with a slow,
leech-like intelligence, where next to strike. The boy was
not afraid of the night nor of the hills behind him, drawing into deep, velvety folds under the moon, but he was
afraid suddenly of that mysterious quality taken on by
the works of man, power ungoverned by sensibility. The
fog, which lay level with the rim of the hollow, shook and
billowed as though the thing under it which men had
made had grown suddenly too big for them and was stirring in its own control.

It stirred and turned upon itself and released a strange,
many-limbed creature that, in the instant of hair-raising
horror, while he looked, wormed its way up the roof of the
nearest tank, the upper side of which was almost level
with the ground. The fog cleared into the moonlight,

however, and enabled him to distinguish the figures of
two men that wrestled and broke apart and clutched
again in a heavy, breathing intensity unbroken by any
other sound. He had hardly grasped the situation, had
not freed it from the start and shock of the supernatural
in which it seemed to have begun, by the time the two
figures had worked over half the space of the thin iron
roof toward the open vent. There was an opening in
every tank, left so for the escape of gases that gathered
above the oil under the steady sun, and it occurred to
Kenneth that one of the men might have been the
watchman closing the tanks against the chance of rain.
If it had been the purpose of the second man to prevent
him, he was making no headway in the terrible, keen
wrestle which carried them every moment nearer the
vent. It was in the instant that they rocked together on
the very edge of it that Kenneth's recognition of the
danger burst from him in a cry, shrilled by his own recent
shock of ghostly fear. It caught the wrestlers in mid-
clutch, and with the start and the loosening hold the
figure which had been pressing the other toward the rim
of the vent, sprang backward, gave a swift, running
leap and plunged into the crawling smother of the fog
not ten feet away from where Kenneth stood. He had
instinctively shut his eyes in the crisis of his astonishment, and when he opened them the second figure was
nowhere to be seen. For a moment he stared at the
empty roof, ribbed in thin lines of light and shadow by
the watery moon. Then suddenly a horrible thing arose
upon him from the vent; black and glistening with its
native slime it crawled blindly out and toward him,
shaking its unrecognizable head and pawing at it with

slimy, shapeless hands. The unexpectedness of the apparition, falling in with all his secret thought about the wells and the strange, unearthly life of the derricks, was stronger than the obvious explanation.

With a sharp sob of terror, Kenneth turned and plunged into the friendly cover of the fog. He ran a long time blindly, falling and rising to run again without pausing to take note of his direction, until, by the process of stumbling over them, he had accounted for the most familiar of the iron ribs that held the place together. Once the accustomed touch of the Escondita pipes had restored him, his feet carried him almost unconsciously in the direction of a yellow smear issuing from the opened doors and windows of a house that, as he approached it, swelled out upon him suddenly, full of running figures and low, excited noises. He saw them pass and repass the blurred squares of the windows and then one, touched with a certain familiarity, leaped out through the wedge of an opened door and was swallowed up by the fog. It was a full minute before he realized that the house was his own home and the figure Peters. It was some minutes more before he fairly recovered his wits; then suspecting that the stir and the anxiety might be on his account, for he had no notion how long he had been blundering about in the fog, he went briskly up the back steps where the light on that side of the house was brightest.

"H—ssh!" Addie warned him; she was nursing a kettle of water over the fire newly kindled. "Where's Anne?"

He was answering her in a usual tone, for the arrangement had been perfectly aboveboard that his sister was to stay the night with Virginia, and he resented the implication of her caution; but "Hush!" she said again. She was listening, strained and anxiously toward the living-room, where now he could make out the figure of a Summerfield doctor and a woman in a nurse's dress who came to the doctor's side for a moment and disappeared again in his mother's room.

"Mis' Brent's took bad," Addie told him; he caught the degree of seriousness from her use of the title. Ordinarily Addie referred to her mistress as "your ma."

"Where's my father?"

"In there." The jerk of Addie's head, as she blew the flame, was toward the door of his mother's room, made all at once mysterious, unenterable.

Kenneth wandered into the living-room where presently, as the doctor and the nurse consulted together in low tones, he thought they must have mentioned him.

"He'd better go to bed," he heard the doctor say; but no one spoke to him nor asked where he had been so long. In his own room at last, he began to undress, but the wall between it and his mother's room was thin; sounds came through to him, unbearable. He sat there on the edge of his bed with his hands over his ears until he heard the noise in the kitchen made by Peters's returning with Anne and Mrs. Burke. Though the night was not cold, he found them hovered over the stove, in some vague world-old movement toward fire, the comforter.

"I'd have come sooner," Mrs. Burke was saying, "but with Cornelius out and no one to stay with the children — and the state he was in when he *did* come — and me telling him he's no business at the tanks when he comes from the lodge. But that's nothing when there's the like of *this* in a neighbor's house . . ." She broke off to hold a whispered colloquy with the nurse who came out of Mrs. Brent's room.

Kenneth caught at some strayed ends of it.

". . . Of course I don't *know* . . . I would n't like to say." This was from the nurse.

". . . No good comes from fooling with them things, ever. Better go through with it, I say . . . That Ballard woman . . . Of course I've had my suspicions . . ."

The children went and sat together on the lounge in the living-room. Once their father came out of the bedroom and caught sight of them there; he turned suddenly as a man struck in the face, and walked away from them.

After a while Anne managed in a dry whisper—"Is she going to die?" But they neither of them knew the answer to that. Presently Mrs. Burke made them both go into Anne's room and lie down. Anne lay on the bed and Kenneth on the window seat. There was no light in the room.

They lay very quietly, until Anne could bear it no longer —

"Ken, you asleep?"

"No. You?"

"I'm not going to. Don't you."

"All right."

And then after a little —

"Ken —"

"All right, Anne, —"

But they must have slept at last, for they had not heard Mrs. Burke come into the room until she stood over them.

"Come now," she said, "your father wants you."

They found him by their mother's bed, sunk in such an intensity of wordless protest at what was going on that he seemed at first not to see them, but presently, as they stood there miserably beside him, he gathered them to him in uncertain, trembling snatches. The sash curtain was drawn, but above it through the narrow panes they could see the fog whitened by morning, hurrying and astir. There was a heavy, druggy smell in the room and the smell of the night lamp struggling with the rakish dawn. Kenneth was aware of the subsidence of the huge sense of disorder which had encompassed the household in the night. It seemed to withdraw from the narrow, thin-walled room with the nurse and the neighbors, clustered together in the room beyond. He dared then to look back at his mother when he saw them turn their backs, for he thought she must be better. She lay there very quietly, with blotched, bluish shadows wavering on her face. He bent, as his father bade him, to kiss her, but the lips that moved in the beginning of the caress shaped themselves to the ceaseless, frightened utterance of her husband's name.

"Steven."

"Yes, Molly." And then, in a moment, as if the assurance had passed out of memory, "Steven," and again, "I'm here, Molly." He held fast to one of the shapely, flaccid hands, and presently the doctor, who from the opposite side of the bed had kept a finger on the pulse of the other, relinquished it to him and moved to join the women grouped all so silently about the table in the other room. The cry from the bed became a mere breathy whisper; it ceased altogether. Presently Mrs. Burke came in and drew a sheet across the so strangely shadowed face; as she touched it the body on the bed gave a tiny leap and a little rasping croak.

All this time Kenneth did not feel anything at all. He watched Anne and did as she did, for he was afraid that people would think he had not loved his mother. He was thankful when he could cry a little as he did sometimes to see the body lying so stark, but he could not think that it was his dear mother who had died. He was continually catching himself up in shamed, trivial interests as to the number of carriages at the funeral and a certain defiance of Addie's toward the women whispering in groups about the house.

Cornelius Burke did not put in an appearance until the funeral; his face was strangely scrubbed-looking and shiny and there was a bandage about his head. Anne told him afterward that Virginia had said that her father had fallen into the tank the night their mother died. Kenneth remembered the figure he had seen crawling toward him across the corrugated roof, but it did not seem worth speaking about. He was afraid to speak of anything but the most trivial and immediate interests lest this hollow shell of insensibility should fall in on him and crush him with the terrible knowledge of his complicity in his mother's death. Thursday, the week of the funeral, it fell. Mrs. Burke had taken Anne away with her because the child was making herself sick. It was a troubled night, full of the presage of rain. Kenneth lay in his bed and heard his father — walking — walking on the long veranda, fourteen paces from the door to the hanging *olla*, five from that to the kitchen wing, then nineteen paces back and one to turn. Kenneth counted them over and over because, when one has lost all capacity to feel, one does not think very much either; he could feel so little that all there was alive of him went into the numbers. He did not believe that he had slept at all, but lying there counting steadily he fell into a dream. It was of a time long ago when his father had been away in San Francisco for a week and his mother had allowed him to come into her bed. In his own bed now, he felt quite plainly her arm over him, soft and firm, and the dear warmth of her body and the faint fragrance of it . . . he had almost slipped off into sleep under the tender certainty — and then all at once he snapped into the waking realization that she was not there, that she would never be there for him again. . . .

He broke out crying terribly at that. Just as he was he ran out into the kitchen. His need of a human breast was so sharp — there was nobody there with Addie but Peters, the two of them sitting solemnly on either side of the stove. And Addie did not fail him. She gathered him into her young lap and rocked him to and fro. "Oh, you pore young one —" The mothering cry of her pierced the heart of his sore reserve.

"Oh, Addie, it was me — it was me that did it! She did n't want to be poor always . . . and I told, and Frank, he told . . . about Burt and Estes . . . Oh . . . Oh!" His whole body wrenched with self-reproaches. Above his shaking shoulders Addie formed words with her lips. Peters rose softly and set the door wide as the pacing steps outside drew nearer. Opposite the threshold they were stayed for a moment by the boy's bursting cry. "She did n't want to be poor always . . . she did n't want to . . ."

"Son, son!"

Kenneth felt his grief cut off, torn from him by the violence of that protest; the sob stayed in his throat and died there. Somehow from his father's white staring face he caught a sense of the community of blame. Between them they had let this thing happen.

"Father, father!" The anguish of it snatched them to each other across the intervening space. He was half conscious of the coat Addie had flung about him, and then the door was shut softly behind them. Down on the steps of the veranda between his father's knees the story sobbed itself out.

"I did n't know it would make all that difference . . . Anne *told* me to keep my mouth shut . . . but Frank teased me, — he was always trying to be so smart." He had no words for the weakness by which the information had been taunted out of him.

"It would have happened just the same," Brent soothed him. "It was n't right for you to tell business matters, other people's business . . . it might have happened differently, but it has n't really made any difference — about — your mother leaving us. You must believe that, Ken."

The boy was uncomforted.

"She did n't want to be poor always . . . she could n't bear it."

"Oh, God! Oh, God!" Brent's heart was racked.

Kenneth crept up with his arms about his father's body.

"I did n't mean anything, father, I did n't think —"

"Oh, son, that's the way with men. . . . We don't any of us *mean* . . . We do what we like at the time we like it, and we don't remember how things are with women. Things *last* so with women. . . . It's all over with us in a moment, but it goes on . . . for them . . . it goes on. You've got to remember that, Kenneth, there's nothing you can do anywhere but it gets back to some woman . . . it gets back . . . and then you sweat and pray, but you can't take it off . . . you can't take it off . . . Oh, God!"

He fairly shook his son by the shoulders in the stress of remembering what it was he could n't take off the dear dead. The boy cried aloud.

"Oh, no, no, father!" He burrowed in his father's arms, stricken with the terrible fret and tragedy of men: never to move out freely, never to strike or to run but to loose somewhere the arrows of desolation.

"You've got to know, boy . . . it would have been better if I'd known it. Not that this you've been telling me had anything to do with — made any real difference. You're not to worry about that any more, Ken. Ken, do you hear me?"

"Yes, father."

"You're almost a young man now, and there's something men ought n't to be left to find out for themselves, and that is that they *can't* make a woman's life for her. Not by just doing the things they like and thinking they can keep the rough ends from her. Things get through to her . . . there's no way in the world. . . . And it's too late when you find it out . . . too late . . ." He broke off, gazing into the thick dark night. Now and then he gave a convulsive clutch at the boy's slim body as if for defense against what he saw in it.

"You think" — he corrected himself — "*I* thought I could make a life for your mother out of my life, a kind of hollow cell in it, where she should be perfectly happy inside of all the things I knew from the beginning she did n't like . . . but they got to her, boy, I brought them to her. You can't go to them without taking something, boy. It rides on your back. And then they leave you . . . you can't blame them for that. They've got to have their own life, Kenneth, they've got to make it themselves if you want them to stay in it . . ." His voice fell dry and whispering; he was beating out the truth against his own breast and dying under the blows.

"And they're worth it all," he groaned; "you know that when you've lost them . . . worth all the things you've lost for them. . . . They leave you with the thing you've sold them for, and it's dust and ashes. And you can't call them back to tell them. They don't come back. Not for an hour . . . one little hour . . . Marcia, Marcia!" Something started back from that cry — the common life of the household was affrighted at the anguish of man. It beat against the invisible wall.

The boy stirred in his father's arms vaguely, protesting. As if in answer something warm and near flowed suddenly over him; he felt himself bathed in tenderness as his lips quivered past his father's cheek.

"She's not mad with us," he breathed.

"Your mother. How could she be — with you . . ."

"With us, with us!" He was sure of it. "Just now — in there — in the bed." Trembling seized on them. "It was like a long time ago, when you were n't here. It was like it was then. She was n't mad with me, father; she is n't mad with us now." He caught Brent about the neck in the eagerness of his insistence. "She knows we did n't mean it, father . . ." Through the dark and the empty space forgiveness filtered to them. They scarcely breathed, not to miss one melting touch of it. Whether from the passing dead or from the deep wells of consciousness in which loving is stored and from which it may be drawn again by the beloved in departing, the power of it rose upon them again with relieving tears.

BOOK SECOND

I

AROUND the years immediately succeeding his mother's death, there was always a numb place in Kenneth's memory. The removal of the family from Petrolia to Summerfield narrowed their circle of intimates to the Burkes and Addie. For with the removal of Brent from the ægis of the Old Man's employment, the family lost ground surprisingly.

In Summerfield there had always been about "The Company," — as it came to be called as Rickart withdrew his personality more and more behind the multiplicity of interests, — a certain distinction, even a distinction of reprobation. The stripe of his financial preeminence was over all his employees, the stripe, too, of his iniquities. In the environment of Steven Brent's new occupation, people fawned upon or defied the Old Man as they imagined that their interests were served or opposed, and always secretly despised him. The Brent children, informed by the sure instinct of youth that he had really liked and been interested in them, shared neither the sordid railings of Jim Hand nor the cheap disloyalties of Ballard. And yet by an equal instinct they checked the quick start of interest, the old sense of possession in his public enterprises that belonged to their memories of Agua Caliente. Between the two they fell back on the reticences of adolescence, which they kept even with one another.

Frank they did not see for the whole of the next two years. The summer after Mrs. Brent's death he went abroad with a tutor; his passage was marked by a trail of picture postcards and an occasional trinket for Anne. There was very little exchange between the two boys, but Anne noticed that at the High School Kenneth made no intimates; Anne was of a noticing disposition.

By their removal from Petrolia they had apparently dropped the affairs of the Homestead Development Company behind them, or rather those affairs had dropped into the capacious jaws of the Capital which had rescued them so hardly from the steam roller of the Rickart interests. Nominally they held their stock intact, but Burt and Estes did what they pleased with it. The Scudders dropped out first, exchanging their shares for a starved, alkalied eighty acres of the newly opened orchard tract, happier, perhaps, than they would have been with a fatter allotment. They had lived life so close to the bone always. Jim Hand took to drink; his bitterness died down to a sullen grudge against Cornelius Burke, and when he was in liquor an inexplicable flare-up of secret exultation.

The Brents spoke seldom of their Petrolia property. Now and then it came to the surface of speculation between brother and sister when they found occasion to wonder whether they would go to college, or by what handle they were to lay hold of life.

"Of course, if father could get what's coming to him—" Anne would begin; but the contingency was too remote even for the large hopes of adolescence. The future had not yet taken hold of Kenneth. When he thought about it at all, it was merely that he would not like to have to spend it in Summerfield. The place which it should have occupied in his mind was filled with wholly pagan revelations of identity. The principal of the High School that year had been a college man, interested in athletics, and he had taken Kenneth with the snare of that strange, intimate delight, the mastery over his own body. To go looping and flying through rings and bars, his feet pointed, his flat young torso arched and springy, brought him to self-realizations such as come ordinarily only through personal passion. The satiny, smooth feeling of his skin and the taut muscles shored him up against the sense of family defeat. He threw himself into physical competence as into the balance against an indefinable weediness, a slackness of his surfaces, which after his wife's death began to come over Steven Brent. Often with some young devotee like himself, stripped to the primary requirement, Kenneth would loose himself to running, and hip to hip pad out for miles of the country roads made elastic with crude oil and sand. Sometimes as he ran he would hear behind or before him the honk of a motor, and Rickart's great car would go careening between the weedy roadside and the young orchards. Then Kenneth would tuck down his head and bend to his running, not to seem to see the figure of Frank's father in the tonneau, timing the circle of his thoughts with his cigar. And always for a little after that, the wings of his running would drop and leave him nothing but the mechanical pound of his heart and the lift and fall of his feet on the highway.

As the second summer passed he grew lathy with exercise, his hair, which had been too light always, darkened, his skin took on a fine clear brown with just a suspicion of down on the cheek. Women who passed him turned to look and said that he was a handsome lad. But he was not yet interested in what women would think of him. All his young loneliness, the vague disquiet of the nights, were bound up with thoughts of his mother. When he would come in late to the sense of something lacking in the house, something sought and not found for all his running, he would turn his head fiercely on the pillow and plunge into sleep as a rabbit to cover. Then he would spring out of bed the moment he wakened, for to lie drowsing was to invite the aching lack, the immanent, terrifying emptiness. But he did not think of women or girls yet save with exasperation; Virginia even — he was very fond of Virginia in the old way, but of late there had come into her manner to him a demand for something — something which he could not put a name to, but nevertheless he did not mean to pay. He put it down, as far as he was able to formulate it at all, to the admitted silliness of girls, but it made him by turns both fierce and ashamed.

As yet the future had not called him; only as he ran the past cleared, the failure at Palomitas, his mother's death, were lifted out of the obscure region of his feelings about them and floated as the outlines of the Torr' clear of the evening haze. He saw them as events merely, hard, reasonless features of the landscape in which he was to find his way about. He did not yet think of any way out and beyond them.

He grew closer to Anne in their social isolation and yet farther from her. She had long since passed him at school, and now she began to lengthen her skirts and to display traits of "silliness," as when she had confided to him her suspicion that Peters was "sweet on Addie."

Peters, deprived of any possible employment under Mr. Brent, had taken to agriculture. He had made a first payment on forty acres and was planting it to prunes.

Three or four evenings a week he would drop in on the Brents and discuss his adventure with the family, of which Addie was an interested and integral member.

Kenneth hoped that Addie would not be misled by it.

"Peters *respects* you, Addie," he took the first opportunity to warn her.

"My land! He better!" Addie flared back at him.

Steven Brent, however, was disposed to take the situation seriously. "I hope you won't think of leaving us just yet, Addie." He put it to her one day while Peters hung sheepishly in the offing.

"Well, you need n't to fear my bein' et up with the idee of marryin' so long as I don't see nothin' but what I *do* see!" Addie soaped her dishrag and polished off the unfortunate Peters with finality.

"But you know Peters *is* fond of you," Anne had insisted privately; "I should n't think you'd have him around so much if you don't mean to take him."

"I kind of hate to," Addie confessed; "he's so humbly."

"Well, I guess he is n't any homelier than you are." Anne had the fine, careless cruelty of youth.

Addie, however, was beyond vanity.

"I reckon that's so," she admitted; "but if we was to have young ones that took after both of us, don't it look like that would be kind of stackin' things up against 'em?"

And Anne found that unanswerable.

Before the second year was out Anne had her own problem. It was to wake Kenneth to a sense of the future. So far it held nothing for him but the rather vague hope of going to college which had been his father's plan for him as far back as they could remember. Anne nipped that bud decisively. It was characteristic of the change that had come to Steven Brent that neither of his children thought of resorting to his opinion.

"Burt and Estes won't do anything while the price of oil is so low, and for father to sell now would be just giving it away," Anne decided.

For want of any light on his own situation Kenneth retorted on his sister.

"What you going to do?"

"There's father to take care of; I don't know whether you've noticed it, Ken, but father's not what he used to be."

He had noticed it; for a long time his sole defense against what threatened in Steven Brent's slacked shoulders and growing uncertainty of manner, had been his own bodily proficiency. He had braced himself against it by personal severities as against some insidious disorder. Now that it was before him in so many words, he was struck suddenly with the futility of all his effort.

"Sometimes," said Anne across the table, "I'm afraid." He dared not ask her of what, but presently she enlightened him. "If Mr. MacEvoy should get a notion that father isn't quite equal to the Mill, if any little thing should go wrong — it would just about kill father to lose this job." Anne's knuckles tightened the way her mother's used to do.

"I could get some kind of work with The Company," Kenneth threw out by way of support.

"Oh, there's plenty of *work!*" Anne flung back at him. "Isn't there anything that you really *want* to do?"

He resisted the impulse to tell her of his secret wish to buy back Palomitas; it was often in his mind as he ran through the countryside, filled with the scent of new-turned furrows and the bubble of water in the *zanja*. He was not altogether free from the notion that doing what you liked and doing it with all that was in you, was not properly a career. He saw that Anne wanted for him a path marked out by blazing ambitions. He would have been very happy to find himself walking in such a one, but there was nothing in himself which pointed the way to it.

Frank came back that winter and the two of them had a week's hunting at Agua Caliente in which the old warmth surged back between them, and Frank talked largely of what he meant to do in the world and with it.

But it was a world unimaginable to Kenneth, a world of stakes and reprisals, of half gods, who neither made nor unmade, but snatched up the things that the million made and threw them about in their colossal rages, as in the old days they had flung the foundations of the earth. All this vast acreage of Agua Caliente, the long, lion-like valley which still held for Kenneth the only sense of home, of the continuity of existence, was to his friend one of the pieces of the game. The river with its fruitful possibilities he would have wound up like a scarf and tossed to one side or the other as the play went.

"I bet you they sit up and take notice when I get going," Frank advised him.

"What of?" Kenneth honestly wished to know.

"Why — Me!" Frank was puzzled to explain himself in the face of such simplicity. He was to make himself felt, to be feared, respected, fawned upon, another and a more magnificent Old Man.

"But what will you *do?*"

"Oh, well," — offhandedly, — "a fellow can do most anything when he has the capital."

They let it go at that. The reascendancy of Frank's mind over his own had brought back to Kenneth the old sense of sufficiency in his friend's achievement. He was not, however, to be saved thus from the necessity of a decision.

That spring the agent squeezed out the last remnant of a deferred payment from Jevens. The first the children knew of it was their father pushing the little heaps of bills across the table to them after supper.

"Your chance in life, my dear," he smiled at Anne. "Yours, Kenneth. It's less than I hoped to do for you, but I have made so little of my own chance, I have come to so little in spite of all I hoped, that I don't feel competent to handle even this for you. I want you to have it to put into yourselves, instead of putting it into property which somebody might take away from you." He folded his hands on the worn cloth and smiled at them still, but sadly.

"You'll find, son," he said a little later, "that what is called Business consists largely in taking things away from other people, and I am not sure you are the kind to take them away successfully. But there's one condition I make with you, and that is that you should n't begin by taking your sister's."

"Father!"

"Yes, Anne," taking the hand which she thrust between his own. "I saw it in your face the moment I laid the money on the table, that you were planning to lend your share to Kenneth for his schooling. Well, that's forbidden. You're to understand, Kenneth, as though it were the last thing I had to say to you, that you are never under any circumstances to take a woman's chance in life to piece out your own, neither her heart, nor her purse, nor her choice of an occupation. It's a poor sort of a man who can't get on without doing that, and if we were n't allowed to do it from the start, we'd find out how poor we are much sooner."

He showed, at this, a tendency to drop into his accustomed melancholy; Anne had her arms about him, accepting his terms at their brightest.

"We'll run a race, Ken and I, to see who gets rich and famous the quickest, and you shall be umpire, Daddy." She seldom used the old, childish term with him.

In response to it he patted the hands clasped upon his breast: "Yes, yes, my dear, I'm sure you'll run bravely." Then he grew restless, after his habit, and rising abruptly he left them. They could hear him outside, pacing the veranda.

Anne looked across at her brother.

"I'm sorry, Ken; if we'd put them together it would get you through college. Maybe," with swift self-abnegation, "you could manage it anyhow. Father could spare you something from his salary; when you're gone and Addie's gone, I could do the work as easy as anything; we could take a smaller house —"

"And of course," Kenneth scoffed, "that would n't be taking anything out of you, would it?"

"But, Ken, what are you going to *do*?"

"I don't know, Anne," desperately; "what'll you do?"

"Oh," said Anne, quietly folding up her bills, "I'm going to buy back Palomitas."

"Anne, you'll never do it in the world! With seven hundred dollars!"

"People have got rich with less than that. Besides, I've got to. Ken, father is n't going to get any better here in the Mill; he's got to get back to the ground again. He's only forty-six. I can't let him go like this . . . and Palomitas is the only thing that will cure him." Anne knew. Then with a transition too quick for him, she exploded a suggestion at her brother.

"Ken, why don't you go to Mr. Rickart?"

Kenneth could n't make the connection and said so.

"Well, if it's like what father said — taking things away from people, I don't know anybody who does it more successfully. And you know he always liked you."

Kenneth did know, and the idea that he should go simply up to San Francisco and demand to be taught the art of getting things away from people, did n't seem on the whole any more preposterous than Anne's scheme of buying back the ranch with seven hundred dollars. He had been stung for the moment by his sister's calm exclusion of himself from that project, which now seemed oddly to shrink to the sort of thing a girl might do.

Thus Anne spurred his nascent manhood, but it was finally to get away from Anne and all she stood for that Kenneth went to San Francisco.

It was the night that Addie had elected, at last, to be married to the faithful Peters. And that was the night that the first rain of the season broke in the hills beyond Summerfield. All day the clouds stretched like a tent from El Torre Blanco, over half the heavens. The Scudders, who drove in early from their barren acres, reported the dry creek beds full and rushing from their far-off fountains. About the hour Peters should have been setting out for his wedding, the rain reached the town in sheets and quick, wind-blown splashes. The bride, ready dressed, sat in the kitchen between her father and her mother; everybody said, of course, that Peters would be there the moment the storm permitted, and everybody knew that he ought to have been there, though the heavens descended.

"I'll bet old Peters has forgotten," Kenneth hazarded, as he and Anne faced each other across the dining-room table spread with the belated wedding-supper.

"He's gone round by the Nacimiento road to avoid the river," Anne was certain.

Things went on like this for an hour. The minister telephoned and a friend of Anne's called to hear her report of the wedding and went away again on learning that it had not yet taken place. He was a longish time bidding Anne good-bye in the front parlor, during which Kenneth began to eat the olives and the celery.

Something in his sister's face, perhaps, or in the occasion, pointed his first question when she came back into the room in time to stop him from the sandwiches.

"Anne, when you going to get married?"

"Never." She was perfectly firm about it.

"Aw — what's Morse got to say to that?"

Morse was the young man who had just called, he had called of late very frequently.

"Ken . . . you never listened!" The question slipped from young Morse unexpectedly, "Anne, when are you going to be married,—" and then, softly,—"to me?"

Kenneth convinced her, however, that his inquiry was purely inspirational.

"But you have to get married sometime," he protested largely. "Girls have to get married."

"Oh, no, they don't." Anne was sure of it. "They only have to when they have n't brains enough and courage enough to get on without it."

This was a facer; it had never occurred to Kenneth that his sister might have what were known as "views." He looked at her now with youth's appraisement. In Summerfield people who did not know Anne, thought it clever of her to have attached herself to the radiant and popular Virginia; but Anne was not really unattractive, she only appeared so against the wildrose flush, the dark tendrils of hair, and the lovely Irish eyes of her friend. Anne had good teeth and a clear skin; her dust-colored hair lay in thick, smooth, almost classic bands about her broad, full brow, and at eighteen she had the body of a young mother, slender still, but full-bosomed and round-waisted.

"You use n't to think that," Kenneth reminded her. The recollection of certain girlish predilections of hers brought other things to his mind. "You used to be sweet enough on old Frank, too."

"Kenneth!" She made almost to leave the room, but at the door she turned on him. "Frank's not our kind," she told him; "he'll marry a society woman and that's the last we'll see of him. Anyway," Anne went on, "I'm not going to marry, and you can make up your mind to it. ... Ken," — she had her back to the door and her hands upon it, — "do you know what our mother died of?"

"Anne ... Anne ... you shan't. ... I'll not hear it. ..." Strange, incredible surmises beleaguered his intelligence; he thrust them from him with a force that sent his chair crashing backward. He leaned both his hands upon the white cloth and stared angrily across the flower-trimmed table.

Anne was white and obstinate.

"You need n't," she threw back; "but I can tell you, Kenneth, I'm not going to tie up my life so close to anybody that anything he can do will make me want to die rather than live, and you'd better be sure before you tie up that you can make a woman's life worth living to her —"

She brought the door open behind her with the vehemence of her protest, and her words were drowned in a burst of anguish that rushed upon them from the kitchen where the bride had suddenly concluded that the matter of life and death, which she had been assured could only keep Peters from her, had actually occurred. "He's dead and drownded," wailed the unhappy Addie. "The crik's riz an' carried him aw-ay, an' I ain't never going to be married at al-ll!" It was amazing to see Addie, who never cried, sobbing with the loud, frank *abandon* of a child. There was desolation in her unashamed wail, "I want to be married — oh, I wa-an't to . . ."

There was a note in it that reminded Kenneth of his mother's "I don't *want* to be poor always." He was pierced for a moment as by a thin little sliver of the fierce, elemental need of women. He was terrified to think what men had assumed who charged themselves with its satisfaction. Addie wanted to be married, wanted it as a man wants to eat or to fight . . . and Anne, did she, too, want something like that? . . .

Within half an hour Kenneth was charging the sheeted storm down the Nacimiento road in search of the missing bridegroom. The wind fronted him like a wall, but he scarcely felt it, so keen was his sudden need of escape from what, in his sister's mind and Addie's, threatened the inviolability of his personal experience. The things Anne must have been thinking all this time! Perhaps she would marry, though ... girls always said they would n't so as to be on the safe side. He had a moment of quite fiercely wanting Anne to marry, to bend her back ... and then he thought of his mother. ... Anne understood things about his mother. ... "You can't do anything," his father had said, "but it comes back at last to some woman. ... " The weight of that lay on his mind like the stiff mud through which he worked, and the wind that faced him. He suffered the need of a world of men.

But even among men there was something. ... Anne must have understood that, too, in her scorn of mere *work*. ... Look at the way Peters worked ... and Jim Hand! It was n't education. ... There was his father ... and there was Burt, of Burt and Estes, a man who for birth and breeding could n't have been distinguished from Jim Hand, forever and completely differentiated from him by the inestimable possession. It was n't money either ... money came of it. He recalled what he had heard; how the Old Man himself had come into Agua Caliente forty years ago packing his blankets. But Burt and Rickart had escaped. They were not driven ... not even by their women. ... Women and land and things fell into their proper relation to men who had ... *what* was it they had?

The Nacimiento road was six inches under water in places, and the stiff adobe mud sucked at his horse's fetlocks as he rode, but Kenneth scarcely felt it because of what rode beside him — the importunate mystery of escape. ... He reached up and along it like a palpable shape, failing of its measure. . . . "*Tell me, I pray, thy name.* . . . " He was aware of having uttered the words aloud, but he did not know from what crypt of memory they were drawn.

It was half-past eight before he saw, through the uncurtained window of Peters's kitchen, that much-worried-about individual sitting peacefully with his pipe before the stove, shining in its unsullied bridal blacking.

Peters confronted him in colossal abashment.

"You don't mean to say you was expectin' — of course I knew it was the day —"

"Well, what in thunder —?"

"Why it was so kind of — damp-like. I thought you would n't have it —"

Kenneth leaned against the door-post and feebly shook with laughter. "You'll have to think up a better excuse than that," he warned, "or Addie won't have you. She's crying her eyes out. . . . Where you going?" But the horrified bridegroom had shot past him like a catapult. Addie crying!

The ceremony was over by the time Kenneth rode again into his father's yard. The rain was quite done and the stars were out; brooding between earth and sky the Torr' showed whitely, touched with the first finger of the snow. Kenneth kissed the bride halfway to the gate.

"Any time you get to hankerin' for the taste of my cookin', you're welcome," Addie assured him.

"I'll be hankering for it lots of times," he told her handsomely, "but I'll have to do without it. I'm going to San Francisco."

"My land!" said Addie.

II

AND yet, after six years of San Francisco, most of which he had spent in the character of confidential clerk to the Old Man, Kenneth had to admit that he had n't come any nearer on his own behalf to the incommunicable secret of success. He had moved forward with the Rickart Company as one moves on a ship through all the points of the financial compass; he had not, however, altered the relative distance between himself and the point in his mind's eye. He felt himself vastly instructed in the manner in which the Old Man, being rich, became richer, but he was not, in any light that he could see the situation, on the way to becoming rich himself.

"You must put something into the game," Rickart had told him on the day when, half sick between shyness and his secret sense of defiance to everything that Rickart stood for, Kenneth had come into his private office demanding direction. "You must put something in — if you have n't money, you can have knowledge — special knowledge." He rolled his cigar in his mouth as though it were the quality of his own success which he thus tried to formulate. "Times," he said, "I would have given one of my eyes for what Frank's getting at college. . . ." He brought himself back from the contemplation of the one unconquered world on his horizon to the matter in hand. "If you had a special knowledge, now, of anything — such as the law — I could use you."

On that hint Kenneth had put himself to the law, to which he added stenography and typewriting. This had brought him, about the time Frank was out of college, to a desk in the outer offices of the Rickart Company. There was no difference between his desk and the one occupied by Frank on the other side of the door that swung into Rickart's private office, no difference whatever in the range of duties nor the salaries attached to them; but there was a difference.

It was not in anything which had sprung up between the two in the interruptions of their boyish intimacy, for if Frank had most to tell, Kenneth was still the better listener. It was not in the occasions made accessible to Frank in having, in addition to his salary, an allowance as his father's son, for all their earlier comradery had grown out of just such differences; nor was it even in such distinctions as that the sons of other rich men who drifted into the Rickart chambers, to sit on the boys' desks and exchange young comment and badinage, somehow never included Kenneth in counter-sessions of sitting on their own. It had to do, so far as Kenneth could formulate it to himself, with the egregious mistake that all they at Petrolia had made about the Old Man. They were all hopelessly and scarifyingly wrong — Soldumbehere, Jim Hand, and the settlers of Tierra Longa. They had known that Rickart had ruined them, but they had recouped their self-esteem in the pride of having struggled with him; they had made, in their small way, reprisals. What Kenneth had faced in the revealing years was the certainty that what Rickart had done, he had done without thinking of them at all; he had done it by his gift of being able not to think of them.

As one or another of the Rickart enterprises swam into knowledge, Kenneth had found himself thinking of them as things a man might well give his life to, — the development of forest lands in Lassen County, the vast reaches of salt lakes in Nevada, — and in the intervals in which he had been sent east or south to examine the titles of other and even more alluring ventures, he found that the first had been milked of their anticipated profits and laid aside. Nothing developed far in the Old Man's hands; it paid toll merely to his faculty of foreseeing its development in a given direction.

Lands, waters, and minerals, he took them up and laid them down again, wholly uninformed of the severances and readjustments made necessary by that temporary possession. The most that he knew of mortgages, overdue installments, foreclosures, were their legal limitations; he did not know that men are warped by these things out of all manhood and that women died of them. It was as if a huge bite had been taken out of the round of his capacity, and left him forever and profitably unaware of the human remainder.

Kenneth had studied law because there was nothing he so much wished as to be used by the Old Man, tempered by him, sharpened. But he was not long in discovering that to T. Rickart a lawyer was a kind of compass merely, by which he found his way about the devious affairs of men. Laws were not human institutions at the making of which men prayed and sweated, but so many hazards and hurdles of the game. He hired men to tell him how to go over the laws and under them, leaving them as intact as possible. He seldom broke a law, seldomer took the trouble to have one made or remade. He could use a suit at law to block a rival's game, but at best he regarded it as unsportsmanly. It was by some native inability to

attain this oblivious frame of mind that Kenneth felt
himself convicted of failure.

He was made to feel it acutely in the sixth year by
events which led to the renewal of direct personal relations with his sister and Virginia, and the discovery of
the extent to which they had both of them established a
sort of working relation with their environment. From
the day that Anne had sent him up to the Old Man, to
receive at his hands the sword which had been turned
against them at Petrolia, he had seen very little of Virginia. Of that little he recalled nothing much but a vague
sense of some demand upon him, to the nature of which
he had never any very definite clue, and an equally vague
and characterless resistance. Her marriage, which had
occurred within a year after the death of Cornelius, had
been inexplicable except on the ground that it was the
business of girls in general to get married. She had announced it to him with dramatic suddenness on the heels
of one of several visits which she had made that year to
San Francisco, on which occasions the swift, warm rush
of her personality and an almost spectacular prettiness
had all but penetrated his young stolidity with intimations of a more spacious existence. It gave him, to hear
of her engagement to Bert Sieffert, a momentary sense
of betrayal, as if she had deserted the adventure of youth
too soon, to cast anchor in the locked port of grown-up experience. After that he had seen her but once or twice,
making out very little except that Sieffert was objectionable and prosperous, and that Virginia's manner denied
him more than a decorative relation to her person. Of her
divorce, which had come early in the second year with an
explosive accompaniment of scandal, he had heard as

little as possible. Partly, because he was away in Arizona that winter on business of Rickart's, and partly because his severe young maleness revolted against the free discussion of the personal equation, which had evidently taken place between Virginia and his sister.

The news, then, that Virginia was about to return from New York — where she had gone to hide whatever discomfiture there had been for her in the necessity of surrendering Bert Sieffert to the superior claims of her maid of all work — had less interest for him than that she was coming back in a new and perfectly defined status as an Agitator. Anne brought it, on one of those occasions which contributed to his feeling too little like the Big Business man he had chosen to be, and too much the younger brother on a salary. For Anne was a business woman. She had the gift of detachment; she could buy land without wanting to work it; she could buy it with the distinct intention of unloading it on somebody else who believed himself elected to work it and was willing to pay handsomely for the privilege. Anne could buy a hundred feet of raw city lot, a mile from any point in particular, and by the addition of two palms, a pomegranate bush, and a cement curbing, dispose of it as a choice residence site. Anne had taken over the Larsen ranch on which Larsen himself had n't been able to raise even the mortgage, and sold it in five and ten acre subdivisions, on each of which the purchaser not only believed he could make a living, but had more or less succeeded in doing it. By such steps, aided and abetted by Cornelius, Anne's seven hundred had easily become seven thousand. It had been the note to take in the circle of the family that Uncle Corny had been the fountain head

of Anne's successes, but now Cornelius had been dead
two years and Anne was doing business privately with
Old Man Rickart.

Kenneth was sure of this because several times lately
he had seen letters go in to the Old Man addressed in his
sister's bold, squarish hand; and the very morning on
which she told him about Virginia she had had a conference with his employer in his private office. Kenneth,
though he knew no slight was intended, could not help
being a little hurt — what business could she have that
he could n't have managed for her? It was part of
Anne's way of doing business that she never could talk of
it, not at least until it was well on the way to accomplishment. She followed faint clues afar off, by some process
that had nothing whatever to do with ordinary commercial astuteness; questions, and the necessity for justi-
fying herself, always threw her off the scent, scared the
quarry. She had learned, and had taught her family, to
pay to the initial stage of her business ventures the tribute of discreet inattention.

So when she had been passed, without any previous
notice of her coming, into the private office, for a brief
conference with Rickart, Kenneth had made the most of
taking her out to luncheon before she caught the return
train to Summerfield, and was rewarded with the piece of
news about Virginia.

"It is the labor trouble that's bringing her." San
Francisco was then in the first throes of the struggle with
unionism. "She's one of their paid organizers." Kenneth made a little sound of annoyance. "Oh, I've no
doubt she's good at it. Virginia could always make
people play her game. Don't you remember?" Anne

smiled and finally sighed. "Of course a woman has to have something to *do* ... but I hoped she'd marry again ..."

"I thought the trouble was that she married in the first place. I never could see why she wanted to."

"Well," — Anne considered, — "it was a way out."

"Out of what? Cornelius was well fixed —"

"That's just it. Virginia was too well fixed; lots of girls are like that; their lives are padded; marrying is the only way they can get out of it into reality, into experience ..." Anne fell into a brown study as she did sometimes with Kenneth, trusting him to follow her uncompleted thought, only to find at the end of it that they had come out at utterly irreconcilable conclusions, as on this occasion ... "And then *you* would n't marry her."

"Oh, I say, Anne!"

"Not that she wanted you to," Anne conceded; "what I mean is that the sort of young men that Virginia ought to have married were all busy like you, making a place for themselves. They had n't time to marry and they could n't afford it. And there was Virginia left with five or six of her best years on her hands. If Uncle Corny had n't died just then ... How it all holds together!" she broke off to exclaim. "Jevens, and our getting into things at Petrolia, and Jim Hand. I suppose he was really the death of Uncle Corny."

Cornelius had finally died from a stroke which had been induced by an old injury to his head, though he had maintained to the last that he had never known how he came by it.

"It was the shock that made him forget," Kenneth reminded her, "and I was the only person who ever *did* know that it was Hand who pushed him into the vent."

"And the loose ends of it hanging over into *our* lives," said Anne, gathering them all into her hand. "You know, we'll owe all we expect to get out of the Homestead property to Bert Sieffert."

"I don't see how *he* comes into it." Bert Sieffert was the man Virginia had seen in the light of a Way Out.

"Well — it was Jennie Hand, you know, who — it was on her account Virginia got her divorce."

"I know — the skunk!"

"Don't be bitter, Ken. After all, he did the only decent thing that was possible. By all the standards of that sort of people he did n't *have* to marry her; he was a married man, and she was in his wife's house — Well, when Jim reached the place where he tried to trade off his Homestead stock for a quart of whiskey, and Sieffert got himself appointed Jim's guardian, he began to think it was a sort of judgment that it should be Jim's daughter who paid Cornelius's daughter out for the part Cornelius had had in wrecking the company. Bert Sieffert is n't exactly the man you'd pick out as an instrument of Divine Justice, but he sort of sees himself that way, and it has steadied him. It makes a lot of difference whether you think of yourself as a plain sinner, or as part of the working-out of a Plan. It's more — dignifying."

As far as a thoroughly nice young man could be thought of as doing anything so common, Kenneth's reply could be described as a snort. He regarded his sister's disposition to seek for subtle and invisible relations as purely feminine — which it undoubtedly was — and as tending to destroy the orderly perspective of human conduct.

Whatever Cornelius Burke as the agent of the Old Man had done at Petrolia, was Business, and for Bert Sieffert to have got his wife's cook with child was a Sin, between which there was a great gulf fixed. His six years of working with Rickart had taught Kenneth that Business was an immense, incontrovertible Scheme of Things; as for the other, it was a simple question whether a man was, or was not, a skunk. Kenneth's feeling of being at a disadvantage with Anne in such discussions kept him from saying anything, except that he supposed that Virginia, on her return from New York, probably would n't make any sort of a visit to Summerfield.

"Oh, she's really here in an official capacity. Did n't I tell you? She's organizing the women's trade unions. She'll go to Los Angeles and Seattle. If you have n't heard from her yet, you will. She'll probably have it in for you for working for a Capitalistic Pirate like T. Rickart."

"Fat lot of good that'll do her!" Kenneth laughed, but he was really a little uneasy in his mind.

Beyond being pleasantly aware of the proximity of the fair and unmated, young Brent knew very little of women. He had the greatest respect and affection for his sister. She had achieved the hallmark of consideration — direct and immediate access to the private offices of T. Rickart. Naturally devoid of the spirit of jealousy, he did full justice to the quality of Anne's success, though he did not see yet that he should have to pay to it the tribute of acquiescence in her social judgments. But he could not argue with her because of a disconcerting way she had of basing her conclusions on the personal instance.

Otherwise he would have cleared himself, by talking

it over with Anne, of a vague sense of menace, of an impending situation involved in the return of Virginia. It had its root in some potential indelicacy which he had realized in Virginia's behaving always, even during the period of her marriage, exactly as though she had not been married at all. Accustomed, as the young are, to regard all relations with the opposite sex as the prelude to adventure, Kenneth had felt himself helpless before Virginia's failure to accept her marriage as constituting her definitely out of the running. Something warned him that she was likely to prove as oblivious to her status as a divorced woman, set apart by a scarifying, if undeserved, experience. But to discuss his own half-recognized trepidations with Anne was to invite such rendings of the ceremonious garments of sex as left him gasping.

Much of what his father had said to him on that strange night after his mother died, had passed out of Kenneth's conscious recollection, but the impress of it lay deep about the source of all his judgments. It had given him to understand how inevitably all that men do impinges on the charmed circle of women's lives; but it had not prepared him to recognize the disturbance of a woman's orbit as arising from a source within herself. It was this separate claim for recognition which, in the person of Virginia, he dreaded to meet again; for he was instinctively sure that when he did meet her it would not be in the character of the betrayed and repudiating wife of Albert Sieffert, but as a human item, as importunate, as necessitous as himself. And yet, when he did see her at last, she made no such appeal to him.

Contrary to Anne's surmise, Virginia had not written him about the time of her arrival, and it was not until the

suggestion of menace it still held for him had almost faded
from his mind that he plumped suddenly into her. It was
one of those divine evenings when the wind comes out of
the Contra Costa country, warmed from the orchard
slopes, and goes walking white-footed on the Bay, looking
for those lost Islands "nearest the terrestrial Paradise,"
as the old tale describes them. It was a wind with a
wandering mood in it, and Kenneth had walked from
his boarding-place along Geary and down Market without any other purpose in his walking than to meet the
wind's need. At Grant Avenue he had paused a moment,
idly attracted to the groups gathered in its open forum
around the fakirs of social solutions, who of late have succeeded the fakirs of medicinal cure-alls in the pageant of
the street. Close to where he stood, a bearded anarchist
brandished his red banner in the faces of a few whose
quest for the material millennium was as wistful and as
futile as the wind's for its lost Islands. Farther up, somebody raucously advertised the Secret of Vitality, as disclosed in the tag ends of some obsolete philosophy; and
highest of all, under the yellow flare of the street lamp, half
a hundred people surrounded a soap box from which a
woman's tossed head and gesticulating arms gave her the
appearance of swimming in their midst. Young Brent
mistook them at first sight for suffragists, until his idle
glance was corrected by the betraying lack of yellow pen-
nants and the determinedly belligerent character of the
audience. As he looked, it swarmed upon itself and gave
evidence of an enthusiasm — whether of agreement or
dissent he could not at that distance determine — which
attracted the notice of a policeman idly swinging his
night stick in the bay of one of the shuttered mercantile

houses opposite. Widening rings of disturbance lapped up the outer circle of anarchists and drew away devotees of the philosophy of Vitality in favor of the nearest manifestation of it. Carried forward by the general movement of the street, Kenneth caught, above the circle of excited exclamation, a high, feminine voice shaking out bitter denunciations of Capital and the Established Order. ". . . Call yourselves Americans . . . call yourselves freemen . . . miserable wage slaves that dare n't say your souls are your own for fear somebody will dock your pay for it! . . . "

"And what pay?" The voice rose again above the mingled growl of corroboration and resentment. ". . . Is it all that you earn with your brain and your brawn and your time . . . is it even a fair proportion of what you earn . . . ? And you call this a free country, and your flag the emblem of liberty. . . ."

"Aw, g'wan, leave the flag alone, can'tcha'!" The adjuration which arose from the outer circle evoked a feeble cheer, overmatched by cries of "Go on! She's right! Shut up, you! she ain't said nothing!"

"I tell you it is the capitalistic flag of a capitalistic —" What followed was too confused to make out. There were cries and scuffling; he judged the speaker had been pulled from her soap box, but whether by her friends or detractors he was not near enough to determine. Evidently she was still going on with her arraignment of the Great American Tradition; scraps of injurious phrase floated clear. By this time the policeman had come up, and Kenneth, following some obscure clue of the voice, plunged into the crowd beside him.

"What's up, officer?"

"Th' iron workers. They're out." Kenneth recalled that he had read as much in the evening papers. "That's one of these here New York organizers. . . . " The policeman bunted his way to the center. "Make way there, make way!" He squared his shoulders outward — and then through the triangle of his arms akimbo Kenneth saw her. She was not changed — she was scarcely changed at all! The gray Irish eyes of her glowed in the flare of the lamps phosphorescently, little tendrils of hair blew out from under her hat pushed awry by her own vehemence. One of her hands was held by a short, heavy girl of an obvious racial type, and with the other Virginia still challenged her audience. It was only thus, close almost to touching, that Kenneth saw the point of the controversy, for with the free hand Virginia shook a corner of the flag that, following the convention for gatherings of that kind, along with the emblems of the organization, draped the impromptu speaker's stand.

"You call it the flag of the free! Free! . . . when you daren't join the Union and fight with your brother workers. . . . *That* for your flag. . . ." She tweaked at it. The police officer caught her by the wrist. . . . "Now, now, Miss."

At that moment the stone was thrown. It caught her fairly on the point of the shoulder.

"Virginia!" Kenneth did not know how he got across, but he was there holding the hurt arm in his own . . . he had thrashed fellows at school for hurting Virginia. . . .

"Order, order!" bellowed the policeman. He had had orders from headquarters which he didn't see, for the life of him, how he was to carry out; from the edge of the crowd he was met by the answering bellow of a fellow officer.

"I know this lady," Kenneth found himself saying.

"Then get her away, sir, else I'll have to arrest her to save her."

"Arrest me? Arrest *me*, officer!" Virginia was blazing.

"Oh, Miss Burke, Miss Burke, you've done all that you could —" The heavy girl tugged at her arm, "We can't spare you, to have you arrested. . . ." Between them they edged her out of the crowd.

"It *is* a capitalistic flag . . ." Virginia insisted. "Ken!" — she noticed him at last, — "where are you taking me?"

"Home. To your hotel. Anywhere you like."

"Do, Miss Burke," the heavy girl urged. "Never mind about going on to the hall; maybe the police won't permit the meeting now. . . . You must save yourself for to-morrow . . . your poor arm!"

Virginia winced at Kenneth's pressure on it; she staggered a little, sick. "Very well," she acquiesced. They walked on without speaking; the heavy girl drifted away from them. Presently Virginia roused herself to give a direction. "No! no! We'll walk." She shook off Brent's suggestion of a car. She began to talk again scrappily. "It's all true, what I said . . . this is n't a free country. We're all slaves . . . slaves to tradition . . . slaves to a system . . . and the wage slaves, they're the worst of all. I've been finding out, Ken . . . I wish that policeman had arrested me . . . I'd have told the judge . . ." She ran on with fragments of challenge and battle, most of it unintelligible to Kenneth. She ran down at last from exhaustion and the pain in her arm. They made the last few blocks of the way in silence.

All this time Kenneth had not been taking her seriously. She was just Virginia. At school they had always
been pulling Virginia out of scrapes into which she had
been led by unpremeditated partisanships of whoever, on
the face of things, appeared to be getting the worst of it.
This time, he thought she had really carried it too far!
If he had n't happened along opportunely, she might
have got herself arrested. . . . Had n't she had enough of
being in the papers. . . .

He was guiding her now up the slopes of Geary, and
with a little of the old exasperation which everybody had
now and then with Virginia, he almost shook her. At the
impatient touch she gave a faint, almost imperceptible
moan. Reduced by it to instant contrition, he followed
her without protest or invitation into her apartment.

It was one of those furnished suites, common enough
in the San Francisco of the period immediately preceding
the fire to have come, all of them, out of the same shop;
— furniture and hangings that might, probably had, belonged to just anybody, with only a scattered feminine
belonging or two and a jumble of papers on the table
to signify its temporary possession by Virginia. Virginia
was not one of those women who give atmosphere to a
room. She did not even, now that she had come into this
one, seem at home in it. She rummaged about in the ad-
joining bedroom and came back with a bottle of witch-
hazel and a clean handkerchief. Kenneth wished now that
the heavy girl had come along with them; he wondered
where they had lost her. But Virginia was incapable of
embarrassment. She saturated the handkerchief with the
contents of the bottle and unbuttoning the neck of her
shirt-waist, thrust it down to the bruised spot on her

shoulder. She sat there opposite him in the Morris chair, with the neck of her waist open, and questioned him about himself, throwing in items of personal information in which she seemed to take for granted the development of her unionizing mission as within the range of his natural interest. She spoke of the iron workers, and of the Cause as though it were some vast, enveloping nexus, of which it was not to be imagined that he was ignorant. She was to address the Friends of Labor to-morrow evening — Kenneth must hear her. That was so like Virginia, to sweep everybody within reach into the lap of her immediate occupation. She conceived him ready to drop into it by the weight of his own experience. Had n't he, she demanded, seen for himself what they were up against there in Petrolia? His own father had n't been able to do what he knew to be wise, he had been driven . . . It warmed him suddenly to recall that even then, regardless of her father's affiliations, Virginia had been on the side of Jim Hand and Pop Scudder. Certainly he would go to hear what she had to say to the Friends of Labor.

Virginia was watching out for him. The place was one of those German-American institutions arranged for dancing and the performance of interminable musical entertainments mitigated by the continuous service of beer and sandwiches, inseparable from the scope and purpose of Turn-verein. He found Virginia in a kind of box, a little above the level of the audience, the center of a knot of tension that, considering the figure the whole performance cut in his eyes, was childishly disproportionate. Her arm was in a sling, which from time to time in the stress of conversation she forgot, and gesticulated with it freely until recalled by a twinge of pain. As often

as this occurred, it brought out in her companions the
commiserating touch, to which Virginia responded —
until some new turn of the excited talk claimed her —
with a becoming deprecation. It was perfectly genuine,
both the forgetfulness and the pain; Kenneth was as
certain of this as he was sure of the feminine response of
her temperament to the touch of martyrdom. It was so
much a part of all that he recalled of Virginia and her
faculty for making everybody play her game, for playing
it herself so absolutely, that he felt for the moment absurdly out of it. She did n't need him even for audience.
Or if she had any use for him at all, it was to heighten the
effect of the audience she had, by showing him how entirely she could do without him; an effect achieved by
introducing the other speakers of the evening as being so
far outside of anything he had attained for himself that
it was n't necessary to explain to him who they were or
what they stood for.

And with one exception he found that he did n't know,
though it was evident in the manner of those who came
and went about the speaker's box, and the newspaper
men hovering in the background, that they stood high in
the immediate expectation. The exception was the official organizer whose name no moderate assimilator of
news could have avoided, any more than he could avoid
an eye acquaintance with Spriggler's chewing gum and
Gibraltar insurance. He was a large-built, easy-moving
man whose pure Anglo-Saxon profile was blunted, as were
all the contours of his loose figure, by a soft, blond fatness, and suffered the further identification of having one
eye missing. It was a touch, not so much of disfigurement
as of deliberate mystification, as of a house in which one

window has been left open for looking out and the other
carefully blinded against the possibility of anybody looking in. You had to *be* in, Kenneth decided, before you
could take any measure of the man or his place in the
movement from which Brent's attention was continually
sliding away as from the smooth face of some great natural promontory, for want of anything he could intel-
ligently take hold upon. It rested longer on a paler type
of man whose name preceded the great organizer's on
the programme, hovering about some elusive suggestion
of resemblance which did not define itself until the man
began to speak. Then it grew upon Kenneth as a likeness
to Pop Scudder, the temperamental Pioneer of social
revolution, far fixed upon the ultimate triumph, and suffering incredible immediate defeat. Around these and
Virginia spread an atmosphere of momentous occasions,
much more momentous than seemed justified by anything that Kenneth knew of the situation. It spread from
them and enveloped the whole audience.

It was the audience — two or three hundred workingmen and their wives filling the body of the hall — that
lifted the hackles of that deep-seated sense of caste that
is in every man. Kenneth could feel his soul, sniffing the
wind tainted by ineradicable difference of type, answer to
the old savage instinct to protect his own by discrediting
the unknown, the unconformable. He was identifying
them by all the marks of Jim Hand and Scudder and Soldumbehere as duffers at the game, men who took their
count from the Old Man as at Tierra Longa they reckoned distance from the Torr', a kind of fluid human element, by its gelid movement at times retarding the sweep
of his enterprises, but upon the surface of which, if it

once became solidified into Class, he might glide the more securely.

Kenneth fortified himself in this soundly American objection to solidification by Unionism, throughout the first part of the programme, during which Pop Scudder's intellectual prototype preëmpted and abandoned one after another of the open ranges of social speculation. He was able, even when the one-eyed organizer stood up amid a storm of applause, to see in him a symbol of the half-blind social struggle, putting the larger interest of the audience as men in peril to their immediate concern as workers. And then, imperceptibly but swiftly, something happened. It was n't altogether in what the man said. He was talking easily and consecutively, like the steady pouring of water in the race; but over his audience as he talked came that kind of aliveness as of a perfectly contrived machine working; slight creakings, the stir of wheel, the tightening here and there of band and pulley. It lifted and lightened somehow; the fluent drops had run together, and out of it had come, not mere Mass, but a Thing, instinct, awakened. It was impossible for Kenneth to trace in the steady trickle of incident and citation the force that had set it in motion — in Idaho mine workers had lain down for nine desperate weeks, and risen to an eight-hour day and time and a half for overtime. . . . Garment workers in Chicago had won a fifty-hour week. . . . Scrub women in an Atlantic seaboard town had gone out at five dollars a week and come in at six dollars and fifty cents. . . . Four thousand men cutters in Indianapolis . . . ten thousand packing hands in Detroit . . . little groups here and there . . . and how slight the gains! The price that young Brent paid for a luncheon added to a week's wage after a three weeks' fight . . . riots . . . bloodshed even! The pitiful littleness of it all, and the inconceivable tenacity . . . inching — inching. The way the audience took it . . . drinking it in, . . . nostrils widened, breath tightened . . .

Kenneth had a moment of terror over it — did the Old Man know . . . did anybody know what was to come out of all this? And then swift on the fluent moment came Virginia. She flashed on them like some bird of plumage; she beckoned, fled, and eluded them down unpathed confidences, resentments, resolutions . . . the Ark of Promise went over Jordan before her — she danced with cymbals . . .

III

But it was not until he was telling Frank about it next morning that Kenneth thought of Virginia as the divorced wife of Bert Sieffert. Frank thought of it first. He rather sensed a connection between the two circumstances. That was a time in America when young men were beginning to talk portentously — the younger the more portentous — about what was likely to happen if somebody somewhere did n't put a firm, restraining hand on women. Virginia was a case in point. First divorce, then labor unions, and insulting the flag. That was what they came to. Not that he blamed Virginia for divorcing Sieffert, — though he did n't suppose Sieffert had done any more than lots of men, whose wives are able to put up with it, — but he held to the general proposition that divorce was bad for women. It gave them a sense of being free to do *any*thing!

And as for all this talk of liberty — well, look at the labor unions themselves! Of course a man had a *right* to belong to a union — but how about coercing others? Look at what was in the morning papers about riots between pickets and strike-breakers. Frank's view was the lineal descendant of his father's, that labor agitations were no more than the bubbling of the pot. If fortunes were to be cooked up, there must be bubbling, and occasionally pots boiled over. A certain amount of cussing must be allowed to the fellows who lost out; cussing was a form of consolation. Still, Frank could n't hold with destruction of property.

This was a point of view to which Kenneth had been officially adopted in coming into the Old Man's employment; but the consciousness of a secret infidelity, to which items of his own experience continually bore witness, kept him from offering any opposition to Frank's argument.

He broke the thread of it, however, with a pleasant excitement, derived from the reading of his Summerfield letters.

"Anne's coming; be here over Sunday."

"Oh, bully!" Frank was always loudly pleased with Anne's short and infrequent visits. "I'll get some tickets to the opera." That was all right, of course, — it was Frank's city, and the Brents had long conceded him the right of playing host in it, — but Kenneth wished his friend would remember that Anne was his and not Frank's sister. . . . The elder Rickart appeared a moment at the door of his private office. "Your sister," he said, "when she comes, she's to be shown in here immediately." This time Anne must really have turned a trick.

Anne arrived on Saturday. Young and pleasant she looked in her tailored dress and a hat of unmistakable Summerfield extraction. She had the clear, warm flush that goes often with thick, colorless hair; her eyes were steady above a mobile mouth; her breasts were as high and firm as Hebe's. Had she known how she might have been beautiful; a little more modeling, the touch of a sharpened chisel . . . as it was she was distinctly nice looking. Sitting happily between the two young men, going up in the Rickarts' car, Frank put his hand over hers and gave it a public and unaffected squeeze.

"Look here, Anne, what *are* you up to?"

"Oh," she laughed, "I knew I should n't be able to keep it; I've bought back Palomitas!" Frank gave one of his accustomed whoops — "That is, of course, if I can make terms with your father."

Kenneth felt himself paling with the sudden clutch of memory and — what was it — something like relief? Anne and his father back at Palomitas . . . suppose they should need him! And then he hid the emotion from himself; he had recognized it as a throb of his constitutional weakness for thinking more of what could be put into a piece of land than of what could be made out of it. He was a business man by his own election; still he could not restrain a certain trepidation of the spirit as Anne went in alone to her conference with his employer.

"It's all arranged," she told him briskly. "Jevens is to take the Homestead stock for his first payment. I've enough coming from the Larsen property for the next. All I want is that you should take over the original mortgage."

In Rickart's eyes a little twinkle of entertainment struggled with his habitual business steelness.

"You mean to work the ranch?"

"To live there. I'm no rancher. Father 'll work it. Father has — come back." She hesitated over the phrase. "You knew, after my mother's death and — everything, father was n't quite himself for several years, but he is all right now; he has — come back." She found, after all, nothing else so expressive.

"You've brought him back."

"It was the land that did it; first the little plantings around the city properties; and then he laid out the

Larsen ranch for me, so that I knew just what every piece of it would do for the owner. You know how father is about land?" He nodded. "And all those people over in Summerfield, they're building and setting out orchards; somebody has to feed them —" She went on outlining her plans, shaping them to something still unconsenting in his eyes.

"Are you taking it all back? All that dry land below the Ridge — there must be a thousand acres of it." He had put his cigar back in his mouth and it traveled the arc of anxiety as he waited her answer.

"We had to. I know there's hardly more feed on it than will pay the taxes; but I think Jevens has shown us the way to deal with that."

"Ah," he cried, "you're not bitten with *that?* You're not going on with that fool craze of his about finding oil there?"

"Better than that," Anne triumphed, — "water! 'Nacio Romero tells me there's water standing in Jevens's old borings. Last season it scarcely fell a foot, dry as the season was. I could put in a pump later." She went on with that for a moment and came back to the flat lands below the Ridge. "Father always said that when the people of Tierra Longa got together and put in a storage dam on the river, that land below the Ridge would be his best property."

"You tell your father to leave dreaming to the next generation and to stick to his muttons and alfalfa." He ruminated while his cigar described the curve of perplexity, and then he said, with more gravity than he had yet shown, "You're not counting on anything of that kind to make the place pay, are you?"

"Dear, no," cried Anne. "There's all those orchards at Summerfield to be fed," — she was brimming with projects, — "we've our work cut out for us for six or seven years."

" Ah, I 've no doubt you'll be equal to it, my dear." He seemed relieved.

"Then you *will* take on the mortgage?"

"Oh, *that*, of course." He reached for the bell to call his stenographer, and thought better of it. "Tell Ken what you want and say that I said he was to fix it up for you."

He walked away from her and for a moment stood staring out of the window at the huddled lower roofs and across the silent stretch of the Bay, before he turned with a final warning. "You stick to your muttons. The water-owners of Tierra Longa are n't ever going to get together."

Anne's steady eyes traveled for a moment across his stiffened countenance, but the light of success was on hers as she went out a little later to join Kenneth at luncheon.

The likeness between brother and sister came out strongly as they sat across the table from each other; Ken's face was narrower, less full about the brows; but there were the same eyes, the same mobile lips not yet shaped by the compelling stroke of fortune. It came out also how much older Anne was, as women are often older than men of about the same years. They were full of the project of rebuilding Palomitas, and of reminiscence.

"What's The Company doing in Tierra Longa?" she wished to know.

Why should she suppose they were doing anything, Kenneth in his turn demanded.

"Because Mr. Rickart was so sure there would n't be anything doing." There was always a marvel in Anne's dealing with Rickart. She dared much, asked for what she wanted and generally got it, liked him immensely and never trusted him. "He warned me twice not to expect anything but sheep and alfalfa."

"*Are* you expecting anything?"

"Naturally. I'm a real-estate agent, Ken I am one the same way other people are musicians and writers. I'm making money at it because I'm a success; but I'm being it because I like it. Land does n't mean crops to me the way it does to you and father; it means people — people who want land and are fitted for the land, and the land wants — how it wants them! I'm going back to Palomitas partly on account of father, and partly because it is the biggest opportunity I see to bring land and people together. I mean to have a hand in it."

"You mean father's old plan, about storing the water in Tierra Rondo for irrigation; you're never going to undertake *that?*"

"I expect to see it undertaken. I don't care by whom; it might easily be a government project. You know it's been recommended to the Department. It might be Mr. Rickart. He warned me twice not to think of it; does that mean, by any chance, that *he's* thinking of it?" Anne considered, tapping the cloth with her white fingers. It was a movement that reminded Kenneth of their mother — so many little ways of hers Anne had. "I'd like to do a big job once, with a man . . . and it is a Big Job, Ken . . . thousands of acres simply crying aloud for men!"

"You're bitten, too, same as father!"

But Anne was not to be put down; it was her day and Kenneth was too good a brother to begrudge it to her. He laughed and was thrilled as she swung into full exposition of her plans. She was to be, she declared, not an agent who sat in the office and waited for people to come to her looking for land, but she was an agent for the land who went abroad looking for the right people to put to it. Over in Summerfield, where she still had interests, they sold you land as they sold calico; they cut off the pieces you selected and you had to put three or four years into it before you found out if it would wash. They sold you land, no matter what you said you might want it for, and if you wanted it for a vineyard and it turned out six or seven years later to be suited only for corn, that was your lookout. But every plot of ground that passed through the office of Steven Brent's daughter had been put to question; a neat little analysis of soil constituents and subsoil and drainage went with the deed to it, and a summary of the things that might reasonably be expected to thrive on it. It irked Anne exceedingly that she couldn't put her clients through the same process. Many a man fancied himself a vine-grower, whereas he had been equipped by nature for general cropping. It took a certain sort of temperament to make an orchardist.

So Anne expounded her theory of real estate as a liberal profession, and Kenneth thought how clever and wholesome she was, and wondered why life was so much simpler for women than for men. Suddenly reminded, he began for his part to tell her about Virginia.

"Oh, she's all right!" he said in answer to Anne's particular question. "She's a crackerjack of an Agitator."

This was his way of saying that he had forgiven her for being the divorced wife of Bert Sieffert. It expressed, too, something of his relief at the absence of all personal appeal in her vivid invitation to walk in the path she had blazed for him. Virginia's invitations had a way of leading to Virginia. If in this case it was to prove only a longer way around, at least he absolved her from complicity. "You would n't know she'd ever been married — or anything," he finished.

"Oh, well, Virginia was n't ever married, really," Anne declared; "you only think she was because of such obvious things as having a ceremony said over her and living with Bert Sieffert. But the only thing that really counts with a woman is her heart and her mind. If a man can't get those he does n't get very much of her."

Ordinarily this was the sort of thing that Kenneth found it very difficult to accept from Anne. For Kenneth's failure to find the industrial world the simple combination of men and jobs he had supposed it, had not in the least prepared him to accept the refusal of his personal world to fall into an orderly perspective of marriage and children and housekeeping.

He had accepted the chafing of the working classes along the coasts of the Old Man's enterprises as one accepts the movements of encroaching tide; he had even moments of anticipatory thrill as to whether it might not yet rise and engulf the Old Man and all his affairs. But it still irked him to find the women of his circle range themselves with the increasing number who did not fit into a perfect feminine perspective. Now, beside his sister's cold refusal of her own place in the picture, Virginia's attempt to secure for herself the traditional evaluation began to show warm streaks and flushes of femininity.

Anne's version of her friend's marriage, as an affair in which only the surface of her attention had been engaged, did much to restore Virginia to their ancient right of fealty and entertainment.

What Sieffert had wanted from marriage was not clear, perhaps the sort of thing for which he had turned to the housemaid; but in the light of Anne's handling of her experiment in matrimony, Kenneth could read into Virginia's attempt to pass through marriage into the flame and fervor of life, something of the same gallantry with which she had won recognition from the embattled industrial forces. All this was a great deal to pass through the mind of a young man between the coffee and the salad. He found it pass too rapidly for articulation. In the mean time Anne was thoughtfully creasing the tablecloth.

"If anything comes up in regard to development at Tierra Longa, you must be sure to tell me," she reminded him.

While he was dressing for the opera that night, it occurred to Kenneth that he ought to have suggested to his sister that the occasion was one that called for evening dress. He was getting himself into the dress suit he had acquired the winter before when he had spent some weeks in Washington with the Old Man, ostensibly as his traveling secretary, but really to snoop about the Land Office in the interest of certain timber titles, and he reproached himself now that he had n't given Anne a hint as to just what was implied in Frank's change — after hearing of Palomitas — from seats for "Don Giovanni" to a box.

Kenneth had never been taken into Frank's social

circle, had never expected it; but he recalled that the relations of the two families in Tierra Longa had been that of neighbors, and the return of the Brents as proprietors would make a difference in the way in which they would be met by friends of the Rickarts at Agua Caliente. He need not, however, have concerned himself. Anne was in evening dress.

Undoubtedly of Summerfield origin, but of a cut that suggested that Anne herself was not oblivious to the value of high, young breasts and delicately turned arms . . . oh, undoubtedly for evening. And withal, something that with all her flagrant prettiness Virginia subtly missed. Kenneth could not say what it was exactly; he supposed it might be the thing his mother had so wished for them, and he thought with a pang how strange it was that their going back to Palomitas should be the occasion of Anne's coming into what Mrs. Brent had always felt Palomitas had stood in the way of her getting.

Virginia had not been invited. It had been in Kenneth's mind once or twice to hint that she should be, but an obscure sense of social fitness overcame him, and neither Frank nor Anne seemed to think of it. Kenneth had always taken his cue from those two, and now to find himself ranged with them in a social order from which Virginia's situation, as a divorced woman who had become an Agitator, excluded her, gave him an odd sense of security. It was true he had seen a great deal of Virginia since her return, at her lodgings and at meetings where he had gone by her invitation. For ever since that first occasion, he had been touched with that flame than which there is no passion more biting, the passion for the people. And he came back for more of it. He kept com-

ing, even though at first he found it constantly flickering
out in that curious hair-lifting aversion which the sight
of massed differences in men excites in us. Always coming
and going, Kenneth thought of the audience as muddlers
and duffers, but he continued to go because now and then
in their midst he would be mysteriously touched with
fire. He could never reason the thing out, but all at once
he would Know. The invisible wrestling Angel would
brush him with its wings. And because that knowledge
is the most precious of all the kinds of knowing that
comes to men, he went to look for it again and again.

It was Virginia who explained to him, after he had ventured to speak of it to her, that what he suffered from was
Class Consciousness. It was the way with Virginia and
her friends that all the homely processes by which men
live had become transmuted into phrases, honorific or
defamatory according as they crossed some mysterious
frontier of the mind. Class Consciousness was one, and
Private Monopoly, Unearned Increment, Economic De-
terminism. They were always handing these about, taking little nibbles as if the mere naming of them satisfied —
fed or drugged — that gnawing desire to know, to find
Order and Direction. Kenneth was always doubtful if he
knew what these meant, even after Virginia's friend had
taken him in hand; lent him books to read, Kropotkin,
and "Progress and Poverty." For always the explana-
tions snagged on that curious mistake they made about
T. Rickart and his kind. They spoke of the Cause in the
terms of personal conflict, employed against employer,
rich against poor, labor against capital. And always it
stuck in Kenneth's mind that the real issue was not in
the points at which they were in direct conflict, but in

the greater number in which they did not come together at all, in the fact that so much of the Old Man's game could go forward without any necessity of his thinking of them.

Fortified by his sister's easy acceptance of the social formula, Kenneth felt himself no longer suspended between two issues that never met, but for the moment at least reclaimed to the Rickart party. His particular problems restated themselves under such obvious solutions as that his mother's death had been incident to his father's temporary embarrassment, that Virginia had married a skunk, and that by the Right Man Anne might be rescued from perversity. Before yielding himself wholly to the music, he gave to Virginia a regretful moment, for her being so completely out of it, and then the opening strains of "Don Giovanni" took his imagination.

Anne returned to Summerfield Sunday night without having said anything to disturb his pleasant complacency, and on Monday morning the Old Man paused at Kenneth's desk long enough to dictate the details of the Palomitas mortgage. "Better make an abstract of the title," he suggested. "I doubt if there is one." He hesitated a moment tapping the desk top with his broadened fingers. "And while you are about it," he finished, "I wish you would look up all the water titles in the valley. It might come in handy."

IV

At the time when it was agreed on all sides that Virginia's expeditionary force should, in the interests of the Cause, become a party of occupation, there was a little hollow of the city shored up between Portsmouth Square and the Barbary Coast, a veritable cove of adventure into which all manner of unchartered craft might run. That lovely galleon which has been caught in bronze and beached halfway up the hill of the Square, had once put in there with R. L. S. aboard her, and there is scarcely any literary port of the world in which there is not at least one great name whose sails have filled to its inspiriting winds and about whose hull still show watermarks of its financial ebbs and floods. There, at the end of a week or two, Virginia moved and established herself, in a studio which had lately been surrendered by a young painter and his wife in one of those temporary reversals to which the sort of business carried on in studios is more than ordinarily liable.

There was no reason why Cornelius Burke's daughter should n't have done herself very well in the matter of lodging, or, if she had, as she said, wanted background, why she should n't have found something better suited to the part for which she had cast herself as the Friend of Labor, five or six streets over in the heart of San Francisco's Little Italy. To young Brent, to whom it cannot be denied the Cove was tainted with the faint savor of decay from strange hulks and unseaworthy gifts, that, barnacled by undigested truth and half guesses, rode at

anchor there, the studio was an affectation. For he had
not yet located her immediate audience, was near, in the
relief of finding himself unaccountably excused from that
category, to forgetting that for Virginia there had always to be a particular audience.

But once he had climbed the breakneck staircase to
her top-lighted loft, he found that, whether or not it was
the sort of background inevitable to a Friend of Labor,
it, at any rate, suited her. It detached her from, without repudiating, her bringing up, and committed her to
nothing. It gave her, by its mere refusal to stand for
anything, to involve her in any particular frame of living,
what no struggles of hers against a more definite background had ever given her, the effect of being just Virginia. Even Frank, who could not be thought of in connection with furnished apartments, called on people in
studios. Perhaps that was why people had them.

Young Brent found himself calling there rather often.
He called on those occasions when she was surrounded by
her friends at interminable councils, which, while they
never seemed to arrive at any point in particular, had
the advantage, inestimable to youth, of setting out very
bravely. They were so immensely sure of themselves.
Virginia's friends, sure of their authority and direction,
slid, on what were as yet, to Kenneth, nearly unintelligible phrases, over vast crevasses of logic and human history. He was aware, in some little separate compartment
of himself, that Virginia's friends were many of them in
that state in which mere words have potency, conjuring
vasty spirits before which they deliciously trembled; and
though that separate part of him bore witness to the
imponderable quality of these visions of social regen-

eration, he did not wish to avoid for himself the thrill of trembling.

He was not yet very well acquainted with the duties of an Agitator, but he saw that things were accomplished. Trades were drawn together, money was raised, strikes organized.

Now and then the forward line wavered and broke in disaster, and again it surged perceptibly toward accomplishment. For himself he saw nothing as yet, could not so much as take the measure of his new experience. He would momentarily be aware of wrestling with angels, and again the savor of unsuccess, to which his apprenticeship with the Old Man had made him particularly susceptible, would drift between him and the Movement, like the peninsular fogs, blotting out the vision.

In these oblivious intervals he found it pleasant to fall back on an old and affectionate acquaintance with a young and pretty woman. It was one of the advantages of studios, he discovered, that the quality of affectionateness appeared there to be divorced from all the implications that, among the few young women that he had known, rendered it prohibitive.

If there was any risk in his so yielding himself to the society of a lovely young woman, with the shadow of unhappiness on her past and the flame of a social crusade in her bosom, it was not, at least, the uncharacterized menace that before her marriage had threatened their every encounter.

About the first of November he had a letter from Anne written from the ranch in the first flush of possession.

It was a curious kind of letter, pierced through and through with the sense of her wanting him, and for some reason more urgent than sisterliness or even the practical need to confer with him about the details of the transfer of the property. She wished to know if he had heard anything from Mr. Rickart lately about his plans for Agua Caliente, and who was this man Elwood who was staying at Tierra Longa, and appeared to be on terms of singular intimacy with Jamieson, the new superintendent of the Rickart property.

Virginia, to whom all this was confided, was not disposed to make as much as he would have liked of Anne's wanting him — Anne who so seldom wanted anybody. "Anne is wonderful," she averred, "wonderful . . . doing without all the things that used to be thought indispensable for a woman, and making a place for herself that men would envy! But let me tell you, Kenneth Brent," — Virginia was always a little given to the oracular, — "the time will come when women won't do without, when they will reach out and take what they want *any way they can get it!*"

Kenneth did not know exactly what she meant; if it came to taking things had n't Anne got Palomitas?

"Oh, that!" Virginia scorned; "economic independence is easy." It was the way of Virginia and her friends that they had always to translate the common experience into their particular argot before they could handle it conversationally. "It's not money or property rights that women like Anne balk at; it's the right to their womanhood."

"Oh, well," — Kenneth was slightly vague, — "I suppose Anne could get married if she wanted to."

"Marriage —" began Virginia, and suddenly, by one of her characteristic transitions, she abandoned the pro-

phetic for the purely feminine. "Who is this man Elwood; what's he like?"

"Man about town, clubman," Kenneth told her.
"Awfully popular and clever, but a regular souse. I
imagine he's gone down to Agua Caliente to get on the
water wagon. He was around the office a few weeks ago
and looked as if he needed it."

"But what is he *like?* "

Kenneth revised his description. "About forty, rather
good-looking when he isn't drinking too much. Had a
wife and family a few years ago, but he went on such
awful tears she had to divorce him. He's rather held
himself together since then; I believe there was something
of a scandal and his clubs threatened to drop him. He's
one of the sort that just *have* to be popular."

"Well, if he is like that," Virginia concluded, "and
Anne is interested in him, it must be because he is up to
something."

"He's often in things with the Old Man," Kenneth
admitted; "funny, too, I don't think he cares about making money. He likes the game, I guess, but he's got to
think he's doing it for somebody else, for the town, or a
bunch of his friends. He's pulled off several things that
way . . . but I don't see what he could possibly be doing
at Tierra Longa. . . ." He broke off, his mind's eye staring down the long hollow of the valley. They drifted
down it on a flood of "Don't you remembers?"

After half an hour or so they emerged again in a warm
glow of recollection. It suffused their meeting glance for
the moment in which it took Kenneth to discover that in
the sort of reform garment she had on, a cut between a
Chinese coolie's blouse and a pinafore, Virginia did not

look a day older than when he had last seen her. Its
luminous, soft green, relieved about the wrists and neck
with touches of lavender, went admirably with Virginia's clear red and white, and the spark, bright and
dancing like a child's, that floated in the wet gray iris of
her eyes. In the light of renewal Virginia preened herself,
shaking out the tassels of her sleeve; Kenneth caught and
played with it as he would have played with a flower.
"You know, that's an awfully pretty thing you have
on . . ."

"It's something I thought out for myself. Clothes
ought to express one's self, don't you think, — the innermost personality?"

Kenneth's rather serious young face crinkled pleasantly. "Think what a give-away that would be to some
of us!" She had become, by the simple device of making
no demand upon him, what every young woman should
be at some time in her life, a delight and a diversion.

"When one stands for a Cause," Virginia insisted,
"one's clothes ought not to distract; they ought to confirm and symbolize the soul of the movement — Well,"
in swift adjustment to his touch of mockery, "that's what
André Trudeau thinks."

"Trudeau?" He recognized the name as one not in-
frequently bandied about among Virginia's friends, but
as yet attached to no distinguishing item.

"The playwright, you know . . ." Kenneth let go the
tassel of her blouse, warned by some subtle shift of all
her effects that around this unexpected corner of the conversation he was about to come into sight of her real
audience. "He's writing a play about me; I mean — of
course, it is about the labor problem, and he has modeled

the heroine after me — my attack on Capitalism, you know . . . my being brought up in the System and — finding myself."

She could not quite carry it off without a flush which somehow kept the conversation on the plane of entertainment and sanctioned a resumption of tassel twirling. Virginia was not entirely clear as to what connection there was between Trudeau's play and her necessity for defining in some subtle and personal way her conversion to the social revolution, but she was perfectly sure of herself.

"A distinctive dress saves you so much explanation," she explained. "I have been thinking this out. Though I shan't wear it, of course, in public in these colors. It's simply astonishing how many of our women are bourgeoise in their notions, just as the men are capitalistic in their sympathies. It's one of the things I do in the play, — that is, the heroine does, — to make them see that, make them revolt against it. It's going to be such a help to me," she concluded, "seeing myself realized on the stage that way."

"Oh, if you are in the play to that extent, why don't you act in it?" Kenneth hazarded.

"Ken!" He recognized the flash and the flush as marking her instant appreciation of a new and fascinating possibility of the game. "I had n't thought of *that!*" Thinking of it now sent her pacing up and down with a sweep and gesture that had already, at the mere suggestion, a touch of the theatrical. Mr. Trudeau, she admitted, was expected on the Coast that winter; he was expected to derive inspiration from the spectacle of Virginia in action, the daughter of Capitalism in the rôle of

the Friend of Labor studied against her native environment . . .

"Oh, well — he'll get his money's worth . . ."

The implication of this speech of Kenneth's and the
look that went with it were the occasion of Virginia's
putting on her most married air, which she occasionally
did with him. "I am very much honored by his interest
in me." Mr. Trudeau, it appeared, was coming West for
his health; he was one of those whose souls ate up their
bodies.

Somehow things were not quite so comfortable between
them after that. Always at the identification of any real
or personal interest of Virginia's with the inhabitants of
the Cove, Brent's Class Consciousness was assailed by
the faint odor of bilge with which, for him, its air was
always tainted.

Kenneth heard more or less of Trudeau in Virginia's
circle after that; he supposed he must have been hearing
it before without taking note of it, and of his democratic
drama for which the world of art had been drawing its
half-suspended breath. Always Virginia's friends talked
a great deal of Art, and in spite of the fact that much of
what was said seemed, and probably was, ridiculous, it
was very good for him. Until now he had thought of it
only in connection with the *works* of Art, more particularly of painting and music, and in respect to the elements of these which were incomprehensible and for the
most part unsatisfying. His youth had been nourished
on the best literature; he had even acquired from his
father a discriminating taste in that which is written,
but he had always thought of it somewhat vaguely as
proceeding from some undetermined source like the

waters of a river. You drank when you were thirsty without reference to the secret springs, the hill streams, and troubled cataracts from which it took its rise. He thought of writers, and less frequently of the great painters and musicians, as existing somewhere in an aureoled mist among scenes and passions inaccessible to the ordinary person. He was now to learn that they lived chiefly in studios where they pinched and starved with Pop Scudder along the frontiers of creative effort; that they fretted impotently with Jim Hand, possessed of inestimable holdings which they lacked the capital to work. He was made to think of them as men who dreamed out great artistic enterprises as his father had dreamed the development of Tierra Longa, and were prevented from realization by just such combinations of personal and financial disaster. They were, quite as much as the Homestead Development Company, and quite as helplessly, bound to the wheel of labor and passed under the yoke of a system gauged only to admit the tribe of Rickart to the full stature of success.

He had arrived at some such stage as this when he felt he could no longer resist Anne's definite insistence that he should come down to Palomitas for Thanksgiving prepared to spend a week. There were still some unascertained items of the water titles which Rickart had told him to look up, which would give to his trip the color of business, but, as a matter of fact, he felt quite free to ask for the week off to be with his family at their reinstatement at Palomitas.

Between T. Rickart and his young clerk there was an admitted if undemonstrative affection. Kenneth could remember being taken onto his knee with Frank when they were children, and in respect to Frank, there had grown up between himself and Frank's father that sort of mutual pride in the Prince of the House which might be imagined between the reigning monarch and his youngest son. Rickart had very definite notions of avoiding, in Frank's bringing-up, the pitfalls which were set for the sons of other rich men. At the same time Frank must not miss those advantages of which his father had most felt the need in his own undefended youth. Frank must cut a figure; and yet Rickart himself lacked the indispensable item of experience which would have enabled him to judge whether his son was cutting just the figure which would insure his success with his own generation. He used cautiously to try out his judgments of his heir against Kenneth's newer conclusions; and their mutual pride and concern for Frank had endeared them to each other greatly.

To tell the truth, Kenneth's estimate of Frank was not altogether the correct one. Not moving in his friend's social circle, he could not know that on that side of his life young Rickart was thought a little lacking in fineness, somewhat overbearing and boastful; and in college he was not close enough to realize that his instructors considered Frank's attainment specious, almost tricky. Measuring him against other rich men's sons, Kenneth credited his friend with a conspicuous clear-headedness and a bluff rejection of excesses which appeared admirable; the narrow range of Frank's ambitions, and the identity of his own wishes with those of his father for him, gave him the effect of simplicity and directness. Perhaps the best thing about the younger Rickart was his steady affection for and appreciation of Kenneth, which

Brent repaid in kind as is the way of the young with affection.

Reasons like these made it possible for Kenneth to state quite frankly that he wished the week for his father and Palomitas; and gave point to a certain reluctance of the Old Man to grant what was so candidly asked for. Years had not taken a heavy toll of T. Rickart. About his frame there was a hint of the sparseness of age, but his face was still well filled out, the eyes even a little puffy, the chin too flaccid. He was, if anything, more inscrutable; more and more in the last few years men had dropped the sobriquet "Old Man" in speaking of him. He was Mr. Timothy Rickart.

In his private office it was Rickart's habit in talking with Kenneth to swing about in his swivel chair, one hand grasping his desk, the thumb underneath, and in any perplexity the strong pudgy fingers tapping, tapping. He swung about now to the boy's request, his free hand groping for the unlighted cigar which lay always somewhere among his papers. He chewed it awhile before answering.

"I suppose your sister feels she needs you?" he brought out at last.

"I can't imagine Anne's needing anybody," Kenneth laughed easily, "but she'd like me to come."

"You've fixed up the papers, about the mortgage and everything? She's not worrying . . . ?"

"Oh — no." At the note of uncertainty in Kenneth's voice the swivel chair creaked slightly. Kenneth had n't been able to escape the suggestion in his sister's letters recently that she was — well, not exactly worrying, but perplexed.

"It's hard on my father, I suppose," — he offered his own conclusions, — "going back there now without — with everything so different." He could never bring himself to speak to any one directly of his mother.

"Yes, of course. I suppose your father —" The thick fingers began tapping. "You know I've always regarded your father as a very unusual man, Ken." He looked straight at the boy suddenly. "That idea of his about storing the river at Tierra Rondo and developing the agricultural lands; — that wasn't a pipe dream altogether. . . ." Over the inscrutable eyes came a faint, deliberate veiling. "Not altogether. . . . In fact," — the eyes met his for a moment in which Kenneth had a distinct impression of having received a confidence, — "I regard the agricultural possibilities of Tierra Longa as distinctly feasible."

"My father's generally right about anything connected with the land." Kenneth took a pardonable pride in it.

"Exactly . . . an unusual man . . . very. Well, you'll want at least a week," — in such terms was consent given, — "and while you are there you might as well —" There followed some details of land and water titles, items of no immediate concern, so far as Kenneth knew, but all contributory to that close watch which the Old Man kept on things in the valley. It had been in Kenneth's mind to inquire whether Elwood was really at Tierra Longa on his own business or Rickart's, but he knew exactly when the interview passed from the personal to the official; he could chat with Frank's father, but never with his employer.

It was not all at once that Kenneth could yield himself to the spell of Palomitas. He had been several times to Agua Caliente, but never once to the ranch since the death of his mother. Now he found, as he walked about with Anne, that the old charm hung about it in rags and tatters.

In the house Anne had changed everything. She had come over, weeks in advance of her father, to accomplish it. There were no traces, in the walls or the furnishings at least, of Jevens's occupancy; still less to remind them of their mother.

"I thought at first I had made a mistake," Anne confessed. "It was dreadful the first day or two the way father went about, seeking, seeking! He never said a word, but he looked — Oh, I felt I could n't bear it! And then he found her garden. . . ." There had been a little fenced square at what was architecturally the front of the house, where Mrs. Brent had once attempted a formal garden. None of them had ever been able to take much interest in it at Palomitas; nor had Marcia Brent really; she had no special sympathy with growing things. The garden was merely a part of her attempt to reconstruct at Palomitas the only fashion of life that had ever appealed to her. In the small city from which she had come, everybody had a garden in the front yard and made it more or less an adjunct of social living. Somehow her half-hearted attempt had survived the devastating Jevens. Ah Sen, so long as he had stayed, had kept and watered it from habit just as he had swept off the veranda. That was how it happened that the roses and pomegranates of his wife's planting were the only reminders that Steven Brent found of her in the house where as a bride he had brought her.

"It was the first thing he began to look after," Anne said. "He went over to Agua Caliente and got slips of the geraniums Mrs. Burke had started from those mother gave her." So she gave the chronicle of small events. "Jevens has let the place run down terribly, but it is almost a mercy for father. It needs him so. He goes about stroking it and nursing it back to life, like a woman."

Jevens, it seemed, had set up a livery stable at Tierra Longa, though Anne could have wished him farther. "I don't see how he lives. . . . Mr. Elwood is almost his only customer. They go driving about all over the country." Anne had not met Elwood yet, but she distrusted him. "He gives out that he's looking for a ranch to buy; he's taken options on several. But he does n't strike me as the type of man who would take to ranching."

"He is n't," Kenneth assured her; "it's some kind of gallery play . . . or else . . ." Something flashed over him and was gone before he could put words to it, the sensation of having the clue in his hand and yet missing it. He thought it would come to him directly.

On Thanksgiving day, which was the third of Kenneth's visit, Addie and Peters drove over to have dinner with them. Peters drove a spanking team and Addie looked comfortable and matronly. Two of their three children had, by some miracle of inheritance, escaped the fate which Addie had feared was stacked up for them. The girl, who "took after" Mom Scudder, was positively pretty. But that was not the real surprise that Mr. and Mrs. Peters had in store for the family.

It was, if you please, that they wanted to come back to Palomitas. Peters had all of his Summerfield twenty set out to orchard, part of it had already come into bearing; but the charms of orcharding were not for Addie.

"Prunin' and then ploughin', pickin' and then packin'; year in and year out; they just ain't enough *to* it." And anyway since the planted land was no longer available for cropping, it was necessary for Peters to seek, until the trees fruited, some other source of income.

"I allow," said Addie, "it's a good *in*vestment for the children, come they want advantages, but me and Peters have got to have something with more bite to it."

It was Peters, of course, who had thought of Palomitas; his allegiance to Mr. Brent was almost feudal. Anne admitted that the future of the ranch was problematical enough to furnish the necessary zest of uncertainty, and as "help" nobody could be more satisfactory.

"I don't calculate to have no more young ones," Addie declared herself; "there's one for me and one for Peters and one extry; I reckon I've about done my duty. And I allow the best thing we could do now, me and Him," — it was so Peters had taken his place in the pronominal category, — "is to tear off a good-sized piece of work that we can get some intrust out of."

It turned out that Anne was immensely relieved by the arrangement. She had n't contemplated giving all her time to the ranch and had n't seen yet how she could leave her father. "I'm no farmer," she said; "my work is with people. But with Addie and Peters here, I need n't worry; and it will be good to have young things about, until your children begin to come." She finished: "Do you know, Ken, in spite of your being a lawyer, I can't get over the old idea we had about your coming back here to have more sheep than anybody and turn the river into Tierra Longa."

"Somehow I can't get over it myself," he admitted. And it was true that when Anne had said that about his children coming to Agua Caliente, he had felt a warm wave go over him, just as if the future had reached out and touched him. And suddenly the clue that he had missed the day before came back to him. "You know it would n't surprise me at all if the Old Man should work out that irrigating scheme of father's. Something he said to me the other day, not so much what he said as the way he said it . . . He's keeping tab on the Hillside Ditch . . . But you never can tell about the Old Man."

The Hillside Ditch was a local irrigation enterprise engineered by a dozen small landholders who had come into a little cash capital, realized in part through the Old Man's tips in the recent Summerfield oil excitement. It had been taken out below the Town Ditch and watered some hundreds of waste acres west of the river. It promised well, but fell short of performance, not so much because of the limited capital of the shareholders as their invincible rurality.

What they severally feared for their enterprise was that it should grow beyond their individual capacity to deal with it.

There were so many reasons why the reclamation of lands outside his fence should enhance the value of the Rickart property that it was easy to believe that the Old Man might be more interested in the success of the Hillside Ditch than in its failure; that he meant, as in the case of the oil tips, to give to the enterprise the final fillip toward its most hopeful consummation.

"If he only would —" Anne kindled; and then she shook her head. It was as if she had tried to match this suggestion with one unspoken in her mind and had not succeeded. "There's something . . . something in the air. Almost the first day I felt it. But it's not that; I'm sure it's not. I've not had time to go about much . . . I have n't the least idea what it is, but I feel it somehow — sinister."

Anne had those flashes of insight which Kenneth remembered in his mother; but where Mrs. Brent could only sense in every enterprise the secret element that threatened her personal issue, crying out against it, Anne, sniffing the offending wind, prepared for battle.

V

On the way down to Tierra Longa next morning Kenneth passed Elwood and Jevens behind one of the livery man's smart teams, driving furiously. Neither of them recognized him, but, as he drew out of the road to let them pass, he saw that Jevens was in that high mood which in a man of his type means mischief. He was engaged in what for him was the soul of all enterprise, the business of "putting something over" on somebody, but for the moment Brent's attention passed him over to fix on his companion. Elwood sat loosely in the wide seat of the buggy nursing his knee; his handsome, dissipated face expressing nothing so much as the satisfaction of an actor carrying off his part lightly, pleased with himself and with his audience.

What that part was Kenneth could have guessed even without the help he had from the ranchers in Tierra Longa; — the part of the open-handed overlord, his weakness condoned by the extent to which he took them into his confidence about it; his strength enhanced by being made to seem mysterious. For Elwood had made no secret of his having come to the country to recoup the waste and loss of his amiable weakness. He offered his friendliness in proof of its amiability; his long bouts of hell-bent driving with Jevens captured their imaginations.

When the Tierra Longans looked out of the windows to see his shining buggy top careening between the gopher hills and the sage, they saw also the devils of thirst that pursued him.

They rose to his game of pretending that he was looking for a ranch, pleased with themselves at having taken
the cue so neatly. It was quite understood that Elwood
did not really want a ranch; he wanted a plaything; he
wanted his mind seized and occupied by new and de-
lightful suppositions about what he would do with one or
another property in Tierra Longa. He had taken three
options already on desirable ranches, but it was not expected that he would buy any one of them. Willard, in
fact, had stated that he would never have given an option at all if he had thought there had been the least
chance of Elwood's taking it up. Willard's was a fat field
and lay along the river. Elwood himself had explained
that the advantage of the Willard property was that if he
wanted to get on the wagon again, he would be near the
water. Such jokes, made possible about a property that
had taken three generations to bring to fruition, tickled
them mightily in Tierra Longa.

It gave them a feeling of opulence to see him toss up
and catch again the very source of their livelihood. And
besides, he paid good money for his options. He paid good
money for everything. Jevens might be said to live by him;
the town's one hotel took on the color of prosperity. He
had an engaging way of thrusting a bill into a man's hand
— any sort of a bill, whipped out of his pocket on impulse,
but never by any chance into the wrong hand — saying,
"Here, old chap, drink this for me," and then dashing off
about the country with Jevens, bestridden by his familiar
devil. The recipient had always a pleasant feeling of having assisted at Elwood's reinstatement without curtailing
any of his own indulgence.

There was no doubt that Elwood had played successfully to the gallery; but there was nothing yet discoverable to young Brent other than the man's characteristic need to find himself *en rapport* with his audience. Elwood had made instinctively sure of recovering his lost control by dramatizing his search for it. Confirmed, by what he heard of him at Tierra Longa, in his reading of Elwood as the constitutional seeker after popularity, Kenneth missed whatever significance there might have been in the figure of Jevens as he had seen him that morning instinct with the joy of meanness. He had, too, his own preoccupations.

All the way down the valley the land had reasserted her claim to him. Under the thin bleakness of November he felt its potential fecundity, he felt its invitation and the advertisement of man's inadequacy. It came and offered itself to the hand, and yet no man had tamed it. Far down, the river wasted seaward; nearer, the insidious growth of sage and camise retook the slight clearings of abandoned claims. He passed the old Scudder cabin, long since stripped of its siding by other and none the less succumbing homesteaders. Out from the town, he saw the Hillside District stretched like an arm along the line of farms, checkered with patches of sand and alkali; and beyond it, pointing the yet untouched lands, the thin blue blade of the new ditch. Here and there scattered homesteads tugged at the dry breast of the valley . . . and over it all the defeating, jealous overlordship of the Old Man.

Familiar as he was with the Rickart methods, nothing had ever fully explained to young Brent his studied discouragement of agricultural development in Tierra Longa. The land which he had acquired outside the

Agua Caliente fence, unwatered as it was, could hardly pay its interest in wild pasture. Yet year after year, at the precise moment of falling courage or failing crops, Rickart through his agents had effected a transfer of titles. It was reported that no one besides Juan Romero and the Old Man himself actually knew how much of the land outside the fence belonged to Rickart. What else could he mean by it except to reserve for himself the moment of releasing it to occupation. As he found his mind possessed by this idea, two distinct sets of emotions played over Kenneth. He thought, as he had been trained to think in Rickart's office, of the enormous profits which could be sheared from the land in the process of turning it back to farm and field and orchard, profits which would legitimately accrue to the long-sightedness of the Old Man, who had foreseen and fended it all these years from lesser claimants.

Handled as the Summerfield property had been, it should yield the income of a principality. Brent's nascent business instinct licked eagerly at the proposition; it was the sort of thing that no man in his senses would hesitate, given the opportunity to be "in" on it.

And along with that there was a small flame singing in him of the new social order. All those patient, drudging people to whom the land must inevitably come, why should it be passed to them through Rickart's raking fingers? What was the difference between Rickart's foresight and Steven Brent's, that the one should pay toll to the other? Was not Pop Scudder's vision of the future of Tierra Longa as good as another's? Was it any less ultimate and inclusive? In the city Kenneth had stood out among Virginia's friends for the right of a man like

Rickart to realize on his natural capacity; here suddenly in the abandoned homesteader's cabins, sun-warped and canted by the wind out of all use as housing or shelter, he was confronted with the absurdity of setting up for the Old Man an especial privilege in futures.

As he rode into the little settlement of half a hundred houses ranked on either side of the highway, overhung by great cottonwoods as by a cloud, it needed only the recognition by the townspeople of how completely he was theirs as against any claim the Old Man had on him, to have cleared his path directly to the attitude he was finally to take and maintain in regard to Tierra Longa.

But the fact was that nobody recognized in him anything other than the shy boy they remembered trotting at Steven Brent's heels, and since become a clerk of the Old Man's. Everywhere he met the guarded courtesy which is paid to powers half feared and never wholly understood. He felt subservience in it which annoyed him, and distrust which hurt his new social sensitiveness. Unable to formulate the distinction, he nevertheless understood that, though he had begun to think for the Tierra Longans, he by no means thought with them. His sympathies suffered a check in finding them so easily diverted from their situation by Elwood's handful of flung coin.

Out along the Hillside Ditch young Brent came into more personal touch through the two youngest of the Scudder boys, working a quarter-section on the shares. Lemuel, who had been one of those with whom he had shared the pagan ecstasy of bodily competence at school, had laid off a land close to the fence and was turning it behind his plough in crumbly, tawny furrows. His lank body swung to the rhythm of the team; power passed from his great, reddened hands on the handles to the steel share; he humored and cuddled it as a musician his instrument. Great flocks of red-winged blackbirds settled in his wake; now and again, as the ploughman shouted to his team, they exploded skyward, there to execute their wheeling wing dances and drop shouting again to the treasure of the new-turned soil. Kenneth tied his horse at the fence and came across to renew acquaintance; they spoke, not of themselves, but of the earth and the sky, as chance-met mariners might of the sea; they took up handfuls of the brown sandy loam and fingered it between thumb and palm. Kenneth took the plough at last and guided it once about the land. He was surprised to find how soft he was; the handles thrust and threw him, but before he was halfway around he began to respond automatically to the sensitive share, he felt the scantly sodded soil curl back steadily.

Lem eyed the deep-turned furrow with appreciation. "Once you've learned the trick it remains on the body till death," — he quoted the gym. teacher.

Kenneth leaned on the handle bar, a little winded. The inexplicable excitement of those born to wrestle with the earth and conquer it tingled in him. They looked riverward along the curved blade of the ditch and up the slope of Palomitas to where the Torr' lifted into the thin blue.

"It's a great country, Lem."

"It sure is, a great country."

Thus having propitiated the *genius loci*, they were free to talk of more intimate concerns. At the end of a quarter of an hour of personal history they came to this.

"Think Elwood is up to anything?" from Kenneth.

"You ought to know." Lem had refused another cigarette from Kenneth's case and was busy with his own "makings."

"What makes you say that?"

"Ain't the Old Man backin' him?"

Kenneth realized that this was a point on which he should have been informed, at least, but he came back with, "What makes you think so?"

"Well, he asks a mighty intelligent lot of questions for one that ain't got no intrust in 'em *except* askin'."

"What sort of questions?"

Lem lit his cigarette and carefully trod out the match in the soft soil. "Kinda in that line yourself, Lawyer Brent, ain't you?" Then he relented. "I don't know as it's anyways again a man to be of an inquirin' disposition, but if there's anything about the Hillside Ditch Company that he don't know, — water rights an' land titles *an'* by-laws, it won't be for want of askin', for all he mixes his questions up with a lot of josh and soft-sawder. An' Jim Hand says —"

"Jim Hand?"

"Ol' Jim. He's ditch-ridin'." Lem made a resounding hollow of his hands and raised a tremendous halloo. "Oh-ee, Jim! — He was there alongside the head gate a *while* ago," he explained. "Jim's son-in-law keeps him over here so he can drink himself to death nice and quiet without causin' no scandal. Sieffert havin' done everything in that line himself that he thinks the family can carry. And Jim's nursin' of himself along so's to keep son-in-law out of the property as long as possible. Being as Sieffert owns a couple of shares in the ditch, we give

Jim the job of *zanquero* just to keep the game going."
No one appearing out of the willows that skirted the curve
of the canal in answer to his call, Lem explained that Jim
professed to have seen Elwood and Jevens up the river,
engaged in some mysterious rite of waving arms, stooping and squinting. They would be at it half a day at a
time with the top buggy drawn close under the dunes out
of range of observation, and though Jim had never been
close enough to identify the instruments they used, he
claimed that there had been instruments. "An' even at
that they might have been photographin'," Lem allowed.
"I see this man Elwood packin' a camera up to Agua
Caliente."

Kenneth was silent, knowing that if Elwood was, as
seemed possible, playing the Old Man's game, it was no
part of his to say yes or no to it. And yet making a mystery of himself might be so easily a part of the game
Elwood played with Tierra Longa; he was perfectly capable of amusing himself at the expense of Jevens's passion for trickery.

When Lem Scudder spoke again it was with a certain
wistfulness. "There's some that allows that the Old
Man's gettin' ready to pull off some kind of irrigation
project. I reckon if he is you'll be in on it?"

"Oh!" Kenneth kindled to the sense of unlimited opportunity in the land that dipped away from where they
stood, and rose again to the round-back Saltillos. "If there
is anything of that kind afoot, we'll *all* be in it!" It really
seemed to him as he spoke that it must be so; he could not
conceive how it should be otherwise.

The business of informing himself as to the exact legal
status of local water rights and land titles along the

Arroyo Verde kept Kenneth in the valley for four days besides those he allowed himself with his family, and involved a trip to Summerfield to search the county records. He saw no more of Elwood, but he heard of him, and nowhere so descriptively as at Agua Caliente. Jamieson, the new Superintendent, was a stiff man who would not let himself be liked for fear he would be the less respected, and the knowledge of Elwood's easy popularity sat sourly on him.

"A man that has to play the fool to get his business done may look to be made a fool himself if he is not careful," said Jamieson; and though he professed to know nothing of what that business might be, he professed it too often.

All these things were talked over with Anne as they happened. It did n't occur to Kenneth that in posting his sister as to the status of water rights in Tierra Longa, he was putting her on the same footing as his employer. It was all information which Anne might have picked up for herself had she hired a lawyer's clerk to do it for her.

It gave him a pleasant sense of being the man of the family to have Anne sit questioning him under the evening lamp, clear-headed and incisive, her well-kept fingers tapping the cloth. Anne was remarkably conversant with land law, for a woman; she bent herself to mastering riparian rights, titles of use and surplusage. Now and then Steven Brent would add something to the conversation out of his well-stored knowledge.

"It is this man Elwood," concluded Anne, "who has the key to the situation. I must really have a look at him." She revolved ways and means for accomplishing that, and then to her brother she suggested: "I suppose if there is

anything on foot, you'll know as soon as anybody? Ken
— if such a scheme should go through I must be in on it
— I've just *got* to be in on it."

"Well, you got what you wanted about the mortgage —" Kenneth's faith in his sister's ability to get
"in" with the Old Man had gone up a notch or two; but
she came at him now from another angle.

"Ken, do you like being a lawyer; like it, I mean, the
way father likes being a rancher, the way I like — what
I'm doing?"

"Well, there is n't anything about it I *dis*like," Kenneth carefully considered. "But I'm not really a lawyer;
I'm only a kind of — legal detective. I go around looking
for dropped stitches and picking up threads. Straker
handles all the cases in court. Yes; I like it. It gives me
a chance to look about me."

It had always been agreed between brother and sister
that Kenneth's apprenticeship with the Old Man had
been merely in order that he might look about him, that
at the precise moment he should find himself in a position
to "get into something" most effectively. In the beginning they had expected this to happen much earlier.
Kenneth did not know quite how to explain to his sister
the sensation he had of being carried along in the Old
Man's financial career, as one is carried by genii in Ara-
bian fairy tales, by the hair of his head. He had seen great
ventures in lands and forests and minerals pass beneath
him, but all too fast for him to select that comfortable
pocket into which he was to drop with his feet under him.
He tried, instead, to express something of his new sense
of social direction.

"I don't know," he said, "that I care so much as I did

about getting 'in.' I don't know that there is n't going to be a bigger piece of work and more fun in getting out and getting others out."

"As — how, for instance?"

"Out of the System. . . . Capitalism, you know . . ." He stated it badly; the terms which passed so glibly among Virginia's friends were stiff upon his tongue, but Anne took his meaning. He was surprised to find that she had read the same books, and to what widely differing conclusion.

Anne was not troubled by any incubus of a System. "There is n't any such animal," she insisted. "It's only the way we look at things. As soon as we learn to see things straight, we'll moult the System."

"But how — straight?"

"Well, the Way Things Are . . . not what we like, you know, or think we ought to, but real values. Society is a sort of mirage, a false appearance due to refraction. . . . I mean most of the things we do and think important only seem so because of all sorts of hang-overs, — political, religious, all kinds of ignorances . . . that's because we have Androcentric culture."

This was a step beyond even Virginia. Kenneth had to have the word explained to him.

"I mean," — she went more slowly, — "because everything has been accepted from the point of view of men only, and that's the obvious. Women have a much keener sense of real values. Take marriage, for instance; — a woman will marry a man because he is clean and honest and will make a good father for her children, but a man won't marry a woman unless she makes him feel a certain way . . . unless there's a — mirage."

There was more of this in the same strain which ruffled
the surface of his egotism. What kind of a world would
that be in which a man could n't do or take because he
felt like it, but must wait always on the essential values of
things? But he was sensible that to admit his irritation
was to admit the argument. He had known that his sister
was a suffragist, but he had n't expected this of her.

"We're getting more sensible about some things,"
Anne admitted. "Look at land; I'm learning a lot about
land, and the first thing to learn is that you can absolutely
find out what land is good for, and in time we'll find out
that, no matter what you feel about it, it only belongs to
the people who can do those things. Say a certain piece
of land will grow prunes or potatoes; then you've got to
have prune people or potato people, or else somebody
makes a fool of himself. I sent some of the Summerfield
swamp soil to the University last week to have it ana-
lyzed, but there's nobody can analyze the man that wants
to buy it from me. And then, when we get into a mess, we
put it on to the System! I can make a Socialist out of a
prune man," said Anne, "by keeping him six years on a
piece of ground that was only meant to grow potatoes."

There was a great deal, Kenneth felt, that could have
been said to this, but he did not know enough to say it.

It was only Anne, of course; and a man is not much
more likely to be moved by his sister's philosophy than
he is by her beauty; still, in default of the absolute thing
to say, he had to go on listening.

"All this talk about the System," Anne exploded, —
"it's only a new kind of devil that's been invented to explain what people won't admit, their own mistakes about
the way the world is made. And even then they can't lay

everything to it. Look at Jim Hand; he's a teamster who failed at being a promoter, and I've no doubt he lays it to the System . . . and what had the System to do with Virginia's making a mess of her marriage?"

Kenneth struck out against the flood that threatened his new-found social consciousness. "You know a lot," he admitted, "but I don't see how you can be so sure of things like that. So far as I know, you've never been in love even . . . and to hear you talk one would think that you and not Virginia had been the married woman."

He was sorry the moment he had said that. There came a whiteness across Anne's face such as follows a blow, and no flush to succeed it. He had an idea that Anne's feelings about marriage were tied up somehow with her recollection of their mother's unhappiness, and the things he would never let any one tell him about the way she died. . . .

"And I'm always telling you," said Anne, "that Virginia has neither been really in love nor really married!" She recovered herself, turned the question back upon him with, "Don't you ever think of marriage for yourself, Ken?"

"Oh, I don't know. . . . I guess I'm a little like Addie about the orchards." He laughed, recalling a characteristic speech of Mrs. Peters: "Seems like I can't bear lookin' at an orchard no longer. It's so kind of *sot;* it don't give you no chanct to stretch your vision."

"Marriage is so kind of *sot*," he confessed.

"Oh, well, that's because you haven't met the right woman," Anne comforted him offhandedly; "she'll stretch your vision for you when you find her."

And still he couldn't help wondering what Anne knew about it.

VI

THE effect of his sister's free stride was to bring out for Kenneth the essentially feminine quality of Virginia's devotion to the cause of labor unionism. Anne herself had contributed something. "It's her baby," Anne insisted; "it has the advantage over a real baby inasmuch as she can't spoil it with coddling, and yet she can neglect it without getting into trouble with the Society for the Prevention of Cruelty to Children."

People who did not know the generosity of Anne's performance found her judgments caustic. She probed like a surgeon, but there was something regal in the way she nursed you back to soundness. Kenneth, who presented the normal male reaction to any sort of feminine acuteness, often winced under her searching hand, but this time he recognized the veracity of her touch.

Confronted with the spectacle of Virginia's fostering of the cause of social revolution, Kenneth saw how inevitably one woman's estimate of another is nearer the mark than any man's!

Virginia's child had grown, had, like an infant Hercules, come to grip its cradle with the python folds of "the Interests," and Virginia, as she patted the young movement and nourished it from her purse, exhibited the most charming maternal poses. The struggle of the labor unions for the mastery of San Francisco proceeded more dramatically, with a swifter recurrence of clinch and climax than on almost any other civic stage. Freer, on the one hand, from sordid pressure of poverty and on the other from the blindness of fatness, it displayed something of the epic quality of the West.

Through its spirited phases Virginia moved electrically, with how much of positive organizing value Kenneth was too little acquainted with the movement to tell; but certainly with an effect. Always, where she went among the workers, exhaling, along with more appreciable odors of beer, onions, and sweated bodies, a faint savor of unsuccess, she was the center of a little whirl of ideas and opinions which, contained like the dust devils of Tierra Longa within a very narrow reach, carried, nevertheless, dust of the cosmos. Insensibly, as the winter advanced, Kenneth found himself drawn into the outer circle of that whirl, with that dust in the nostrils.

Unionism, Socialism, Syndicalism, how many of the hot ploughshares which were trodden by the young men of the early twentieth century are cold to the light-footed radicalism of to-day! They were many of them cold then to Kenneth except as they were warmed for him by Virginia's triumphant personality. Virginia had so many ways of getting at him.

There was her old childish trick of laying hold of a wrist or a knee or an elbow when her swift imagination outran the speed of words to express it; a trick that the almost family nature of her relationship to Kenneth disarmed of familiarity. It answered with them, as it has with millions of the young; — those swift, deceptive short circuits of sex attraction, offering themselves as a superior intellectual sympathy, and serving nature quite as much in the one thing as the other. There was a trick she had of drawing out of their common experience illuminating instances, to lay alongside the immediate problem of in-

dustrial agitation. She would make these excursions into
his past with a swiftness and verve that prevented his
realizing that, while she seemed honestly to be illustrating
her case with examples of the Scudders and Jim Hand,
she had only restated it in terms of her personal prejudices. But one way and another the salient problems
of the day got themselves stated for him. From time to
time, while Virginia's hot little hand, under the influence
of some flaming diatribe, worked along the coat sleeve
into his palm, or while from the shouldering crowd he
watched Virginia's self shaking her brave pennant in
the face of the Established Order, the miracle of oneness
happened; he felt for a moment the pulse of the world
of labor in his own breast.

But a little before the holidays the sense of the world
movement was obliged to give place to more personal
and poignant emotions set in motion by the coming of the
playwright André Trudeau and his sister Ellis. Their arrival, of the date of which Virginia for some reason had
neglected to be explicit, took place during one of Brent's
short trips out of town, and the first glimpse that he had
of Trudeau was of a physique, which to the practiced
California eye presented all the characteristics of a
"lunger," a pair of eyes gentle and wide apart, a mouth
too full and pouting, barely made to seem masculine by
the pointed beard and mustache and a crop of dark,
springy hair spraying out like a fountain. He was making an address at the time in that same Turn-verein
hall where Kenneth had once listened to the one-eyed
prophet of Industrialism, and the general ineffectual-
ness of his exterior was heightened by the plucking
gesture, many times repeated, of a man between whom

and his audience gathered successive veils of formless hypothesis.

The address, however, had not begun when Kenneth, finding every seat occupied, had slipped into the space between the wings of the rather tawdry stage, where he hoped to find a packing-case at least within sight and sound of the speakers. Moving in the half light he had come plump upon a slender, anxious girl with a man's heavy overcoat trailing from her hands, looking out, evidently in great perplexity, at the group already seated on the stage in full view of the audience. At the sound of Kenneth's blundering in the back stage obscurity, she turned with instant relief; she might, indeed, have taken him for one of the hall attendants.

"Oh," she said, "if you would be so kind as to take this coat to my brother, to Mr. Trudeau — the third one from the left. . . . He did n't realize the hall would be so draughty."

Kenneth took the coat and dropped it unostentatiously about the playwright's thin shoulders.

"Oh, *thank* you!" she said again, this time with a sense of the enormity of her proceeding, due to her discovery, as he stepped into the full light, that Kenneth was not an attendant. "My brother's health is so precarious," she apologized. And then, suddenly struck with Kenneth's manner which was hardly that of a stranger, "You know him?"

"I have heard of him. At Miss Burke's," he added, and thereby acquired merit, for it was evident that Virginia was in charge of the evening.

"Oh — " she began to say, and then, "Hush," for the meeting was about to begin. She was full of a quiet kind

of excitement, immensely concerned for her brother, and
yet ready, when the intervals of applause permitted, to let
shine for him the light of appreciation which sprang from
her for whatever had brushed, even with the wing's tip,
the subject of Virginia.

"You're fortunate, if you're a friend," she whispered,
under cover of the storm that greeted Virginia's rising to
open the meeting.

"Quite the oldest —" He smiled down at her enthusiasm.

"Ah —h!" the exclamation died down for Virginia's
introduction and rose again at the end of it. "Isn't she
wonderful! I suppose you've heard—" for Virginia had
left nothing unsaid about the playwright and his connection with the Democratic Drama except her personal
relation to it. Kenneth signified his familiarity with
the extent to which Virginia actually did figure in her
brother's play. "It's just gorgeous for Andy to have this
opportunity to study her," Andy's sister confided. "He
has such *liberal* ideas about women. But mostly the types
where we've lived have been such frumpy, so — bourgeoise." The word which circulated so freely in Virginia's circle came a little hesitatingly as if she flinched
before its possibly injurious import.

"Where you've been —" Kenneth began to question,
and then covered the potential impertinence with the
first thing that came into his mind. "Your brother
doesn't look in the least foreign," he explained.

"Oh, but he isn't! At least, not for a hundred years.
We're French Huguenots, I believe originally, but now
we are just Connecticut. My brother's name is really
Andrew; he took the French form for — commercial rea-

sons. It is so much more interesting." She took this supposititious demand that writers' names should be interesting with the same simple seriousness with which her brother publicly accepted his rating as the exponent of Democratic Drama. Even before Virginia found them, at the end of the meeting, and formally introduced him, Kenneth had decided that Ellis Trudeau was a nice little thing.

That she was also a pretty little thing did not occur to him until Frank had spent an afternoon at the studio and, having dismissed Virginia's high color and vitality as merely continuing her claim to be "as good a looker as ever," discovered in Miss Trudeau the quality of unusualness. Brent observed then that her hair, which she wore coiled neatly about a small head, was the color of Anne's, soft ashy brown, but in place of Anne's steady blue her eyes were pale brown, and her brows had a winglike sweep at the outer corner. Her skin was colorless rather than pale and her lips not red, but a clear rosy pink, folded and thoughtful. One hardly noticed these things, however, in Virginia's presence unless attention was called to them, or in the presence of her brother. She was so taken up with that gifted pair, with observing them and admiring them and making sure that they wanted nothing, that she turned the attention back to them by a kind of personal refraction. She was not often at the studio, but always when Trudeau addressed meetings, or when, notebook in hand, he fluttered in the wake of Virginia, there was Ellis, with an extraordinary sensitiveness to draughts and a finality on the subject of damp pavements that belied her promise of softness.

Sometimes before or after meetings, the four of them

would go up the hill of the Square to eat chop-suey in the teahouses of China Town, or, somewhere about the borders of the Cove, turn into one of those Italian places where the food is excellent and the wine execrable.

Always Virginia played to them. She had an almost unlimited capacity for keeping the game going and for shaping her part to the requirements of the audience. What the part was, over and above what she was supposed to stand for as the Friend of Labor, was the Spirit of the West. It was not all at once that Kenneth recognized it as such, for she played it in the only key in which the Trudeaus were accustomed to see it manifest, in the key of Owen Wister and the Sunday Supplements. He would break in upon her at first, not as to matters of fact, for Virginia was incorrigibly honest as to fact, but with some notion of freeing her interpretation of life at Tierra Longa from a swagger foreign to the spirit in which it had been lived. Presently he gave over such attempts, discovering that to the Trudeaus the West, stripped of this hand-woven fabric of Romance, bared its teeth. Except they could see it in the color of literature, they were unable to see what endeared it to him, could form no notion, from the little they did see, what it was about. Almost they were terrified by it, as he could recall he himself had been when — once while he and Frank had been lost for a whole day, hunting in the Saltillos, or often on his lonely walks about the heights above Petrolia — the veil of familiar use had dropped and left him face to face with its immensity, its immutable purposes. Confronted with this necessity for defining the West, for rendering it intelligible, he fell more and more into Virginia's trick of handling it in the terms and colors of fiction. Once he had dipped his brush in that medium, he recognized it for the color of dreams and found himself suddenly enriched by the possession.

All this was immensely good for him. He began to handle the stuff of his own life and pronounce judgment on it; as if, where it had been but clean clay and water, he could see it now as the material from which vessels are moulded. Until now he had sat where many young men on salaries sit for the whole of their lives, before the human pageant as before a painted picture. He had admired the picture as it was presented to him in books and on the stage, been stirred by it. Now the canvas itself stirred, the tapestry trees waved their branches, the figures moved in and out under them. Times when he and Virginia would sit before the entranced Trudeaus, playing each other off in some dramatic recital of life in Palomitas, he would catch himself turning quickly, under the impression that now . . . at a word, at the stretching out of her hand . . . the painted surfaces would yield . . . they would be "in," gloriously in together. And always after that he would leave her with a sense of the evening's being suspended, incomplete. Gradually he came to seek, as a solution for this delicate bafflement, the possibility that Virginia was already "in"; that she had been by some gift of her natural constitution, always in the picture, and that the demand which she had made on his adolescence had been nothing more or less than an invitation to him to come in, to be a part of the world-old pageant and the show. She had held out her hand to him. . . . Ah, let her but flutter that signal again, she would find what she would find! There were moments when it seemed she was about to do just that, and drew unaccountably back again. One night, when they had put the Trudeaus into a cab at Dupont Street, — for there was a wet fog trailing up and down the streets and André coughing with every breath of it, — they trudged down the Square together, past the fountain, paused for the passing salute which Virginia would insist always upon giving it, and he drew the hand on his arm into his, drew it finally across his breast to clasp it in both his own with gentle, intermittent pressure. So they came and stood for a moment at the bottom of the dark stair which led up to the studio.

"Oh, Ken," she half laughed, "why were n't you always like this?"

"Like this?" He gave her a little pull toward him, as though, if he could not come into the picture, she at least should come out. "Oh, well," — he laughed fully, — "give a man a chance to grow up!" He was feeling particularly grown up, full of a fine male exultation and perfectly sure of his intention.

"If you were . . . if you really were . . ." She panted a little, she swung him about by the shoulders, searching his glance by what light there was, almost with desperation, then suddenly, by one of her swift turns, she put him from her.

"Boy . . . oh, Boy, . . . Good-night!"

She fled up the stairs away from him.

He recalled this incident afterward with a kind of prideful embarrassment. He had meant, he had surely meant, to kiss her. He would have kissed a married woman! For Virginia, in spite of her divorce and the retaking of her maiden name, was technically a married woman . . . and he had almost kissed her. He behaved himself toward her for the next few days with great circumspection touched with extenuating tenderness. . . . She was Virginia, of course, . . . but she was something more, a creature of experience, the mysterious source and occasion of "situations."

All this was the warp and woof upon which was embroidered the figure of Virginia as the heroine of Democratic Drama. Under the influence of the West, and the inspiration of Virginia in action, the play went forward leapingly. There was constant talk now of a "try-out" production on the Coast before trusting it to the hazard of Broadway. Most of the talk about it was too much in the professional patter for Kenneth to follow, except as it reminded him of the talk during the early days of Petrolia.

They would sit, as Jim Hand and Scudder and Soldumbehere had sat around the table, in one of those cafés about the coasts of San Francisco's Little Italy where execrable wine is balanced by an excellent cuisine, talking, talking . . . and all their talk was tinged as that other had been with the need, the inexorable need, and the impossibility of satisfying from any known source, the need of Capital. Committed as they were to a social system that would forever prohibit the formation of pools and hidden veins of wealth, they still desperately required, for the success of all their enterprises, to dip them in those reservoirs. Times like these, Kenneth, whose mind had swung with them through all the quarters of social reconstruction, would swing, with a round turn, to the side of the Old Man. He would see, in a flash, Rickart and his kind as a work of nature, gigantic, inevitable, like the epoch which stored the oil under Petrolia.

They were sitting so in the upper room at Campi's a day or two before Christmas, when, in response to some discussion which had arisen, the tables were pushed back, — it was very late and they were almost in full possession of the restaurant, — for Virginia and André to play out before them the scene which terminated the second act. Trudeau could n't act, and had the sense not to try, but Virginia dashed through the part of the heroine with a spirit which, considering that the whole scene was but a shorthand report of Virginia's daily performance, was not without verisimilitude. Through the round of applause which followed, — for by this time the audience had been augmented by the waiters and the half-dozen remaining diners who had felt themselves quite free of whatever entertainment was offered, — somebody could be heard triumphantly. "There's your leading lady, Trudeau! She's simply *made* for it."

"It was made for *her*," the playwright admitted handsomely.

Virginia included them all in the modest acknowledgment of success.

"Mr. Brent suggested it some time ago," she confessed, "but I was afraid—" Renewed hand-clapping interrupted her. She came directly over to Kenneth, taking him by the elbow in a way she had, making herself altogether of his party. "Of course it would save expense," she agreed with the air of being willing to consider it with him from all sides; "we have to think of that."

It appeared from this that the plan for a San Francisco try-out was much farther along than Kenneth had imagined, and for the life of him he could not say why the plan was not a good one, except as he had a notion that what Virginia had just done was not acting, and he more than suspected that Trudeau could not write a play. For he had not wholly accepted the current explanation of Trudeau's failure to produce anything which had been professionally accepted as such, as due to the capitalistic influence which hung like the traditional millstone about the neck of American Drama. In view of the way in which Virginia had pulled him publicly into her boat, he could not very well explain the pure mockery of his original suggestion that she should play the part for which she had sat, and it was only on the way home, that Ellis Trudeau aroused him to the extent to which she was practically involved by it. It frequently fell out that he walked home with Ellis while Virginia was taken away by the playwright, always, of course, in the interest of "copy"; an arrangement with which Kenneth could have found no reasonable fault, except for a suspicion that Miss Trudeau had accepted him, not so much in order to enjoy his company as to afford her brother uninterrupted possession of Virginia's.

"You think it's a good plan, really? I mean a good *business* plan? Of course it would be wonderful *any*way for Andy to have his play tried out at a real theater, but I don't want him to do it this way if it isn't good business."

"You mean if it doesn't pay back what is put into it? I'm sure I don't know, but there ought to be ways of finding out."

"Couldn't *you* find out? Andy isn't very good at business. He always thinks things are going to be better than they turn out. Artists are that way," she stated without bitterness. "But, you see, Virginia has done so much for us already."

"Virginia!"

"If she — capitalized the — the production," — she hesitated over the professional patter, — "I should n't want her to lose by it. When she's doing so much for us." The speculations which this innocent statement gave rise to, kept Kenneth silent, and presently Miss Trudeau asked again with an arresting irrelevance, "Do you think your sister could tell?"

"Anne!" Kenneth felt that he was not sustaining his end of the conversation, but the exclamation was of sheer astonishment.

"Yes. That nice Mr. Rickart said she was a *remarkable* business woman. He says she *is* all the things that Virginia and — the others — spend their time trying to persuade other people to be. I should *so like* to meet her."

"Oh, well," — Kenneth laughed tolerantly, — "old Frank always was a little sweet on Anne. She'd like *you*, though; she'd have you down at Palomitas the first rattle out of the box." He drew the talk off in that direction until he could account for the queer start it gave him to consider just what was the "so much" that Virginia had been doing for André Trudeau. If she had advanced the money, as these disclosures seemed to indicate, for his visit to the Coast, and if she really meant to put up money for the play, she was going some. He reflected that he did not really know anything about how the Trudeaus lived except that they had housekeeping rooms and that Ellis's time seemed to be largely taken up with the care of her brother's health and diet. About the financing of Democratic Drama he really knew nothing, though he thought Miss Trudeau's wish that Virginia might not lose by it rather fine; and he resolved in his mind to speak to Frank about it the very next morning.

He had been shy of talking with Frank of his new interests, as shy as he had been of all that had lain always at the back of his mind about the Old Man. Nobody would have been more surprised than Frank to learn that there were, for Kenneth, two distinct figures of T. Rickart, for one of which he entertained a well-seasoned, half-humorous regard, and another about whom his thoughts revolved in cold and slowly enlightened speculation. So far this double perspective had not flawed his young loyalty to Frank. Brent's failure to speak freely of what had come to him through the renewal of acquaintance with Cornelius Burke's daughter really was due to the realization that she was, in the nature of things, out of the circle of Frank's social interests. But on the subject of Virginia's projected invasion of the professional stage, Kenneth thought he could appeal to his friend as a patron of the drama, whatever drama was available in San Francisco. Better than any one of Kenneth's acquaintance, Frank would know whether what was in the air was the sort of thing that Virginia's friends would wish for her. And Frank emphatically thought it was n't.

It is true that Frank's ideas on the subject were more or less confused with impressions of the type of actress whose photograph is oftenest seen on the front page of the ten-cent magazines; and the histrionic gift was by association identified with a kind of provocation which the daughter of his father's former superintendent pointedly did n't have for him. As for the exponent of Democratic Drama, Frank had not been favorably impressed by him.

"That chap with the sister . . . quaint little thing,

is n't she? Reminds me of Anne, sort of. Chap looks like
a lunger. No pep to him. That's what a playwright has
to have these days; pep and punch. Besides, you can't
make a play out of labor unions; they're not dramatic."

Kenneth would have disputed this; there was Haupt-
mann's "Weavers." Rebecca Lovinsky had recently
given it to him to read.

"Ever heard of it on Broadway?" Frank demanded.
"Well, there you are. . . . I tell you you have to have
heart interest . . ."

Frank waived the discussion of the larger aspects of
drama to come back to the personal instance. "Virginia
ought n't to get too thick with that Trudeau fellow; looks
to me like one of these decadents." Neither Frank nor
Kenneth was quite sure what this implied, but it sounded
knowing. "Virginia thinks every sort of animal is a
parlor pet until she gets bitten. Tell her to look a little
out."

This being the sort of thing it was fatal to tell Virginia, Kenneth resolved to do the looking out himself.
He had a healthy male prejudice against a man's taking
support from a woman. The suggestion that Trudeau was
financially dependent on Virginia — and it accounted too
aptly for the discrepancies between Virginia's known income and her way of living to be easily dismissed —
brought a touch of contempt to the feeling with which he
was beginning to regard the playwright. He found himself sniffing the other's words for that faint odor of de-
cadence which Frank had hinted at; it seemed to him that
he had been missing the full significance of much that was
going on under his eyes.

Kenneth's own ideas about women had been strongly

tinged with that Americanism which is nearly Oriental in its insistence on keeping them a race apart. They existed for him in two tribes of good and bad, in the first of which were enthroned all those who could possibly be thought of as touching his own life. He had not, however, lived six years in San Francisco without realizing something of the ease and the occasions by which the line could be crossed; he had even been made to feel, through the talk that cropped up in the office between Frank and other rich men's sons, that the lines were uncomfortably close. He knew, for instance, that there was an address in Alameda, known only to Straker, the firm's senior attorney, at which the Old Man could be found in emergencies, and he recalled, with rather a burning sensation, the incident of a certain canary-blonde stenographer who for a brief three weeks or so had held the corner desk of T. Rickart and Company's outer office. She was a Santa Rosa girl and this had been her first city employment. It was to simple *gaucherie* that he had attributed a certain trick she had of putting down his mail over his shoulder so that her hand dragged the lapels of his coat, and the obvious invitation of her banter with young McRae, of Dent, McRae and Company, who frequently dropped in to sit on Frank's desk and discuss "skirts" and polo. He had even put his clean young interpretations of the girl into the form of a remonstrance to McRae, having seen them dining together once or twice at public restaurants, to that young gentleman's great entertainment. His "Oh, come now, Brent, a slice out of a cut loaf —" had barely been swallowed by Kenneth, being seasoned with wholly irresponsible Irish laughter; and then one day he had come into the office to find the girl with her skirt caught up on a nail as she tiptoed on a high stool to reach a row of office files, disclosing a surprising length of stocking. She had, in truth, recovered herself with commendable modesty, but not before Brent had had time to be struck with the more amazing revelation of the quality of the exhibition. He knew what silk stockings cost; Anne was rather partial to them; she had said that she would know when she was rich enough when she could afford to wear them every day; he had just made her a present of a box for her birthday . . . and the stenographer, at twelve dollars *per*, was wearing *silk* stockings!

Kenneth was not a fool; therefore it was a relief to him, after a week or ten days' absence from the office, to find that the canary-blonde had been superseded by a brunette in spectacles, and when he ran onto them later dining at the Cliff House, neither McRae nor the girl noticed him.

Now at Frank's suggestion that Virginia ought to look out a little for André Trudeau, Kenneth experienced something of that sense of affronted confidence with which this incident was always associated. If the playwright had, under cover of the gospel of democracy, crept into his own and Virginia's grace, with any suspicion of sliminess, it was Kenneth's part as the long established friend to be the first to fix and repudiate it.

VII

Looking out for Virginia in connection with the prophet of Democratic Drama was by no means the simple matter of precaution that it sounded. Kenneth's first effort in that direction was to put the case to Anne on the occasion of her Christmas visit. Originally she had planned to have her brother at Palomitas; but it was characteristic of Anne always to keep well within her capacity. Anne could manage a household with the same clear confidence with which she handled her real-estate business; as a mother of twelve she would have been notable, but she quailed before the feminine necessity of keeping her father's first Christmas at Palomitas free from reminders of his widowed condition. So they made three days of their holiday and spent two of them buying cultivators and alfalfa seed. Incidentally Anne found time to insist to her brother that Virginia's dramatic adventures were none of their business.

"There's no reason why Virginia should n't put her money into a play the same as into an oil company. I understand that some plays are very good investments. And if she spends her income on Mr. Trudeau, that's her affair also. She probably would n't do it if she was n't getting something out of it."

"I don't see what she can expect to get from a chap like Trudeau. Unless you mean she expects to marry him."

"Goodness, Ken, what an old maid you are! Do you really think marriage is the only thing women want from men?"

"I don't know what else she can get that would justify her spending her money on him." It was really shocking the way Anne talked; if you did n't know her very well you might think —

"It's a matter of values," Anne interrupted him. "Women have always had a different set of values from men. But I don't see why they should n't assert their right to what they value at the market price . . . if they *have* the price."

"You mean you think it all right for a woman to — to *pay* a man for — for —"

"For dramatizing her life for her? I don't see why not. Men have always paid women for the same sort of thing . . . being an inspiration to them, don't they call it? I should n't wonder if there are women who have done that, too, though maybe they don't talk about it."

He should think not! A wave of his old fierce desire that Anne should have a husband, and that he should beat her, surged over Kenneth. It was intolerable that a woman should talk so about men — as though to serve the needs of women were one of the things for which they had been expressly created.

"You don't know anything about men," he told her angrily.

"Maybe not," Anne agreed amiably; "but I know three, anyway, and I know a lot about women."

Afterward it occurred to Kenneth to wonder who the third man could be. Himself and his father were two, of course, and the other — yes, it must be old Frank. Anne could always do exactly what she liked with old Frank. In view of the brilliant match it would be, he wondered why she had n't done the obvious thing and had him marry her.

Somehow with those two it would have to be obvious; you could never think of old Frank and Anne ensnared in that warm, delicate web which — well, which might so easily be spun between himself and Virginia. And yet Frank would have married Anne like a shot if she had told him he ought to. At least he would before a certain Miss Rutgers of New York appeared upon the scene. Could it be that there were really women who did n't care for marriage, with whom it was not a mere courageous pretence that they liked to knock about and do things? He tried to get a line on Virginia, as far as he might, by getting a line on his sister from her friend.

"I used to think she and Frank would hit it off," he confessed diplomatically; "Frank's awfully fond of her."

"Oh, yes, he's *fond* of her." There was always a touch of professional antagonism in all Virginia's references to the heir of T. Rickart.

"You don't suppose there has been anybody else, anybody Anne herself was fond of who sort of — disappointed her?"

"Well, Kenneth Brent, do you think I'd tell you!"

"She'd tell me about you fast enough! She'd know that I would really be interested," he hastened to add.

"She would n't! Would n't tell, I mean. Anne would dissect me all to pieces the way she does everybody, but she would n't tell you one single little fact that she thought I did n't want you to know." Virginia was magnificent.

"Well, I don't see why she should mind *my* knowing; after all, she's my sister."

"If somebody she cared for had disappointed her — if he had n't even seen? Of course she'd mind. If there's anything Anne wants you to know she'll tell you herself."

Kenneth reflected on the amazing certainty women had about their own kind. Look at the way Anne and Ellis Trudeau had taken to each other! For among the results of Anne's visit had been the one that Kenneth had foreseen; within an hour of knowing her she had invited Ellis to Palomitas.

Abandoned by his sister in his fine young resolution to stand between Virginia and the tainted weather of the Cove, Kenneth had to fall back on the playwright's own utterances and Rebecca Lovinsky, one of those curious types whose souls are snared in the raveled fringe of art, from which no single shred of its creative spirit redeems them.

Miss Lovinsky was a purveyor of book news and reviews, writing about writing, deriving a kind of literary sanction from the process of laying one gift alongside another and comparing their breadth and thickness. Miss Lovinsky was consumed with the desire to become the nurse and inspiration of a work of distinction, and her notion of accomplishing such for André Trudeau consisted in sitting before every word of his, as it were with the tongue of her mind hanging out, and to all he said yelping, "Yes, yes!" so passionately that Kenneth felt like nothing so much as taking her paws on his knees and stroking her ears.

It was to Miss Lovinsky that Trudeau had largely given over the business at which Kenneth had first discovered him, of plucking veils from between his audience and the thing he had in his mind to say. Like many another unready talker, he depended upon women so to dispose the drapery of his thought about him that they, at least, gave him credit for what he would like to have said.

And it was Miss Lovinsky who, more than anybody else, plucked all reticences from the sort of thing that in Kenneth's opinion threatened Virginia's niceness.

Next to the patter of Labor and Capitalism, in a gelid solution of which Virginia's friends lived and moved, no word was so tossed about among them as the name of Freedom. It passed from hand to hand like a crystal ball which nobody could quite see through or very far into; and when Virginia caught it in her turn, sending it high on her fine, flushed enthusiasms, he had no doubt of the crystal quality of what she handled. But when Miss Lovinsky snatched it, she was forever giving it ineffectual dabs at somebody's coat or skirt, to clear its smooth surfaces, dulled by too much handling. And by the very coats and skirts she chose, revealed specific violations of much more than the liberty Virginia had elected for herself by wearing queer clothes and talking of just whatever came into her head as if there were no reason on earth why she should n't talk of it.

Art, it appeared, in the vocabulary of the Cove, was the product of Self-Realization, from which it followed, in the course of much tossing to and fro, that for all True Realization there must be Freedom. This was Miss Lovinsky's cue for wanting to know whether women had never been truly great in Art because they had never been truly Free.

"They have been great on the stage," the playwright would remind her; and Miss Lovinsky would yelp, "True, true!"

On the stage, it was conceded, woman had asserted her right to herself, she had cast off the shackles of convention, she had been Free.

"What you say is so True," murmured Miss Lovinsky.

"Even in my little experience," — Virginia would hesitate prettily for the general commendation of her modesty, — "I feel how true it is that, for the woman who uses her personality as the medium of her expression, the great necessity is Freedom."

"She must" — the playwright laid down as an axiom — "regard the achievement of that freedom as her Contribution to the Race."

"She must enrich her personality," Miss Lovinsky solemnly agreed; "she must eliminate as a sacred obligation everything which impedes the full development of her Ego." Sometimes she said that, and at others she offered the bit about the Contribution to the Race, and it was the playwright who laid down the sacred obligation.

Nothing was further from Kenneth than to imagine that Trudeau and Miss Lovinsky had taken for themselves any of the liberties with life and behavior which their talk condoned in conspicuous members of the confraternity of art and social science. What he really feared was that, as the crystal flashed, Virginia might have a glimpse of things which it is against every code of niceness that young women shall see. What he thought he feared in her connection with "The Battle," under which name the Democratic Drama was to be introduced to San Francisco, was that she should be publicly seen in juxtaposition to things which would invalidate the claim to niceness which every instinct in him set up on her behalf.

In Nature's whole bag of tricks, nothing is prettier than this impulse to bestow on the object of our interest all the enhancing virtues; and on the whole nothing is sounder than the instinct of young women to wear with grace the qualities in which they find themselves tricked out to advantage. But Kenneth had not played with girls enough to remember that the thing that was logically expected of her was just the thing that Virginia could n't be expected to do. He went so far out of his way to find an occasion for warning her against a too public identification of her interests with Trudeau's, that he gave her time to approach the subject first and with her mind already made up.

Almost the only professional recognition young Brent had had from Miss Burke was the readiness with which, when she found herself in need of professional service, she expected him to render it on the same basis on which everything else in their long acquaintance had been rendered. It fell out quite naturally that she should give him, early in January, a commission to sell some of her Petrolia oil stock in the open market. About three thousand dollars' worth, she thought. Not that they meant to put so much into the initial production, but it would be a pity, — did n't he think? — if the play showed signs of catching on, to have it fail for want of a little extra backing.

"Then you really are going on with it?"

"My dear Ken, I thought you suggested it!"

"Your acting in it." He really had never had the courage to tell her that he had n't expected to have his suggestion taken seriously. "But is n't that enough? Putting yourself into it, I mean, without putting in your money?"

"Oh, but if it is worth myself," she triumphed, "isn n't it so much more worth money?"

"Only, if it's a failure," — he put it to her, — "you can take yourself back, but you can't take your money back."

"Why should I want it back — if it helps the Cause the way I think 'The Battle' is going to help it? I can't take back what I put into the shirt-waist strike last winter, but you have n't heard me say I want it back, have you?" She sailed far over him; he cast about for something to bring her to earth again.

"But are n't there managers who put on plays and back them? I always thought it was a regular business —" he groped.

"It is," she agreed. "A capitalist's business. That's why plays like this one —"

He saw they should never get anywhere in that direction. Once Virginia sniffed the wind of industrial conflict, she would have cast into the ring the last shred of that comfortable cloak of vested capital in which Cornelius had wrapped her.

Kenneth ventured once more, and more successfully, with the personal argument.

"You mean you don't *want* me to have this play?" She puzzled over his remonstrance. She had been so sure of him; so full of a sense of the play's importance, of the completeness of her whole performance, herself the inspiration, the backer of the play, and its vivid exponent.

"I mean I don't like the idea of your being so mixed up with this André Trudeau, acting in his play and financing him — and — everything." He finished weakly.

He was pacing up and down in her studio, as he talked, and Virginia in her swift, fearless way came straight at him. She had on one of her loose silken pinafores of wisteria silk with touches of bright cerise that matched the red of her bitten lip and the sudden flag that fluttered in her cheek.

"I don't understand what you mean — 'everything.'"

"Well, you don't know much about him," — Kenneth had already heard from Ellis how much she knew, — "and he is n't — that is, his views are n't the kind that — that — well, you know they are n't the views of people generally."

"I thought there were a good many of them your views. But I know what you mean, you mean his views on personal freedom . . . on the freedom of love."

"People might think you agreed with him" — Kenneth hastened to get it out — "if you were associated with him in business." He breathed easier, feeling that they were past the worst.

But Virginia was by no means past it. She stood working one hand in the other, her foot lightly tapping.

"Oh, they might think I agreed with him, might they? Well, would it surprise you, Kenneth Brent, to know that I do agree with him? I agree with him *perfectly!*"

"Oh, I say, Virginia —"

Really, somebody who has the interest of the feminist movement at heart ought to think out a formula by which an earnest young man can readily convey to an equally earnest young woman that, while he knows, of course, that she means absolutely everything she says, he knows at the same time that she does n't mean anything. And yet it must be a situation frequently cropping up in these days when young women are nothing if not earnest. It must, to judge from the ensuing remark, have cropped up in Virginia's experience a sufficient number of times for her to be ready with the best substitute for the formula in general circulation.

"I know what you are going to say," she forestalled him; "you are going to say that it is not what I think about such things that matters, it's what people will think about me for thinking them!"

This was so exactly what he had been trying to avoid saying, that for the moment Kenneth said nothing, and when at last he did venture found he had but blown her strangely flaming anger.

"You know what people are," he extenuated.

"Yes, I know. There are lots of them who would n't care at all for my thinking it, if only I did n't say it, and there are more who would n't mind its being said if only I stopped at saying. But there are n't any of them would forgive me if they thought I was honest enough in what I said to *live* it."

Yes, certainly the advocates of the New Womanhood have been neglectful in not providing a formula. How on earth is a thoroughly nice young man to explain to a young woman that nothing, not even the degree of honesty implicit in her living up to her Sacred Obligation of Freedom, can assail his belief in her niceness? After several fruitless attempts Kenneth fell back on the one certain note with Virginia, her natural concern for others.

"Think how your friends would feel, having you misunderstood . . . think how I should feel."

"Oh, *you!*" She moved away from him with one of those explicit native gestures which their childhood had caught from Ignacio Stanislauo, a gesture in which the tossed palm and a light puff of the breath says much better than many words, that the wind of our adversity will divide the grain of our friends from the chaff. A gesture which, besides being expressive, is, at the hands of a pretty young woman in a wisteria silk pinafore rather severe treatment for a young man who is moved at the moment by nothing so much as a proper male protectiveness.

"Of course, I know liking and respecting you does n't entitle me to anything —" he began, injuredly aloof.

"Oh," she flung out, "*liking* — liking and respect! You think that's all a woman needs . . . to be liked and respected, and to wait . . . wait . . . until some man gets done fussing about and finding what *he* likes, what *he* wants to do and can make of his life . . . and then comes and invites her into it!

"And she is n't supposed to have any feelings while she waits, nor to make anything of *her* life . . . nor to change, nor to think . . . and all she gets out of it is to be liked and respected!"

She came toward him again with such an impetus that he caught himself back-stepping to avoid her, and involuntarily put out his hand so that she came to rest against it, her soft bosom panting under its thin silk as though for the moment she had offered it in confirmation of her protest.

He was immeasurably moved, beyond his young embarrassment, by the vehemence of her outbreak, a vehemence which under his hand grew quieter and gained in intensity.

"Don't you ever say things like that to me, Kenneth, don't *you* . . . Have n't I always been the kind of girl who could be liked and respected? And what did I get for it? . . . My own kitchenmaid! . . . Do you suppose women are going on making good . . . and nothing, *nothing* certain in return!"

It was the first time she had ever spoken to him directly of her trouble, but before he could find the thing to say she had moved away from him with a dignity that touched the quick of his new perception of her as the vehicle of inestimable experience. He was moved by a remorseful sense of the waste of her treasure of young womanhood — pricked by some sense of the slight implied in our traditional setting of it aside, like a flower in a vase — conscious of inadequacy.

"It is n't true," she said, "that women are like that . . . it is n't true, Kenneth. They can't just wait . . . and wait. If they seem so, they are most of them pretending . . . and there are some of them too honest to pretend." She dropped, spent with the energy of protest on the low couch which ran along one wall of the studio; her wrung hands stretched across the cushions.

He went to her in a swift movement of contrition for all the things that women suffer at the hands of men.

"You must n't take things so hard, Virginia, — things, I say." He wanted desperately to convey to her something of his newly awakened sense of personal blame for the wastage of her loveliness, but nothing better occurred to him than to draw her locked hands upon his knee and delicately to stroke the warm inner surface of her arm where the blue vein ran into the curve of the elbow. "You must n't think I want you to pretend, ever!" he assured her.

"Oh, yes, you will, Ken; there's nobody who will want so much pretending as you." She laughed a little as if to cover the recollection of her outbreak. "I don't suppose a woman really minds pretending if she gets something out of it."

Kenneth, not knowing quite what was expected of him, and moved by more things than he could easily name, remained quietly stroking her arm.

Presently she drew it from him.

"If you were to offer that stock in Summerfield, you ought to get at least three thousand for it."

"At least that," he agreed with her.

VIII

THE taking of Anne and Ellis Trudeau to each other had been like the joining of streams on the slope of the Torr'; a flash between the willows, a riffle of foam — and there were those two setting out for the ploughed fields as if they had always known they should do just this and no other. As pretty as that and much quicker.

The acquaintance had begun at the Studio where Virginia had invited them all in for a dinner which had been sent in "hot and hot" from Campi's. Anne had put up an umbrella against the rain of suggestion as to where, and in pursuit of what entertainment, she should spend the three days of her holiday.

"I've a week's shopping to do," she protested. "You forget I'm a rancher, or at least that I'm living with one. Father needs a guardian when he gets among gardening requisites; he always wants all of them."

"I recommend you to turn all that over to my sister," Trudeau contributed; "she's farmed all the best catalogues in the State of New York, and I'll guarantee that she can lead you to the nearest nurseryman's by the sixth sense only."

Steven Brent turned on her with one of his rare smiles out of the ambush of his beard.

"If you are addicted to the pleasant vice of catalogue farming, Miss Trudeau," he said, "I shall be pleased to have you with me. When my daughter buys she buys exactly what she wants and that is the end of it; she knows nothing of the delights of indecision."

"You wait until I get my hat," — Ellis rose to him.

Anne, looking at her directly for the first time, caught the flash of an equal spirit.

"If you know what you want to do as promptly as that," she declared, "I'm not afraid you won't know what to buy."

"What she really wants," supplied André, "is an abandoned farm or an unimproved quarter-section, something she can coax and coddle and put rubbers on and dose with fertilizers — *I* know her!"

And by the time Anne's holiday came to an end it was actually determined that the visit should take place almost immediately, before rehearsals began and André would be needing her.

On the last evening of their stay, the Brents had dinner with the Rickarts at their apartment, where poor dear Fanny's place, which Mrs. Ballard had felt herself so unappreciatedly competent to fill, was supplied by the Japanese butler. It was an occasion on which the Old Man was disposed to make much of Anne, whom he toasted as the guardian angel of Tierra Longa.

Anne laughed and denied it. "It's you who are that; though I'm afraid the settlers don't always recognize your angelic quality."

"Well," he chuckled, "I'm told the devil was an angel once."

"They don't think as badly of you as that," Anne assured him; "it's only that they don't always see what you are driving at." Kenneth wondered if she were really going to try to draw the Old Man at his own table; Anne certainly was a cool one. "They'd feel a lot better just now," she went on, "if they knew whether or not Mr. Elwood is working for you."

"Why, is Elwood working them?" Rickart kept his end up lightly.

"That's just what they can't find out. If they were sure he was working for you, they'd probably think so." Anne's sally brought quick, appreciative laughter.

"It's because your power for doing them good is so enormous," Mr. Brent extenuated gently, "that they are always afraid it might be evil."

"That," said T. Rickart, "is why some people fear God."

But he reckoned without Anne if he hoped by that to turn the talk away from Tierra Longa.

"I'm apprehensive myself," she insisted; "I've a notion if you keep out of it long enough, I may be able to build that storage reservoir at Indian Gate, that father dreams of. That's why I'm keeping my eye on you."

"My dear Anne," — Rickart raised his glass to her, — "don't keep it on me too close; I might have to take you into partnership to keep you quiet."

"That," said Anne placidly, "is exactly what I'm after."

"For he is up to something," Anne insisted to Kenneth; "I can feel it when I'm with him. Now I've let him know I want to be in, and if he won't let me in through the door, I'm going to find a crack somewhere. But I've got to have something definite to go upon."

Nothing more definite having transpired, the Brents returned to Palomitas at the end of the week, with the understanding that Ellis Trudeau was to come down as soon as she could be spared, and to stay as long as possible.

The visit when it came off was, to judge by Anne's letters, in every way a success. Miss Trudeau had supplied somehow the missing element between Anne and her father, the little important things that Anne knew she missed, and ached for, without being able to lay hands on them. "I could almost put up with the brother for the sake of having her again," she wrote. And then about a week before Ellis's return, Kenneth received another and very singular letter.

There was nothing in it whatever except the urgent request that he should come down to Summerfield the next Saturday.

He was to leave, his sister wrote, by the first train after office-closing hours, which on Saturday would be at one-thirty, to have his dinner on the train, and to get off at the Saltillo Crossing. Above all he was not to mention to any one where he was going nor for what reason. Small chance, Kenneth thought, seeing he could himself form no sort of a notion. He was to be returned to the city by the Sunday night express, which would bring him back safely to office hours Monday morning.

Well, Anne generally knew what she was about. He left his bag Saturday morning at the restaurant where he expected to lunch, not to excite question by taking it to the office with him, and got away without having to account to any one but his landlady for his absence. The Saltillo Crossing was a mile or two out of Summerfield, where the county road left the town limits and began to climb toward the Draw. The distance to Tierra Longa had been shortened of late years and the road greatly improved by the use of crude oil, so that Palomitas could be reached in about four hours of steady driving. From the instruction to alight there he supposed that he was to be taken directly to the ranch, and possibly that it was not desirable that his presence should be noted in Summerfield. Accordingly, when a little after seven that evening he signaled the train to stop at Saltillo Crossing, he was not surprised to have Anne's voice hail him high up from some dim bulk of vehicle, which he presently made out to be the spring wagon, with Peters driving behind his best team of bays. They were off almost before he had seated himself in the back seat behind Anne, and it was not until the team had settled to its stride that he turned and kissed her.

It was characteristic of the odd, wordless communication between those two, which still operated in moments of crisis or tension, that Anne made no effort to relieve his mind in respect to his sudden summons. With a brief inquiry after members of the family, he relapsed into silence and the pleasures of the swift movement and the road. These were mostly of the fresh air, the country sounds, and familiar roadside scents. For the first mile or two they had the ancient, oily smell of Petrolia, then the canebrake by the water-gates, and the miles and miles of orchard beginning to drip sap from branches newly pruned. Finally, where the swell of the hills first sensibly began, he caught, off to their right in the soft dark, the rank smell of a flock and the thin trickle of wood smoke from a herder's fire. As it came to them across the open pastures it had the power to include them once more in the interests and intimacies of Palomitas.

"I did n't want you to be seen in Summerfield," Anne abruptly began. "Elwood is there . . . he filed to-day on the surplus waters of Sanchez Creek."

"Ah-ha." Kenneth indicated by the rising inflection his sense of the pertinence of this information. Sanchez Creek was one of the smaller streams that took its rise within the boundaries of Agua Caliente and poured, in wet years, its waste waters far below the fence upon the un-preëmpted plain.

"Last week," she went on, "Jevens filed on Wacoba. 'Nacio found the filing notice when he was looking for the colts that broke out of the south pasture."

"Elwood and Jevens as thick as ever?"

"Thick as thieves . . . and that's more truth than figure I'm afraid." She plunged at once into her story. Elwood had been taking options on property right and left, tossing them up and catching them again like a boy with a new ball. He had even let one or two of them drop, and the people who gave them had been tickled to death to come into a bunch of money so easily; they had simply run after him with their tongues hanging out with eager-ness to renew.

Gradually the impression had gone about that to get two or three hundred dollars on one of Elwood's options was like finding it in your Christmas stocking. He had a form all his own which he would write out in the presence of the owner, with enough nonsense in it to carry out the idea that he was just a big boy having the time of his life.

"I was talking with Willard about it," said Anne, "and he seems to think the option is a sort of gentleman's agreement, and not much good in court anyway, but I had a look at one — I just want you to see it. I've had to know something of the nature of a contract in my business, and — well — I asked 'Nacio to invite Pedro Gonzales from the Tulares to come up to-morrow and bring his option with him."

"You can be certain if Elwood puts his name to it, it's a water-tight contract for Elwood," Kenneth assured her.

The road began now to climb the hills, so that Peters could give the team its time, leaning over the back of the seat, making himself, as indeed he always had been, one of the family council, while he enumerated the properties covered by Elwood's options, and, as nearly as he could gather from general gossip, the terms for which they were given.

It was all too indefinite, however, for Kenneth to make much of. "The thing is to see one of them," he said; "I'm glad you thought of that. But the most important thing of all is to know for whom he is working, himself or Rickart."

"Ah," sighed Anne, "I was hoping you could tell us that by this time. But I can tell you one thing, and that is he is not working for the good of Tierra Longa." There was more to this, all of which was unfolded as they rounded curve after curve of the brown-breasted hills, treeless and scented with the faint suggestion of new growth and recent rains. Somehow — but nobody could trace it to its sources, Anne said, there had sprung up in Tierra Longa the impression that Elwood was about to undertake some scheme of local development which bubbled up in him and at times quite unconsciously over, and that the great plan, whatever it might be, was starred with his bright friendliness and his easy capacity for putting Tierra Longa on the map.

It had come out so naturally for the bucolic imagination that, as Elwood had lived with the land, he had become possessed of a sense of its possibilities; its voice, so compelling and to them so inarticulate, had spoken to him in terms of canals, highways, towns, so that what to the Tierra Longans had been in the nature of an enslavement, had become to Elwood the clear call to realization. It was as if they had cherished all these years, in the hope of what the valley might become, a very noble and lovely lady, too exalted for any of them to mate with, but who yet might be persuaded to look favorably on this more accomplished suitor. All the air, Anne said, was full of such cheerful prognostication for everybody but the Brents. And here, with its touch of that intrinsic feminine quality which came out in her so surprisingly at times, came Anne's own story.

From the first, she said, she had distrusted Elwood. The wind of rumor that blew up from the town had, by the time it reached Palomitas, been purged of the dust of romance with which the man's opulent personality had dazzled the eyes of the townspeople, and carried a clear tang of mischief. All this time she had never come any nearer to him than an occasional passing on the road between Agua Caliente and the ranch house. A little blunt in her immediate personal relations, Anne had, in respect to things moving at a distance, remarkable intuitions. But as if to compensate for the frequency with which her mind at the moment of grappling, failed of its intuitive perceptions, she had kept the discerning touch. However much her somewhat depersonalized intellect missed of you, her firm, warm hand seldom failed of its true report. It was an old, old secret between brother and sister that it had never been any use for Kenneth to lie to Anne once she had hold of him, and no secret at all from Anne herself that wherever she distrusted her judgment or her temper, there was nothing for it but to lay hands on the subject of her indecisions. But after all it is no simple matter for a perfect lady, such as Anne undoubtedly was, to walk up to a perfect stranger of the known temperament of Elwood, and lay hands on him. Much as she wanted a moment alone with him in which, by the sympathy of sense, to shut out all confusing impressions, she realized that it was important that such a meeting should, when it came, appear accidental. If Elwood, as she surmised, meant mischief, he would too easily be put on his guard by having a well-known business woman like Anne Brent lie in wait for him.

Kenneth could hear his sister chuckle in the dark as she told how she had finally achieved the moment of revealing intimacy. To Anne the stalking of a man's secret thought in his mind was an exhilarating sort of adventure. He had heard the Old Man chuckle like that sitting quietly at his desk, revolving his business piracies; and he was struck, through the association of that odd little note of laughter, with certain likenesses of method. Kenneth did not really believe that his sister understood what was in people's minds by touching them; he thought that she used the personal contact as a means of picking up little things that almost any person might have noticed who had a noticing disposition. He had long ago discovered that there was seldom anything known to T. Rickart which was not also known to his business rivals; it was the way in which inconsiderable items jumped together in his mind that gave him his advantage, and constituted the likeness he noted now between his sister and his employer.

Anne had discovered that when Elwood was at Agua Caliente, as he often was for two or three days at a time, he usually spent his evenings at the Company's store.

This was the supply station for the Rickart ranch and its employees and the families of a dozen or more lank mountaineers who had their cabins on the crest of the range above its fences. Sometimes the Brents sent over from Palomitas for small matters when there was not time to fetch them from the town or Summerfield.

Between the wings of the low adobe building which constituted the store, a wide, uncovered *patio* had become the lounging-place of the *vaqueros* and ranch hands, and an occasional prospector or hunter who passed that way. Here Elwood loved to loaf after the early evening meal, feeding his humor with the quaint philosophy of cow-punchers and herders. And this was the setting Anne chose for her first encounter.

It suited her better than she knew, for Anne on horse-back as she came cantering up along the Palomitas road was a taking figure. Tall and thin-hipped, the brown-laced riding-boots and the knee-length riding-coat, over brown corduroy breeches, gave her distinction. She had her mother's full bosom and the lovely Greek joining of the throat and chin, and above that her father's placid forehead with classic bands of hair folded neatly in at the nape of the neck without a trace of coquetry. As she forded the creek with the pale gold of the twilight behind her, her hat was off and the collar of her silk shirt, rolled back over the brown corduroy, revealed the tanned line of her throat.

She rode lightly with bridle dropped low and the tassel of her quirt trailing the water. As she pulled up at the outer edge of the *patio*, Elwood, in the shirt-sleeved undress of the ranch afternoon, rose instinctively, and the storekeeper, in the custom of the country, introduced them. They went all three into the store together, for that also was the custom of the country that the newcomer should be made to feel part and parcel of the occasion. Anne had counted on Elwood's interest in her as a type to engage him in conversation, but she found her work easier than she expected.

She appreciated his ready conquest of the townspeople in the instinctive, unpremeditated effort which she found herself make to stand well with him. In spite of the ravages of dissipation, the loose lip, the puffed lids, the man had quality; he moved easily as a mountain lion, his eyes glittered. Anne had made herself a quarter of an hour's errand at the store, which could have been stretched if necessary, but it wasn't necessary. Elwood was too much a man of the world, too steeped in news of the neighborhood, to have missed the right note with Miss Brent of Palomitas. One or two of the store coterie drifted past the door as Anne stood waiting the fumbling service of the keeper, and drifted away again.

Thoroughly at their ease with each other, Elwood and Miss Brent had come out of the narrow door at the same moment; the sleeve of his shirt brushed the shoulder of her corduroy with a thrill that pricked warningly along her consciousness.

Elwood was saying, "I've wanted to call on your father, Miss Brent; one hears inviting things of him — and Palomitas." He was too expert to add "and of you" so early in the acquaintance, but Anne was amusedly aware of the implication.

"Oh," she said, "Father will be pleased to see you; he has very little company. But I'm not sure of Palomitas. From what I hear of you, one should n't show you a piece of property one is anxious to keep in the family."

He laughed in his turn.

"You've heard of my little weakness. The truth is I know so little about ranches that I can't for the life of me make up my mind which one I like the best."

"Well," ventured Anne, "I'm a real-estate agent, — when I have time for being anything but my father's daughter, — perhaps I could help you." And to herself she had said, "Now let's see what he will make of that."

He made a very good imitation of boyish eagerness as he snatched at the suggestion, "Would you? I don't really know *any*thing; I've no doubt I shall get fearfully stuck. If you'd just go over a few of the most promising with me —"

"I think I see myself," thought Anne, "playing your game for you." But aloud she said, "It all depends on what you mean to do with a piece of property, whether you want it or not. If it's general farming, I recommend the Willard property, but if it's live stock —"

"The truth is," he engagingly confessed, "I'm thinking of everything. I take them day and day about, but I never get any nearer a conclusion."

"In that case," said Anne, "come and see my father. He's going in for sheep, and he has more ways than any man you ever saw for making it appear the one occupation for Tierra Longa."

"I'll come," he promised. "But I *would* be obliged to you, Miss Brent, if you'd look over some of these properties with me —"

He was doing it very well, Anne thought, but not quite well enough to pass with a woman who has had professional experiences with the *nuances* of prospective buying. "He does n't *want* any of them," she decided. Even though she liked him, perhaps because of it, she found she distrusted him more than ever.

They moved to the edge of the *patio* from which the fall of the land was toward the creek, and from that to the river. All down the boulder-strewn banks the heaps of wild vine and the buckthorn thickets were bursting full of buds. The sky was still alight, the tip of El Torre Blanco delicately glowing, but along the ground darkness crept like an exhalation. Over beyond the Saltillos lay a streak of citron-tinted cloud within which floated a silver disk of moon. The man's fluent sentiment which was at once his strength and his undoing swept them together for a moment.

He waved his arm boyishly toward the crescent wonder. "*That's* what I want . . . I've always wanted it."

"Oh, that's mine," Anne laughed indulgently, "but you may have it to play with."

Under the web of leafless vines, which spun spiderwise from tent to tent of the ancient willows, as he helped her to her horse, Anne, who more often than not vaulted lightly from the ground, scorning assistance, hesitated, broke through the hold, but took the saddle at last with her hand on his shoulder, surprised to find herself a little breathless. He kept her hand a second or two longer than was necessary, as Anne, being entirely honest, admitted to herself he had a right to do after the advances she had quite shamelessly made.

"I may come, may n't I?" he insisted.

All this, modified as one does modify things of that kind for telling to one's brother, Anne retailed to Kenneth along with her general deduction. "He does n't want a ranch," she was certain; "he is n't interested in land nor in what can be done with it. He's simply holding those properties until he can *do* something, find out *something*. That was why I thought of getting hold of one of those contracts; I thought you might make a better guess at it if you knew for how long he wants them and on what terms."

"He might n't, after all, want them for any harm to the owners. There's all sorts of moves in the game," suggested her brother. "These big operators often cover ground they've no notion of using, as a blind, or simply as a way of making themselves safe."

Anne considered that for a while in silence.

"No," she concluded at last, "he means something definite and he means it now. The man is simply bristling with mischief. You must n't try to talk me out of it, Ken; you know how it is with me . . . I would n't have sent for you if I had n't been perfectly sure." They all knew that once Anne had had her swift prevision it did n't come again, and whenever she had been overruled in it, it had always been to the family's disadvantage.

"You know how it was with them colts — " This was Peters's contribution; he had had his turn at combating what he termed "the female instinck" with male reasonableness and knew what he got by it.

Kenneth paid his own tribute handsomely. "I was n't trying to talk you out of it; I was only hoping. I must have a look at that contract to-morrow."

They were silent a long time as the horses strained up

the last pitch of the hill, and when the loosened tug and the renewed rattle of the harness marked the point at which the road began to wind down into the Draw, Anne spoke again.

"Whatever it is this time, Ken, you *must* be in with it."

He knew she was thinking of Petrolia and of all that she had sent him to T. Rickart to learn. He wondered if as long ago as that she had had one of her flashes of fore-knowledge that his chance would come at Tierra Longa.

"I'll be in," he assured her, "if I have to pry my way in with a pick."

The waning moon rose later and lighted the valley, but within the Draw they still traveled in deep shadow. Below them they could hear the soft clash of budding boughs and the creek's incessant gurgle. Here they smelled the bush lupin and there the crosiers of the fern pushing up along the water border; now the wild grape and then the Judas tree sent them wafts of sweetness. Old scents, old sounds tugged at Kenneth's sense with the one ineffable word which the spring tries to say. Somehow the place at his side which his sister filled was achingly vacant; it lacked some warm, vivifying presence which he could draw within the circle of his arm. As they crossed the Ford of Mariposa, which ran at flood, the horses stopped to drink and he thought of Virginia. He remembered, as though it were yesterday, how he had wrestled with her.

It was past the turn of the night when they drew up at the ranch house and the morning coolness had already begun to flow from the watching Torr'. Below them in the hollow of Tierra Longa a lost mist from the sea crept and fumbled.

The house lay all asleep like a crouching dog with one

eye awink at a little window. They spoke and moved softly all of them under the weight of the moonlight and the cold drag of the earth on its axis. Steven Brent, who had roused to the soft clink of the harness and the eager stamp of the horses, hungry for their stalls, came out to meet them.

Never a demonstrative man, he managed to get his arms about Kenneth's shoulders. "It's good to have you home, son," was all he said, and it seemed to Kenneth more of home than any place since as a child he had left it.

"You'll have to sleep in the west wing, Ken," his sister warned softly; "Ellis has your old room."

And for the first time he remembered that Ellis Trudeau was still his sister's visitor.

IX

WAKING late Kenneth heard Ellis singing in his mother's
garden: —

> Señor San José,
> A carpenter so fine,
> He built a pretty cradle
> All underneath a vine; —

and knew she must have learned it from 'Nacio, or his
wife singing her brown babies to sleep in the *potrero*. He
looked between the curtains and saw her moving happily
from shrub to flower, pruning a little here, loosening the
sandy loam, crooning over the seed beds. She was as
busy as a nurse and as important; presently his father
joined her and then she was the nurse, competent and
respectful, at the elbow of the visiting physician. From
little snatches of their talk which came in at the open
window while he dressed, Kenneth gathered that they
played at some such whimsical realization of themselves
in relation to the garden, and that much of her charm for
Steven Brent lay in just this capacity for taking seriously
their pleasant pretense of not being serious. They mocked
each other over the question of a water allowance for the
begonias, and they could afford to mock because they
both so pointedly did care whether the begonias had water enough, as they would have cared about a young child
or an animal.

Kenneth was not without a young man's sentimental
appreciation of the extent to which a pretty girl and a
garden set off one another. At the belated breakfast which
Anne served for him, he gave her an opportunity to ex-

tend to him her conspicuous approval at having been even remotely the occasion of bringing this particular girl and garden together.

"How long," Anne wished to know at once, "do you think her brother can spare her?"

"Not long, I imagine. There's nothing settled about the play yet, but he looks to me as if he had n't had anything since she left but cigarettes and — inspiration."

"For goodness' sake, don't tell her." Anne was alarmed. "Maybe he'll learn to appreciate her." She mused awhile chin on palm. "I'd be almost willing to put up with him here for a while, if it is the only way of keeping Ellis."

"You could n't and he would n't." Kenneth felt always bound to restrain himself in speaking of the playwright, conscious of a desire to do him something less than justice. "He thinks he loves the big, free West, but he'd die if you got him off the asphalt. And I can't see you being an inspiration to him."

Anne shrugged. "Is he any good, do you think?"

"How can I tell? That's the worst of geniuses, you can't tell until it's over."

"And by that time they may have used up several perfectly good ordinary people. Oh, well —" Anne threw it off. For that day it was the only time she could spare her brother which had not to do directly with the business which brought him to Tierra Longa.

In the middle of the morning 'Nacio brought Miguel Gonzales with the Elwood option carefully done up in several wrappings of a black silk handkerchief. 'Nacio with his Indian instinct had attached himself to the land. He had worked for Jevens and now he worked for Steven Brent. But with all his faith and affection he served

Anne. He still called her "Anne" to her face occasionally, to show that he was as good as anybody, but to every one else she was "The Señorita," the lady of the hacienda. 'Nacio introduced Gonzales as his cousin; a convenient term to cover all degrees of the complicated and far removed kinships of their kind. The Gonzales ranch was the alkalied, adobe remnant of an early grant, lying along the river flat, stiff soil and unworkable, but it carried a very ancient riparian right. The option which he produced with due regard to its preciousness was, at first glance, just the sort of thing that might have been dashed off by a man in a high good humor, so sure of himself that he could be careless of formalities, and Miguel had no uneasiness about it except such as had been engendered in his race by two or three generations of dealing with Gringos. He had already spent half of the sum he had received for it and was apprehensive lest it should, in case of any slip, be demanded back of him.

"My cousin he want to know eef Elwood not buy his ranch he mus' geeve back the *dinero?*" 'Nacio interpreted, on which point Kenneth reassured him.

"My cousin he say, eef he get any more money from Elwood? He say, Elwood gonna buy his ranch anyway?"

It is doubtful if Miguel understood Kenneth's explanation of an indefinitely renewable option, but he appeared to appreciate the opinion of a lawyer of such distinction, 'Nacio having laid it on rather thick in the family interest. To his sister Kenneth said privately, "If they are all like that, it simply means that Elwood has them tied up as long as he wants them *at the present price of property in Tierra Longa.*"

Anne, the business woman, nodded. "If anything happened, an oil strike, or an irrigation project, he could sell them out for twice or three times over what they cost him."

"Well, that's business," Kenneth reminded her.

"It *might* be oil. . . . Mr. Rickart seemed anxious that I should n't get any such notion . . . and that might be interest in me, and it might be interest in getting the first whack at it himself. But you notice, Ken," — they had the map before them, — "that every piece of property he has under option carries a first-class water right. The two he let lapse had secondary rights only."

It was all very perplexing. The Scudder boys and a neighbor of theirs called Baff came up for the midday Sunday dinner. It was Anne who had contrived that their all being there on the occasion of Kenneth's visit should seem anything but a contrivance. Baff came to consider a job of fence-building. It was the first time the Scudders had had a meal there since Addie and her husband had returned to Palomitas.

While the ranch was still running half-handed, their fashion of life was very simple. 'Nacio, who plumed himself on the title of head-shepherd, ate at home; Demetrio, who had been hired to assist at lambing-time, boarded with him. The bunk house had not been reopened. Anne and her father had their meals alone, Peters and the ploughman in the wide old kitchen, an arrangement which relieved Addie of the necessity of keeping the children up to the standard of behavior which would have been required at the Brents' table. Thus any arrangement which was demanded by Anne's own personal fastidiousness was put on a basis that salved Mrs. Peters's social sensitiveness.

"'T ain't noways right that young ones should have the burden of their elders put upon them all the time," was the way Addie explained to her family an arrangement which in their improved social status seemed to demand an explanation. But to-day the big dining-table had been pulled out its full length to accommodate the chicken dinner that was Addie's *tour de force*. After it they sat about and talked, with Anne tapping the white cloth as her mother used to do, only where Mrs. Brent had barely endured these occasional visitors, Anne studied them and their effect upon Kenneth.

It was all so like Petrolia; as if it were too much like for him to endure it, Steven had pushed back his chair almost as soon as the meal was concluded, and catching Ellis Trudeau's eye had carried her away with him to the south pasture, where on its sun-steeped slope 'Nacio was herding the first of the season's lamb-band. The Scudders smoked. Baff, who being more of a stranger was under the greater obligation to show himself at home among them, tilted comfortably in his chair, picking his teeth with one hand and stroking his ankle with the other. The conversation dropped, after some disappointing sallies on the part of Baff and Lem Scudder, — made with intent to discover what connection, if any, between Rickart and Elwood might be extracted from Rickart's junior clerk, — into the general contagion of hopefulness.

They were not, they wished Kenneth to understand, of that stripe of Tierra Longans who had been taken in by Elwood's game, rather of those to whom the fact that he *was* playing a game had been clearly established. Their superiority consisted largely in being cer-

tain that Elwood did not play with himself only, his
own amiable and — to the holders of options — profitably unstable impulses. Somewhere behind his incon-
sequence they divined the shaping hand. If the Old Man
was not the god of that machine, then it was some one
very like him; one of those half gods whose divinity is
conferred by dollars. On the whole, it seemed most likely
that the Old Man was about to satisfy the perennial expectation and "develop the property," an expectation
founded on little else than the extent to which the property loudly called for development and would so conspicuously repay it. As for those who had given options,
the spectacle of whose possible beguilement it gave them
an unadmitted feeling of superiority to contemplate, if
they lost out in a rise of prices, that was their business.
In the moment of seeing most clearly, under Anne's suggestion, what their neighbors stood to lose, Baff and the
Scudders ranked themselves, by virtue of the unchal-
lenged American right to keep your objective to yourself,
on Elwood's side.

"I allow a man's got to be mighty close-mouthed,
a-handlin' one of them big businesses," Mr. Baff gave it
as his opinion.

"I allow so," the younger Scudder gravely conceded.
"It stands to reason that whoever does develop the property has got to have something to kind of settle back on.
I allow they ain't anybody goin' to put no amount of
capital *in* Tierry Longway, without he stands to get some-
thin' *out of it*."

"The way I dope it out is this," Mr. Baff explained to
the company; "the proper play when anybody like this
Elwood comes pussy-footin' about, is n't to fall *for* him

the way them river ranchers did, but to fall *in* with him. There ain't anything he can do to the price of land in the valley that he can keep all to hisself."

"I allow you said an earful," Lem Scudder agreed, judicially tapping out his pipe on his boot heel. "If it pays Elwood an' his friends to hold on to that much farmin' land, I reckon it'll pay some of the rest of us."

The company lapped itself in complacency; — all but Peters, who exhibited signs of having the case of them colts still on his mind and was heard to rumble throatily about the female instinck.

Anne checked him. Last night in the dark it had been easy to win credence from Kenneth, but what could she say in broad day to Lem Scudder and a man called Baff which would not look ridiculous. And there was nothing Kenneth could say which would not be read as pique at not being himself wholly in the Old Man's confidences.

"So far as I can make out," — Baff voiced the general sentiment, — "we ain't got no call to mistrust Elwood *pusonally*. There ain't anything he's done which is out o' the ordinary way o' doin' business. He's smart as they make 'em; you have to keep in with them Capitalists; but it looks like *pusonally* he's an all-right fellow."

"He sure is," — Lem capped the situation. "He's a regular fellow."

Peters, not to be wholly silenced, contributed something. "We got this ag'in' him, that he's thick with Jevens."

"Oh, well, now," — Baff extended a large tolerance. "We only got Jevens's word for how thick they are. Jevens drives him an' Elwood pays for it. It's my opinion," — Baff had the air of offering this modestly, but with the conviction that the company was very much mistaken if they did n't come to it, — " it's my opinion that if Elwood did n't do more than hire Jevens to black his boots for him, Jevens would give out that they was intimate." With which stroke of wit the whole question appeared, for the time being, to be disposed of.

It was like nothing so much as the meetings of the Homestead Development Company in Petrolia. As a boy Kenneth had derived a vast sense of affairs from those sessions about his father's table; now he perceived that, like them, these men of Tierra Longa plotted without knowledge and imagined childishly. They were as much the victims of their own limitations as they were likely to be of the machinations of Rickart or Elwood.

That earlier experience, as well as the recent extension of his vision over the field of Labor, had prepared him for the revelation of this moment, which rose upon him out of his own hesitances and resentments as a reflection from below the horizon is lifted on the heated air of summer.

For he liked these men and understood them: the instinct which made them look to the land for their living, their impulse to fall in behind the Old Man, to be herded and led by him; taking rank with the old tribal impulse that had driven Brent himself to take service with Rickart, and the instinct which pulled him back, at any pause in his allegiance, to Palomitas. Facing the certainty of their defeat by the very elements which made them good farmers, producers rather than players of the game, all Kenneth's young contempt for unsuccess went from him as the tide from a rock. The difference between what they fancied lay behind Elwood's schemes and what his experience taught him was Elwood's likeliest motive, gave to inevitable defeat the quality of ancient tragedy; the tragedy of men defeated, not squalidly by other men, but by forces within themselves which had the form and dignity of gods.

Such an interpretation of the situation did not yet shape itself in words; it lay all about him in the warm light and air which came in through the open door, the scent of the Banksia rose over it and of the fresh-turned earth of the garden beyond. It was so mixed with the associations which had freed the vision in his mind, that for a long time he was not able to think of it without at the same time recalling the flick of Ellis Trudeau's dress across the pastures and the image of Baff rocking complacently on two legs of his chair, his thumbs in his armholes. And because it was still so formless he was not even able to produce it to offset Anne's own notion, which she put to him succinctly when the session had broken up at a sign from her to Peters.

"There's nothing you can do *against* him that Elwood wouldn't turn somehow to his advantage," she said. "That man Baff is right when he says the only thing to do is to go with him. And Lem Scudder is right when he says that if it is to Elwood's advantage to hold property in the valley, it's equally to yours to hold the same kind. Now it is perfectly plain that what Elwood is after is water, and the only unappropriated water in the valley is the river surplus. You must file an appropriation notice to-day."

"The river surplus!" Kenneth found the proposal staggering in its simplicity. Thousands of cubic feet of water over and above what was claimed by the local ditches ran to waste every season, on wet years it reached even to the sea, and it was on this waste that any scheme for reclamation of Tierra Longa lands must be calculated. As the laws of the State were then, the surplus waters could have been claimed by any person making an appropriation of them according to due form, and could be held as long as the appropriation was shown to be based on actual use of the waters.

"I don't know why Elwood hasn't filed on it himself, unless it is to avoid suspicion. He'd have to begin work in sixty days, and that would be such a give-away."

"Well, I'd have to work it too," Kenneth objected.

"I know. We'll have to risk it. You notice that those options were for six months; some of them have already been given for two or three; I think whoever is back of Elwood is about ready to strike, and we can't risk their getting ahead of us.

"You can make your appropriation just below the Tierra Rondo Gate. Father says we can get the water from there onto the land below the Ridge, and it's all Government land in between." She went on explaining the practicability of her suggestion. "You've two months' leeway, before you have to make a beginning, and it won't cost more than a few hundred dollars to hold it for the first year. At the worst I can carry it for you for as long as that."

"Then why not you do the filing?"

Anne shook her head. "Mr. Rickart has been awfully decent about the mortgage. I'd not like to cross him; he'd take it harder from a woman. But if you do it, — don't you see? — you will be sort of in with him; you can put your interests in his hands, make it a favor to him."

"I don't know that he'll take it so much of a favor for one of his employees to block his plans." Kenneth was merely beating about for time: the whole proposal had taken his breath away.

Anne was prompt with him. "Don't you see that the point is that you *don't* know that it is his plan. Not yet. And if you make it plain to him that you did n't know, he'll think it clever of you to have put a spoke in Elwood's wheel. It's perfectly simple. You come down here for a visit and find Elwood up to *something*, and you just take a hand on general principles. A man is entitled to take an interest in his home town. And then, if it turns out that Rickart is interested, you can put yourself on his side. . . . He'd be hopping mad if Elwood really is doing anything here without his knowledge. . . . Whatever happened you must be on Rickart's side. Oh, Ken, —" she was vexed at his slowness, — "have n't you had enough of going *against* him?"

She was so right as Rightness is viewed in the business world . . . but there was more than the slower pace of his mind that divided them. He wished to say something of what had been in his thoughts a few moments before, of being on the side of the ranchers, of using his knowledge of the Old Man's methods, not to his own interest, but to serve the larger claim. Before the thing could shape itself in words, Anne swept it away with the details of her plan.

"I've all the papers in the house. You can't do anything to-day, Sunday, but if you post your notice a few minutes after midnight, Peters can still get you to the Express . . . it's nearly all downhill . . . and you've ten days in which to get to Westerville to the recorder's office. You can manage that, can't you?"

"I can send it to the recorder by mail," he admitted.

The point at which the water appropriation was to be made, just crossed the line into another county of which Westerville was the county seat. It began to look really plausible.

Anne sighed with relief. "After all there may be nothing in it. . . . It's queer how everything that goes on in Tierra Longa always seems so important. . . . Anyway, we might as well have that water right in the family."

It was when they went out to look for their father that she proposed that he should go up to the gate before dark and look for the point at which the notice of appropriation should be posted. "I've made a monument," she said, "but you'll never find it in the dark unless you know where to look for it." And after a moment she added, "Take Ellis with you — no, she won't know unless you tell her. She's fond of riding; and anyway, she's company." Then, as they caught sight of the girl and Steven Brent hovering over the season's new plantings in the orchard, she added: "It's wonderful how they get on together. She understands things in him that I wouldn't have thought of." Kenneth had no clue to the momentary sadness that shadowed her. He did not know that there was always a fear in the back of Anne's mind that she might miss her father as her mother had missed him. Manlike, he shared his father's feelings that they had missed understanding their mother. "After all," Anne concluded without relevance, " you are the one that's like father."

Anne carried their visitor back to the house, and father and son walked between the young almonds and the olives.

At the bottom of the orchard they were stopped by the

waters of Vine Creek which ran a slender stream of overflow from the ditch as the sign of a wet season. Far below
they marked the shining waste of the river, and heard
as always the clear call of the empty land to be put to
human use. But though they were nearer than they had
ever been to realization, they said next to nothing. It was
just as they were turning back toward the lambing corral that Brent spoke almost lightly, "So you're going to
get into the big game, son?" He had taken it for granted
that Anne's counsel would prevail; and Kenneth gave him
Anne's answer.

"It may not come to anything . . . but, anyway, we'll
have that water right in the family."

"That's the way to go at it," Brent approved. "And
do it while you're young, so if you find you can't play the
game it won't quite ruin you."

Kenneth opened his mouth to say what had recently
come into his mind, that he might have a better chance
to play it successfully if he played it for the people of
Tierra Longa instead of for himself, but it swept over him
suddenly that just such protective impulses must have
moved his father toward Jim Hand and Pop Scudder. At
the bottom of that experience at Petrolia must have lain
something of the same desire to cover their lack with his
own larger outlook, and the sick result of leading them out
of their own restricted field to a more signal disaster.
Checked in his motion to speak of what he now realized
would have led chiefly to painful memories, Kenneth
slipped his arm within his father's and was rewarded with
a cordial pressure, and the evidence that they had been
nearer in their thoughts than he might otherwise have
imagined.

"I doubt you are too much like me to play the game according to the rules," said Steven.

Kenneth gave the arm a boyish squeeze. "I don't know what you think you are, Dad, but I'm glad I'm like it."

"Oh, well," the elder Brent laughed as he led the way to the lambing corral, "for one thing, I'm a first-class sheepman." For an hour the talk was all of the lambing and the chances of the spring market.

All this time something at the back of Kenneth's mind was busy with the personal problem. Was there, then, no middle ground between being the kind of a man T. Rickart had become and the sort that was fleeced by him? If gifts like Rickart's had n't notably been used for the advantage of the tribe, was it in the nature of things that they could n't be? Was a man like his father, too intelligent to rank with the Hands and the Scudders on the one side, and too fine to be ranged with the Old Man on the other, to become, as Steven Brent had been for the past ten years, neither bird nor beast, but batted about between them? Preoccupations like this, together with his real interest in the details of his father's business, quite put out of mind his promise to take his sister's guest riding until he was reminded of it by seeing Peters bringing up the horses for saddling. He excused himself then with Brent's quick approbation.

"It's I should make excuses," he said; "I must be getting an old codger, not to remember that you would want some time with your young lady. Oh," — he put out an excusing hand as Ken's exclamation protested the possessive, — "it's only my way of saying how heartily I endorse her."

"But she's not . . . but it is n't . . ." Kenneth found himself unaccountably blushing. "Miss Trudeau is Anne's friend; we're hardly more than acquainted."

"I beg your pardon" — Brent himself colored; "I thought something your sister said . . ." Not for the world would Steven Brent have intruded into the personal life of his children. "It's probably my mistake, I find her so utterly charming. . . . However, there's no harm done."

"I hope you have n't —" Kenneth began. He was furious with Anne; it was n't like her to be silly.

"Oh, dear, no," — Brent laughed a little; "I was only thinking how I must have bored her; I've talked of you more than a little."

It was not a fortunate frame in which to set out for a ride with a nice girl, to feel the possibility of having been put in a fatuous position. He wondered if the fact that she had been bored accounted for the circumstance that as they rode out by the Agua Caliente Gate, she did n't seem in the least interested in him. She asked a thousand questions of the land and the trail and the new life that came crowding to her quick, excited notice, but she displayed none of the consciousness of his being an extremely nice young man to which the nice girls he had met — at places where he had boarded, for example — had accustomed him. He recalled now that he had never talked much with Miss Trudeau except about Virginia and her brother, and he was piqued to realize that she had so successfully all this time kept from him what his father and Anne had found in her.

It was almost as if she had n't thought him worth it. She had disguised herself within her interest in that gifted pair almost as completely as her slender figure was muffled in the riding-skirt which he recognized as one of Anne's, too big for her. He tried to think that he probably had n't noticed her more because of an unfeminine lack of that desire to please which in the rather restricted society to which a young man boarding in the city is admitted, was the recognized hallmark of thoroughly nice young womanhood. He would have thought something like this if she had given him time to think much of himself or her, but she wanted immensely to know; she must have everything named and placed for her and related to the life at Palomitas. He told her the names of plants and their natures; all that he could remember of the lore of childhood.

"Oh," she breathed, full of a child's delight, "only 'Nacio tells me things like that." And it suddenly tickled the native humor of the junior clerk of T. Rickart to find himself ranked flatteringly with his father's head shepherd. Presently he found her a horned toad, and before he let it go again to lose itself in the clean mesa dust, he said a little charm which 'Nacio had taught him, after which, if you turned the toad about three times and looked closely in the direction he scrambled off, you were sure to find an Indian arrow point; and sure enough when they looked, as Ellis insisted on getting down from her horse to do, they found a small, shapely point of obsidian quite perfect except for one corner gone. A few minutes later they went in by the way of the burrow of a brooding elf owl and past the downy owlets to come quite out on the other side in the land of fairy wonder.

Neither Agua Caliente nor Palomitas lands were touched by the river, which rose in another country and burst through into Tierra Longa about a mile above the

Brent ranch where one of the roots of the Torr' showed in a great basalt dike. Above this point lay the little round valley of Tierra Rondo, from which the river had once poured in a cascade over the dike which dammed it, but now tunneling under tall chaparral it came out between basalt pillars, the ruined buttresses of the ancient dam known as "Indian Gate." There was a tale about those two pillars, of which most people had forgotten everything except that they were Warrior and Maiden, and had stood there so long that four-hundred-year-old oaks had rooted in their crevices and climbing vines had masked all but their tall, crested heads.

From the foot of the gate the water poured in a white torrent over the rubble of the broken dike to reach the floor of Tierra Longa, and it was from the top of this torrent along the middle mesa level that Steven Brent had always thought the river could be led around the front of the Torr' and turned into the upper valley lands. Once the gate was shut again by a concrete dam, Tierra Rondo would resume its ancient use as a lake bed for the stored waters of the river, which now ran all at large in a wide, shallow gorge far seaward, and in wet years mingled its freshness with the tide.

It was late in the afternoon when young Brent and Ellis Trudeau came, with slack rein and shining eyes, across the middle mesa to the foot of the gate, an afternoon in which they had by some divine chance recaptured the old magic of young wonder. They were so touched with it that they scarcely disturbed by their coming the brisk, small life of the mesa; they answered the burrowing owls and were answered by them as their own kind. Hand in hand they climbed up the buttresses of the gate to look

down on Tierra Rondo, stiff with chaparral, blue with
wild lilac, and filled with airy shadow. From the Warrior's very shoulder they made a fire to signal the un-
numbered fairy tribes . . . all of which takes time, as does
also lying close together and face downward on the brink
of a vine-covered ravine to watch the raccoons playing
tag and "king's excuse" in the hollow, so that it was much
too late to have kept a nice girl out riding by the time
they rode back again to Palomitas.

"It's all my fault," Kenneth called out to Anne, who
was looking for them down the Caliente road a little
anxiously. He thought it a pity the girl's fun should be
spoiled by being blamed for anything. "Ellis wanted to
come back an hour ago, but I made her climb to the top
of the Warrior." And in an aside, to make everything perfectly secure, he said, "I had the deuce of a time finding
your old monument." Then at something in his sister's
face, to himself he added, "Confound it, I don't see why
I can't call her Ellis if the rest of the family do it."

He had another long conference with Anne after supper, and finally a little before midnight Peters drove him
by the river to the precise spot agreed upon so that he
might post his notice with the first tick of Monday morning, and from there on to the Saltillo Station. The next
morning at nine-thirty he was sitting at his desk at Rickart's and nothing whatever appeared to have happened.

X

It was a week or ten days before he saw Ellis Trudeau again, the evening after her return from Palomitas, and the first word he heard from her was a reproach.

"Oh, why did n't you tell me!"

"Tell you —?" His mind flashed back over the lapsed days for the source of the real anxiety that rang in her fresh young voice.

"My poor Andy — he is looking dreadfully!"

Kenneth had run across them at Gianduja's, Virginia and the playwright, dining with two or three others whose air of being habituated to the public eye gave to their appearance here, in the undistinguished character of diners, an almost undress effect, as if they had been caught stripped of some indispensable garb of manner without which they should not be looked at too closely. Ellis, he could see, was not looking at them, but sitting more than ordinarily detached from the group, her eye brighter and her cheek warmer for weeks in the open. Roving the long room of Gianduja's for some more attractive food for her attention, she had drawn him to her side before the others had looked up or become aware of his entrance. Directed by her glance, Brent took stock of the playwright and admitted that he did, indeed, display a degree of gauntness, a nervous distraction more than the part required.

"He smokes too much," Kenneth assured the sister, hoping devoutly this would content her. He would have been at a loss to explain his own feeling for Trudeau as a man consuming himself by emotions too pretentious for the slim restraints of his personal constitution. He could not have explained anything that he might be feeling about the playwright at that moment without touching on the source of a new and deep resentment against Virginia.

He had come up from Palomitas with the new light on his own problem shed by the reappearance of his boyish dream above his horizon, aching to establish it more solidly in line with his future by means of those long, intimate conversations with a young person of the opposite sex, in which, though nothing is clear, everything appears to be wonderfully cleared up.

Always a little baffled by his sister's more swiftly moving mind and incisive methods, Kenneth felt that he had been yoked to the Palomitas scheme without having come into fruitful relation to it, but he was not without appreciation of the extent to which it might yet divert him from the ends which he thus far pursued. The law as a profession meant very little to him. If, at the time, the Old Man had suggested that he study medicine or mechanics, he would have gone at it with the same clear simplicity and doubtless have passed as creditable examinations. As affairs were arranged at the office, he had become, as he himself recognized, a sort of legal detective, a searcher of records, a trailer of clues. The best of his work came to him through contact with T. Rickart, who, liking to have this clean, personable youth about him, and moved paternally to do the best by his son's chum, had made use of him on semi-confidential errands, loosing him now and then for some executive flight over the field of his unlimited enterprises.

But for the last year a latent restlessness, the thing that had made him susceptible in the first place to all that Virginia's new range of interest offered him, had reached the point of demanding something more personal and explicit.

Competent as Rickart's hand was at the reins of his life, Kenneth felt the normal young man's desire to shape something, even a poor thing, but his own. Power, the sort of power the Old Man had, of driving men before him in herds, of rounding on them, fleecing them, and scattering them again to depleted pastures, made no appeal to him. He did somehow see himself, in his prophetic fancy, as the hope and center of the harmonious group, the leading citizen, the head of the family.

It is not young women only who walk companioned by little feet, warmed in their young imaginings by hands thrust invisibly into theirs. The dream of fatherhood in young men is as sacred and endearing, possibly as explicit. Kenneth had a way with children; Addie's oldest adored him. As he walked a week ago in the camisal a whistle would bring 'Nacio's young brood to trot in his trail like amiable brown puppies, and it was so in his dreams that he saw himself, accompanied and companioned. Now, by his actual proprietary contract with Tierra Longa, a background had leaped out in the picture with a wealth of detail that led him to suspect that it had always lurked somewhere in the unmapped region of his future. And all of it inextricably mixed with Virginia. He did not relegate her to any specific place in the picture, but he could not clear it of their long-established intimacy.

He had, by his brief dip into the past, been reimmersed

in the old relation in which the ascendancy of her mind over his had passed without question, and was never so near the point at which she could have snatched it from him as of old she had snatched every suggestion, to make it into the serious drama of their lives. And by her failure so to take it she had disappointed, not only the expectation of their established intimacy, but the honest expectation every young man has of every likable young woman, that she will become, on any appropriate occasion, the oracle and intimation of his destiny.

But this was hardly the sort of thing he could say to the sister of the man to whose totally irrelevant affairs he owed his check with Virginia.

"He smokes too much," he said, "and does n't take exercise enough in the open."

"Andy loathes exercise," she sighed, "and taking his breakfasts in restaurants. I suspect he's been going without any. And all this worry about the theater has been so wearing." She dropped again to the note of gentle reproach. "You ought to have told me."

"But I thought," Kenneth protested, "that that was all arranged; that" — he glanced at her dinner companions — "the rehearsals were already started."

"Oh, they'll go on with it, even if they have to build a theater themselves to give it in," she assured him.

The tension of the trades union fight was at that moment at its tightest; when it had become known, through Miss Lovinsky's rather injudicious flaunting of it in the papers, that "The Battle" was supposed to strike the very roots of Capitalism, there had been difficulties; difficulties which, it must be admitted, had been made the most of by the Friends of Labor as an evidence of their being taken seriously. "Virginia is so — so gallant," was Ellis Trudeau's tribute to the spirit in which the question of a proper stage and auditorium had been met.

Opposite them at the table which was reserved for Virginia's coterie, he recognized the man who had been engaged to play the lead with Virginia — of whom nothing could be said except that he was the sort of actor who might be found looking for employment so far from the Rialto of New York — and Dickman, the producer, who had been a figure in the theatrical world of more than local reputation. For the reason why he was not still ranked with the great names of the stage, one had to seek no further than the man's drink-fogged countenance, or the faded, pretty face of his wife, turned to him now with a confidence nobly supporting itself beyond the evidence of failure. It was so much a younger sister to the look that he had marked often in Ellis Trudeau, that, moved by his old disgust for the sort of flabbiness that needed so to be supported by the love and faith of women, Kenneth began, quite deliberately as his dinner was served, to draw off her attention from the others and engage it in a report of the progress of the season at Palomitas.

They kept the talk there easily for half an hour, question and animated answer as to the flooding of the creeks, the number of new lambs, and the first appearance of mariposa lilies in the *potrero*. Finally, poised before the subject as if the slightest intimation on his part of a wish not to speak of it would send her flying in the opposite direction, Ellis ventured: "That Mr. Elwood called on your father."

"On Anne, you mean." He gave her a fleet look of intelligence, sure by the "that Mr. Elwood" that Anne had told her much. He was collecting information about the sheep business, Ellis told him.

"Much he cares for the sheep business," Kenneth laughed; "the kind he fleeces are two-legged."

The girl nodded, smiling slightly. "He's a mighty well-informed man," she said; "he was informed about your visit, and about that ride we took Sunday." She added demurely to the quick interrogation of his eye, "I told him my brother was a writer and I was collecting Indian legends."

"True, true . . ." Kenneth laughed out.

But her folded lips held something more of amusement. "Anne offered to take him to see the Warrior."

"Oh, by Jove, that was a stroke!" He could see how Anne's quick wit would see the advantage in making the invitation, and how she would take Elwood wide of the point at which his appropriation notice still stuck among the lupins. "I suppose my sister must have told you something of what is afoot," he supplemented.

"Not much, but enough — I think it is glorious!"

This was grateful. He hardly realized how little Anne would have left to tell after that Sunday under the Warrior.

"It's going to mean a lot to me —" His legal caution reasserted itself: "some time I'd like to talk it over with you."

They were claimed the next moment by some noisy discussion which broke out about Virginia's end of the table. In any case it would have been impossible to keep wholly outside the whirl of Virginia's excited interest.

Quite beyond calculation they found themselves swept up and relegated to their proper places as audience to her

rôle, admitted on all sides, to furnish a singular peril for
the onlooker. Kenneth would have let himself go much
further in the direction that the new red of Virginia's lip
and the new flash in her eye signaled him, had it not been
for the evidence offered him on every side that André
Trudeau was there before him.

Modified as it was by recent association, Kenneth's general view of the conduct of life for young ladies ran true to
form and divided the quality of appreciation by the number of the audience. To a personal and excluding view
Virginia, flushed from rehearsals, relaxed and, tender with
spent emotion, would have enchanted; passed about from
Lawrence the actor to Dickman the producer, smacked
and savored, she savored of nothing so much at last as
commonness.

And Trudeau was always about; he appeared almost
to live at the Studio, — "sprawled" there, Kenneth expressed it to himself, though there was really nothing in
the way Trudeau sat or stood to justify the note of disgust. It was rather in the effect he had of having settled
himself on Virginia like some sea creature of a formless-
ness that permitted its complete adjustment to the environment. To Kenneth, whose character was still stiff
with young intolerance, the spectacle was not a pretty
one. It was rendered positively objectionable by the
extent to which Virginia was taken in by it, accepting
Trudeau's temperamental preciousness as an excuse for
much the fellow must have been male enough to know had
quite another genesis; whether or not he was man enough
to admit it.

And yet every attempt of Kenneth's to interpose a
restraining consideration resulted somehow in his being

more than ever bound to the wheel of Virginia's progress as a woman of genius. It was not, however, until within a week or ten days of the first night of the production that he gave over attempting it. He had come to the Studio hoping to have Virginia to himself for an hour, only to find Trudeau, Miss Lovinsky, and the others ensconced there, cutting wide swathes in the theory of human behavior in the interests of what they conceived as artistic freedom. They had worked through the Cosmic Consciousness and the Development of the Ego, and the playwright had just laid it down as the last word in Modern Thinking that there can be no True Realization without Experimentation. As if this marked the point beyond which the feebler feminine spirits could not follow him, the conversation dropped off to a general murmur in which the voice of Miss Lovinsky, offering the names of Wells, Ellen Key, and Gorky, was the only intelligible item. As if it marked, too, the limit of what Kenneth could patiently hear, he had risen and walked to the far end of the room, looking out through a little window there across the flat, intervening roofs, at the Bay's blue and amber. Fresh and flowing it looked, flecked with great sails, and must have moved him had he not been too much moved at the moment by inarticulate annoyance. And in a moment his resentment went from him at a touch, as Virginia came in her old way straight up to him and laid her fingers lightly on his breast.

"I'm sorry you think so badly of my acting, Ken."

"But I don't! I don't see why you say that!" He protested against the suggestion of giving pain by an opinion which he obviously had n't expressed. "I have n't even seen it!"

"That's just it. You have n't been to a single rehearsal. If you would come and see what it means to me, what I am trying to do with it, you'd be more — sympathetic. I wish you would come, Ken." That was Virginia. She had everybody playing her game just by being genuinely unhappy if you did n't play it.

"It is n't your acting —" he began. He meant to tell her it was Trudeau that he could n't endure, but he began badly. "I know you don't care a rap for my opinion —"

"It's because I do care," she caught him up. "I care ever so, Kenny. That's why I hate so to have you misunderstand me — and my friends. I don't always follow them; they're miles beyond poor me; but I've gone far enough to realize that artists must make sacrifices, often of things they'd really rather believe and be . . . that is, if they want to accomplish anything." She played with the button of his coat and there was a faint suggestion in her sagging hand of instinctively and unconsciously seeking his support. "We women have to go so fast these days . . . People don't always seem to realize that when a woman finds herself carried out beyond what she was brought up to believe in . . . that she sometimes . . . suffers, Ken."

She let him go at that, gathering herself against her womanly weakness. "There'll be a full rehearsal Tuesday. I wish you would come, Ken."

There was no doubt about it, when Virginia gave her whole mind to the part of a woman of genius, she did it very well. In his heart Kenneth knew that he should not be able to keep away from the rehearsal.

In keeping with the pretensions of Democratic Drama, real workingmen had been secured for the strike scenes, which rendered night rehearsals obligatory. Accordingly, when Kenneth found his way into the theater, which actually had been hired with very little difficulty after the first flourish of opposition, he found a considerable audience of supers already collected, filling the pit and being herded on and off the stage in the interest of the mass effect. Virginia, in her character of leading lady, was keeping herself sacredly apart. Avoiding Miss Lovinsky, who as press agent sat about snapping up tidbits of appreciation with her customary eager yelps, Kenneth made out Ellis Trudeau sitting apart in one of the boxes and joined her there.

He thought she looked less well than when he had last seen her and was struck with the fact that he really had n't seen her since the meeting at Gianduja's and said as much. She seemed constrained; said that the rehearsals made great demands on her; that she had all her brother's notes to take, and tapped her stenographer's book to point her excuse. She came back to that book after some desultory talk about the progress of the play, showed him her neat shorthand, and asked if he thought she could get something to do in that line.

"I take all Andy's dictation and type all his manuscripts. I can really spell." She was both shy and anxious. "I should like to earn something."

"But with the success that everybody says the play is going to be —" he began.

She cut in hastily. "All the more if it's a success; they'll take it on the road. Nothing will stop Andy; he'll head straight for Broadway." She seemed to wish Brent to take it for granted that she was to be left behind, but before he could take up the point with her the full rehearsal was called.

Kenneth wandered about, viewing it from different angles of the house, interested in the unfamiliar technique, but unable to get any thrill from the performance. He thought it distinctly unpromising, and was surprised to find that others felt that progress had been made. The cast, made up as it was of chance-met material, he judged not particularly a good one, but it at least brought out to advantage Virginia's unpracticed vigor. He guessed that the professional actors rather resented her, and none of them were especially pleased with their lines. Trudeau sat beside his sister, gabbling corrections and alterations, and at times affectedly tearing his hair.

Dickman went about with a lighted cigarette continually adrip from his lips, exhaling alcoholic fumes; Kenneth saw Ellis Trudeau shrink once as he bent over her.

There was a vast amount of propaganda in the lines, which the workingmen supers duly applauded as it came, and so contributed to the sense that the play was really getting on very well. It ended indeed, for them on a triumphant note to which Kenneth could scarcely rise, and after waiting about for a time for producer and playwright to be done with Virginia, he found himself instead walking home with Ellis Trudeau. They talked very little and that little was all about the chances of her getting paid employment.

As he thought this over later, it struck him as singular. Kenneth had drawn up Virginia's contract with Trudeau and knew that, in addition to royalties, he was to receive a sum for directing the production. Brent had supposed, on no better authority than his client's, that this was right and customary. It appeared from his knowledge of the contract, that the success of the play would make

Trudeau independent, and his sister's sudden and importunate sally after employment, on the very eve of that event, added one more twist to his feeling of being at last at grips with the complicated process of modern living. Before he had time to do more than think it over, Anne added a turn to the screw in a letter in which she practically commanded him to bestir himself to find Ellis a situation.

He went then for the first time to call on her at her lodgings, and was so moved by the poor plainness of it that he forgot to be vexed with Anne for overlooking the embarrassments which might easily beset a young man in search of employment for a pretty girl of his acquaintance. But if Ellis suffered any embarrassment in his calling so, it was not for any impression that was made on him by her environment. She had none of the traditional attitudes of a young lady forced to seek humble employment, neither bright bravado nor self-pity nor the fine pretense of economic independence. She wanted typewriting or stenography to do because she wanted primarily to get out of her present situation, and wanted it with a desperation that nothing Kenneth knew of that situation could explain. She was so bent upon it that she had neglected to think that her urgency might have to be explained, and accepted gratefully his suggestion that her willingness to be left behind by her brother grew out of her love for the West and a wish not to leave without a deeper draught of it.

She was very reasonable about her chances of getting work, full of practical suggestions which uncovered, affectingly for the young man, the extent to which her clear surfaces, which he had mistaken for the placid niceness generic to young ladies, mirrored an ever-present anxiety.

And in the mean time, her quiet acceptance of the severances to be wrought by the success of her brother's play, brought him face to face with the loss out of his own life of Virginia. For Virginia was so much a part of his life that he had accepted, as part of the universal scheme of things, her reappearance in it just as the adjustments of his own business gave him leave to attend to her. He had found, after the first strangeness, that the things which she had been doing in the interim — getting married and divorced — had scarcely affected the renewal of their relations, had been no more than the temporary diversion of interest which must be allowed to young women when their young men are battling for support and professional standing. Anne had said that Virginia had married because there was n't anything else for her to do, and in a way Anne was right.

Lively girls like Virginia had to be up to something. . . . Here she was now "up to" this play. And suddenly the play promised to develop a vitality capable of snatching her away from him bodily into those regions from which so recently he had recovered her.

Daily intimations of such an issue of "The Battle" multiplied. The newspapers had been disposed to be interested in Virginia, her beauty and supposed talent, and to exaggerate the quality of social success from which she had turned to become a Friend of Labor, and to be silent about her divorce, of which possibly they had n't heard. Labor was interested. Local organizations bought advance seats *en bloc*.

Capital was interested. The one-eyed organizer having

reappeared on the Coast, Trudeau had offered him a box and Virginia had daringly offered Frank another. Frank had accepted the dare; he was giving a box party in honor of Miss Rutgers of New York. Miss Rutgers, fully alive to being in the West where one did a great many things one would n't have thought of doing at home, was tickled with the idea of being a patron of Democratic Drama; and whatever Miss Rutgers of New York did, a great many people in San Mateo and Burlingame did also. So the tide rose triumphantly.

And after all, the play failed. Not all at once, with merciful certainty. It flared up at first with the brave show of "Society" and the thunder of a packed house, Labor loudly applauding everything that Labor approved. But under it was heard the faint snicker of Capital at the Mumbo Jumbo caricature of itself, and under the damping effect of the next morning's press the flare died down in a gray smudge. It appeared that Trudeau did n't have a play and that Virginia could n't act.

She gave, *The Chronicle* admitted, an excellent imitation of herself, which had the sole advantage of being an imitation of a very charming person. The *Examiner* dubbed it a second-rate piece of self-exploitation, and the play a mere lumpy mass of propaganda unenlivened by crude melodrama.

Biting criticism, easily explained on the ground of a Capitalistic bias; but unhappily Capital, which had gone with one hand up to guard and the other for defense, came away with both hands comfortably in its pockets, to send its friends to see the show, — "So perfectly naïve, you know."

By the third night the snicker was fairly audible in the

audience and Labor began to wonder if after all it hadn't been made to look the fool.

Kenneth, who, in the deceptive glow of the first night, had tendered his congratulations with a queer clutch at his heart, dared not go to Virginia. He was indignant for her, and relieved, and considerably mixed as to his own relation to the incident. He called instead on Ellis Trudeau to tell her about a place that was vacant with Kline and Kauser, brokers. He found, in the hint of the inexplicable in her attitude, something which matched his own secret trepidation.

"It has n't come home to him yet," she said, admitting without preamble all that Kenneth's polite inquiry about the author of the play implied. "And naturally I have n't the heart to force it on him. All I'm hoping for is that they can keep it going till he finds out for himself; he's quite capable of finding out, you know, and of taking it off because it is n't worthy of him."

Kenneth saw that her affection had hit upon the saving note in the situation. "Ah," he said, "we must do what we can to keep it going."

"It depends, of course, on whether Virginia—on what she thinks of it."

"That's just the point; how does she take it?"

"Oh, I hoped you could tell me." He saw a dull flush rise unaccountably along her cheek. "They have such different ways of looking at things — Andy's friends — you never can tell. But she could n't have meant anything unkind . . . It's the way she really would feel . . . that it was heroic, advanced . . . Miss Lovinsky, I mean."

"Miss Lovinsky?"

"She was here yesterday, full of something. . . . Andy

did n't see her — Oh, you must believe he would n't have
had anything to do with it . . . to make use of her trouble
that way! As if it were n't bad enough for her husband to
leave her, without making an advertisement of it —"

"What!"

"Oh," — she said after a dismayed interval, — "don't
tell me you have n't seen *The Bulletin!*"

There were a good many reasons why a clerk of T.
Rickart's might not be absolutely on the hour with the
news in a city that published its morning papers at 11 P.M.
the night before and its evening papers at 11 A. M. He had
run into the Trudeaus', being in the neighborhood, on his
way to lunch, and had not seen the paper which she now
held out to him folded to display sickening headlines —
"Talented Leading Lady Makes Sacrifice of Husband —
Considers Mother of Child Has First Claim."

"——" said Kenneth, unaware that he had said anything not suitable to be said in the presence of young
ladies, consumed with the pure horror of the American
male to find his own women made the subject of newspaper sensationalism, and by an equally poignant regret
that, as things were, he could n't kick the writer.

He came out of a red cloud of anger presently to catch
the last of what Ellis Trudeau was saying, to the effect
that after all it depended on how much Virginia had cared
in the first place, whether she would be more or less hurt
by it.

"I don't know . . . Sieffert was a skunk . . . I don't
think she cared much one way or the other. But, of
course you understand, she could n't have consented to
this, — she is n't capable—" He choked; not from knowing that Virginia was incapable of making capital of the

circumstances of her divorce, but that she would be incapable of realizing that it would be making capital; she would take it, as no doubt the writer had meant she should, as her contribution to the cause of the New Woman. It was Lovinsky, of course; who else could have so dressed up the item of Bert Sieffert's intrigue with a kitchen-maid in the phrases of sex emancipation, — how Lovinsky had wallowed in them — with Virginia figuring as the partisan of the right, even of a husband, to the full Development of His Personality. He felt that he must get to Virginia at once; he must make her understand that the Lovinsky woman must be suppressed. He was so bent upon getting to her that he neglected to reassure Ellis Trudeau of his entire belief that her brother had had nothing to do with it. Come to think of it, he was n't so sure; there was n't much that he'd put past that bunch. Two or three times on his way to the Studio, for there could be no stopping for lunch, the girl's troubled face came back to him with a faint suggestion that it would have been better to talk it out with her, that there might be things even yet that he did n't know; but he was obsessed with the idea that the one thing was to stop talk of every kind. Fortunately he had n't to break it to Virginia. She had the papers; she had all the papers; and she was a little scared. She exonerated Trudeau and defended Miss Lovinsky; it did n't occur to Kenneth until afterward that she was a little too apt, a little too well prepared against attack. But whatever sanction she had given the newspaper woman, she had n't expected it would be like this.

"She must have had the best intentions," she insisted; "she thought it would — interest people."

"Oh, it will, it will," Kenneth groaned. "She's made

sure of that by making it appear an affair of only a few weeks ago instead of two years." But he was softened to the situation by perceiving that Virginia had cried.

"Look here, my dear," he said with a fine male largeness, "you must get out of all this; cut the whole bunch. Oh, I know Lovinsky has n't done anything to you that she would n't do by herself; but that's the point. They're not your sort. They're not good enough, and it's only your being too fine to see what they are that gets you mixed up with them." He believed that; she had been too fine for Sieffert and she was too fine for Trudeau.

"You must get out of this. I must get you out," he repeated. He did not know how much of the appeal she had for him at the moment was due to recent tears and the frailing effect of the wisteria pinafore. He walked up and down in a glow of indignation and protectiveness, and at last he took her gently by the arms. "I must get you out right away. The reporter will be after you in an hour . . . You put on your hat and come away with me. We'll lunch in some quiet place, and go out to the park. You must not — you positively must not see any newspaper people to-day."

She went very prettily; few women could resist the flattery of an attractive young man who cuts his employer half a day in her interest. Virginia in a tailored suit, her beauty subdued by consternation, lost every taint of theatricality. There was nothing Virginia hated so much as to miss her cue, and if, as the critics said, André Trudeau had turned out not a playwright, then she had missed it — oh, unforgivably. But it would not be herself that Virginia would n't forgive; it would be André.

They went out to the Cliff House after lunch and

walked past the bathers far down the beach and lost themselves amid the dunes. The lazy reach of the sand, the cradling swing of the breakers, and the veiled sun suited Virginia's mood. She felt relaxed after the strain of the production and the high faith with which she had kept the suggestion of failure at bay. She snuggled in the sand at Kenneth's shoulder and felt the soreness of the past few days penetrated by the comforting warmth of a wholly feminine ascendancy. He let her see that as Virginia she charmed him infinitely more than as Trudeau's leading lady; incidentally in the course of the afternoon he unbosomed himself of all that he had felt and done at Palomitas. If he referred at all to the obvious fate of "The Battle," it was only to let her see that it meant neither more nor less to him than that she stayed in his vicinity. They had dinner at the Cliff House and went straight to the theater. Of all that might have been said under the circumstances by a young lady and gentleman but one deserves chronicle.

Reluctantly, he let her go at the stage door, in view of the tremendous lark it had been for them to be so together in the face of other calls on their attention.

"We'll have more of them when you get this confounded play off your hands." He gave those same hands a squeeze. " You don't know how I've missed you."

"If I'd only realized how you felt about things" — She broke off, leaving him to infer that in that case things might have been entirely different. No doubt she thought so; no doubt she was in a measure right.

That was on Friday of the first week of "The Battle." From Saturday until Monday evening Kenneth was out of town on business. Tuesday afternoon Ellis Trudeau called him up by telephone; her voice was frightened, but declined to give him any clue to the urgency of her request that he would come to see her immediately. He did up his work as quickly as possible and found her wringing her hands in her plain little sitting-room with a contained and quiet desperation.

"I was afraid you would n't get here before Andy comes back — he's trying to catch her — Virginia. I thought you might know — she's gone away."

"Gone — where?"

"How do I know? How does anybody know what that kind of woman does." It was the first touch of bitterness that he had heard from her. "She's gone and left Andy in the lurch with his play — she's gone and left *him!*"

She grew quieter under questioning. The play had been going better. Miss Lovinsky had been within her reckoning as to the value of her kind of publicity. The audience had picked up. And quite unexpectedly that afternoon Andy had received a note saying that Virginia had gone away. Andy had rushed off, — to the Studio, she thought, and to see Miss Brooke, Virginia's understudy. Before everything there was the play. They thrashed it over two or three times without making anything more of it; they were disposed to lay a great deal at the door of Miss Lovinsky. And in the midst of it André Trudeau came back. He came in looking utterly done; and at the sight of Kenneth the dull smears of color on either cheek flared scarlet.

"So," he said, "you 've come to see the effect of your work, have you? You did n't like my exposé of your class and your employer's . . . you thought you would spike my guns, did you . . . you damn bourgeois!" His voice dripped with fury; all of his face that was not scarlet was dead white. Like a sword the question leaped out of him, — "What have you done with her? What have you done —"

"Andy! Andy! Mr. Brent had n't anything to do with it. He did n't even know —"

"No. He did n't know that I knew of his sneaking, undermining tricks — trying to break up my play because there's too much truth in it for his stomach! Oh, there's a lot of things he does n't know." He gave Brent no opening for an answer, and yet the other's silence seemed to enrage him the more. "Thought she was too good for me ... Did n't know that she was mine ... MINE, I tell you. ... Could n't take her from me honestly like a man ... took her by a trick." He shuddered sick, and the others waited on the progress of his rage as on a man afflicted. "Take her," he said, pitifully, "take my leavings!" He retched once like a man drunken.

"Andy! Andy!" She was at his side, tender, imploring; she entreated him dumbly with her hands. "Andy, you don't know what you are saying!"

Suddenly he wheeled on them both. "I'll get her back, damn you, I'll get her ..." He choked and relaxed weakly on the girl's shoulder. She turned to Brent with a frightened cry; before any of them she had seen that his lips were flecked with blood.

XI

By the time Anne reached the city in response to Kenneth's telegram, he had had time to realize that his impulse to send for her had been quite as much on his own account as on account of anything that had happened to the Trudeaus, and to reflect that he could never really tell her what it was that had put him so acutely in need of her. He was relieved that she found excuse enough in Ellis's need and took hold of matters there with a high hand. André she packed off to a hospital. The case called for expert nursing; more than anything else it called for obliviousness to the occasion of his plight, which only the impersonal hospital service could throw consolingly about his still raw and aching egotism.

"Give him a good nurse, and a pretty one," Anne had said to the house physician, and as an afterthought, — "one who won't lose her head."

The physician surveyed her cool firmness with satisfaction. "You'd make a corking nurse yourself," he said.

Anne shook her head; like all perfectly well people, she had a secret conviction that sickness was n't in the least necessary if only you kept a hand on yourself. Her next step was to close up "The Battle."

There had been a check in Virginia's note, rather a magnificent one, that must have left Virginia embarrassed on her own account. The girls had found it in André's pocket.

Ellis shrunk back. "Andy can't touch it now!"

"Oh, come," said Anne, "if things were the other way

about and your brother had left Virginia in the lurch, with the play on her hands, you'd think paying his share of the loss would be the least he could do about it. Anyway, you would n't want him to leave it for Mrs. Dickman to pay, and it comes to her in the end if Dickman does n't get his."

Ellis surrendered. "You always think things out so much further than anybody else," she sighed, and set her softly folded lips, "but you can't think anything out that will make *me* think Andy could take anything for himself."

"You don't know me," declared Anne; "I've already got it thought out that it would be fairer for Virginia to pay his hospital bill than for you to pay it." But she made no objection to Ellis's taking the work, which Kline and Kauser kept open for her, the day that André went to the hospital. "It will keep her from worrying," she said to Kenneth; "I'm going to have her in Summerfield with me as soon as we can dispose of the brother. I must have somebody; the ranch and the office together are more than I can manage."

And having paid off everybody and closed up everything so far as Virginia's check would do it, she had an evening to give to her brother.

"Now," she invited, "just how much did you have to do with this whole business?"

It was a relief to have her begin, but that was not quite the way to go about it. If she had only said, "How much has this business to do with *you* —?"

"What makes you think I had anything to do with it?" he fenced.

"Well, from what Virginia said —"

"Virginia!" He could only echo the word in astonishment.

Anne nodded. "She's there at Summerfield, with her mother. From what she said I gathered you had everything to do with her throwing up the whole business."

"Oh, *that!* The play was a flat failure. And all that rotten publicity —" He gave her an account of the particular "rottenness" of Miss Lovinsky. "That bunch! Publicity's their dope; they'd die without it. It was the only thing Virginia could do, to cut and run."

"Virginia was as keen as anybody for the kind of publicity *she* liked," Anne reminded him. "Virginia knew what they were when she went in with them; she'll have to have a better excuse for kicking over the board than that comes to. What I am trying to find out is whether you gave her a better excuse."

He did n't know what she meant by that and said so. He would have liked to say further that he did n't see why his sister should jump on *him;* why Trudeau could n't have provided the excuse; why it was n't excuse enough for Virginia to have got to the place where she simply could n't stand him. But he had no idea how much his sister knew of what Virginia had "stood" already. He found he could n't tell her any of the things that Trudeau had voided in the sickness of rage and jealousy. He would never be able to tell anybody. He was sick himself when he thought of them.

But you never could tell about women. Ellis he thought would have been too much alarmed about her brother's health to have caught what he was saying; it was n't in the code that girls like Ellis Trudeau should understand things like that even when they heard them . . . still you

never *could* tell. And Anne had talked with Virginia . . .
women told each other everything . . . things that men
— the right sort of men — would n't tell to anybody . . .
So he came around at last to saying, "I don't know what
you mean by a better excuse."

"Well," Anne considered, "self-preservation is always
a perfectly good excuse. I mean that when a woman goes
into things that involve the personal welfare of other people, she can't kick over the board just because she finds
she does n't like it. But when she finds that going on with
something she has begun is going to stand in the way of
her getting the best thing in life, what everybody has always agreed is the best thing, I suppose she can cut and
run, without being blamed for it."

This was both explicit and ambiguous; for while it left
him in doubt as to how much Anne knew of the things
Virginia had done in her private character, it applied perfectly to all that everybody knew she had done as a
Friend of Labor and as leading lady in the Democratic
Drama. If he let it go at that, Kenneth felt he need n't
shrink from discussing his own part in separating Virginia from what, he had told her that day on the dunes,
threatened all the things that his sort of men valued most
in women. On that safe supposition he began to tell Anne
all that he had said.

They were sitting in his own room after dinner; having
dined early to let Ellis Trudeau get off to the hospital to
tuck Andy in for the night, and the soft gloom of the evening almost shut them from each other. Under such circumstances, further mitigated by a good cigar, a man may
talk freely to his older and only sister. He put it to Anne
that if Virginia's recoil from the situation had in any way

been affected by his appeal to the traditional, intrinsic niceness of young women, he would take his share of the responsibility light-heartedly.

"I suppose," said Anne thoughtfully, "it all depends on what Virginia thinks you meant by it."

"Ah, what does she think?"

"She thinks," said Anne, "that you want to marry her." Waves of his shocked silence must have reached her through the dusk to soften the note of Anne's final, belated inquiry, "Do you, Ken?"

"I don't know, Anne — I — I never thought of it."

"Well," deliberated Anne, "I guess we'd better not talk of it again until you have."

Perhaps Anne knew as well as anybody that it was not strictly true that Kenneth had n't thought of marrying Virginia; rather that he had thought of himself as being married to her, but thought of it left-handedly, without letting himself take notice. He had thought of it the day he went down to the Studio to rescue her from the doubtful offices of Miss Lovinsky, thought of it as the practical obstacle in the way of just snatching an attractive young woman from a parlous situation and shutting her up in the round tower of her own preciousness. Society did n't permit a young man to do so until he was in a position to maintain her in it, as against all comers. Until this moment Kenneth had made himself believe that the objection which persisted in his mind against marrying Virginia was quite the general prohibition he had himself set against marrying any one until he found himself quite and unmistakably "in" the game of Big Business. And on top of this creditably reasoned version of his indecisions had come the rage of possession, into which he had been thrown by Trudeau's revelations, as the most unprecedented thing in his experience.

His first instinctive impulses had been to stop the fellow's mouth, and to stop it finally and more effectively than the hemorrhage had done; but, such has civilization made us, he had found himself instead helping Ellis to lay her brother carefully on the couch, and telephoning frantically for the doctor. His personal animus toward Trudeau had not lasted beyond the moment when he had seen the fellow hanging in a faint on his sister's shoulder. But the things he had said, they must be stamped out, utterly discredited; and no way occurred to Brent at the moment but to snatch Virginia to himself and dispossess even the idea of the playwright by a public and exclusive possession. Virgin youth as he was, there was no doubt in his mind as to the nature of that possession. He had had, in the two or three hours succeeding Trudeau's outburst, as he had paced up and down in front of the lodging, in case Ellis might need him, a revelation of the force and reality of a great many of our stock phrases of sex that rendered him by turns hot, ashamed, and rampageous. Had Virginia been at hand there is no doubt he would so have snatched her out of the pit which Trudeau's admission had seemed to dig for her, would have obliterated by the surge of his own passions every track which led between it and her, as the wave destroys a slimy sea-print on the beaches. Out of the reach of that blind faith of passion to re-create and reëstablish Virginia had removed herself, and by as much as she could not be his she remained, in his mind, something of Trudeau's. Sitting there in the dusking room with his sister, the sudden tumult of his blood deafened him, . . . things Virginia had said . . .

"Women are n't like that — they can't wait always . . . " things he had noted between her and the playwright, looks . . . touches . . .

He had told himself several times since that a man who would say what Trudeau had said about a woman would also lie about it. This was the code of the world of men as he knew it. He recalled how he had complained to Frank once of the slighting way young MacRea had in speaking of the blonde stenographer, and Frank had said, "It does n't mean anything so long as MacRea says it. Mac is just stringing you. If there were anything between the girl and him, you'd never hear a word out of him." And true enough, after she had left the office Mac-Rea had never mentioned her. Oh, there was no doubt about it, the sort of a man who would tell was n't the sort to be believed.

And on the other hand, his intelligence warned him that in Trudeau's class the rule of his own would n't necessarily hold. People like that told everything — more than anybody thanked them for — dissipated their souls in confession. Had n't Virginia just told Anne that she thought Kenneth wanted to marry her? . . . If he only knew how much more she had told! But, of course, if there was a question of marrying, he could n't ask. If he had any idea of making Virginia his wife, he could n't discuss her even with his sister. As if she had accepted the situation on that proviso, Anne began to talk of affairs at Tierra Longa.

Anne had been at Summerfield, as he knew, when his wire reached her, and her news of the valley was three days old, but pertinent.

"Elwood's game is about over," she said, "and, I suspect, before he has played out his hand. He played it well as far as he went. All sorts of rumors got about, of local development, power plants, and direct railroad connections. People got a notion that Elwood had it in his power to bring these things about, and if they got behind him somehow and gave him their options as a sort of vote of confidence, it would come back to them in the final division of profits. You know how the valley people are!

"And then all in a minute things changed. Jevens was in liquor and talked too much for one thing, but it was those Maxwells, who had the old Crane place, who were the cause of the slip-up. They were heavily mortgaged and everybody was expecting a foreclosure. Elwood, who has n't been able to get in under the Town Ditch, offered to lend them the money; offered it in that free-and-easy, I'm-a-good-fellow-and-you're-another way he has, and they surprised him by turning it down. . . . It seems Mr. Maxwell had had a little legacy from somewhere back East that they had n't told anybody about; but not being able to find out made Elwood uneasy."

Kenneth recognized a familiar situation; he knew how the Old Man and his confrères sniffed the faintest taint of "outside capital," keen as buzzards for carrion. "But it was a mistake if he let them see that he was afraid," he concluded.

"It's the kind of mistake he made," Anne told him; "I don't know just what happened; we're not very close to the valley people at Palomitas; but I think he made some kind of a gallery play for sympathy against an outsider."

"That's Elwood," Kenneth agreed; "if he meant to

cut their throats he'd want their sympathy while he was
doing it. I've seen him get it."

"Not with Tierra Longans," Anne was certain; "outside capital means competition and that means higher
prices. Even after the Maxwells told, there were plenty
who did n't believe them. Elwood will get no more options at the old prices, and the more he offers now, the
more they will suspect him. The point is that if anybody,
who is behind Elwood or opposed to him, really means to
start something in Tierra Longa, he's blocking his own
game now by keeping dark about it. If Mr. Rickart is in
it, one way or another, — and I don't see how he can
keep out of it, — he could carry the whole valley with him
by a straight-out declaration. A little more of this uncertainty and he'll have them stampeded. That's one
reason why I came up; I wanted to have a talk with him."

Rickart was in Chicago; it would be another week,
Kenneth said, before he was expected. "Well, then,
you'll have to tell him." Anne considered thoughtfully,
"Tell him as coming from me . . . though that's almost
too formal. I could have made him think he had found
it out . . . anyway, tell him."

"Don't you suppose Jamieson tells him everything —
if he does n't hear it direct from Elwood?"

"Jamieson is a — an Englishman. He does n't know
any more what the people of Tierra Longa think than he
knows what the buzzards are thinking, flying over."

"And you think —" Kenneth waited for her to fill out
the suggestion. If he had but known, he was nearer the
reason for Anne's urgency that Rickart should declare
himself than she intended to admit to him. The truth
was that Anne did n't know what she thought. For the

first time in her clear-cut life, Anne had found herself unable to think definitely about a man because of what he was able to make her feel about him, and the certainty that this was the case humiliated her. Elwood had called twice at Palomitas and she had ridden with him to Tierra Rondo. They had climbed to the edge of the hollow, and looking down on it had told each other freely all they thought of the possibilities of river storage; she had talked of it as an old dream of her father's and he had talked of it as a new dream of his own growing out of his long session of idleness; and neither of these two astute business people had been able to keep from the other that it would be a glorious sort of thing to do together.

Anne did not trust Elwood; so far as she knew him, she did not approve of him; but all the time she was aware of the glitter of his eye, his easy seat as he rode, and the quick play of his intelligence. The things his hand had said to her as he helped her up the hill had not been at all the sort of thing it had said the first time she had gone seeking touch with him, as it brought the hot tide to her cheek, sitting there in the dark, to remember. She rallied herself to support the evidence of her intelligence against the secret hope that when the Old Man declared himself, it would prove to be in a direction that would remove the necessity for opposing herself to Elwood.

"I think, from the effort he is making to smooth things over, that Elwood has n't got all he wants yet, that there's some really important reason why he does n't come out directly and tell what he is after."

"Think he's found out about my filing?"

"I've no reason to." She did n't think it necessary to let Kenneth know that she had accounted for his last visit by permitting Elwood to think that it had been prompted by a desire for the company of the very pretty girl who was staying with his sister. It was a natural sort of thing for any one to think, who had seen Ellis Trudeau and Kenneth riding off together, and as a matter of fact everybody on the ranch did more or less think it. And Anne had her own reason for not wishing to discuss her personal impressions of Elwood. She led the talk away after that to family concern and finally to make some natural inquiry after Frank.

Ordinarily Frank conducted himself as though Anne's visits were expressly arranged for the purpose of letting him see a great deal of her, so that a reference to the tennis tournament of Del Monte had been part of Kenneth's greeting to her, as a way of accounting for Frank's failure to claim his customary share of her attention. If she came back to it now, it was apparently only to round out her trip with a touch of his affairs, such affairs being for the moment chiefly in the small but extremely competent hands of Miss Rutgers of New York.

"I've a notion old Frank's a goner, this time," was Kenneth's friendly summing-up. "Though I don't suppose anything is settled yet, or you'd be the first to hear of it." This was his way of putting his private conviction that his sister could have coppered old Frank if she had tried for him, but Anne wasn't the marrying sort.

"Oh, yes, I'd know," she agreed, matter-of-factly. He noticed she did n't say "hear" — well, she was cold enough to old Frank to have one of her flashes about him; he'd noticed she never had them about people she was really fond of.

"It's exactly the kind of marriage I've always expected Frank to make," she was saying; "I mean, with all she stands for; beauty, family, social prestige. Men like Frank don't come very close to women; don't have much sense of reality about them. They are very likely to pass right over the sort of woman who *is* all the things they think it is desirable for a woman to be, and take the sort that is dressed up and certified to be refined, exclusive, and all that."

"Oh, Miss Rutgers is the real thing, I should think. I've met her." Really it almost sounded as if Anne meant to be catty.

"Well, let's hope, for Frank's sake, she's not too real. There's a limit to what Frank can live up to in the way of refinement."

No, decidedly, if she could analyze him like that, his sister wasn't likely to be hipped by the news of young Rickart's engagement.

Anne got back to her work next day without again mentioning Virginia, and the moment he had let her go Kenneth realized that he should at least have pressed her for some clue. He quite understood that when a young man has come to the point of letting a girl think that he wants to marry her, there shouldn't be any apparent hesitancy about his next step. It might be overlooked by Anne — who was acquainted with Virginia's capacity for thinking things on the slenderest grounds — that he hadn't met the question as to whether or not he wanted to marry Virginia with an instant affirmative. But would Virginia overlook it? Wasn't her flight from Trudeau a sufficient indication of what she wanted! Could he do any less than follow the invitation of that flight and cover

the publicity of her preference by a public possession.
For it was public. Trudeau had understood.

It blazed upon him in retrospect that Ellis had come to
some conclusion about her brother and Virginia about the
time of her return from Palomitas. He recalled that he
had n't seen her at the Studio since . . . and then her
sudden sally for employment . . . and what Anne had
said! ". . . Men have been paying women for things
like that . . ."

Had there been things known to Anne so early, or was
it just one of those blinding flashes of hers which outran
the fact by as much as the unformulated wish outran it?

"Why should n't a woman pay a man —" Oh, God!
And being in bed at the time, staring sleeplessly into the
dark, young Brent rolled on his face and bit his fingers.

Curiously the rush of conviction carried him to Virginia's side. They knew, those two clear-headed young
women; and the divine chivalry of youth prompted him
to raise between their knowledge and Virginia the ægis
of compelling faith. Oh, there was no doubt about it, he
wanted to marry Virginia, but he wanted to marry her
now! He could have done it then and there and had it
triumphantly over with. What he could n't do was to
spend hours, even days, in the process. He thought of
his work and the distance to Summerfield. He thought
of weddings; he was under the impression that they took
a vast deal of arranging; thought of Virginia's mother,
her commonness, her noisy affectionateness, and her disposition to insist on a great deal of talk.

At the idea of explaining to Mrs. Burke his necessity
for marrying Virginia and marrying her quickly, Kenneth
sank back into bed — he had been sitting on the edge of it

with some notion of getting forward with the business of marrying Virginia — and covered his head with the blankets.

In marriage as in finance it seemed that nothing was simple; you could n't just pick out your girl and your job and have them by being able to please one and do the other. . . . All sorts of stupid people. . . . all sorts of shifts and waits and indirection . . . Nothing was simple, nothing *square!* . . . not even Virginia. . . . How was he to know what she wanted of him, going off like that? He perceived suddenly how true it was that women were the real movers of the game. Here he was, led up to the crisis of his personal life and left hanging in the air. . . . Anne ought to have talked; if she knew anything at all, she knew that he did n't know what was expected of him.

The truth was that Anne knew very little except what she had guessed through a long familiarity with Virginia's methods. That sudden flight to the maternal nest, that swift resumption of maidenly preciousness and alarms; what could they mean except the rising somewhere on Virginia's horizon of the prospect of honorable marriage? There had been an hour's conversation between those two, in which whatever conclusions she came to about André Trudeau, Anne at least came to the conclusion that she must keep it to herself.

Anne loved her brother. It is possible she understood him, and on this occasion, at least, used toward him that feminine indirection which all her life she had disdained with other men. If she left Kenneth to work out his relation to Virginia unaided, it was probably because she knew that that was the way to have him work it out to her satisfaction.

Deprived of both his sister and Virginia, Kenneth had left, for his consolation, only Ellis Trudeau; and from her he was more or less divided by the nature of things.

He saw her almost daily; it seemed his duty to, considering that he had made himself responsible for her with Kline and Kauser, and that she was still in great anxiety about her brother. Within a week, however, there was news.

"It is n't at all what we feared," she told him; "not lungs, you know, it's only bronchial." It had been arranged that André was to go to Indio as soon as he was stronger, for the open-air treatment, sleeping with very little between him and earth and nothing but a blanket between him and the stars.

He was quite thrilled by it; he would expand his soul in the Silent Places. Something notable in the way of a book or a play would come out of this encounter of the desert with the literary temperament.

"It *is* his temperament that is mostly the matter with him," Ellis explained. "You see, life is twice as hard on people with creative imaginations. They have all the things we have to put up with, and the other things beside, the — the situations they — create." She was able to say it; she was able to look at him quite directly, unaffectedly, quite as though it were all as simple as it sounded. "They are so *real* to them, the things they create," she said; "they are with Andy. I've seen him *suffer* . . . I've seen him made positively ill over things that were just — sort of — made up."

They were dining together, not at any of the resorts affected by Virginia's coterie, which they by common consent had abandoned, but in a clean, light place, where

there was music, and well-dressed men and women coming and going, people with obvious, cheerful interests.
It was the best moment she could have chosen to discuss
her brother, since it was inevitable they would have to
discuss him sometimes; but for the life of him Kenneth
could n't help a little stiffness as he said that he supposed
it was so, but for his part he had to have things real.

"Yes, you would," she agreed, not at all as if there
were any special merit in it. "It is difficult for people like
you and me to understand. I never saw anybody not an
artist who *could* understand it, except Virginia." It was
the first time her name had been mentioned between them
since they had last heard it on André Trudeau's blood-
flecked lips, and it was wonderful, on the whole, how
naturally she said it, and how at the mere pronouncing
of it a little of the old warmth colored her reference.
"Sometimes," she said, "I think Virginia is the most
understanding person I know, except your sister. Her
going away — I was dreadfully angry at first. It seemed
like desertion . . . but that was only my short-sighted-
ness. The play was a failure . . . they had to get out of it
somehow; and only Virginia had the sense to get out of
it dramatically."

"Oh, if you look at it that way —"

"We *have* to — if it has turned out that way. You see
it was just *dragging* out, leaving everybody in the dregs of
discouragement — and suddenly Virginia pulled it around
into something else. Even the public sees it as something
else — the leading lady being called away, and Andy's
illness. Every day there's been something in the paper
about how he is getting along; they are really interested.
Of course, it was too bad of him to make such a fuss just

at first — not to see what she meant by it." (It was indeed, thought Kenneth.) She sighed. "That's where his temperament has it in for him — making something up on the spur of the moment to account for everything —"

She was looking at Kenneth quite steadily, almost too steadily. But it all might so easily be *so;* it was so confoundedly plausible!

"It's given him something to think about besides the play; it's helped him to get over it," she said. "He's got a whole new set of — imaginations."

Well, if Ellis Trudeau was paying a debt to Virginia, she did it handsomely. She had put them all back where they were three months ago . . . nothing whatever had happened. Were n't women wonderful . . . simply *wonderful!*

He was able, on the strength of that conversation, to take up some phases of their wonderfulness with Frank when he came back from the tennis tournament bursting with health and spirits. They were always, those two after any separation, undisguisedly glad to see each other. If there were two or three things which they had not talked out together, such as Kenneth's preoccupation with the problem of Labor, and his secret feeling about the Old Man, it was because they belonged to that part of their lives which, as clerk and heir to T. Rickart, they could never have together. On all points where they mutually touched they had perfect communication. That evening in Frank's rooms they came naturally to talk of women and marriage because their minds were full of it.

"The trouble is," Kenneth postulated, "nobody tells you anything about it, not anything important. For instance, whether it is something you ought to think out, like choosing a profession, or whether it ought to just happen."

Frank was of the opinion that any man of any experience at all, by the time he was old enough to be married, knew that it was n't a thing which could be let happen without any reference to the facts. "Take my case. I'm going to have a pile of money. . . . Money! Have you any idea what my father is worth? I have n't exactly; but I know there are princes over in Europe who have n't his income. Well, that's the biggest fact in my life. I've got to think of that when I marry; it's up to me to choose a wife who will know what to do with all that money. She's got to be used to money; she's got to understand it."

"If you think money is so important —"

"Would I think a hump was important if I had it? I've *got* the money — or at least I will have as soon as Dad blows out — long life to him!" He blew a salutatory ring of smoke. "I'll have to live in the house with it. There'll be three of us, myself, my wife, and my money; we've all got to get along together."

This was the sort of astuteness over which the Old Man had been accustomed to whet his delight; but to Kenneth it was too much of a special instance.

"There are times," he insisted, "when a man's feelings can be the biggest kind of a fact."

"All kinds of women can give you feelings," Frank objected. He might have added how many kinds attempted to give them to young, attractive heirs of wealthy men. "Sometimes I think the kind that get you going easiest are the worst kind to marry . . . the kind that plays the game . . . keeps you guessing."

This was an approach to illumination. If there was anything about Virginia which interested Kenneth it was the way she kept him guessing; but he made a stab in self-defense.

"Is n't it a woman's business to keep a man stirred up — her game, if you put it that way — to keep him stimulated, inspired?"

"Not so darned much." Frank slid his hands into his pockets and elevated his feet comfortably to the window ledge. "Not if he's a regular fellow."

Frank himself was perfectly regular as could be determined at a glance. His large, somewhat gangling frame had begun to take on solidity without undue weight. He had a high color and a big manner which passed with people like Miss Rutgers for "Western." He was particularly straight in the back and conspicuously well-tailored.

"You know, *I* think," he delivered, "that a lot of this stuff about women keeping men stimulated — being an inspiration, and all that — is mostly bunk that they've made up between them; the women because they have to do something to keep in the game, and the men to hide their general flabbiness. Loving your wife and having children and getting your job done is something a regular man ought to be able to manage just by himself, without being eternally chucked up to it. Do you get me?"

Kenneth supposed that a lot of them did manage it; how else could you account for the large numbers of perfectly commonplace men and women who were getting married and making a living and having children every day? Still, a woman ought to be something in a man's life that he could n't get along without, else why marry at all? And when a man came to his own personal case he wanted something to go upon; if he was n't to trust to his own feelings, what could he trust to?

"Find the biggest fact in his life." Frank put it oracularly. "If she does n't square with that, I don't care what his feelings are, he 'll come a cropper. Now, you take my case —" What Frank's case amounted to was an admission, as far as a young man can make it without having yet ascertained the views of the young lady, that Miss Rutgers of New York squared, not only with his facts, but his feelings.

Kenneth heard without taking note. For almost the first time he was reflecting that, while Frank's fortune had never interfered with their affection, it did prevent their coming together on any permanent interest of their lives. The biggest fact in Kenneth's life was that he did n't have a fortune, and he felt that such items as that a girl might have been previously married to one man and have had "an affair" with another might seriously disturb him in the process of acquiring a wife. Something nearer his need was supplied by the Old Man, writing from Chicago that Kenneth was to proceed at once to Tierra Longa and take up the work that Elwood had been doing there. He was to put himself in touch with the farmers, and win their confidence; Elwood, the letter said, had unaccountably fumbled matters. Further instruction would reach him by way of Agua Caliente where he was to stay, not to be too far removed from telephone connection with the city office. If the letter afforded him no clue to the bearing of the work that Rickart expected of him, it at least would bring him again into touch with Virginia.

XII

"About this man Elwood," said Mr. Baff; "it's this way, the valley ain't holdin' out nothin' on him for the way he got them options. Maybe he did let on he was funnin' more than he was, but they was willin' to take the joke so long as they thought it was on him, so they ain't got no kick comin' when it turns out it's on theirselves.

"*Of* course," — Mr. Baff raised his liquor to the level of his eye for the traditional tribute to its quality, and having inducted more than half of it into his capacious throat, ritualistically wiped his mustache, and concluded, — "of *course*, there's some of 'em kickin', anyway, but the valley don't allow they've any call to."

"I certainly agree with you, Mr. Baff," acknowledged Rickart's junior clerk, waving his own glass with a gesture which he hoped would be accepted in lieu of his drinking from it. "I do think the people who gave Mr. Elwood options on their property have no cause to complain of him."

"None whatever," — Mr. Baff threw off the remainder of his liquor with a gesture of confirmation so large that it left the now emptied glass in the best possible position for the bartender to refill it, which he did without waiting for the permission of Kenneth's half-lifted eyebrow.

From under twin green domes of cottonwood, the barroom of the Arroyo Verde House reached back into grateful dimness, a clean, old, earth-smelling room with traces of an earlier and magnificent régime in the tarnished gilt of the bar-fittings and the fogged old mirrors, and a thin gleam of prosperity along the brass footrail polished by the boots — or perhaps it would be more exact to say by the boot, for the conventional negligence of attitude permits of but one boot on the rail, the other fitted comfortably into a hollow of the much-scrubbed pine flooring — polished by the boot of such as Baff, the Scudder boys, Willard, Jevens, and, on this occasion, the neat Oxford tan of Rickart's junior clerk.

Kenneth leaned an unaccustomed elbow on the black-walnut bar, caressing his glass to conceal from the casual comer how little he had really drunk from it. This was the fifth day he had ridden down from Agua Caliente, only to find that neither his newly awakened social sympathy nor the late reduction of his Class Consciousness carried him so far into the confidence of Tierra Longå as the shared and inhibited weakness of Elwood. In respect to this gentleman, too, he found himself in a quandary, not being able either to account for his motives or his whereabouts. Two days before his arrival, Elwood, following a protracted long-distance conversation with the city office, had disappeared in the direction of Toyon County, and though Kenneth was now openly committed to Elwood's policy, there was nothing Jamieson, the Superintendent at Agua Caliente, could tell him; practically nothing. Jamieson was a stiff man, not letting himself be liked much for fear he would be less respected, on whom the knowledge of Elwood's popularity sat sourly. "My business is the cattle business, Mr. Brent," he had explained himself; "and though 't is not ranked with the business of promotin', there is this to be said of it, that you can succeed with cattle without playin' the fool to them." So, for all that Kenneth could contribute, speculation still hung on the irreducible item as to what the Old Man, who was more or less recognized as the source of Elwood's activities, might or might not be up to.

"It's this away," explained Mr. Baff. "If so be he was expectin' to develop on his own account, there's no call for him to act like the valley was ag'in' him. One or another of 'em, they've had their fill of *that*. And likewise, if this is a Gover'ment projeck, what call has anybody to suppose that Tierra Longa is ag'in' the Gover'ment? An' if Elwood is representin' the Irrigation Bureau, how comes the Old Man to be in with him?"

"What makes you think this is a Government project?"

Kenneth had asked this because he really wished to know. Even before his arrival in the valley he had heard that a party of Government surveyors, who had been working on the Toyon Reserve, had moved down along the upper waters of the Arroyo Verde; and they were now at Tierra Rondo. But the moment he had put the question, in all honesty and with no intention to divert an equally honest inquiry, he was aware, on the part of Jevens, of some subtle emanation as of delight at mischief well executed. It was all part of a disposition he had noted and rejected during the past five days, of an attempt of the liveryman to set up with him, through the medium of his cast eye, a secret and sinister communication. He had, however, to give his attention to Baff.

"Well, if it ain't," demanded that gentleman, "what in tarnation is a United States survey party doin' in Tierra Rondo?"

"You're sure they are Government men?"

"Why, ain't they?" Baff was genuinely surprised.

"They're the same fellers that done the survey work on Toyon, leastways, Pedro Gonzales says he can swear to three of 'em. They're wearin' the same kind of clo'zes. Lattimer, their boss, he's a Gover'ment man, everybody knows."

"Lattimer has gone back to Washington," Willard contributed to the general information. "I was over to Westerville last week and saw him gettin' on the train."

They considered this rather baffling circumstance in silence for a while, and Baff burst out at last: —

"Well, if they ain't Gover'ment men, who in hell are they?"

"Oh," said Kenneth, "that's what I asked you."

He was really concerned to know. News of this surveying party had reached Anne at Summerfield and he had had a letter from her the night before which, while it had answered the first part of Baff's demand, left him more perplexedly in doubt about the latter. If such a party was at work on a dam site or reservoir, it was not likely his appropriation notice could remain long undiscovered. About that same notice he was beginning to be apprehensive; whether or not it would appear to the Old Man in the simple light it had presented itself to Kenneth and to Anne, depended very much on the way in which he came to know of it. Kenneth had rather indefinitely expected that, before matters in the valley came to a crisis, there would be opportunity for a talk with his employer in which he could have placed himself in just the right relation to whatever his project might prove to be. He might have made a clean breast of it as soon as he received his commission to buy land and water rights in Tierra Longa, but somehow it had not seemed just the thing to communicate by letter, and in any case he waited to get a fuller account of the business from Elwood. Just now, as some slight but subtle movement from Jevens had apprised him that the liveryman was probably acquainted with the pertinent item of Anne's letter, he had been seized with a moment's panic about the Old Man's possible connection with the survey work going on at Tierra Rondo. Confronted with Baff's reiterated question as to what, if anything, that connection might be, he cast hastily about in his mind for a term that would be within the letter of his instruction and yet not commit him to too much.

"Not being in the Government's confidence," he threw off, "I can't say; but as for Mr. Rickart, I know that he would like very much to be with you in this."

"The question being," drawled Lem Scudder, "just what *this* is a-goin' to be."

"As to that," Ken put it candidly, "I can't go into details. Mr. Rickart is in Chicago, but I expect him within a few days; all I know is that his feeling toward the valley is most cordial." In his young ingenuousness he really believed it.

"Well, now, sirs," corroborated Jevens, "ain't that what I always said? If Mr. Rickart and Mr. Elwood want to be *with* us, ain't that proof enough that things is comin' round our way? You don't ketch the Old Man on the side that's gettin' the worst of it; now, do you?" They did not, indeed. Logic like this was irresistible. At least it was irresistible to those who had not committed themselves in advance. To Willard it had a certain dubiousness.

"If the Old Man wants me with him, why did n't he say so before he put a paper on me? If this is a Govern-

ment project, it's got up for the benefit of the taxpayers
and there had n't ought to be any millionaire staking out
the ground ahead of it. If it's a private undertaking,
there's no clause in my option that says where I'll be if
things fall out for a raise. Any way you take it, looks like
I'm out before I know where the ball's coming from."

Jevens settled comfortably back against the black-
walnut bar. "There ain't no Tierry Longway court goin'
to uphold the option that's ag'in' a Tierry Longway
man," he opined.

In the face of this cheering certainty, Kenneth knew
Elwood or Rickart would have kept silent. If the people
fooled themselves it was none of their business; perhaps
if just at that moment he had not caught again that
slight but significant movement of Jevens's wall eye —
as it was he spoke out sharply.

"Your option is perfectly regular, Willard; the courts
would have to uphold it." He modified his instinctive
revolt. "In any large undertaking it is necessary to con-
solidate the interests. Whatever Mr. Rickart wished to
do in the valley, he would feel that he had to have something he could depend upon." In his young perturbation
he had let his glass go, thereby disclosing, in the full two
fingers of red liquor left in it, the shallowness of his own
participation in the fellowship of Tierra Longa. Recalled
to his obligation by the sight of his untouched drink,
Kenneth hastily gulped as much as he could manage at a
mouthful, and to cover the involuntary movement of
distaste, he joined himself to Lem Scudder assembling
his long limbs for departure.

Together they issued from the shadow of the twin green
domes and crossed the wide plaza full of light, emptied

of all else but sleeping dogs and an occasional loafer, chair tilted against a shadowed wall. At the public hitching-rack where his team was tied, Lem stood slapping his long thigh with the hitching-strap, with the air of a man with something weighty on his mind, and not quite sure of his moment.

"You're workin' for Rickart, ain't you?" And after a longish interval he followed Kenneth's slightly surprised affirmative with "Elwood's workin' for him?"

"He works with him," Kenneth corrected. "I mean they often pull off things together, but Elwood's not employed. He's working with Rickart on this," he added at last, seeing Lem got no further.

"Well, then, can you tell me this much, are they workin' for or against Tierry Longway?"

Kenneth considered this perplexedly.

"If they were against, do you suppose I'd be allowed to tell you?" he put it at last. "Well, then, what good would it do for me to tell you anything?"

"I see." Lem balanced the strap carefully on his hands. "Well . . . as man to man, if I was to sell that eighty of mine below the ditch for what I can get for it, at the present prices, would you say that I was or I wasn't goin' again' my best interests? Mine and Ab's. Rememberin' that all we got's right here in Tierry Longway, an' Ab's a family man?"

"Well, that's a hard proposition for me to answer, Lem."

"It's no harder than what I'm up against myself. We put all we had an' two years' work already into the Hillside Ditch, and we ain't taken hardly anything out yet. Ab's wife she's been right sick this spring; her baby come too soon. . . . I was kinda lottin' on gettin' married myself soon as I could see my way to it. . . . It's pretty hard sleddin' — but if things is anyways goin' ahead —?"

"I can't tell you, Lem, I — I don't know, really."

"If they ain't, you see, I reckon I'll have to sell that lower eighty and the water stock that goes with it. I allow the stockholders will take it hard of me, sellin' to Rickart. He ain't never got in under the Ditch, an' they allow he ain't never goin' to, but I do need money mighty bad. . . . I reckon these development schemes is slow, anyhow."

Kenneth knew he should have closed the bargain at once; if Rickart wanted anything in the valley he wanted the Hillside Ditch, but neither Elwood nor Rickart had gone to school with Lem. "I can tell you one thing, Lem," he admitted, "there's nothing in that notion of a Government irrigation district. I knew they had Tierra Rondo on their list, but the moment Anne heard of these fellows surveying, she wired to the Department and got a letter saying the Arroyo Verde project has been abandoned on the recommendation of Lattimer."

"The hell it has!" Then, with a sudden gleam, "If Anne had to write to Washington, it can't be Rickart —"

"Don't be too sure, Lem." Kenneth knew it was a popular conception in the valley that Anne could get what she liked out of his employer. "The Old Man never tells anybody everything; but I do know that he wants to be friends with people in the valley. You set a price on your eighty and I can fix it up for you."

Lem shook his head, thoughtfully.

"There's a nigger in the woodpile, looks like. I got

to study over it. Folks on the East Side won't anyways like my sellin' to Rickart." He climbed heavily into his buckboard and then turned for a smile of unimpaired friendliness. "So 'long, old man . . ." Kenneth found his own shoulders settling to the depressed sag of the other's as he rode out toward Agua Caliente.

A mile or two out of town, where the East Side Ditch was taken out of the river, he saw Jim Hand looking for gopher holes in the bank below the drop. As he had last seen Hand in Summerfield he had been a beaten man, but in small, furtive ways, rebellious. Drink had robbed him of the sense of the time that had elapsed between the occasion of his pushing Cornelius Burke into the oil vat and the death of Cornelius from some unexplained cranial injury; he thought the two things had followed close on one another. Times when he was very drunk he would boast of what he had done to Cornelius, and finding himself disbelieved would weep inconsolably. Kenneth was always uneasy lest somehow his own surreptitious knowledge of the incident should come to light, and he should be called upon to confirm the puppet of the gods in his one successful reprisal. As soon as he caught sight of Hand now, blundering about the banks, Kenneth dropped his head and looked attentively between his horse's ears; but Jim must have been looking out for him, for the next moment he disappeared from the canal and presently broke with a cautious rustle from the willows which here approached almost to the county road. He called to Brent in his cracked, bibulous voice, and made mysterious signals for him to come alongside.

"Wanna tell you sumpin . . . wanna tell *you* . . ." Kenneth allowed his horse to drift into the tall grass and

humored Hand's portentous demand for secrecy by pretending to cut a riding-switch from the willows. "Wanna
tell Steve Brent's boy . . . fine boy . . . fine father . . .
partner o' mine. . . . Tell you sumpin you don' know
'bout that —— " He lost himself in obscene profanity
which prefaced the introduction of Rickart's name. It is
probable that Hand knew of Kenneth's employment by
Rickart, but when in liquor the tendency of his mind was
always to telescope the present into the situation at
Petrolia.

"What was it you wanted to tell me, Jim?" Kenneth
recalled him.

Hand made the solemn and pitiful struggle of the drunk-
ard for the recovery of his own members, peering a little
for the malign Powers who might at any moment reduce
him again to subjection.

"Say, you know that Elwood? Damn city feller . . .
damn cap'list, been buyin' ranches, buyin' ever'body's
ranches. Workin' for Rickart, he is. Workin' for
Rickart. Thass what I tole 'em . . . tole ever'body. . . .
Damn teetotaler workin' for Rickart."

"Elwood's working for Rickart; I get that. What of
it?"

Jim gazed at him with fixed solemnity.

"Steve Brent's boy . . ." he affirmed. "All right,
feller. Never go back on Tierry Longway . . . I tell *you*."
He rocked a little and brought up with a hiccough which
seemed for the moment to carry off the confusion of
drink; he came nearer and laid a cautioning hand on
Kenneth's rein.

"You know them Gover'ment men up in Tierry
Rondo?" He waved his arms and took a squint through

his hands in a rough indication of surveying. "Well, they ain't workin' for the Gover'ment."

"Oh," said Kenneth, "they're Government men and they are n't working for the Government!"

Hand leered up at him; for once he had done mischief undetected by the Powers.

"I'll show you." He produced, after some fumbling, a crumpled paper. "I's fishin' th' other day, feller came along — Gover'ment man, same feller on Toyon 'zerve, gimme this; wanted cash, — gimme this." He waved the check about for Brent to see that it was for a trifling amount, but drawn on a bank that the Old Man used for enterprises he did not openly father, and signed by Elwood.

"You say this was a Government man; how do you know?"

"Same feller over on Toyon 'zerve last winter; knew ol' Jim. Did n' wanna cash check in Tierry Longway, made ol' Jim promise." He poked it insinuatingly at Brent, "You cash it . . . ol' Jim needs money . . . father's partner . . . ought to be rich . . . am rich . . . damn Cap'list." He trailed off in cursings of Rickart and his son-in-law.

Wishing nothing so much as to be rid of him, Kenneth cashed the check; he thought he would show it to Anne. He recalled Anne's first impression of Elwood as sinister . . . Anne's first impressions held. Circumstance and her friends sometimes jockeyed her out of them for a time, but in the end one had to acknowledge their truth. Anne had said that Elwood meant no good to Tierra Longa, and Elwood was paying the surveyors at work in the round valley above the Gate. He thought he would go up and have a look at them the next day.

Accordingly he rode to Palomitas the first thing in the morning, knowing that his sister was expected some time toward the end of the week; but this time she had sent Ellis Trudeau in her stead. Kenneth found her with his father deep in the entertainment of a new card-filing device for the ranch accounts; so many lambs dropped, so many days between planting and harvest, the rise and fall of waters, kept like a court lady's diary. It occurred to Kenneth that it would give a new validity to his excuse, being caught by Elwood's men at the Gate, if he took Ellis with him; it is always excusable for a young man to be wandering by river-banks with a charming young lady.

"Certainly, my dear, you must go," urged Steven Brent; "it is part of your job to know the land. We'll see when you return how much you can tell me."

"My land!" said Addie when instructions about the lunch she was to put up reached her; "get away before Luella M'ree sees you; she'll howl the roof off."

The girl's soft eyes sought Kenneth's with lively interrogation. "It'll seem ever so much more like a picnic with children," she suggested.

Kenneth laughed and agreed; he was the adored of Luella M'ree and was immensely tickled by it.

As they went out, the three of them, by the Agua Caliente gate, the morning-warmed air of the mesa began to move before the cooler currents from the Torr'; it stroked the cheek like soft fingers. In the clear sky above the valley buzzards wheeled and tilted. Outside the gate they did not at once recapture the fairy wonder into which more than a month before they had delightfully stumbled; they noted where the filaree had curled, and stooped to tie the bunch grass to a shelter for a lark which had miscalculated its shadow for her nest. They rode into the widening day and felt their private anxieties shrink with their shadows. As the trail slanted down the lower mesa to strike into the river above the Agua Caliente bridge, they saw two little Romeros digging their bare heels into the flanks of their buckskin pony and affecting a profound obliviousness to the presence of the picnickers.

"They're tagging; the little rascals!" Kenneth laughed; "shall I send them back?"

"Oh, there's lunch enough," Ellis consented; "I've great sympathy for taggers; I've tagged all my life disgracefully."

Kenneth raised a shout which admitted the little copies of Ignacio and Pedro Demetrio to their hereditary privilege.

From the mesa Arroyo Verde presented itself to the eye as a winding inset of wild vines and willows; the trail that broke over its shallow cañon dropped then out of sight in a river of green that flowed and glinted in the wind like living waters, but the stream itself spread thinly over clean sand, or collected in trout-abounding pools about the roots of ancient sycamores. Spits of dry rubble and banks of fern and spiked monkshood divided the channels; blue herons nested there; by night raccoons could be heard bubbling under the tented vines. By the time the picnic party reached the bottom of the cañon, the high sun on tender foliage filled it with translucent shadow; fleeces of willows edged the runnels, or floated in the golden air.

Kenneth and Ellis fished up the river from channel

to channel thridded with still pools; the children were left to bring up the horses slowly, wading and splashing to their hearts' content. After an hour or two of this, Kenneth made a singular and interesting discovery; it was, that after long looking at brown streams through golden air and mellow light, it is possible to slip deep into the pale golden-brown of a girl's eyes as naturally as the sun-warmed water slips from pool to pool. You work up a still, golden shallow, with the dun note of wood pigeons overhead and an occasional echo of the children's laughter far behind you, and then, across some trout-ringed, gliding reach, your spirit dips into condoning quiet, — no troubling spark, you understand, — no sort of nonsense about it, — just a comfortable word or two about how the sport was going and the proper fly to use, and that still flowing of glance into glance . . . and the faint, far-off reassurance of young laughter.

All this was the more remarkable for the ease with which, about a mile below the Gate, a passage was effected from the point of meeting eyes to the business of cooking trout between two stones, and the final consideration as to whether Pedro Demetrio ought really to be allowed that last piece of pie just because he seemed able to hold it. Exactly as Ellis had said, the presence of children made the occasion much more like a picnic; as they lay stuffed to repletion on the sand with their toes in the warm shallows, comfort stole upon him, beatitude of the Distributor of Benefits. Ellis, who had wandered away out of sight for a drowsing interval, came back with her hands spattered with pollen of pine which she had culled from the ripple edges.

"Your father was right," she concluded, reading the

signs as he had taught her. "It is going to be a good season."

"Anne was right," he affirmed, "when she chose you for assistant." Think of her picking up things as quickly as that!

"Oh, Anne's nearly always right," — she blew the dried pollen from her palms, — "*always* when it's people."

"In an hour," he said, "we'll know how right she was about Elwood."

By this time Ellis knew everything the Brents knew and all they surmised about Tierra Longa. But it was nearer two hours than one when he came back from the Gate with confirmation.

"He's there all right?"

"Elwood?"

Kenneth nodded. "There's a surveying party, running levels in Tierra Rondo. Elwood's in charge. They've found my appropriation notice. While I was looking . . ." They spoke in the hushed tone of conspiracy. She had been alone with the felt presence of the wood and the river, and their spell was on her. Kenneth said he thought the discovery had been considerable of a jog to Elwood. He had n't known what to make of it. He could see him trying, on the spur of the moment, to make something of it that would prevent the men from supposing that Rickart had slipped something over on him. Well, anyway, it settled one thing.

"Yes?" she interrogated.

"That whatever they're up to they are deliberately trying to keep me from finding it out, and at the same time they're using me." He scuffed the sand in perplexity. "I don't believe Elwood has been to Toyon," he thought out finally. "He's been right here all the time, trying to avoid meeting me."

"Well," she said at last, "Anne was right, then."

"Right? Oh, yes . . . if they don't want me to know, it can only be because what they're up to is no good to Tierra Longa."

XIII

It was Ellis saw it first as, with the shadows beginning to fleet before the coastwise hills, they climbed up out of the Arroyo — the cloud of dust far down the valley, and the black, scurrying insect that from time to time, as the wind shifted the cloud, outran it.

"It's a car," Kenneth agreed; and then, desire and apprehension leaping together in his mind, "Rickart's car?"

It might have been; there was a passable road from San Francisco which the great roadster could have covered in six or seven hours. Now, they concluded, things will begin to happen. But as they watched it, riding in to the ranch house, the car displayed unfamiliar lines and a rate of going that spoke more of the driver's concern for his machine than of Rickart's obsession for annihilating the distance between places. Decidedly not Rickart's car, they agreed; and as it came charging on toward Palomitas instead of turning off across the Agua Caliente bridge, it was Ellis again who recognized the machine in which Anne from time to time went careening among the orchard estates of Summerfield. "It *is* Anne," she decided finally.

They worked out, to account for her coming from the direction of Arroyo Verde instead of up from the Draw, that Anne must have telephoned to headquarters and been told that that was where she would find Kenneth.

"If she had anything to say important enough to bring her all the way out here in a hired car," Ellis insisted, "she could n't want to lose any time over it." With so much in the air it was possible that something might have happened to commit Anne to just that extravagance. Kenneth no longer doubted that this was his sister.

"But who's that with her?"

"I don't know," Ellis hesitated. But she did know, and Kenneth perceived it in almost the same moment that he recognized the second veiled figure as Virginia. The riders had hardly more than dismounted at the house gate when the car overtook them.

Anne, with a single motion, alighted from it and claimed her brother's attention. "They told me at the ranch that you were in town. . . . I went straight on from the Draw. Read that." She thrust a folded San Francisco paper at him.

"Good — God! Anne — it's not possible. . . . I'll not believe it . . ."

"You'll have to. Mike Williams did it; I had a line from him this morning. . . . You know Mike . . ."

Instinctively the brother and sister walked apart. Without a word Ellis took the bridles over her arm and moved off with the horses toward the corral; Virginia sat still in the tonneau.

When Ellis Trudeau first took charge of Anne Brent's office at Summerfield, she found, among other accumulations, two or three months' back numbers of real-estate and farming journals which Anne, in the complication of her interest with Palomitas, had been obliged to leave unread. "Save anything that has to do with local interests, and everything in connection with irrigation projects, and mark it for me to read," she had instructed, and Ellis had faithfully saved for her the report of a paper by the

Government irrigation expert, Lattimer, on San Francisco's water supply, read at a recent convention.

Ellis's attention had been stayed by the mention of the expert's name, for she had already heard how Tierra Rondo had been placed on the list of possible Government projects for investigation. It happened to be this report that claimed Anne's freshest attention, and something in the wording of a paragraph, which stated that there was a plan on foot among public-spirited business men for a supply from some unconsidered source, held her a long while in silent speculation.

She could never really say whether or not her conscious intelligence took hold of the possibility that this slightly indicated source might be the waters of the Arroyo Verde, but, obeying some obscure impulse, Anne had blue-penciled the paragraph and sent it with a note of interrogation to a man she knew on one of the city papers. He had been for a time in charge of one of the local news-sheets, and had found in Miss Brent's keen intelligence the one substitute for the stir and tension which is one of the perquisites of the journalistic calling. Young Williams knew enough to know that if Anne sent him an item like that, it was because she had more reason for finding it pertinent than appeared on the surface; he had made it, therefore, the subject of a personal investigation, which had resulted in the two-column announcement of a plan by which the waters of Tierra Longa were to be brought through a cement conduit across the valley and tunneled, through a flanking coast range, to the city faucets.

The name of T. Rickart did not directly appear, though there was mention of his large holdings in that district, and a great deal more about the public spirit and prophetic genius of Elwood. Very little of the detail, of which there was a surprising amount, got home to Kenneth at the first reading.

"But you can see," said Anne, "how it explains everything."

"It explains why I was n't told . . . why I was sent here, not knowing, to win the confidence of the people —" A wave of sick indignation went over him, recalling the Old Man's calculated glance of quiet confidence, his "I've always thought that scheme of your father's perfectly feasible . . ."

Anne caught the passing thought that whitened her brother's countenance.

"We've got to tell father!" They were moving off together.

"Ken, oh, Ken!" Virginia was getting out of the tonneau and calling them.

Kenneth's shoulders hitched with impatience. "Ah! — why did you bring her?"

"I did n't. She just came."

Mechanically they waited, remembering their manners. Virginia came between them and caught them each by an elbow.

"Oh, I know just how you feel! This dreadful Capitalistic System —"

"Ah — ah!"

"Oh, I *know* how you feel . . ." Mercifully they lost her as they entered the house to look for Steven Brent, walking at sunset in his wife's garden. He took it very quietly, with the look of a man who sees his beloved hurt and may not help her. He handed the paper back after a cursory reading.

"If Rickart says he'll take the water away from Tierra Longa, he'll do it."

"He has n't," said Anne; "he has n't even said. It was I who got it into the paper." She explained briefly. "I don't believe he was expecting to have it found out so soon."

"He was n't," agreed Rickart's clerk; "there was a lot more he wanted. What it tells here is what he meant to do." Item by item he mentioned rights and properties accredited to the promoters of the scheme, which the Brents knew were all in the hands of original owners.

"But if it's like that, if he has n't everything in his own hands, yet, is n't there something —?" Steven Brent looked from one to the other of his children and with a sigh turned his eyes toward the breach in the encircling ranges by which the threatened waters reached seaward. Below them they saw the wind on their own olive trees, the river's winding green, the fan-shaped shafts of light that played through the coast hill cañons, and the land — the land that was so much a part of their every thought, that bound them to it through the nurture of common experience —

"Over there," said Steven Brent, "from the top of San Anselmo, the Spanish padres blessed it . . . where the town stands there was a roadhouse when Frémont forded the river. Fifty years ago, when my father drove over the Pass, there was this house here and the hacienda at Agua Caliente. . . . Even in those days they dreamed of a dam at Indian Gate." . . . And again, "Water," he said, "water and power . . . and farms . . . farms, not cities. . . ." He fell silent, his thin hand plucking at his beard.

"Farms," said Anne; "farms and people . . . people.

And to think that there's nothing we can do about it! Nothing!"

"Nothing?"

"The people of the valley, yes, ... perhaps, if they could get together. But who's to lead them? There's nothing *we* can do ... how could we? Ken working for Rickart and I — when I think of the terms on which he let me have that mortgage ..." Whether for or against, how trapped they were and impotent!

Brent took the paper again. "It says here that the surplus waters alone.... But I thought you had the surplus, son? Does n't that put you in ...?"

Brother and sister exchanged one swift, veiled interrogation.

"Oh, there's no doubt about it," Kenneth agreed; "I'm in on this scheme to take the water away from Tierra Longa, — I'm in."

And Anne, the undaunted, broke into sobbing, hysterical laughter.

Ellis Trudeau came out of the house and stood behind Anne's chair, unobtrusive, serviceable. She took off Anne's hat and dusty veil and pinned up the masses of her hair. "The chauffeur says he must be starting back in an hour. I think I had better go with him."

"Ah, do," Anne urged with relief; "I think I must stay here."

Anne's assistant nodded.

"Addie's giving the man some supper; we'd better have ours."

They came into a more natural relation to the situation during the meal. Mr. Brent had to read the paper aloud for the benefit of Addie and Peters.

"My land!" said Addie; "there's folks in the valley that fit for their places once, and I reckon they ain't so tuckered out but what they can do it again."

"But what can they do?" Virginia demanded at large; "I've always said there ought to be a farmers' union. They are as much the victims of the Capitalistic System as anybody; they've just got to organize against it."

"Why *against?*" said Steven Brent. "Does n't the land need Rickart as much as it needs the rest of us? All this struggle — all this plotting and contriving —" He mused in his beard. "What the land needs is that we should cherish and work it. . . ."

"'T ain't Christian, that's what it ain't," Addie rampaged. "It ain't any ways Christian, if you ask me. I allow it's called that, but callin' don't make it so, long as things like this 're goin' on. Ain't it in the Bible that we're all children of one Father? Ain't it in the law that the children share an' share alike? The earth *and* the sea an' all that in them is! Ain't them the water an' the oil an' things? It don't stand to reason Them that's Above would be so set on havin' Ol' Man Rickart for a fav'rite child. Howcome we got the laws fixed so's he can just natur'ly snatch the innards out of everything, an' leave the husks an' the peelin's for us?" she demanded.

Virginia was of the opinion that what the farmers needed was Class Consciousness. "They must develop their Class Consciousness," she insisted.

Nobody said anything. After a longish interval Steven Brent addressed himself to Ellis.

"Well, my dear —"

"I was thinking of the herons," she said; "we saw

them coming home to-night, long flights of them. I was thinking how many hundred years they've nested there, and one day they will come and there'll be only a cement aqueduct . . ."

Almost by concerted movement the three Brents pushed back their chairs; they went out of the low room by different doors. Somehow the homely touch had brought the relieving rush of tears.

Almost immediately Kenneth left for Agua Caliente; he had reflected that he ought not to remain so far from the telephone; the premature publications of his plans might bring new orders from Rickart's office. Anne walked out to the corral with him while he saddled, but there was little to be said.

"I must see Rickart first," he told her.

Virginia joined them. "I know how you must be feeling," she comforted; "it's another victory for Capitalism, but every victory brings them nearer the end. It teaches the people to see how they must unite against a system that makes such things possible. I know how you . . ."

Kenneth gloomed at her as he gathered up his reins. "Sometimes, Virginia," he told her with brutal conviction, "I think you don't know *any*thing." Good Heavens! he thought, as he rode, could n't the woman understand that this was n't a social problem; this was Frank's father and Tierra Longa.

Instinctively Kenneth was prepared to find Elwood at Agua Caliente. By what means he had already been notified of the premature announcement of his plans it was impossible to guess, — he would naturally have been, all this time, in close touch with the city office, — but it was plain that it had been a jolt to him. It had jolted him clear out of that seat on the water wagon from which he had so successfully appealed to Tierra Longa. In the four or five hours since Kenneth had discovered him at Indian Gate, Elwood had sopped his temperamental need to feel always the perfect *rapport* for his objective, with as many drinks as served to dissolve the figure of himself, as he must now seem to the cheated ranchers, in the rich picture of San Francisco's most public-spirited citizen — last most serviceable resort of the romantic imagination — paying his devoir to his city.

For Elwood, by the time the junior clerk joined him in the long gallery of the old hacienda, the waters of Arroyo Verde were already pouring through the city mains, a libation to that peculiar cult of the West, the pride of Locality. Hymning his Queen of the Golden Gate, he exalted his own services. He, Elwood, had done this thing. He had looted the wilderness; he had led a river captive.

It was a tremendous thing to have done, a man's-size thing. The sort of thing a Man's Own Town expected of him, as a witness to its superiority over all other towns.

There was more of this and all in the same epic strain. Kenneth endured it. Jamieson pulled intermittently at his pipe.

Nearby the wind fretted the broad leaves of the figs, where it ceased they heard the steady purling of the creek. Finally, as a sense of their unresponsiveness began to make itself felt through the Dionysian raptures of the successful "booster," Elwood consented to take them into the conversation. He was driven to take them in by his need of *rapprochement* with his audience. He betrayed

the discomfiture he had suffered, on the publication of his
project with so many items of it unaccomplished, in the
lengths to which he went to prove that the announcement
must have been sanctioned by Rickart. How could information, which might render prohibitive a scheme the
public utility of which even the press admitted, get past
two such men as himself and his working partner? He
said that so far as he was concerned, he might easily have
blundered; to give the thing away prematurely was just
the sort of blunder that he, with his willingness to credit
everybody with his own devotion to the Good of the
Town, might have made. But of Rickart, or of a man
transmuted by such a partnership, it simply was n't
thinkable.

Oh, was n't it? Kenneth wanted to know.

Well, now, *was* it? Was n't the fact that Rickart had
got publicity for his plans, proof that he wanted it? Not
that a pocket-souled, sensation-mongering press would n't
have published anything with the Old Man's name to it;
but had anybody ever known him to give out information
except as it was to his advantage? In this case information was too detailed not to have been authorized. And,
anyway, look at the long time the work had gone on under
cover of their joint astuteness.

He said that it had been his own scheme originally.
He had conceived it on the earliest of those retreats to
Tierra Longa made necessary by his own neglect of the
element in question as a beverage. He had climbed up
Indian Gate and from thence he had had a vision; a
vision of the river dammed and stored, not to unend-
ing fruitfulness, as Steven Brent had seen it, but of an
arched, concreted aqueduct leading from the Gate to the

city's faucets; a vision worthy of the most exalted cult of Locality. It was a vision, moreover, which had come triumphantly through the Old Man's searching test as to what there was in it. It had proved itself, in fine, a Business Proposition. Then there had been the Interests.

Elwood admitted that there were interests in San Francisco which did not absolutely demand the waters of Tierra Longa for their fulfillment; interests whose vision was speckled with considerations of immediate and personal profit. And there was the game of city politics; pieces to be placed on the board where they might easily be brought up to flank and cover the final, crowning moves. They had had to have help there. But it was none of those who had been so included in their confidences who had betrayed it to the newspapers. No; *that* would n't have been their way of spilling the beans. They would have cut in and blocked the whole scheme by buying land and water at points of vantage. For proof of their loyalty, look at the free hand they had given Elwood in the valley. For they had all recognized that the ticklish point had been the possession of lands with water rights in Tierra Longa. Actually, he said, a tentative survey of the line of the aqueduct had been made and rights of way secured before any attack had been made on the local problem.

And then, when everything had been done to commit them to work, and yet nothing which insured its accomplishment, there had come this staggering news that the Arroyo Verde District had been reserved for investigation by the Bureau of Irrigation. Here again it was Elwood who, by his extraordinary faculty for organizing the weakness of men, had found a way to divert, not only the

investigation, but all its labors in his direction. Not that
he put it in the terms of weakness. His narrative was
lit up as by a phosphorescence of decay, the decay of
that fine instinct for coöperation which had made it
indispensable for him to stand well with Tierra Longans
even while he fleeced them. It *is* rather fine, that exalted
cult of Locality, by which so much is forgiven so long as
it is done in the name of the Good of the Town. But it
had required a high percentage of alcoholic dilution to
carry off the process by which the interest of the Government expert was transferred to the city in which recently
acquired property had established the Good of the Town
as his prime moral necessity.

It was, no doubt, due to Elwood's being not quite
drunk enough that there were so many gaps in his account of how the views of Lattimer on the advisability
of creating a national irrigation district in Arroyo Verde
had been made to coincide so exactly with the views of
Elwood on the necessity of establishing it as a city water
supply.

But there the expert was now, by the possession of
valuable suburban properties, in the ranks of the *Kou-
retes*, the armed and initiate dancers around the nursing
Empire of the West.

That the spoiling of Tierra Longa actually had some
such significance for Elwood was the sore point of Kenneth's realization of it. It put the Tierra Longans so
completely out of the game. There they were, like the
figure in the group of the Laocoön he had once seen,
serpent-wrapped, their mouths open and no cry to issue
from it. At least, none that the half-gods of business
could hear. All their dear human hopes, — Lem Scud-

der's to get married, — Ab's wife and her baby, — an ant-heap in the way of Elwood's foot! . . . Anne's work . . . and his mother . . .

By one of those swift fallings-together of incidents far divided in point of time, Kenneth knew perfectly what it was his mother had n't been able to endure in the face of Rickart's overthrow of the Homestead Development Company. . . . He came back from the sharp wrench of anguish to find that Jamieson, in the middle of Elwood's account of how he had managed to conceal the withdrawal of the Government enterprise by taking their surveyors and chain men into his own employment, was tapping out his pipe on the railing preparatory to going to bed.

"'T is vary instructive to hear you, Mr. Elwood, vary," — there was a burr in the Superintendent's speech that was the index of his dissatisfaction; "but I'm thinkin' there's a great deal in a business man's life would never come into the head of a cattle man."

He went off without waiting for an answer, and, left alone with the junior clerk, Elwood dropped into the inconsequential confidences of the partly drunken. As between the two of them he did n't mind letting Kenneth know that he was a little uneasy about the effect of this newspaper blow-out on affairs at Tierra Longa. Of course if it had been Rickart, — but that was the rub; Rickart was somewhere on a train between the city and Chicago and they could n't be sure — of course it might have been the Hetch-Hetchy interests, there were some big men in that project. And, of course, it took a sizable man to beat a man like Rickart.

"Oh, if you want to know who had that article put in

The Chronicle," Kenneth advised him, "I can tell you. It
was my sister."

"Your — sister!"

Up to that moment Kenneth had n't thought of telling,
but at the glimpse of Elwood's face by the flare of his
cigarette, between the words, he was glad he had done it.
He said to himself that *that* would give the fellow something to think about!"

What Elwood thought showed in the sudden sobriety
of his next question.

"And just how does your sister happen to be so well
informed of the business of your employer?"

"Oh," Kenneth threw off, easily, "I was given to understand that she did n't know anything except what she
got from you. She was the first to tell me anything; in
fact, so far as knowing what you were up to here in the
Valley, she is the only one who *has* told me anything!"
He had n't meant to drag Anne into it, but now that she
was in, he thought he might as well make a good job
of it.

That he had made a good job he could tell by the
effort Elwood made to throw off his own question as
lightly.

"And what, may I ask, does your sister expect to make
of bucking the Old Man's plans?" Elwood was rapidly
reviewing his memories of the ride to Indian Gate to see
if it was possible he had given himself away to that extent. Momentarily his condition overcame him. "The
fair Anne!" he fatuously laughed. It goes with the type
that he should be the kind of man who could condone an
indiscretion due to such fairness.

"Miss Brent," Kenneth corrected him, "is a successful real-estate dealer; she does n't consult me about her business undertakings. But she was on to *you* as soon as you began giving those options."

He said to himself that *that* ought to be a settler; but immediately Elwood opened his mouth again, Anne's brother wondered if he had n't gone a little too far with the proof of Anne's acuteness.

"Then I suppose it was your sister who —" Elwood began, and left off, making a to-do about finding another match for his cigarette. Kenneth understood that he had meant to ask if Anne had put him up to the appropriation of the river's surplus which Elwood had that day stumbled upon, but was unwilling to be found ignorant of anything that might have been done under instruction from Rickart. Instinctively Rickart's partner fell back on the least discomfiting attitude, that of amused masculine appreciation of Anne. "She sure did slip one over on me . . ."

But he did not talk any more, and as he went off to his room presently he went about through the dining-room where he helped himself liberally to Jamieson's whiskey and soda.

The whole house was quiet before Kenneth himself rose and went out by a little gate at the corner of the *patio* toward the open hill, sloping riverward. There was a sound from it at times of the wind moving intermittently down the Arroyo. Nearer the steady rush of the creek was like the pulse of the season's vitality.

Lights twinkled here and there among the ranches and went out. Lights under the Torr' that was his home marked where Anne kept her thoughtful vigil. A white planet hung over the Saltillos and under it the flare of a sheep herder's fire, Soldumbehere making his annual round. In the darkness the sleeping earth suspired.

It was one of those nights which to the young seem full of mysterious portent, presage of their own burgeoning powers.

Kenneth told himself that he had come out here to think; that there were decisions to be made, a course to be thought out. But now that he was here, his thinking seemed all to have been done. He seemed never to have done anything else but think, never to have really lived or experienced, merely to have said his life through to this point like a lesson, and the lesson was now learned. He quivered still with resentment, disgust with Elwood, young revolt against social injustice, against chicanery and indirection. But somewhere, deeper than he could divine, lay his answer. He knew that when he should be called upon, it would come, letter perfect.

As he threw himself on the grassy hill it was as if he had laid his head upon a breast, and it was the bosom of his own destiny, his own profoundest fulfillment.

All the time Elwood had been talking, Kenneth had held himself to listen by sheer intention to possess himself of all the items of the plot against Tierra Longa. But with these all in hand he was not thinking; at least, he was not thinking what he should do about it. He went on, as he had been when Elwood left him, thinking of Anne, her swift instinct, her clearness, and of her handicap of womanhood and want of opportunity. He had not thought much of women except as every young man thinks of them, in relation to himself. He had accepted for his sister, as most men had for all women, the necessity that one or the other thing in her should waste; and he saw now that it was n't necessary, but simply stupid. It was n't in the least that a woman could n't be both as big as Anne was, and as womanly, but that men were n't big enough to afford her both within the scope of their lives. In a way Elwood was big enough . . . her mind ran neck and neck with his . . . the recollection of Elwood's fatuous laugh sickened him. It had n't been the quality of her mind nor her equal spirit that had condoned for Elwood the check Anne had given him.

Overhead the blue of the sky deepened toward midnight, full of wandering stars and a light that beyond the earth's penumbra flowed between the vaults. So outside the reach of his own interests and resentments his spirit cleared and lightened. Elwood's estimate of women, Rickart's of natural resources; what were they measured against the essential use of things . . . the earth's shadow in the starlight spaces? Too small a measure. Anne had called it a man-made world, and all he had seen of it went to show that men had made it badly. But what could men do in a world in which lands, waters, the worth of women, had no measure but a man's personal reaction. It was a moment of deep but revealing humility. If it dropped him wholly outside that circle of material success it had been the object of his lifelong fumbling to be "in," it had at least dropped him consolingly into the lap of an ultimate reality, not realized or measured except as he felt it sustain him.

He did not know what he should do about it; what he should say to Rickart, or how he should meet the crisis of affairs at Tierra Longa; but he knew where he should be, where he had always been, on the side of the unseen, the immeasurable. And knowing it, he was taken with the aching need of completion, something stronger than the desire of the young male for his mate, something wider than the common human wish for a home and off-spring . . . He stood up and stretched out his arms to it in the darkness, and from afar off, beyond the reach of material sense, something answered.

It was not until he was dropping asleep in his bed, an hour later, that he remembered that he had met Virginia, and without thinking once of her relation to himself or of her affair with André.

XIV

RIDING down to Arroyo Verde the next morning, Kenneth, instead of crossing by the bridge into the county road, kept to the trail which ran close to the Agua Caliente fence on the west side of the river. It had hardly been a conscious choice, rather an instinctive movement toward the more solitary way wherein he should have leisure to think of the details of a plan of which he had found himself possessed on the awaking. It had lain there at his hand, — when about an hour after sunrise he had snapped wide awake, — new and shining like a sword which the night had forged for him; and strangely, it was shaped out of all the doubts and indecisions of his life. He had lain in his bed for an hour playing with it as youth will with a sword, and had risen at last singing the song of the sword. Breakfasting alone, for Jamieson was already at the branding-pens and Elwood had not put in an appearance, he spent some time at the telephone, dictating rather a long telegram to the Summerfield Western Union, and had packed his trunk and his bag — for he had come to the ranch prepared for an indefinite stay — and ordered a horse saddled.

Elwood joined him a few minutes before he rode out, still a little under the influence of drink, and not so much so as not to be uneasy about what he may have let out the night before in his pæan of self-congratulation; a little afraid to trust himself with the ranchers again, and yet beginning to rehearse with Kenneth the part he meant to play to them. He was sympathetic almost to tears. Nobody could regret more the trick he had been obliged to play on them, but there he was, the victim of a larger loyalty . . .

He was ready, as he had been with his dissipations, to let his noble weakness for his Own Town condone what he had done to theirs. The pitiable part of the performance was, as Kenneth could n't help knowing, that there were Tierra Longans who would so let him dissolve his practiced deceits in a tepid bath of sentiment. It irked the junior clerk exceedingly to suspect, as he did, that there was something in Elwood's weakness that was even more akin to the spirit of Tierra Longans than his own stiff young idealism.

But once he struck into the trail his purpose retook him. He rode, tossing it up and catching it again, feeling himself strong and able to make his own advantage.

It was a wide day full of light. Below him he had the Arroyo as he rode, with its windy river of green, and on the other hand, close up, the coastwise hills from whose tops it was possible to make out the sea and ships sailing on the rim of the world. It had been a good year, and outside the fence, where the cattle had not cropped, the wild oats brushed his stirrup.

As he rode he saw all the pleasant farms spread out on either side the river, and he fitted them one by one into the plan he had found waiting for him. It was a good plan, which lacked nothing of necessary knowledge of land and water laws; as if he had served his apprenticeship to Rickart and Rickart's expert attorney, Straker, for no purpose except to be furnished for this hour. Yesterday, in the course of the desultory conversation around his father's table, Anne had mentioned two or three points of possession covered by clients of hers, and though she had not said so, he inferred that these had been taken by her advice, acting on her instinctive guess at what Elwood might be about. These, too, he recalled and fitted into his own project. He knew now that this plan, which he shaped and smoothed as he rode, had been in him almost from the moment of hearing what threatened Tierra Longa, and that his not mentioning it to any one was merely the evidence of his no longer needing any other mind. He was neither Rickart's clerk nor Anne's younger brother, but his own man.

From a mile or two above the Agua Caliente bridge, the river sunk so far below the general level of the valley that the trees with their feet in its runnels scarcely topped its crumbling, clayey banks. To a horseman on the trail they afforded no screen whatever between it and the county road. It was about half past ten when, at the ancient ford, the one by which Frémont had crossed, a mile or two above the town, he saw issuing, from among its encompassing orchards, a singular cavalcade. Not quite long enough for a funeral, it had nevertheless an air of solemnity.

At its head, deployed on either side a top buggy, rode four horsemen, with rifles laid across their arms. Behind the buggy were two led horses, and following that a buckboard with a trail wagon and another led team. Two more riflemen brought up the rear, and, as the procession issued into open country, several pedestrians who tailed it dropped back to watch it out of sight. Leaving his horse among the willows, Kenneth climbed, concealed, to the top of the nearest bank; but long before the cavalcade and its escort came opposite he had recognized the black horses, the black-topped buggy, the jet mustache and the cast eye of Jevens, all the blacker for the paleness of his countenance.

Even without the account of it which he afterward had from Lem Scudder, Kenneth could guess what had happened.

Jevens, in a spirit of mean triumph, and a little, no doubt, under the influence of Elwood's amiable weakness, had flaunted his own complicity in the theft of the river, an admission which had been followed by the prompt expulsion of himself and his property from the town. It was evidently the intention of the escort to see him well on his way to the county line, if not actually across it.

Seeing in the evidence of public resentment the best possible augury for the success of his plan, Kenneth, when the cavalcade had past, rode openly into Arroyo Verde.

He was still, when he thought of it, sore with resentment at the way in which he had been used by Rickart, from whom he had a right to expect a better employment than that of decoying his father's friends and neighbors into Elwood's net. There was a deeper, more personal feeling against being so used by Frank's father, but for the moment his new-forged purpose pushed it aside. Watching Jevens driven out, he had felt the click within him of a sympathy by which he was locked finally to the interests of Tierra Longa as against every other claim; but it did not occur to him that, riding into town on one of the Caliente saddle horses, he was still under the visible sign of Rickart.

There were ranchers and cattle men gathering in the plaza, and from group to group of them an intermittent flow of sullen and excited talk.

It fell off as Kenneth approached, and was succeeded by strained silence. Behind him it began again, with here and there a note of sneering laughter. He spoke to one of the river ranchers whom he knew, and for answer the man shot a long squirt of tobacco juice which struck the fore-flank of his horse. The quiver which passed over the sensitive animal shook for a moment in young Brent's soul, but in the faces about him there was something that restrained the personal impulse. At the public hitching-rack he came upon the Scudder boys, who ducked their heads and made as if to pass without speaking, but Brent sung out to them.

"Hello, boys!"

The habit of old friendliness was too much for Lem. "'Lo!" he said, and sidestepped again.

"Look here, Lem, I want to talk to you."

"You?" sneered Lem. "What do you want with the likes of us? You're workin' for Rickart."

"You're a liar, Lem, if you never were one before. I quit working for Rickart yesterday afternoon at half past four, exactly."

"Fired you, did he?" gibed Ab; "was n't quite smart enough, coaxin' your old friends into his net."

But Kenneth's high mood was proof even against this.

"I fired myself the minute I found out the game he was working against Tierra Longa," he corrected. "Ab, you fool, do you suppose he would have dared to send me down here if I had known what he was up to?" Two or three of the bystanders, who had refused Kenneth's greeting, stopped to listen, curious but unconvinced. "I came," he explained at large, "because I was led to believe — or at least I did believe," he corrected himself in full justice to his employer — "that Mr. Rickart was really interested in some scheme of local development. And I quit him because there is n't money enough anywhere to hire me to work for a man who is working against Tierra Longa." His burning desire to be understood by them led him into their own simple phrases.

Ab gave him back a short, barking laugh. "Pretty good for a first attempt, Lawyer Brent, but it ain't quite good enough. You'd ought to take a few lessons from your friend Elwood when it comes to soft sawder. Damn him!"

"Shut up, Ab," Lem interjected. "There ain't no cause for us makin' worse fools of ourselves than we been a'ready."

"Oh, let him get it off his chest," Kenneth conceded. "And while you're cussing, Ab, you can cuss a few for me. I don't know that you've got anything on the Old Man worse than I have, sending me down here, sight unseen, to pull the wool over my friends and neighbors. But don't waste too much time cussing; we've got to get busy now and beat him."

This got home to them.

Kenneth experienced a strange, inward thrill at this new rôle of personal ascendancy which came so easily. He hooked his arm through Lemuel's. "Come over here," he urged aside, "I want to talk to you."

At the end of a quarter of an hour Lem was choking between the lust of battle and an occasional backwash of suspicion. "It listens good," he admitted. "If there's any way of buckin' Rickart's game, looks like that's the way to do it . . ." He fell back on the tradition of the valley, "There ain't nobody in Tierry Longway ever went up ag'in' the Old Man and got away with it."

"No one man," Kenneth agreed, "but all of you — solid!"

Lem spat reflectively. "There ain't all of us in Tierry Longway ever agreed about nothin' yet."

"But they'll have to, or else surrender. You'll come in, you and Ab . . ."

"Oh, sure . . . Don't take it noways hard about Ab . . . he was up 'most all night; the baby like to died on 'em. I guess you better put this up to some of the big owners."

All morning men kept arriving from the isolated ranches, and were fused in the common resentment. It was agreed that there ought to be some kind of a meeting. The townspeople who were responsible for the expulsion of Jevens broached it first; action had whetted their appetite for action. But the farmers suffered, even in betrayal, a need of the genial bond which Elwood had forged for them, such a need as a woman has for the lover who has abandoned her. Had he come among them at that moment, those who had already felt it would have stooped again under his stroking hand. Actually their craving for the consoling community of interest which Elwood's shared weakness had created for them, was issue of that same root of tribal solidarity which had moved Kenneth to throw himself on the side of the threatened valley. But Brent's medium was strange to them.

The solitary, rural habit which admitted them to a community of beguilement could not lift them to a community of enterprise. Not all at once. But by mid-day the altered demeanor of three or four who had talked apart with young Brent began to spread, about the plaza and under the cottonwood domes, a faint irradiance of anticipation.

About two of the afternoon the schoolhouse bell was heard clanging slowly, and there began to be a general movement in that direction. Some forty of the towns-people and the threatened ranchers gathered, with a fair sprinkling of women. Just as the meeting was called to order, the party from Palomitas came in, Steven Brent and Anne, and Peters; and before the chairman had con-cluded his opening remarks, the meeting took on a touch of grimness from the entrance of the Jevens escort, who came stamping in at the back and stacked their rifles.

After the opening the meeting sagged back like a horse at the end of a stake-rope. There was the hot, life-less smell of unused buildings; blue flies droned at the windows.

In the half-hostile silence Willard arose, and shuffling on his feet called for a few remarks from the son of our esteemed friend and neighbor. A sudden murmur went over the crowd as though a choppy wind played upon it, shaking out assent and remonstrance, and then a curious, strained silence.

"Friends and fellow citizens," Brent began; and then from the back of the room a lumbering hulk of a cattle man, one of Jevens's escort, heaved himself to his feet and claimed the chairman's attention.

"What I want ter know, Mr. Chairman, who air we listenin' to? Are we a-listenin' to a emmesary of the Old Man, or are we a-listenin' to a skunk in sheep's clothing?"

The chairman shuffled in his turn and passed the ques-tion on to Kenneth.

"I am not," he said, "in the employment of T. Rick-art."

"Since when?" said another voice from the audience.

"Since the moment I read what is printed in this paper." He waved the betraying sheet before them. For the first time he looked over at his family. Steven Brent gravely nodded; Anne looked at the fingers of her gloves.

Kenneth had never conducted a case in court, but he had watched Straker, that most expert of special pleaders.

Half-consciously he modeled the first embarrassed moves of his speech on what he remembered of the firm's senior lawyer: driving straightaway to the point until it was established, a shining mark, the focus of all attention, and then coming back to pick up his audience and drive them toward it, a handy missile. And the point was, not what they might feel and think about Rickart or the method by which he had nearly stolen their river, but whether they meant to let him get away with it. Item by item he laid it out for them: as matters stood, Rickart did not own enough of the water of Arroyo Verde to pay its carriage to San Francisco.

Find a way to keep him out of possession of any more of it and the river stayed in its arroyo. Was there, then, such a way, defended from Rickart's practiced cunning and their own need which from time to time betrayed them to him?

There was such a way; one that had behind it all that young Brent had learned of law in six years with the Old Man under the hand of Straker. It all depended on their sticking together. They were to put their land and waters in escrow, tying them for a price which would render Rickart's scheme practically prohibitive. In the unlikely event of his rising to that price, it would, at least, let them all out of Tierra Longa together; it would protect them absolutely from the slow defeat, the dwindling values, the long-drawn bitterness which confronted them. They had only to stick together. It was as simple as that. Too simple by half.

Tacking always toward its objective, blown out of the course by prejudice and slanting back on a partial idealism, what more natural to the rural mind than to suppose that whoever first reaches the goal does so by an excess of cunning — a more complex indirection? To catch Rickart-birds one must make nets and snares; they were not to be arrested by the simple device of ring around a rosy.

Perhaps Brent, as he talked, knew that he did not have his audience with him. He might have seen, as he faced them, how, by as much as they had given of themselves to the soil, they were made defenseless against this attack on it. For a man lives with his land as with a mistress, courting her, suiting himself to her humors, contriving as he can that her moods, her weathers shall drive for and not against him. And in time he becomes himself subject to such shifts and seasons. He cannot handle himself; he is to be handled.

But if Kenneth understood that this was the case with the farmers of Tierra Longa, he gave no sign. If he felt in them, what had struck so sorely on his father, the waste of what they had put into the earth, the irredeemable waste of it, he was silent on that also. Beyond some streaks of whiteness which came into his face as he rose to the first challenge, his whole bearing was free from emotion. The fire which forged his sword had gone out; it was the clean, cold blade he offered them. He took all for granted, their love for the land, their right to it; spoke as man to man, neither Rickart's clerk nor the tool of Elwood. He was

Brent of Palomitas. He had the poise of three generations of landholders.

That was how he struck, all unaware, the secret which
it had been his six years' quest to discover, the secret of
the Old Man's success; the trick of taking the shortest
distance between two points, ignoring the human element. But being so sure in his heart that he worked in
the community interest, he failed, almost as completely as
Rickart had done, to win the community's coöperation.

So at the end of three quarters of an hour he came to
the end of his statement with his audience cold. They
shuffled a little at his close, broke out here and there in
half-audible comment, and fell silent. Lem Scudder,
carefully instructed thereto, moved a resolution favoring
Brent's plan and calling for the appointment of a committee to formulate it. Discussion was called for, which
gathered and broke in short, irrelevant flashes. Nobody
questioned much nor proposed any alternative; nothing
could lay hold on minds so preoccupied with anger. A
more practiced speaker would have known how to draw
their resentment to the explosive point, clearing the way
to action. Brent himself knew it, but his defense was too
much in the manner of Rickart's own campaigns to appear adequate. They had damned Rickart often as the
passionless embodiment of money-grabbing; but it was
not so they realized him. Such damage as they stood to
meet could not have been plotted in cold blood, not without passion be defeated. To sign their names to a paper
and sit tight was too tame a medicine for their burning
sense of injury.

The river rancher who had first challenged Kenneth's
loyalty put the sense of the meeting.

"Mr. Chairman: I don't know as I've anything to say against the proposition Mr. Brent has put up to us. I reckon he's a pretty fine lawyer and knows the straight of it. Looks mighty slick the way he's read it out to us; but that's just the trouble with it. Looks like them options some of us been signin' lately. Mr. Dutton, here," — Dutton was the town's own lawyer, who had pompously, if somewhat reluctantly, expressed his entire legal agreement with Mr. Brent, — "Dutton has given it as his opinion that that's the law of it, but what I want ter know is, whose side the law is goin' to turn out to be on, ours or Rickart's?"

He sat down amid grunts of agreement and one or two voices raised in protest. Lem Scudder was on his feet, but the chairman passed him over for Baff, who was disposed to be judicious.

Nobody, it appeared, had a higher appreciation of the legal skill which had been exhibited. Mr. Baff allowed it was a right smart statement. But the human mind, according to Mr. Baff, required humoring; it wasn't possible, now, was it? to switch off as they had been required to do within an hour, thinking of Brent as employed by the Old Man, and think of him as working for Tierry Longway; he'd leave it to Mr. Brent if it was easy.

"I certainly admit the difficulty," Kenneth met him good-humoredly.

"Well, then," Mr. Baff put it rather intimately, "it's this away; if we go into this, I allow we got to go in bag an' baggage, puttin' all we got into the pot, Mr. Brent certifyin' that it's the sure dope for what we got stacked up against us. Now, I put it to you, gentlemen and Mr. Brent, don't it look like Mr. Brent'd ought to be in with

us? Don't it seem like we'd be easier in our minds if Mr.
Brent had something he could put in with us? Don't it
sort of look that way?" It was the sense of the meeting
that it did. "I ask you, fellow citizens," demanded Mr.
Baff, growing easier as he felt his audience with him, "to
what extent, if any, Mr. Brent is in with us."

"Well," the chairman agreed by way of passing it on
to Kenneth, "I reckon that's a fair question."

"Oh, yes," Brent conceded, knitting his brows slightly,
"it's fair enough. If I have n't stated to what extent I'm
willing to come in with you, it is because I have n't been
sure this was the time and place for it. I rather thought
the committee" — he looked at Willard and the Scudders, but though he must have known what it meant to
her, he did not look at Anne. The attention of the meeting
stayed breathless on the point of his indecision; it rose
perceptibly as it watched him catch consent from the eyes
of two or three who knew what was in his mind. "Well,
if you think best, gentlemen, . . . I'm with you to the
extent of thirty thousand cubic inches of the river surplus."

If he had dashed it over them he could hardly have
taken them more by surprise. They were startled by it,
half a dozen of them, into following Lem Scudder's lead
of applause, but sharply stopped to hear what else the
speaker had to say.

"I'm with you further than that, gentlemen. I'm
with you to the extent of being willing to transfer a controlling interest in the river surplus, which I filed upon in
my own right six weeks ago, to any properly constituted
company of those of you who will develop and use it."

He broke forth largely into an account of how they

might bring about for themselves all those things that
Elwood had made seem bright and easy of attainment.
Though he did not know how much Elwood had worked
for him there, kneading the stiff stuff of the rural imagination, they were fired at last; touched with that passion
for togetherness which is the ravishment of noble souls
and the refuge of weak ones. So for as long as it served,
he achieved the miracle of coöperation. The resolution
was passed and cheered. Tierra Longa was awake, and
the Old Man had been caught napping.

"Well, Dad?" Kenneth shook himself free from question and congratulation to clap his father on the shoulder.

Brent beamed upon him.

"Very well, son!"

"Well, Anne, — can you give me a job at the ranch for
my board and clothes — Anne?"

Anne was crying.

"Oh, Ken, your one chance —"

"You bet it's my chance. You watch and see what I'll
do with it!"

Being at his most triumphant he was most male, and
a little obtuse. It was arranged, however, that 'Nacio
was to meet Kenneth at headquarters about five, to
take away his trunk. He would not spend another night
under the same roof with Elwood.

Kenneth, after a short session with the committee,
found nobody at Agua Caliente but Jamieson, smoking
over the day's accounts. "I wired my resignation this
morning," he said by way of explaining why he was leaving. He saw it was not necessary to tell the Superintendent anything of the afternoon's proceedings. Nobody
knew how news was carried to Agua Caliente; it was

thought Tom Dinnant, the fence-rider, might have something to do with it, but there was nothing could go on in
the valley and the ranch not hear of it.

"Eh, well — you know your own business, Mr. Brent,"
was the Superintendent's only comment, but he came
out to see the boy off with his baggage.

They stood together while 'Nacio fumbled with the
trunk, looking out over the valley now filling with the
evening light, banded and barred through the coastwise
cañons. Kenneth, who liked the blunt Scot, sought for
just the phrase to justify what might easily seem a dis-
loyalty to his employer, but found nothing better than
"There's something, you know, about a man's own country . . . the country he was born and grew up in —" and
fell silent watching the homing flight of the herons.

Jamieson grudged him nothing. "'T is a great country;
a man might do much for it."

"Sure," Kenneth rose to the local slogan, "it's a great
country."

Encouraged, he ventured a discreet suggestion:—

"If I knew when Mr. Rickart is expected, I would try
to see him myself, before — anybody else, I mean."

Jamieson nodded. "Man to man; 't is better so. If I
knew myself I'd tell you."

But it proved, after all, unnecessary for Kenneth to
contrive to meet Rickart at Agua Caliente. About mid-
afternoon of the next day, while the committee was sitting in the town's one hotel, Rickart's car came careening
up the valley with a begoggled, dust-disguised chauffeur,
and Rickart chewing his cigar in the tonneau. With his
usual imperviousness to the local feeling about him, the
Old Man stopped his car at the hotel for a drink. Or

stopped for his own purpose to bring on this encounter
with his former clerk. The committee, issuing from the
green and shadowed cave of the bar, came plump upon
him. For his own purpose Rickart chose not to take the
meeting seriously.

"Well, Ken," — he worked his cigar to the corner of
his mouth the better to clear the way for any expression
the occasion seemed to call for, — "been stirring up the
town against your employer, eh?"

"Well, not until I had sent you my resignation," Kenneth corrected him. He was more moved at this unexpected encounter than he had expected to be or cared to
show.

"Well, my boy, it seems to me you might have waited
until I had accepted your resignation. I have n't been
such a bad employer as that comes to." He had n't, as
Kenneth miserably knew.

"I should have preferred that myself, sir. But the
situation here — the people, seemed to need me."

"Uh — the people." Such people as were within reach
strained their ears. They knew they had no business to
listen, and pretended not to, but a consuming curiosity
had them in its grip. "T-h-e" — long drawn out —
"p-e-o-p-l-e." The cigar came round to an angle slightly
skeptical. Suddenly there was a change of tone. "Look
here, Ken, jump into the car and come down the road
with me a piece. I want to talk to you."

Kenneth colored and was firm. "I'm sorry, Mr.
Rickart. It has n't been easy for me to make the people
understand that I actually have come over to their side
and am against you in this fight . . ." Sweat of pure dis-
comfort broke out on his forehead.

"I see. And you can't have a few minutes' chat with your second father for fear the p-eo-ple . . ." Rickart took his cigar out of his mouth and sat for a while as if taking counsel with it. "What's this about Anne?" he broke out abruptly. "Elwood tells me it was she that spilled the thing to the newspapers."

Kenneth cursed himself for having brought his sister into it.

"Anne's on your side —"

"Anne has sense."

"She was so much on your side that she thought Mr. Elwood might be putting something over on you. She was only trying to find out what he was up to. The paper found out the rest."

He had it on the end of his tongue to say that it was in his, Rickart's, interest Anne had suggested his appropriation of the surplus waters, but he feared to involve her further. "Anne," he finished mendaciously, "does n't approve of me."

"I've always said Anne was the business man of the family." Heaven send he would go on thinking so. "Well, I did n't see your resignation; they told me it was in the office, but I suppose you complied with the usual formalities."

"Formalities?" Kenneth was puzzled.

"Turned over all the papers, properties, et cetera?"

"All the papers and the power of attorney are in my desk at the office, — I shan't put in any claim for salary or expense after the tenth, if that's what you mean . . ."

"And the surplus water appropriation that you filed as my agent, have you turned that over?"

"As your agent —" Kenneth saw the pit open beneath him. He should have been first to mention that appropriation and as whose agent. He gathered himself in one concentrated effort not to look as confounded as he felt.

"Why, yes," Rickart pleasantly chatted, "rights and properties acquired by the agent, you know . . . but I need n't quote law to you. Straker said the transfer had n't come in yet, and I told him if he did n't get it in a few days to write to you."

XV

EVER since Ellis Trudeau's first visit to Palomitas the deep veranda opening on the formal garden had become the place of family councils. It was, Anne openly averred, largely for Ellis's gift of laying hands, soft and service-able, on the hidden centers of personal relations, that Anne paid her; the stenography and bookkeeping were thrown in for good measure. For Anne, seeing in the shut gar-den, refurnished from all that they could recall of their mother's preferences, only the place of regretful memo-ries, would have swept the family life aside and apart from it. The pomegranate hedge stood breast-high about it, but the slope of the land gave them full from the veranda the perspective of the valley. It looked a little away from the river, toward Mariposa, and took in above its western hedge the line of the Caliente fence and the breach in the Coast Range, curving seaward. Or, if you chose, sitting low, it took in nothing at all but the banks of red geraniums, the new-planted beds, and the red rambler working close under the waves, with here and there a lifted, inquiring streamer. Cushions and hammock had made their appearance there, a low table where Addie took her mending; a place cleared for Steven Brent's pipe and paper; all this within three months from the time Anne had come hurrying in from the *potrero* to find that Ellis had received there some former friend of her mother's calling from Rancho Toyon, and that her father, to whose sensibilities Anne had feared a wound, was gravely pleased by it. "Land o' livin'," said Addie, who was placidly preparing a tea-tray under Miss Trudeau's direction, "it's your ma's memory they're callin' on, anyway!"

"It lets them know," Ellis explained, "that he did n't fail her; that he's keeping right along with the sort of thing she liked best — she would have liked it, would n't she?"

"Yes," Anne considered; "she would have liked it. It's exactly the sort of thing she tried to get out of us when we were children . . . some kind of social ceremonial . . . we were as wild as little Indians, but I don't see how you knew!"

"Oh, well," — Ellis was serious, — "knowing what other people like is my profession, I suppose." She made a little *moue*. "Andy has given me lots of practice."

That was how it happened that the first intimation Kenneth gave to anybody of the new turn affairs had taken was given to Anne and his father, about four of the afternoon that Rickart came to Tierra Longa. He had hurried away from the town not to give room for widening rings to spread from the shock his talk with Rickart had occasioned him.

"But, Ken, what can he do?"

"Sue me for recovery of rights acquired while I was acting as his agent."

"But you were n't. If anything, you were *my* agent; I put you up to it."

"If you could prove that . . . but I was in Rickart's pay."

"Not out of office hours, surely. I can prove that I sent for you, that I brought you out here, and my hired man took you to the point where the filing was made. Why can't your best answer to his demand be that you have turned your rights over to me?"

"You forget I've promised to turn over a controlling interest to the Citizens' Committee."

Anne choked at that.

"I'm not sure you had any right to do that without consulting me."

"Oh, Anne, surely you see that I could n't just hold on to it as a plum I'd picked out for myself?" Perhaps because he was doubtful whether he had been right, Kenneth was the more anxious to appear so. "I *had* to go in with them, if I wanted them with me."

Anne waived discussion.

"Even then I don't see why it would n't be a good move for me to claim you as my agent before Rickart does?"

"Well, I've already told him before witnesses that you don't approve of me."

"Ken! How could you?"

He could easily, he said, because he did n't intend she should be mixed up in this. Did she suppose, just when she'd built up her own business so successfully, she was to be allowed to risk it on him? "Besides," — he hesitated for the least offensive phrase, "I don't want you, Anne. I don't want any help, and — don't think me a thundering egotist, sis, but I don't want any advice. I've got to see this thing through on my own . . . I've got to *come* through. I don't want to be influenced by fear of what would happen to somebody I'm tied up with."

"He's right, Anne; we must n't tie him in any way," Steven Brent agreed.

Anne tapped with her fingers on the arm of his chair.

"But if it is to my interest to fight this scheme for taking the water away —"

Well, it just was n't, Kenneth told her. Palomitas was n't affected, or, if it was, it could n't be unfavorably. It would take two or three years to build that dam and aqueduct; she was to think of the profit she'd make selling her produce on the spot without hauling it to Summerfield . . . and all the land that would be turned back to wild pasture for the sheep . . .

"But, Ken, how will you manage; about money and everything?"

"I've some stock, things I've picked up in the office. I could realize two or three thousand —"

"Two or three thousand for a lawsuit with Rickart!" Anne scoffed.

"Oh, to tell the truth, I don't think it will come to that. There's something I'm much more afraid of. Something that will come cheaper than a suit at law and serve his purpose exactly as well; and that is the *idea* of a suit."

"You think he simply means to throw a scare into the committee?" Anne's quick mind caught him up.

"Well, he said it where they could all hear him, Willard and Baff and Scudder. It is n't Rickart's way to threaten. If he means to sue, he just sues."

"If he makes that play so early," Anne concluded, "it's because he is somehow pressed for time. But we can keep on for a year or two and hold that surplus water right even without the Citizens' Committee. The thing for us to do is to fight for time. I'm having Peters file on that eighty between us and the river. Within six months I can have somebody on every unpatented acre that the surplus ditch will cover. We can give water for work on the ditch and if he scares off Arroyo Verde, make a community of our own."

"Anne, you're a wonder! Rickart ought to have taken you into partnership."

"He ought," she admitted; "as it is I could give him a run for his money." She alternately drummed and frowned as she planned, having full sight of the quarry and all the moves of the game. Kenneth stretched himself and paced up and down the veranda.

Clever as she was, her brother was not moved to join forces with her. He did not want Anne, he did not feel to want anybody on his side; for it was not so important to him at this moment whether he won or went down, but to know with what he fought. He suffered the need, so inexplicable to women, of aloofness; to see straight, to swing clear, and to come to grips.

In the hour or two which had passed between the passing of Rickart and his own flight from the town, which he had delayed just long enough not to make it seem precipitant, Kenneth had not had time to think out this new phase very clearly. He thought slowly for the most part, and was more than pleased with this new instinct in him, which, working ahead of his intelligence, had operated to keep Anne out of it, since the end of such thinking as he had been able to do was, that at any cost to himself she must be kept out. She must be kept in touch with that better side of the Old Man from which had sprung his support of her undertaking at Palomitas, and as far as possible from that revealing acquaintance with Rickart's methods which gnawed at the root of his own lifelong association. Let Anne think as long as she would that Rickart's threat was mere bluff, to frighten the ranchers of Tierra Longa. It was not unlikely that it should be so; Rickart had no claim upon him, absolutely no legal claim. But the certainty to which Kenneth measured his pacing was, that if it became necessary to the Rickart Interests that a case should be found, there would be a case against him.

All that flood of competency upon which the Old Man's enterprises floated, stirred by this menace, turned up, as the white undersides of poplars, glimmering bay, and dark shades of oak, were revealed in the stirring of the Arroyo's leafy surfaces. Incidents of old cases turned up, half hints and guesses, letters which the defendant denied receiving, copies of which showed between appropriate leaves of the letter-press . . . instructions protested, but sworn to by one or another in the Old Man's employ . . . conversations overheard and noted; turned up a current rumor about the office that the Old Man's private sanctum was contrived for the express purpose of overhearing; turned up inexplicable rises in fortune of certain witnesses, inexplicable disappearances. What was a case against a junior clerk to men who had effected the shift of a Government bureau and yet saved the face of an unimpeachable civic loyalty!

If Rickart offered him fight, Brent knew that he must fight to a finish; but he knew also, in reason, that he could n't win, and that was the reason Anne must be kept out of it. For it mattered to Anne whether she lost or won, and at the moment nothing mattered so much to young Brent as that he should take his own measure. Whatever he was up against, — laws, institutions, the passions and prejudices of other men, — he must know once for all its nature and its name. All around him for the past few days he had felt the questions he had put to life falling in with their answers, two and two. In a little while, if nobody stopped him, he would swing into his own proper stride . . .

"Look here, Anne, you've got to promise that you'll keep out of this. Has n't she, father? If you don't, I'll not stay around. I'll go down to the hotel and live until this is settled."

"Ken, as if we would *let* you!"

"Unless you promise. Is n't that right, father?"

"I think he's right, Anne."

"Oh, well,"—Anne conceded the point; "but there's no necessity for your behaving as if we'd disowned you. Mr. Rickart is n't so small as *that!*" And no one making any answer to this she was off in a new direction. "I'm glad you have all that money, Ken. Of course I could have spared you a little, but I think I'm going to buy a car." They laughed at her characteristic thrust against misfortune. It was always Anne's way, in the face of threatening, to make a sudden new assault and recoup in another direction what she stood to lose. If she thought now of buying a car, it was because she foresaw the necessity of lifting her business to the point where a car would become indispensable.

The laugh brought Virginia out of her room, where she had discreetly lingered while the Brents discussed this new check to their affairs. It was intolerable to Virginia to be kept out of things, but even to Virginia it was plain that the rape of Arroyo Verde, the outrage of which had brought her in swift, warm partisanship to his side, had dropped like a cold curtain between herself and Kenneth. If in his reasonable hours he did full justice to the impulse which led her to range herself with him and the ranchers of Tierra Longa, his appreciation was, for any purpose that would have served Virginia, much too reasonable. Far from throwing them together, as in her unpremeditated flight to him she had no doubt imagined, on the crest of that indignation which the spectacle of social injustice so easily excited in her, Virginia had found herself cast away on the coast of a situation to which not even Steven Brent's grave agreement with her resounding phrases admitted her. It was not that they slighted her interest in them: the Brents were far too polite for that; but with all their politeness they were unable to make out of Virginia's feeling *for* them anything that would take the place of just naturally feeling the same thing at the same time. Nothing, not even the releasing laughter with which Anne's sallies in the face of financial discomfiture were greeted by her family, could give to Virginia's reappearance anything but the status of an old and well-intentioned friend of the family, who had chosen a rather inopportune occasion for making a visit.

"It's the best possible cure for that poor feeling," Anne was maintaining, "to go out and buy something you can't afford."

"I know, I know," — Virginia felt eagerly for her cue. "It corrects your vibrations; puts you in harmony with the stream of abundance."

"Possibly," said Anne. "Don't you and Ken want to go down and bring up the letters?"

The Palomitas letters were dropped by the lately established rural delivery in a box at the Ford of Mariposa Creek where the county road came out of the Draw, and were brought up with the lamb-band by Demetrio.

It was hardly a reasonable assumption that Anne's anxiety about her business could n't brook the further hour's delay before the drawing-in of the flocks would have brought her letters to her hand. But it was in the air that whatever there was between Kenneth and Virginia, they must have it out together. If there had been, on the part of Anne, any anxiety as to what this hour could hold for her brother, she had so far successfully concealed it. Yet it was with an odd, misleading tenderness that her gaze followed them down the orchard. Steven Brent, who saw it, came and put his arm around her. He thought her very beautiful, this tall daughter, fit to be the consort and mother of men. Now, as his eyes moved tenderly over her soft hair, her fine bosom, he wondered afresh, with ever-present pain, what far-wandering dart from her mother's unhappy destiny had struck Anne's chance of happiness to the heart. She was so tremendously sure of herself, and yet little things — this new wistfulness with which she watched her brother and Virginia — set him agrope.

"You don't think that they — that Kenneth" — he floundered. "I had an idea, in fact, I rather hoped it was the other one. She seems — more suitable."

"Oh," said Anne, "that's nothing. There is n't anybody for Ken, yet."

"There's time enough," he admitted. "It's you I'm thinking of . . ."

"Oh, father . . ." She put up a hand to his cheek, went red and white, inwardly stricken. "Are you going to mind it so much, my being an old maid?" She saw it on his lips to say that he minded only that she should not be unhappy, and checked it with her hand. "It is

not," she said, "as if I did n't know what I am missing
. . . " Always uncommunicative about herself, she could
get no further.

She moved away from his consoling arm, setting the
chairs in order, but she had no heart to leave him
troubled.

"You're not to think things, father — it's just that
I'm happier this way than I could be with anything that
is likely to happen to me." Staidly she went in to help
Addie with the supper.

Kenneth, at the Wash of Vine Creek, was disposed to
be reminiscent. "I was nearly drowned here once," he
recalled, "saving a three-weeks-old lamb, which was afterward sold to the butcher." He laughed, being in the
mood in which the mind seeks signs and omens. "I
wonder," he said, "for what the ranchers of Tierra Longa
are fattening."

"Whatever it is, you will save them from it just as
you're saving them now from Rickart!" Virginia's pen-
nants were all out again. "Oh, Ken, I can't tell you how
splendid all this is —"

He met her dryly; all his young energies pent up. She
was to remember, he said, that as yet he had n't saved
anything. It would come, indeed, to the Tierra Longans
saving themselves; the most he could do was to point the
way for them. It was no new thing, he said, to be in a
fight with Rickart; only where he had been before on
Rickart's side, he was now, by the merest accident,
against him.

"You feel," she insisted, "the pressure of the System."

But neither would he have that as an explanation.

If he fought, it was not as a reformer, but simply by instinct. "I hit back," he said, "because he's hit me where I live."

"Where you live," she exulted, "is among the people."

"Oh, the people!" If it came to that, he said, there were plenty of people whose relations to the land were exactly what Rickart's were. They were simply holding it to make the most out of it. It was n't so much a matter of numbers as of capacity. The greatest common factor of the Tierra Longans was their general inability to rise to the Old Man's measure; they were inferior stuff of the same pattern.

He would admit, since she insisted, that the system by which land and water became subject to the greed or caprice of men like Rickart was a bad one. But she must admit that a part of its badness lay in subjecting it to the ignorance and greed of men like Baff and Jevens. No, it was n't any feeling about the System that had got him, it was a feeling for the land. Land was to be cherished, to be made productive. . . . It did n't make so much difference under *what* system it was bandied about, if you lost sight of that consideration.

He lit a cigarette and threw it away, needing no stimulant but his own embattled prejudice. "Land!" he said, sniffing the new-turned furrow which in the face of defeat from a new quarter spoke to him consolingly. "That's where I live; on the land and working it. Don't pull any of the hero stuff on me, Virginia; all that I've been doing is finding out that I've always been a farmer."

Renewed association with the things about him bred a conscious sense of security; the grazing flocks, the ribbed hills, the steady fall of the valley seaward. "It's just," he said, — and the phrase touched him with a fleeting recollection of its appropriateness, — "that I've come up against the biggest fact in my existence. I'm Brent of Palomitas."

Dry fuel this for Virginia's flame. She felt back among the kindling phrases to feed it. "But, of course, you'll realize that you can't stop with just getting after the individual; it all comes back to the Cap —"

His newfound sense of personal value struck out against befogging phrases.

"*That's* the mistake you make, Virginia. All the time, — there in San Francisco, — I could n't, somehow, say it, but I felt the mistake of dividing people up according to what they get out of it. Rich against poor, I mean. It is n't the Old Man's capital that the people of the valley are up against, so much as it is their *idea* of it, and their idea of the situation, or their lack of ideas. . . . I'm just seeing it. The System — what system of land and water there is — is on their side, and circumstances are with them . . . but I don't know that that will save them, if they don't come to *see*. Oh, Lord!" he broke off, recalling that it was he who should presently have to depend upon their seeing.

Virginia's hand stole under his elbow and worked along his arm by slight, slow clutches and releases. It was a witchery which had worked well enough in that old ground of inducted social passion. "I know," she murmured, "I understand."

Kenneth took his arm quite away from her, ostensibly for the uses of the smoke that he had just rejected.

The trouble with Virginia was that she was sometimes genuine. Where she was dramatic, as in her flight from

Trudeau, she was irreproachable. Even with Kenneth's failure to follow, it had still been open to her to hear the clear call of her consecration to the cause of Labor sounding above the note of personal passion, against which her only resort had been flight and cloisture. Out of this unimpeachable attitude she had been flung, by the genuine rush of her sympathies, toward Tierra Longa where she had been born, and to the Brents who were nearer to her by association than any of her own kin. Where it had flung her at last was against the cold surface of his preoccupation. And how was he to know, how are men ever to find out, — since with them the case is quite otherwise, — that with women the rise of the social passion is but a flare to their personal intensity? Kenneth had taken his arm away from Virginia, not because of the failure of his instincts to respond, but because he felt the nature of that response a hindrance to clear thinking. His need of getting this thing stated to himself overrode even his youth and its importunate demands.

It was not, he was certain, what people got out of things that determined their relation to a given situation, but the way they went at it. He drew upon the nearest thing in his own mind for a figure of comparison, the one that Elwood had furnished him.

"It's like the way some men are with women," he said; "if they think of them as just a kind of trimming, why that's the way they use them." By the sudden flick of fear in the eye that she turned toward him he saw what he had done. There had been, in point of fact, but the merest tremor, the almost imperceptible veiling of her audacity, but it hurt him to see it. So far as he had been conscious of anything in his talking, it had been to avoid

the implication of there being anything like a situation
between himself and Virginia, and here he had walked
deliberately into it. It was only by the sense of shock
that followed on his break that he became aware how
completely the situation had been there all the time for
Virginia.

"The way men are with women," she said, "is n't always easy for a woman to discover. I can't even tell," —
she tried and failed, for the note of brightness, — "unless
you tell me first, what you are up to."

"Oh, what I'm up to?" That was easy. He was up to
this water fight, and to cutting something out of it for
himself to live by.

"You mean — to live *here?*"

"What else is there for me? If I'm done with Rickart,
it's because I'm done with his way of doing business.
I'm done with business. From now on, I'm a producer.
I shall produce" — he took it all in, the rich rural prospect, Anne's new fields, his father's flocks, the refurnished
orchard — "alfalfa and mutton. Maybe I shall produce
an irrigation canal and a farming district, but the thing
I feel I have a talent for is mutton." He said it gayly;
more gayly in fact than he felt it, as he was willing a moment later to show her. "It won't be so easy," he said;
"it means years of work and short commons. All this
belongs to father and Anne; I've really nothing. I shall
just have to stick at it. . . . It will be years before I can
marry . . ."

Well, if Virginia had not dished herself by the affair
with Trudeau, this very world-spirit which she had
worked to produce in him had done it for her.

"It's fine, of course, Ken," — she could n't quite let go

of her preferred attitudes, she clutched at one of them, indeed, as a plank between her and drowning, — "your being willing to join the ranks of workers; but I hate to think of you burying yourself out of the big world."

"Oh," he protested, "I shan't be entirely out of it. You'll be there, and that will always give me an interest . . ."

It was, however, the end of his interest in her for the moment. They had reached the mail box, and, as he lifted the letters from it, he saw that one bore the familiar superscripture. Straker had lost no time in reminding him that he was expected, along with his other papers, to turn over his appropriated rights to the surplus waters of Arroyo Verde.

XVI

RICKART's master stroke in dealing with Tierra Longa was to take Elwood away with him. The third day the great car, like the passing of a sinister portent, raced northward, dust at its tail as if the land had yielded to the primitive impulse to defile what it found contemptible.

Followed a few lowering days lightened by subtle intimations of triumph; succeeded to these a general slackening of the tension of opposition. And then doubt.

The visible presence of the party of attack had whetted the fighting humor of the Tierra Longans; its removal to regions whence no sign issued, and to which the rural imagination could not follow them, left both sentiment and opinion absurdly toppling over an empty chasm. It is true young Brent professed to know what the enemy might be about and from what quarter they could be expected next to strike; but considering that they had known Brent since he was knee-high to them, was it likely? To the rural mind, a proper sense of caution demands that you suspect something. Deprived of Elwood and Rickart, they suspected the device which would have bound them to concerted opposition. Most of all they suspected its even-handedness. According to Brent it made you safe against every contingency; its weakness was that it provided an equal security for old man Tuttle who was suspected of being a Mormon and Sturgis who made you ridiculous by succeeding with his silo in the face of your confident prediction.

Not for mere poetizing has the ancient word for coun-
tryman come to be the word for unbeliever, for Chris-
tianity is a religion of togetherness, and, pagan to the soul,
the ranchers of Tierra Longa preferred to trust to the
partial gods of their own boundaries, the secret stroke of
fortune.

That week saw the end of the Rains. They blew in on
the coast winds through the vent by which the river found
its way to the sea, ran halfway up the Saltillos and broke
over the Torr' in a succession of quick, steady showers
followed by warm, bright days of surpassing clearness.
As though it had been loosed on them from the super-
heated air, dry discontent settled over Tierra Longa.
Young Brent, working from ranch to ranch in search of
signers for the Land and Water Holders' Agreement, felt
it come like a dust-storm at the turn of the season; a
sense of rasping tension, and then an imperceptible
curdling of the air, and suddenly they were lost in it out
of sight and sound of one another.

It began with the givers of options. Many of them had
wanted badly to sell. Men who had bought into the valley under the stimulus of one or another of the rumors of
local development, men who begrudge the tying-up of
their capital in profitless fields, began to see themselves,
by the success of Kenneth's defensive operations, done
out of a sale. For it was plain that if Rickart was forced
to surrender his scheme of taking the water away, their
property would be thrown back on their hands. And
after six months of him, Tierra Longa missed Elwood.
He was the enemy, no doubt, but he was also Illusion, the
satisfaction of that incurable desire of men to be played
upon, to be handled. What were all young Brent's sober

calculations, compared to the bright air of cities which Elwood diffused about him? As the second week closed with no sign from him or Rickart, reaction took the form of resentment. At the meeting at which the final measures were to be taken in behalf of the Land and Water Holders' Agreement, practically nobody was found to have signed it. The few faithful did so with the understanding that, unless a certain quota of property holders eventually added their names, the signatures were revocable.

"'T ain't," Lem Scudder explained, "that we're anyways holdin' out on you. But it don't seem any use if it ain't unanermus."

"Of course, it would have to be practically unanimous."

"I'd kinda hate to have you get sore on us —"

"I'm not sore, Lem; I understand."

"Naturally, if it was any way unanermus . . ."

"Oh, the others will come to it in time; they'll see that it's the only thing for them."

Brent took that way with them partly because he believed it, partly to cover a certain shame he had to be the witness of their strange, self-defeating grudges. Of the two exhibitions he thought their attitude rather less tolerable than Rickart's self-defending cunning. He was close to the turn of mind which compels our allegiance to successful villainy largely because it is successful.

That week he began work on his water appropriation. So far he had not been entirely abandoned. Baff sent a team; two of the river ranchers came up with scrapers; the Scudders promised him a turn before the fall ploughing. This was something in a measure understood, a familiar medium. But when, the third day after work had begun, Rickart brought suit, under one excuse or another they fell away from him.

"It's this away," Mr. Baff explained; "we all allow this is a good scheme if you can work it; but we ain't none of us hankerin' to have it turn out that we've been workin' for Old Man Rickart."

"Why, I'd feel much freer, Mr. Baff," Kenneth answered him, honestly enough, "with the rest of you out of it. But, you see, I'm going through with this thing, and I did n't want it said in the end that I'd elbowed any of you out of it."

Baff eyed him with admiration not unmixed with concern. "Ain't bit off more than you can chew, have you?"

Kenneth laughed. "Ain't seen me spitting any of it out, have you?" he answered in the idiom of the country.

Kenneth had a month in which to prepare his case. "More than I want," he declared to Anne; "the sooner it is settled, the sooner you can begin your campaign for settlers under the Howkawanda Canal," — which was the pleasant name they had agreed to call it. Old Howkawanda, the Warrior of the Gate, stood over the point at which it issued from the river. Kenneth kept up like that with Anne always. All they at Palomitas said it was wonderful the way he kept up; and then that the wonderful thing was that he was not really keeping it up at all. He was, by his own account, keeping himself down.

The way he put it to them was that his plan for saving Tierra Longa was a perfectly gorgeous plan; the more he contemplated it, the more he was overcome by a sense of its gorgeousness. The only trouble was that the people did n't seem willing to try it; but it would have worked; it would work perfectly.

It would be more to the point, Anne considered, if he could think of a plan the people would be willing to try. She had something of her mother's lack of patience with any sort of failure. Anne went white and strained those days; took the defection of the Tierra Longans much to heart. If she made what she felt about it cover a trouble of her own, there was none to know of it but the Keeper of Women's Hearts, who must by now be inured to the keeping of pitiful secrets, and did not tell on her.

She bought a car, and though it was used chiefly for keeping in touch with Palomitas, — every member of the family learned to drive, including Peters, — she did somehow pull her business up to the point which justified it. Anne, so Kenneth averred, had gone on a regular jag of business; she drowned her sorrows in it.

Ellis, who heard him, arched her eyebrows.

"Anne is never sorry," she protested. "She might have disappointments and feel pain, but she would n't be sorry."

"Well, then, I wish she did n't feel so disappointed about this business. I heard to-day that Tuttle had sold, but I hardly dare tell her."

"To Rickart?"

"He does n't know. To a stranger. That's the beginning," he said; "next they'll stampede it. First one inconspicuous sale and another, and before they know it they'll be falling over themselves to sell. That's what the Agreement would have saved them from, Rickart in disguise, but they can't see it."

"What Anne can't see is, why you are n't more disappointed yourself."

"Well, I'm going to be, I suppose, when it gets through

to me. But just now I can't think of anything much except to be pleased with myself because I *am* able to think of a plan that would have the Old Man buffaloed. For it would — if they had tried it. I thought of it in twelve hours, and the more time I have to think of it, the better it looks to me. And that's something. He'll beat me; he's got me beaten now as far as my scheme goes; but the point is that I knew just what it would take to beat him. He may beat me, too, out of this water right. He can do it by a trick; but I'll know exactly what the tricks are. I could have thought of a better trick if I'd been doing tricks. Anne could have written me a properly dated letter authorizing me to make this filing as her agent . . . but that's not the point. The point is that I'm only twenty-six and I know what I'm up against. That's the difference between me and Tierra Longa. They are afraid because they have n't found out; the whole thing is mysterious to them and they're afraid of it . . ."

"I know," agreed Ellis; "I used to be afraid of almost everything."

They were sitting in Kenneth's camp under the very shadow of the Warrior, from which the work required by law for the holding of his appropriation proceeded. Out from the white torrent tumbling through the Gate, Kenneth's ditch followed the contour of the Torr' at the level of the middle mesa, a thin ploughed line which here and there was scooped into the shallow semblance of a canal. Kenneth himself had staked out the levels, by the aid of some simple instruments and the characterless capacity which had enabled him to acquire a knowledge of the law on no better excuse than that Rickart could use it.

Slight as it was, taken up and cradled in his imagination, the project fulfilled every requirement, not only of the law, but of a sufficient occupation for a young man who had been clerk to T. Rickart. It was a job; it was the curved edge of his weapon at the throat of destiny. Self-imposed was the condition of his sleeping there and subsisting on his own cookery and such alleviations as Addie from time to time sent out to him. It was so he kept formally from implicating Palomitas in his situation. It supplied the need he stood in of healing and reassurance, the ineffable consolations of twilight and the stars, the healings of the mornings. He grew brown and leaner and at ease with himself, a kind of ease which was inexplicable to Anne almost to the point of irritation. Which was perhaps why, when it was necessary for some one to go down to him with bread and letters, she so often sent Ellis.

They had talked out, brother and sister, all the possibilities of the situation, and to Anne, who valued talking solely as a means of arriving at conclusions, it was intolerable to sit sifting the dry dust of speculation. To Anne, once she had learned all that was necessary to the construction of the work in hand, of the depth of the soil and the basalt ribs of the Torr', the interest her brother and her secretary took in the intimate properties of the earth, the burrow folk dispossessed, the shrubs uprooted, the endless talk they had about it and the books they found it necessary to read, were a sort of sublimated mud-pie making. Still there was the period of suspense before Rickart's suit to be got through, and if mud-pies would do it — for they were all inextricably caught up in Kenneth's suspense, Kenneth's stake in it, and Kenneth's reaction to its possibilities.

As for Kenneth, he gave no sign, except it were a too pinching leanness and the way in which, at every moment when he was free from bodily labor, he plunged into the play of his work, and an unqualified demand for Ellis to play with him. Not that anybody denied him; it was wonderful, in fact, the way everybody at Palomitas conspired to give him Ellis to play with. You would have thought it was for that Anne paid her a salary.

All this on the theory that he was "keeping up"; that, genuine as his interest was in the play of his work, perhaps just because it was genuine, quite to himself he faced the dreadfulness of its being snatched from him, and his being found with no status but that of brother to his sister. It was a situation that neither his sister nor her friend could face for him. They were quite resolved there should some way be found of his not facing it.

And in the mean time the unexpected stampede of property to Rickart had not happened. There had been two or three transfers of titles, but all to strangers, or to persons so well known that the supposition that they were intermediaries of Rickart's was untenable. Rickart, it appeared, was n't interested in Tierra Longa property. And when the date of Kenneth's hearing arrived, Rickart secured a postponement. It was all very unsettling because it was so little what had been expected.

"He's meaner than I thought," Anne gave it as her opinion of the Old Man; "he's playing a waiting game. By September" — which was the new date for the appropriation claim — "Kenneth will be at the end of his capital and his patience; and the people of Tierra Longa will drop into Rickart's hand." But though she drummed incessantly with her fine fingers, she could drum up no expedient for diverting the course of events.

Ellis, who had adopted the family point of view that the only figure on the screen worth considering was Kenneth, planted a fruitful suggestion.

"If somebody could only get *at* Mr. Rickart!"

"I can't," said Anne, "after all he's done for me. And, besides, Ken has forbidden me."

"Oh, I don't mean to beg him off — but anybody who had his own reasons for not wanting him to go on with that suit — anybody who could influence him?"

"It would n't be any woman . . . I think my mother tried once."

"But suppose young Mr. Rickart —"

"Frank? But what reason would *he* have? You know, he's never answered Ken's letter. Ken wrote, of course, as soon as it all happened, and it's just been passed over." They were sitting in Anne's room in Summerfield on an evening when she had come in from the ranch, reporting Ken looking strained and thinner than was good for him. Anne had her hair down, twisting long ropes of it and biting them in her perplexity. "I know he cares tremendously, but he won't have Frank blamed; naturally, he must side with his father."

"I don't see why . . . I don't see why he could n't bring his father around to side with *him*." Ellis took a brush and began to brush her employer's hair as she often did when Anne was overdone. "And it would be easy enough to bring Frank over to your side," she let fall.

"I — oh!" And after a longish interval, in which the brush went rather wide of its mark without either of them noticing it, "Ellis — I can't — you don't know . . ."

"I know there's nothing *you* could do would make any difference in Frank Rickart's friendship and respect for you." After that the brush went on with steady, even strokes in silence.

And in the end it was a very little thing that brought them around the corner. One of Elwood's options expired and was not renewed by him. The giver of it, a poor soul whose struggle with the soil had robbed him of much that gave him title as a man, met Brent in town the day he heard that Elwood was no longer interested in his property, and took out his disappointment in cursing Kenneth. Peters, who heard it and had to be restrained, told Addie, who told Ellis, who drove the car in alone that afternoon to tell Anne.

It was wonderful, she said, the way Kenneth had taken it. He said that the man had a right to feel disappointed; that it was probably true that Rickart was waiting now until prices, under the menace of his water steal, dropped to the breaking figure; said that he'd always been afraid that if the ranchers did n't adopt his plan of selling out together, they'd all be sold separately, but that it was up to them. Said he knew just how the man felt and he was sorry if his own efforts to help had turned out badly.

"A hell of a lot of good that'll do me, you ―― ――."

It was at this point that Peters had to have his manners reinforced by the bystanders.

Anne heard it out, leaning her chin upon her hand, ― she was still in her office and the day's work was lagging to a close, ― and then, without raising her voice at all, or any hesitation, she wanted to know if Ellis was too tired to run the car over to the station and reserve a berth for her on the express passing through about midnight to

San Francisco. And please to say as little as possible
about it.

That was all, absolutely all there was between those
two young women, except a rather singular conversation
that took place while Anne was lying on the edge of
Ellis's bed, waiting for midnight, not having been able
to persuade the girl to go off to sleep and forget her.

"I suppose," she said, "you'll marry some time,
Ellis."

"I suppose so," rather faintly.

"And have children."

"I hope so."

"I'd like," said Anne, "if you did n't think it unfortunate, to have one of your children named after me."

And if Ellis did n't understand much more than was
said, or than anybody else would have imagined, it was
strange that she should lay Anne's cheek to her hand as
she did and cover it with a warm rush of tears.

Speaking of it afterward to Ellis — and it was very
little she *could* speak of even to her, — Anne said that the
first definite assurance she had that she actually would
get through with what she had come to do, was in the old,
unaffected delight in her company which streamed up to
her in Frank's voice. Knowing the place so well and
being known, she had come in without any announcement
and stood at the corner of his desk. She had one clear,
bracing moment of warm recognition in his "Hel-*lo*,
Anne!" before realizations of the later phases of their
intercourse pulled him back to a formal "Is there anything the matter?"

"Nothing," she said, "that I can speak to you about

here." He rose at once and showed her courteously into the private office, where again she had time to measure the depth and freshness of the tie that she had come, perhaps, to destroy, in the elder Rickart's customary, "Well, Anne?" and the unconscious shifting of his cigar to his left hand, as though he had meant to shake hands with her, a movement which she made no answering movement to confirm. If it showed her how successfully Kenneth had kept her out of his quarrel, it at least showed *him* that she had no intention of taking advantage of it.

Frank was rather grave.

"I want to speak to Anne privately, father, if you don't mind."

"Oh — ah-um!" He bit hard on his cigar while he eyed them with a certain speculation. "All right; I'm just going."

Between father and son there passed some mute half gesture relating to the use of the room, in which, though she forgot it immediately afterward, Frank appeared to exhibit anxiety, and to ask, to entreat something which was neither granted nor denied. Rickart was inclined to chat.

"All well at home, Anne?"

"Quite well, thank you."

"Crops coming on well?"

"As well as could be expected."

This was apparently thrown in to cover a period of embarrassment while he retrieved certain papers from the confusion of his desk; but Anne was aware that all the time he had her under the closest scrutiny, which — having exhausted all reasonable pretexts for prolonging — he had finally to leave unsatisfied. He went out by the door of a still more private office, but it was not until they heard the clash of an outer door opening on the corridor that the two young people felt free to speak.

"Well, Anne . . .?"

"Frank — can you tell me why your father has postponed his case against Kenneth?" Anne was nothing if not direct.

Frank stiffened.

"That's in my father's department."

"But you know."

"I should think you could understand, Anne, that under the circumstances I'd try to know as little of it as possible!"

Anne looked him squarely in the eyes.

"Yes," she said; "for if you knew *all* about it you would n't be able to go on with it."

A dull red stung in his cheek and mounted to his forehead.

"I know," he answered with some heat, "that my father has been done by one of his most trusted employees."

Anne said she supposed that was what he had been told. But she could n't for obvious reasons push him too far on that line. She could n't in any case make out his father as a liar. She hoped, she said, that he'd see that if she did n't take it up on that basis, it was because she did n't need to do so in order to prove that Kenneth himself was far from supposing that he had received any commission from his employer in respect to the waters of Arroyo Verde. "He could n't, you see," she threw off, "because he was at the time under commission from me. I suppose" — she went further — "that your father knows it was I who set the newspapers going."

"Oh, yes, we know that!"

"Well, then, you might have guessed that it was I behind what happened in Tierra Longa. Poor old Ken, what's he ever done that you should suspect him of plots and counter-plots?"

"We thought"—Frank was honest, and honestly relieved—"that he had picked up something around the office. Lots of employees do, and cut in with the hope of cutting out a slice for themselves. And all old Ken had to do was to *ask* for a slice —"

"Exactly! And all *I* had to do. . . . But the one thing we did n't know was that Elwood was working for your father . . ." She went on then to tell him what she had known and what surmised, and how she had arranged for Kenneth to do what he had done. "And mind you, it's all legal enough. Your father has n't a ghost of a claim if I should put in *mine*. And that's just what Kenneth won't consent to do. He's afraid of anything that would get me in wrong with your father."

"If my father could only hear this —" Frank walked restlessly about.

"I've promised he shan't hear it from me, and as for Ken, he'd die first. Perhaps you can imagine that after six years' faithful service it is something of a jolt to him to be accused of bad faith."

"Well, it's a jolt to my father to have his wheels spiked like this. After all he's done for Ken!"

"And after the jolt you gave us in the Burt and Estes business."

"Oh!" said Frank, and then "Oh," again.

"No," she answered to the tone, "Ken was n't thinking of that; he's forgotten it. But I've thought of it a good many times, and the share it had in my mother's death."

"Anne!" he cried; "Anne! Is this fair!" And then, with a man's instinctive avoidance of personal blame, "If Ken could n't afford it he should n't sit in at the game."

"Yes," she admitted, "if he had been playing the business game." She was silent awhile to let the sense of what she had said sink into him. "How much do you suppose your father would have paid Ken for that surplus right if he'd offered to sell it instead of giving it to the people of the valley?"

"Nothing — now."

"Ah, you mean —" But she did n't know what he meant.

"I mean that you've done for us. You. Oh, nothing that happened in the valley. Here in San Francisco. Giving it all away like that, it gave the Hetch Hetchy people the tip and they've cut the ground from under us."

"And the water stays in Tierra Longa?"

"So far as we're concerned."

"Well, then —" But she left it for him to say.

To all appearances he found it difficult. He said there were a number of considerations beside the fact that they did n't really want the water of Arroyo Verde. There was his father for one; his father was sore. He was sore at Kenneth and he was sore at having his plans interfered with. And there was the question of discipline. Word had gone out that Brent had "snooped." It was a thing Rickart never forgave his employees, — knowing more than he told them — and what could he say to them if he backed down on the suit against Brent? And there was Kenneth. If he would n't make any plea for himself, how

could Frank, how could anybody make a squeal for him?
"How would old Ken like that?"

"He would n't like it at all," Anne admitted; "that's
why you must ask your father to dismiss this suit on *your*
account; not because of any feeling you have about Kenneth, but because you think it right."

Frank did n't see himself at that. He had n't taken to
editing the Governor's morals *yet*. Well, then, he must
do it, she said, because she asked him. To which Frank
insisted again that he did n't see where she came in.

"Ah," she said, "then it's extraordinarily stupid of
you, not to see what it would mean to me to have Ken
discredited the way he would be if he lost this suit. It
is n't true what Ken said to your father, that I don't approve of him. I think he's splendid; I did n't know he had
it in him. But it is n't what I wanted for him. I wanted
him to get in with your father. It was I that sent him
here in the first place, and now, if by something I've put
him up to, he loses everything —"

Frank said he could see *that*, of course; what he did n't
see was why she should n't put it up to the Governor;
why she should put it on *him*.

"Because," said Anne, "I've promised, and because
it's the last thing you can ever do for me."

He did n't see that either. If she meant that because
Ken had got at cross-purposes with the Old Man, it was
to be the end of a pleasant friendship between *them*, he
would be sorry; but was it fair to put it to him at that
price, was it fair to *him*?

"I had n't meant," she said, "to put it at a price; it
is only, as things are, the last thing I shall be able to ask
of you." She stood up then, as if so near to the end of

what she had to say that once the end had come there
would be nothing for her but to go. He stood up with
her, honestly puzzled, saying that he had hoped there
were still many things —

"It's not," said Anne, "that you would n't do them if
I asked you, but as things are I shan't be asking."

"As things are —"

"As they are with me. You see . . . I love you."

"Anne! Anne . . ." Some delicate instinct in him, or
was it fright, leaped to prevent her.

"I don't know," she said quietly, "when I have n't
loved you. It is n't anything you have done. . . .I think
sometimes it isn't anything you are. . . . There are times
I don't approve of you. It's just something that *is*, and
I don't want you to think of me as sorry about it . . . or
be sorry for me . . ."

"Oh, Anne!" he could only say, "if I had known . . ."
He was distressed beyond measure, he was ready, she
could see, to go any length, take any step . . .

She made haste in the tenderness of her heart to release
him.

"But I could n't let you know," she said, "until I was
sure that you had found something for yourself that would
help you to understand me."

"You know?" He looked at her in grateful wonder.

"What is there about you that I have n't always
known?"

They looked at each other as if for the first time, and
in a clear sincerity which made him for the moment more
wholly hers than if their glance had been warmed by
any more personal passion, such as in men like Frank
Rickart must have always a taint of their baser natures.

It was a moment she had the wisdom not to prolong, and yet she could not let him go without a bridge thrown out by which, for his comfort, he might return to the consoling relation.

"That's why," she said, "I thought you'd like to do this for me. It's something you could save me from; this anxiety and disappointment about Ken. . . . I suppose it is about all anybody will ever save me . . ."

"Anne, Anne . . . I can't tell you what you've been to me." It was plain he had not known himself until that moment. "What you'll always be . . . the best . . . the noblest . . ." He had her hands, and not knowing what else to do he kissed them.

"I hope," she said, "you will be very happy. Shall we see you at Palomitas this summer?"

"I think not. I'm going East. Miss Rutgers wants me to meet her people."

She gave him her grave approval. But when, as she moved toward the door, she saw what was in his face, there was something in hers that was as near to fright as for Anne was possible. She put up her hand as if mutely to say that that was the one thing he must not ask of her; and in the same moment the mother in her rose to meet his need of a tangible restoration to his status as the old and valued friend. She lifted her face to him where she stood and kissed him quietly.

In the decent interval which Frank allowed himself before he faced the office force again, he realized that before he had time to consider how he would go about it, he would be obliged to give some account of his interview with Anne. He heard the door opening into his father's private retreat; but before he turned to read the confirmation of his suspicion, he had time for a swifter realization still, that there had been no preliminary click of the outer door, and to gather himself for what, when he did finally wheel from the window out of which he blindly gazed, confronted him.

"Father! You never listened!"

"Ah, when I saw what she had come for, what she would probably do to you . . ." He was ashamed, though it was not at his eavesdropping, and there was a queer kind of exultation mixed with his shame. He was pleased as men always are when by sheer force of her womanhood a woman outwits them.

"Well, then," — Frank was rather high with him, — "you are prepared to hear that she did 'do' me; that I've promised to use my influence with you to have this suit dropped . . . that it is to *be* dropped?"

"I did n't hear you promise — " The Old Man put up a protesting hand. "Oh, that's all right . . . I'll go you. I only meant that the promise was n't necessary." He broke into a queer sort of chuckle, "To think of her hitting on the one thing that you'd *have* to come to . . . the courage of it . . . the damned courage . . ."

"Father, if you please —"

"All right — all right . . ." He looked speculatively at the cigar which he had taken out of his mouth as if wondering how it could be got to express his sense of that courage. "I'd forgotten," he said, "that there are women like that . . . the courage of it! . . . I'd marry her myself if I thought she'd have me! I don't know why men don't marry women like that . . . why in hell don't we . . ." He gave it up and restored his cigar to its accustomed angle, looking a long time at his son tenderly. "Of course," he said, "I'm pleased about — the other young lady. Any reason why I haven't been told?"

"Except that nothing has happened; that is, nothing formal. Miss Rutgers wants me to meet her people before anything's announced."

"Oh, quite right, quite right. We must do the correct thing. You must let me know what's expected of me." His mind ran to diamond bracelets or a sapphire pendant or even a tiara. He had an idea a present from the young man's father was the proper thing. He was immensely pleased that his son had done so well for himself. "I hear her people are quite the top-notchers," he hinted.

"If you please — I'd rather not . . ."

Well, that was quite right, too; showed the boy had a decent feeling.

"I heard you tell Anne that we've done with Tierra Longa. I suppose we may as well go the whole figure. I'll speak to Straker. What'll you tell Ken? I suppose you'll have to tell him."

"I suppose so; at any rate, he's not to be told that Anne has been here. You understand, father. I'll tell him you've withdrawn the suit because you've become convinced of the sincerity of his motives."

"The hell you will . . . Oh, well, go ahead, I suppose that'll please Anne — I suppose I can eat dirt if my own son tells me to . . . Hifalutin young beggar! If he'd have stayed with me I'd have made his fortune." He settled to his desk again. "And tell Anne — tell her the next time I want to pull off anything in Tierra Longa my first move will be to make her a partner."

XVII

It took time, as much as a week or two, after the receipt
of Frank's letter announcing that the water fight for
Tierra Longa had been abandoned and the suit withdrawn,
before it was borne in upon Kenneth that the situation
created for him by the sudden release of opposition was,
for him, practically no situation at all. If, as he had said
to Virginia, he was done with Business, it was equally certain that Business was done with him. There was no
prospect whatever of his being taken on by the Rickart
Interests, and no likelihood that his life would supply him
with any other opening into the world of finance half so
good. The law as a profession had never interested him
enough to be thought of as a sole means of livelihood,
and though he had enthusiastically declared his devotion
to the cause of mutton and alfalfa, the only opportunity
open to him for coming into a productive relation to
either of these was as a hireling on his sister's ranch. After
six years with one of the most successful capitalists on the
Coast, he had nothing more creditable than a scant two
or three thousand dollars and this water right to show, a
right which he might as easily have acquired without the
necessity for quarreling with Rickart.

It was a right and not a possession. He had, as he
humorously saw with that new capacity for playing with
his work which had arisen for him out of the stroke of
necessity, proposed himself as a consort for as much of
the River as was not claimed elsewhere. His being married to it depended on his being able to support it in

that style to which rivers turned to the use of men are accustomed. If he was able to see, in the way he had been pitched, by the falling of his house about his ears, into this adventure with a lady who had been singing under his window all these years without so much as a penny of his attention being thrown to her, something of that designing Hand which men like to feel at the crisis of their lives, he was so far fortunate. Quite as plainly he read the conditions of hard labor, years of time, and more capital than he at the moment saw his way to, required to make out of his appropriated right a creditable achievement.

This was the situation as he had made it, which, as news of it circulated through Tierra Longa, bit slowly home to him. It turned him obstinate at first, refusing Anne's seductive invitations to new planning, and finally, after the first half-humorous appraisement of it, turned him silent.

If his first conscious instinct, confronted with this crisis, had been to strike himself free from every sort of personal entanglement; on its final resolution his first conscious necessity had been that of coördination. And the result of his first tentative cast had discovered him to himself as more solitary than he had supposed it was possible to be. He had n't, he admitted to himself, expected that Tierra Longa would be wholly with him, nor yet that he would suffer a complete misunderstanding. What he had expected was that he should become in a small way the center of a new community of interest, and the nucleus of a robust opposition. "As it is," he complained to Anne, "if they think of me at all, they think of me as a good deal of a fool, and if I've got nothing out of it for myself, that it serves me good and right for my meddling."

"Oh, well," Anne consoled him, "as fools are judged they're partly right. After all, what *have* you got out of it?"

"I've got myself; that's something." It was, indeed, Anne thought, seeing him lathy and full-chested, young stubble on his chin, clear-eyed, but being his sister said nothing.

"And I've got a lot of things settled," he argued, "what I think, and all that."

"You have n't," — Anne insisted, — "you have n't settled *anything*. You've just escaped."

"But — escaped?"

"If you want to have it that way, — escaped the necessity of settling anything, of having to decide things that are important to be decided. You like this, don't you?"

She could bet he liked it! He liked ploughing through the mesa because it turned up soft and crumbly, he liked cutting through the basalt because it was n't soft, and he liked the smell of sheep and getting up with the sun and being all sweaty and as tired as a dog. Anne said he need n't tell her all this because it was perfectly apparent to the observer.

But it was no sign, because he liked going without shaving oftener than twice a week, that anybody else liked it. Nor that, having dropped by a fluke into the kind of thing he liked, anything on earth was settled by it. It was a mistake, she said, that women had always made, thinking that, because they enjoyed being ordered about by their husbands and cuddling their babies, it was their God-appointed destiny and they were therefore excused from any further responsibilities. So that if it was a notion he had of being a Heaven-built farmer, he could be one, just as Baff and Willard were. He could homestead a hundred and sixty acres under his own canal and be happy in it until she or Rickart or somebody of the same stripe came along and took it away from him.

"I could have stopped Rickart this time if they'd only pulled together," he affirmed.

"Yes, if you only had."

"Me?" he said; "well, I like that!"

"Yes, you, honey. It was a lovely plan and a fine feeling, but how much did you actually do?"

"They could n't pull together."

"Oh, I *heard* you, Ken. It's true they were n't with you, but then you were n't within a mile of *them*. Maybe if you'd been a little closer, they could have come the rest of the way." Anne, he thought, hit harder than she knew. But Anne thought she knew exactly.

"If he slumps now," she said to Ellis, "he's done for." Actually the greatest restraint she had put upon herself was that she might not swamp him with expedients to fortune such as sprang incessantly from her active brain.

Two influences combined to weave for Kenneth the frame of mind into which his young manhood had fallen as into a snare, influences proceeding out of that secret, submerged childish life; the consoling, sufficing presence of the Torr' and the corroding touch of his mother's private dissatisfactions. The one of these sustained him in the feeling he had of being born to live upon the earth and work it; the other obscurely served to push him farther still from Tierra Longa. Though he did not recognize it as such, there was something of his mother in the resentment he cherished against Rickart, who, after so many years of almost parental interest, had been willing to make him the victim of self-interested misrepresentation, and in the instinctive though concealed contempt in which he held certain of the Tierra Longans. For when, through those mysterious channels by which the Old Man kept himself informed of local affairs, and permitted as much or little of his own as served him to be known, report had represented Rickart's abandonment of the water steal as a mere turning of the back upon them, there had been toward young Brent a recrudescence of that suspicion with which they had viewed his earlier appearance among them.

For to all of them, whether they had hoped most or feared most from Rickart's ascendancy in the valley, there was left in the cup the dregs of disappointment. Life, business, chance and change, the excitement even of opposition, had again passed by them. They were dropped again into the humiliation of being too poor to steal from. It was n't that they did not fully realize their own failure to rise to Brent's lead; that was exactly what they did realize, and for that they could n't forgive him. They had fallen away from the Howkawanda Canal, a controlling interest in which had been so freely offered, so long as they thought of it as likely to "get them in wrong with Rickart," only to find that it was the one thing likely to have raised them in Rickart's estimation, putting them in possession of something Rickart had valued. Rickart's withdrawal had given to their vacillations an antic appearance which, in their invincible rurality, they visited on Kenneth.

Much of this state of theirs was hid from him by unfamiliarity; he saw only that they withdrew, and plunged protectively himself into silence. He went seldom to town, saw nobody but the household at Palomitas,

worked prodigiously at his canal, exceeding the requirement.

Anne and Ellis used to come out to him of evenings,
since Anne's car made it possible for them to be often at
the ranch house, to sit on the edge of the mesa and watch
the summer moon climb its slow arc above the valley.
But their talk on these occasions was mostly of what
Anne had been doing, or of the night owls nesting above
the Gate, or the raccoons bubbling in the cañons. Now
and then it touched the personal note, as when Anne
brought him word that Virginia had gone to Los Angeles.
She said her work had called her, but Anne chose that
occasion to add that André Trudeau was there also.

"Ellis is afraid she means to marry him, but she
need n't be," said Anne; "Virginia won't marry a man;
she 'll marry a situation." And Anne had put it to herself
that Virginia must have seen by this time that André
Trudeau was n't the man to provide her with that sense
of the dramatic which Virginia's temperament demanded.

This was too subtle for Kenneth, but he thought it
did n't matter. "At any rate, you were mistaken about
her thinking of marrying me," he affirmed, "she never
had any such idea." It was the best he could do for her.
Perhaps by this time he believed it.

"Oh!" said Anne; and then after an interval, "Anyway, it would n't have done. Virginia's all right, of
course, — but it is n't enough for a farmer's wife to like
him; she also has to like farming." Pronouncements of
this sort from Anne had ceased to be a red rag to Kenneth; he had all the appearance of taking this one seriously.

Things went on like this until the middle of August,

and then all at once the deadlock on Kenneth's spirit was broken. Lem Scudder broke it with his team and scraper and bag of dunnage; he came up one morning out of a mist of heat and joined Kenneth under the Warrior.

"Well, old scout," he hailed, "how's things progressin'?"

Kenneth gasped at him in amazement.

"Lem," he said, "Lem, I — I — thought you'd gone back on me."

"Well, now," — Lemuel looked appreciatively at the thick shade of the oak under which the camp was pitched, and the not too distant river, — "I told you I'd get along as soon as it was any way convenient. Did n't allow to get here much before fall ploughin' time, but it's pretty hot down the valley; I allowed a week's campin' would n't do me no damage . . . an', anyway, Baff says he's comin' to do his turn in September —"

Kenneth's arm went around his shoulder. "Lem, — you old son of a gun, — give the team a rest, and let's go swimming!"

At the end of two weeks the two went down to Tierra Longa together, and a week later, Kenneth burst into his sister's office at Summerfield in the very pink of spirits and condition. "Well, sis, what do you think? I've got an office in Arroyo Verde and I'm going to be there one day in a week, anyway, as president and attorney for the Howkawanda Development Company —"

"Ken! You've never —!"

"Absolutely! Company's all organized. I'm here now getting myself made notary public. And I'm going over to file a homestead on that hundred and sixty below the fence —"

"Too late, Ken, I filed on that six weeks ago, and Ellis took the one next to it. You won't get in under your own ditch at all if you don't look lively."

"Anne," he said, in the most unstinted admiration he had ever given her, "you *are* a hummer." They plunged into an hour of happy planning.

The next most natural reaction of Kenneth's restored state was that he wanted somehow to have a talk with Rickart. He made many excuses to himself for bringing it off, not the least sincere of which was the sense he had of what, after all, he owed to the Old Man's tutelage. And finally, without any excuse at all, he went up early in September and presented himself at the Rickart offices. Frank was still away on the Atlantic Coast, in the train of Miss Rutgers to whom his engagement had already been announced, and there was a new stenographer in the outer office, which gave an unwonted strangeness to his being asked to wait there until Rickart could see him. He waited an unconscionably long time, which the Old Man made up to him by taking him out for luncheon.

It was not until the meal was ordered, the drinks brought, and napkins tucked in that they got around finally to the meat of the occasion. "Well, now, young man," — Rickart folded his large hands on the cloth before him, — "suppose you tell me all about it."

"I'd like to try," Kenneth admitted, "though I don't know if I can explain —"

Rickart tucked his cigar away into the farthest corner of his still finely cut mouth to make room for a flicker of a smile. "Shoot," he said; "I'll do my best to understand you."

It was a long explanation lasting fully through the meal, and brought from time to time little beads of sweat on the young man's forehead, but somehow he had managed to make clear his conviction that the earth was the right and property of those who worked it, and that its values should accrue to them if to anybody. Incidentally he said something of his newfound appreciation of the need and power of working together. "It's only a glimmer I've got," he admitted, "but it's enough to go by. It's as much as most people have, I imagine."

"Oh, then this is n't just something you've thought out for yourself? There are others?"

"Thousands," Kenneth told him; "so many that I'm beginning to think I've been a back number."

Rickart dry-smoked for a time in silence.

"I'd begun to suspect something of the kind," he confessed. "This 'Progressive' business, — I suppose that's something in the same line?" Kenneth nodded. "And women wanting the vote . . . I sort of thought that would knock things endwise. Women have a way of showing you that there really is something that gets at you, deeper than business. Your sister Anne —" He broke off, remembering what it was he must n't say of Anne. "Me, too. I think I'm for business purposes only, and then something gets me. . . . Well, was this what you came all the way up here to tell me?"

"Well, I thought it was," — Ken smiled across at him shyly, — "but I guess the fact is I was just homesick to see you."

After that, though they carefully avoided any mention of Kenneth's own business, they drifted into quite a comfortable chat about Palomitas.

"There's something I've been meaning to tell Anne," Rickart said, "ever since she came into the property. There's oil on your land. Jevens didn't look in the right place for it. It's on the other side of the Ridge, and it runs pretty well down into the valley. Years ago I had the whole place experted . . . what Jevens struck must have been a seepage basin. I guess it pretty well broke him. He had that young fool Hartley Daws snooping round the place and I fixed Daws so he would n't trust his own judgment, or so, if he did, Jevens would n't trust *him*. I don't know which way it worked, but I know Jevens did n't find it.

"Well, I'm counting on you to keep this confidential. We don't know how much oil there is, nor how good it is. With the Petrolia fields running so strong and the price crude oil is, there's no good going after it now. But you tell Anne that when there's a chance of a railroad, or when she gets good and ready, I'll go with her . . ."

Kenneth listened in silence to this extraordinary statement with its mixture of friendly good sense and the entire absence of what is ordinarily called conscience. He thought of his mother and the strange chances of his youth, all so long buried past resentment. It came over him again that the key to the Old Man's success was, after all, knowledge, knowledge of land and minerals, knowledge of law, and, more than everything else, knowledge of men, knowledge of everything except that strange, ineradicable quality of men called righteousness; the thing which he could n't always calculate in others or get the better of in himself. It was a moment of revealing poignancy through which he sat, and though it took something of warmth from the handshake with which he finally parted from his former employer, it sent him back to Tierra Longa in a new and humble sense of hope in the people among whom for the rest of his life he had cast himself.

It was a mood which lasted him at intervals all through the four or five days' revisiting of old friends and associations which he allowed himself, and followed him to Summerfield and well out on the Palomitas road, for it was Saturday afternoon and his sister and Ellis Trudeau had already left the office. He rode out himself with the mail carrier, and felt again the nameless stir of incompleteness which had troubled him that night ride with Anne the time she had sent for him about this surplus water appropriation.

It merged in a need that he had felt growing on him all that summer for something warmer, more understanding than the tardy coöperation of Tierra Longa or even his sister's active business partnership. It drove him silent at last and with a strange pricking to get down from the carrier's buckboard, a mile before there was occasion, to seek on foot, along the ferny creek, the Ford of Mariposa.

It mingled, the pricking in his blood, with familiar, poignant images . . . his reluctance to lend himself wholly to Virginia's version of Jacob and the Angel, the fascinations of 'Nacio's *diablo negro* coming out of the Draw, the drowning lamb, and his old feelings about his mother. One by one the images wavered about him and were reabsorbed as shadows into the landscape.

It was the long hour of twilight. The creek ran a slender rill, and the grass of Mariposa, ripe and burned with summer, lay furry and lion-colored over the swell of the meadow; the wind stirred it like the waterings of some

great creature's coat, and the sound of the wind in the
Draw was like the earth purring. And then, down the
hollow of the swale where the lamb-band had frisked, he
saw her coming. Her dress was white, and she walked as
one seeing the end of the way and not the path before her.

She saw him and stood still, waiting; the hem of her
dress lay in the grasses, and the grasses stirred about her
feet as though she had just risen, so blossom white and
softly brown, out of the earth to be the final answer to all
his indecisions. As he moved down the swale and across
the Ford of Mariposa, it was, indeed, as if all the tread-
ing of the years since last he played there had been but
stepping-stones of the path that led to her. And as he
went he felt a sudden stir and a sigh of the air as of the
passing of great wings, and the angel of his struggle went
from him, and he knew at last the ineffable name by
which alone Heaven prevails against us. And though he
felt in going that he should always limp a little on the
sinew of material success, he knew, too, that he should
never come this way again and not feel the magic and the
triumph of this hour.

"Ellis!" he said.

"Oh," she sighed, "I knew you would come. Nobody
expected you, but I knew . . ." But it was not until he
spoke her name again that she moved within the circle
of his arm that closed softly round her.

"If you knew," he said, "it was because you must have
known how much I needed you."

"Oh, my dear, my dear . . . I thought you would never
find it out . . ." And suddenly the arm went very tight
indeed, to still her trembling.

The wing of the dusk had spread well over the valley,

the sky above the Torr' was muffled by its pinions by the time they came to the bottom of the orchard lane and saw Anne and his father looking for them.

Ellis had a moment of flurry.

"Let's not tell them yet; they could n't have the least idea . . ."

"Nonsense," he said, taking a firm proprietary hold upon her. For once he had one of his sister's flashes of insight. "I should n't wonder," he said, — "I should n't wonder if it turns out Anne has been meaning something of the kind all the time." Which proved to be the case.

THE END

Mary Austin, 1906. Reproduced by permission of the Huntington Library, San Marino, California.

Mary Austin (1868–1934) came to California in 1888 after graduating from Blackburn College in Illinois. With her widowed mother and brothers, she homesteaded in Kern County, adjacent to the Tejon Ranch in the Great Central Valley, where she concerned herself with the local history, Indian cultures, and environmental issues that provided the material for her thirty books of fiction, nature writing, and autobiography. Her first book, *The Land of Little Rain*, was published in 1903. She spent most of her adult life in California and New Mexico.

California Fiction titles are selected for their literary merit and for their illumination of California history and culture.

The Ford by Mary Austin	0-520-20757-2
Disobedience by Michael Drinkard	0-520-20683-5
Skin Deep by Guy Garcia	0-520-20836-6
Fat City by Leonard Gardner	0-520-20657-6
Continental Drift by James D. Houston	0-520-20713-0
In the Heart of the Valley of Love by Cynthia Kadohata	0-520-20728-9
Golden Days by Carolyn See	0-520-20673-8
Oil! by Upton Sinclair	0-520-20727-0
Who Is Angelina? by Al Young	0-520-20712-2

Forthcoming titles:

Thieves' Market by A. I. Bezzerides
Chez Chance by Jay Gummerman
The Vineyard by Idwal Jones
Bright Web in the Darkness by Alexander Saxton